THE
CEDAR VALLEY COVENANT

BARNA WILLIAM DONOVAN

This is a work of fiction. Names, characters, places, and incidents are products of the author's imagination or are used fictitiously and are not to be construed as real. Any resemblance to actual events, locations, organizations, or persons, living or dead, is entirely coincidental.

World Castle Publishing, LLC
Pensacola, Florida

Copyright © Barna William Donovan 2020
Hardback ISBN: 9781951642846
Paperback ISBN: 9781951642853
eBook ISBN: 9781951642860
First Edition World Castle Publishing, LLC, September 28, 2020.
http://www.worldcastlepublishing.com

Licensing Notes

Cover: Alisha Moore from Damonza Covers
Editor: Maxine Bringenberg

CHAPTER 1

The Handlers had relented. At last, they gave in, and they would let the Predator have her. He couldn't function if he couldn't have her. He couldn't carry out his mission if he wasn't allowed to dream about her. She had taken over his fantasies. She had come to possess him, to take over and control his thoughts as much as he needed to take over the thoughts of his targets tonight.

But the Predator's Handlers had given in. They, too, after all, were in his head. They understood the condition he was in. They understood his need. If the Handlers wanted the Predator to kill the two men sitting across the restaurant, they had to let him take the payment he demanded.

Jessica.

Her name rang through the chambers of the Predator's mind. He was picking up flashes of her, images of her, the closer he got to his targets.

He needed Jessica.

If they wanted the Predator to go through with it, they had to let him take Jessica.

Sure, the Predator realized they could just as well kill him and find someone else to carry out the hit, but that would take too long. They needed the Predator for his very special qualities. They needed him for his very special modus operandi. They couldn't let all of his previous work go to waste. It would take too long to set up another assassin to take his place.

For now, the Predator had the upper hand. The Handlers needed those two men—sitting there and drinking, discussing science and philosophy, teaching methods, the price of South Illinois real estate—dead as quickly as possible. They especially needed Dr. Nelson Danziger dead. His companion, Dr. Brock Randall, was merely a secondary target. The Handlers hadn't cared about Randall originally. Or rather, they didn't care about him enough to want him dead just now. But the Predator had the power to force Randall's execution. If the Handlers wanted Danziger eliminated, they had to let him go after Randall too.

Brock Randall had to die because of what the Predator had discovered in his mind. When he read Randall's thoughts, the Predator found Jessica. From the moment he found her, everything changed.

Jessica. Brock Randall's beautiful daughter. Randall and his estranged daughter had started talking to each other again. The Predator knew because he scanned Randall's mind every day. He could see Randall looking at Jessica's pictures when he was on the phone with her. The Predator saw her exquisite photo sitting on the desk in Randall's office. When the Predator shared Brock Randall's vision, when he intruded into his thoughts, he saw Jessica, he heard Jessica, he saw her photos all over Randall's house.

But Jessica was so far away. The Predator had to get to her. He needed to bring her to Cedar Valley right now. She had become his addiction, his madness. He knew that Randall's sudden tragic death would bring Jessica to town.

The Handlers wanted Danziger dead, and the Predator was going to kill him before the night was through. But Brock Randall would die at the same time. The Predator would not be denied. Not even the Handlers could stop him now.

CHAPTER 2

"Brock, to tell you the truth...," Nelson Danziger said, and looked Randall square in the eyes. He paused, raised his snifter of scotch, and smiled affably. "The impression Cedar Valley State has made on me is really great...."

Brock Randall swirled the rum around the bottom of his glass. He thought he heard a "but" about to be tagged onto the end of Danziger's remark. Of course, Randall wasn't supposed to be the one apprehensive about what Danziger was about to say. Randall, a representative of Cedar Valley State University, was supposed to have been the one with the upper hand here. *They* were the ones about to offer Danziger a job.

Except the truth was that Danziger, no doubt, had several other offers waiting for him. He wasn't a desperate new Ph.D., fresh out of grad school with a few years of adjunct teaching, a pile of student loans, and maybe one or two conference presentations under his belt. Nelson Danziger's CV read like a novella. He already had five books published, two of them with commercial houses in New York. And, despite the subject matter he wrote about, his mainstream success only stood to help the school, to boost enrollment. That success was the reason a small school like CVSU was willing to spend as much money on Danziger as had been allocated for him in the hiring budget.

"Glad to hear that, Nelson," Randall replied, but paused quietly. He could sense Danziger had more to say.

"So now I wait and hope for the best. I hope the search committee's been impressed," Danziger said.

"Oh, I'm sure about that."

Although Randall had been asked to take Danziger out for his farewell dinner, he wasn't actually sitting on Danziger's search committee. Danziger was interviewing for one of the rare full-professor openings in the psychology department. Randall was an interpersonal communication specialist. Cedar Valley State being so small, however, almost made the school a big family. Every department took an interest in every single full-time faculty hire. Danziger's guest lectures, his research presentation, and discussions with the psychology department's search committee had been observed by representatives from every other department.

Now that Danziger was about to go home to Tampa while the search committee deliberated, Randall had been asked to take him out for a farewell dinner.

"You have to admit, though...," Danziger said and paused.

Here comes the "but," Randall thought. He was annoyed by how much trepidation he felt, but the fact was that this entire interview process had been a seller's market. And Danziger was the seller. The college needed him desperately.

Randall just raised his eyebrows and waited for Danziger to complete his thought.

"They did ask a lot of nervous questions," Danziger said.

"Nervous?" Randall asked, sipping some rum.

"I think they're asking themselves if they're hiring a psychologist or a writer from a supermarket tabloid."

"That's not the case at all," Randall said and chuckled, regretting the words the moment they came out of this mouth. He'd made himself sound defensive. The key to this entire hiring process was not to make Danziger feel too powerful, too needed.

"Well, how do you think they feel about my work?" Danziger asked bluntly. "I'm sure my books have impressed the school to a certain degree, and I guess at this point it's up to the psych department's search committee to make its final decision, but they take input from all the faculty members who've observed me."

"I think they're trying to figure out how to deal with...with the implication that you don't seem to think people who've experienced the...."

"The unexplained?" Danziger asked, and drank some scotch. "That they're not all insane?"

"Well, *you've* got to admit that your arguments for the objective reality of parallel worlds and the spirit world are fairly radical," Randall said.

"Yes, I suppose they are," Danziger said, and stared off into some distant corner of the nearly empty restaurant past Randall's head. Then his focus came back to Randall. "I suppose they really are," he reiterated. "But I don't necessarily think it's a bad idea. Do you?"

"What do you mean?" Randall chose to evade Danziger's question.

"Our line of work. Research, higher education, isn't it supposed to be a battlefield of ideas? Nothing is supposed to be too radical. We're supposed to throw all ideas out there and see how they can be defended."

Randall shrugged. "Well, you don't really have a hostile audience here, you know. *My* department has a couple of committed post-modernists."

"Aha, the post-modernists," Danziger said, and chuckled. "Nothing exists, nothing is real, we can't trust any rules and any reality. So my candidacy's not entirely a lost cause."

"It's the people in your own hard-sciences you have to watch out for," Randall said, and finished the rest of his rum.

"Should I be very worried?" Danziger asked, and smiled lightly.

Randall thought he smiled a little bit too lightly. There was a cockiness emerging from this guy now.

"You must have met Tom Lancaster from the physics department, right?" Randall asked.

"Can't recall his face."

"Tall, dark-haired, good looking...."

"Snappy suits, right?"

"Yeah, break those scientist stereotypes. No pocket protectors on that one."

Danziger laughed. "Looks like a yuppie stockbroker."

"Yeah, that's the one," Randall said, and guessed that Danziger must have been wondering how many students Lancaster was sleeping with. Randall, though, was certain that the answer was none. Lancaster was a real stand up guy, he had to admit. He always pegged him as highly ethical, if not a bit stiff. He was, of course, a zealot when it came to certain aspects of his work, but he was a straight shooter, nonetheless. Maybe that's why Randall thought he would have been happy setting him up with Jessica.

"But anyway," Randall continued, "he wrote a book a while ago called *The Naked Ghost.*"

"Yes, of course," Danziger said with a knowing smile. "Now, I remember."

"Well, he's still trying to save the world. Shining the light of science."

"Yes, he's the one," Danziger said quietly. "Good for him if he's trying to save the world, though. Even if sometimes he writes outside of his area of expertise."

"He would probably take issue with some of your ideas."

"Who knows?" Danziger said, and shrugged lightly.

Randall thought he could sense that cockiness again.

"Maybe he, too, believes in that battlefield of ideas," Danziger said.

"I'm sure he probably does."

"Yeah," Danziger said slowly, and drained the last of his scotch. "I remember the reviews of his book. Very zealous guy, indeed. His book was pretty successful."

"Not as successful as your books," Randall said.

Danziger returned a humble smile. "Well, whatever differences I might have with someone like Tom Lancaster, I hope CVSU will decide it's a big enough place for a diversity of opinions," he said diplomatically, leaning back in his chair.

It was time to wrap up this farewell dinner, Randall realized, glancing at his watch. He still had to drive Danziger to Cedar Valley Municipal Airport, from where he would take a commuter flight to Chicago and catch his connection down to Tampa.

After settling the bill to be placed on the school's account, Randall and Danziger left the nearly empty restaurant.

Only one other patron haunted Bertucci's Tratoria this late at night, Randall noted as they headed for the front door. A man sitting in the farthest, darkest corner of the restaurant seemed to be staring at a barely-touched plate of pasta in front of him.

CHAPTER 3

Cassie Brynner leaned toward her microphone upon getting the first cue from her producer in the control booth. When the second cue came, it was time to get back to the show.

"Welcome back to *The Facts of Love*, syndicated nationwide on the Superior Broadcasting Network. And we have Jessica Lafayette in our studios once again. Real advice for real relationships, ladies." Cassie glanced at Jessica, ensconced behind her own microphone. "So, we'll take one more call then, Jess?"

Might as well, Jessica thought. The show had gone well enough, and she was feeling less self-conscious by now, sitting under the gaze of her own enormous, overbearing photo framed on the wall in the corridor outside the studio, "staring" onto the proceedings in the studio through one of the sound-proof windows. Cassie, Jessica noted, was lucky enough—in case she was bothered by these things—to be sitting at such an angle as not to be watched by her own photo from the "Wall of KBLA Stars" lining the corridor outside. Jessica had originally liked the photo of herself, but after sitting through her first guest appearance on *The Facts of Love*, the slightly over-glamorized picture had started to make her feel off-kilter. She could hardly have been able—or would even care to—keep her blonde locks so dramatically wavy all the time, for instance. That toothy, perky, life-loving smile had been captured after some thirty shots, and it was somehow unnerving how the computerized manipulation of her eyes seemed to give them such an other-worldly glitter.

"Oh, absolutely," Jessica spoke into the microphone, replying to Cassie's question. "Let's try and squeeze as many in as we can. I love to talk to your listeners."

"All right!" Cassie said. "How about that, ladies? What a trouper. So, Johnny, who's our next caller?" She glanced at the computer screen next to the microphone. "All right. Johnny, the intern, tells us it's Annie from Sacramento. Annie, you're on the air with Jessica Lafayette. What's the real relationship problem you have?"

"Hi, Jessica," a woman's voice came through the headphones. "I just wanted to tell you how much I love all your appearances on Cassie's show!"

"Thank you, Annie."

"I mean, Cassie, you're just so great and everything," Annie tagged on breathlessly, obviously nervous and flustered by her first opportunity to have a call placed on the air. "But when Jessica's on, it's like a special treat."

"Thanks, Annie…I guess," Cassie said with a mock annoyance.

"For real, Cassie!" Annie blurted across the line from Sacramento.

Jessica saw Cassie grinning at her.

"I know," Cassie said. "And I'm glad I'm appreciated, Annie."

"I mean, sometimes I just feel like you're my big sister and stuff," Annie continued complimenting, still sounding overwhelmed. "There's just so much…. God, you can't believe how many crazy times I made it through by listening to your show, Cassie."

"Thanks a million, Annie. So what's your question for Jessica?"

Annie took an audible breath, her gasp susurrating through the headphones. "Okay...Jessica! What I have a question about is how you're telling us that we have to keep our relationships real."

"Uh huh."

"So now what I wanted to ask you about...aren't relationships supposed to be, like, about give and take? That both you and your lover have to give, and then you have expectations in return."

"Sure," Jessica said.

"But it sounded to me before like you were saying that a woman should have her list of expectations and never compromise. I mean, I don't really understand how you can get what you want if you're going into a relationship just making demands and never being ready to please your man. Because a guy's just gonna leave at that point, or you *know* what else he's gonna do, right? And then you're alone." Annie paused for a breath. "I just thought it sounds like you're taking a real radical turn on us here when we're supposed to be all about keeping it real and real solutions to real relationships."

When the silence after Annie's litany seemed to be stretching, Jessica realized the caller was through. "Well, Annie," she said at length." I think you just tossed more than one really complicated problem out there."

Cassie chimed in with a friendly chuckle. "She certainly said a mouthful, Jess."

"First of all, Annie," Jessica said. "I do believe that a real relationship is something both people need to work on, and it definitely *is* a case of some major give and take."

"Yes?" Annie asked simply.

"However, what I was saying is that I'm afraid too many women, especially too many young women, let the balance in the give and take relationship tilt against them. We need to understand and prioritize what we can compromise and negotiate on, and where we need to hold the line in a healthy relationship. So, for example, you need to know whether it's your career, education, children, or whatever those things that are important to you, how do those things rate, and once you decide what's on top of that list of priorities, you have to commit to it. And yes, there are some things I would urge you *not* to compromise on. I think you owe yourself that much. There will be many issues in a healthy relationship, a real relationship, that are definitely a matter of give and take, but you need to have a clear idea of boundaries and what you have to do on your own terms."

"Thank you, Jessica," Cassie suddenly exclaimed as Jessica wrapped up her monologue. The signal had come from the control booth that they were running out of time. "And thank *you*, Annie. And Annie, we will send you a copy of Jessica's new book, *Jessica's More Real Advice for Real Relationships*. That will have to wrap it up for us tonight, but I will see you...I guess *hear* you, tomorrow night at the same time, same bat-channel. I'll give you all the details on getting involved with this year's Wings of Angels walk across America for breast cancer programs, *and* one of the sizzling topics for tomorrow's guest panelists will be...bedroom games! *The Facts of Love*, ladies. KBLA Radio, San Diego."

Cassie's producer gave them a thumbs up from the control booth. The show had gone well, but it was over.

"And that's a wrap," Cassie said, pushing away the microphone and pulling off her headphones.

And none too soon, Jessica thought, removing her own headphones. "That's a wrap," she exhaled. "What a day." She was glad her status at the station was still that of a regular guest star on Cassie's *Facts of Love*. It was thrilling to hear the progress coming along in the development of her own show, but Cassie's nightly schedule still looked like a killer.

"Exhausted?" Cassie asked, running her fingers through her long mane of bright red hair and massaging her neck.

"Yeah. Just some crazy feedback from my publisher," was all Jessica chose to say at this point. Cassie had been listening to people's problems for the past two hours. Jessica figured she didn't need any more right now. And Jessica didn't particularly feel like talking about her own issues in too much detail right now.

"You look like you need a strong one."

"Probably do," Jessica said. Despite trying to be reticent, she thought her walls were about to crumble, and she would unload a speech as strung-out as Annie's had been.

"Join the gang for drinks over at *Fred's Place*?"

Jessica thought about that one, but the cracks in that wall had run too deep. "Yeah, I probably *need* to join you for a strong one."

"Are you seeing Dave afterward?" Cassie asked. "Maybe you shouldn't join us at all—"

But Jessica cut her off. Not only were the cracks deep, but now the dam collapsed. "No!" she blurted out vehemently. "*Definitely* not."

Cassie arched an eyebrow. "Wow. That doesn't sound good."

"No, it's not good," Jessica understated, but her tone told most of the story of her disaster area of a relationship with David Holloman.

"Is the bad news really from your publisher?"

"Yeah, that too. But the real issue is...."

"Yeah," Cassie said with a rueful grimace and a shake of her head. "The real issue is Dave. It figures."

"No!" Jessica said strongly. "It's not an issue, okay, Cassie? Dave is no longer an issue for me. Our issues have been settled for good."

"Is it over?"

"Yeah," Jessica said, and waved her papers outlining tonight's show at Cassie. "You know, some things in a relationship we can not compromise on," she said, mocking her own clinical, professional voice.

"Like what? Oh, wait a minute, let me guess…?"

"This is one issue I'm not *capable* of compromising on. Unless I decide to be understanding and patient about this so-called sex addiction *problem* he developed all of a sudden now that his ex from New York lives just a two-hour drive away in L.A."

Cassie returned a disgusted look. "Sex addiction? Really? Does anyone still use that excuse?"

"*And* he's been dealing with anxiety since he didn't get that role on that…. God, what is it called? That lawyer show with what's his name playing the prosecutor."

Cassie nodded vigorously. "Oh, yeah, I know what you're talking about."

"Yeah," Jessica said, frustrated for a moment that her voice sounded more glum than agitated. She had every right to be angry over what she got back from Dave Holloman after all the work she had put into their relationship. "Dave was auditioning for that thing, and he was among the last three people being called back for something like the third reading. He thought he had it in the bag."

"So now he's an unemployed actor again. And his ex is so understanding that he became a sex addict all of a sudden?"

"It's not like he's an unemployed actor," Jessica insisted, "because he can always do that gig at the La Jolla Dinner Theater. And it's hardly like he has to starve. He can just go back to working for his father's company any time he wants to. But, of course, he doesn't want to do that, because that would be like selling out and admitting defeat."

Cassie rolled her eyes. "Well, then he should be glad he's dating someone who just bagged a six-figure book deal," she said with a flat, annoyed tone, and shook her head. "But of course, he can't handle that either, now that he didn't get his big break. Right? He can't handle it, *especially* now."

"Nope," Jessica said simply.

From the look on her face, it appeared as if Cassie was about to blurt out something stinging about the oversized, yet pathetically fragile, male ego, but she was cut off when the studio door abruptly swung open.

Helen O'Brien, Cassie's producer, barged in.

"Jessica!" Helen gasped, wide eyed. "Jessica, you gotta take this call in the office."

"What is it?" Jessica asked. Almost in an instant, a cold, prickly sensation came alive on the back of her neck and seemed to sweep over her back.

"It's your dad," Helen said. "There's been some kind of an accident."

CHAPTER 4

"Since Brock left us, not only is our school, our Cedar Valley State community, less of a place, but I believe this world has lost one of those people it needs the most," Tom Lancaster recited. He had placed a sheet of paper in front of him on the lectern, but he'd barely glanced at it since taking his turn remembering Brock Randall. "He was a builder. Brock had dedicated his life to building connections, to bringing people together. He had the ability to connect with all points of view, to erase disagreements, to erase conflicts, and help everyone around him find our common strengths, our shared commitment to knowledge. I will miss Brock as a colleague and a friend."

After a solemn nod and a glance at the urn holding Brock Randall's ashes on a podium at the front of the Benjamin-Mead Funeral Home chapel, Tom Lancaster returned to his seat among the mourners.

Jessica's eyes swept the crowd as Lancaster, a surprisingly young-looking member of the Cedar Valley State University faculty, returned to his seat. She saw heads nodding slowly, distant, thoughtful glances appreciative of his words. It made Jessica's impression of her father's funeral service all the more bittersweet.

These people were remembering Brock Randall with such shared affection for his skills as a facilitator of communication—"bridge-building," as Tom Lancaster had said—as a man who brought others together. They were sincere about it, too, Jessica could tell. These words were more than just funereal platitudes. They had loved Jessica's father for the way he could build connections between others, for all the skills he was somehow incapable of summoning in his own private life.

Jessica's unease haunted her all throughout the aftermath of the wake as the crowd, made up largely of CVSU faculty, staff, and a number of undergraduate and graduate students, headed over to the house of Murray Hamilton, Chair of the Communication Studies department. For appearances, this affair was something Jessica would have been unable to characterize as anything but a "good funeral." This was the way anyone would wish to be sent off into the great beyond.

But it was something Jessica felt detached from because she hardly had the opportunity to be a part of what these people were celebrating. Having rarely seen her father while growing up, Jessica was incapable of feeling anything more than an empty, detached objectivity here. She wanted grief. She wanted to feel loss, but it just wasn't real. She had made an obligatory appearance at the funeral of her father, her last living relative, yet, in truth, she had come to see a ceremony for a stranger.

Unfortunately, the bittersweet emptiness of the wake then gave way to the claustrophobic, overpowering awkwardness of the reception. Since this had basically been an affair by and for the grieving members of Randall's CVSU family, Jessica was an intruder strangers were obligated to talk to when they really didn't want to.

One of the professors—Jessica forgot her name—made a vague comment about her books. She admitted she hadn't read any of Jessica's work, but for some reason, she found them worthy of mentioning.

An actual pattern in the way Jessica was addressed by the

locals emerged soon enough. First, the members of her father's department greeted her. His closest colleagues came to shake hands, offer their condolences, recall outstanding memories, and tell her they were sorry they never got an opportunity to meet her before all this. So was she, Jessica had told them, curtly, politely. There was no need to discuss the bumpy details of her relationship with her father.

Then Tom Lancaster, the youthful and final speaker at the wake, approached Jessica, and the impressions of this entire oppressive and surreal affair turned notably conflicted.

"I never actually worked with your father," a smooth, mellifluous voice caught Jessica's attention, elegantly cutting through the din of the background noise in the reception room. "But I do miss him a lot."

Jessica turned to see Lancaster standing next to her. She, of course, had recognized his voice from the previous speech.

"We got the chance to become good friends, though. This being a small school. Everybody knows everybody."

The youthful professor stuck out his hand, and Jessica shook it.

Again, just like when seeing him deliver his recollections of Brock Randall, Jessica was taken by how much of a contradiction Tom Lancaster was to everything, *everyone* here. He was tall, fit, and remarkably handsome, whereas the other academics were a somewhat nondescript lot. His handshake was firm and muscular, hinting that the rest of his angular, big-boned physique underneath the well-cut dark suit must also have been this sturdy and athletic.

An uncomfortable feeling nagged Jessica again.

"I'm sorry for your loss," Lancaster said, giving Jessica's hand another shake like he was reluctant to let it go.

Jessica noticed that she didn't mind.

"This is certainly a great loss to our school. To his department," Lancaster said, at last slowly releasing Jessica's hand. His fingers glided over her skin like a quiet, clandestine caress.

"Thank you," Jessica said softly. "I appreciate it," she found herself adding after a beat.

She couldn't help studying the rest of Lancaster's features as he barely stood a foot away from her. His light grey eyes, fixed on her with a fascinated intensity, appeared friendly, gentle, while at the same time promising a powerful, uncompromising intelligence. There was a sturdy, self-assured calmness about this man, Jessica realized. It seemed to come from a strength that was not physical at all but psychic, cerebral. He must have been a man who commanded others' respect by the weight of his ideas.

Upon closer look, Jessica noticed other tiny details about Tom Lancaster that added to his overpowering charisma. She saw the white streaks in his dark brown hair and lines around his eyes, noticeable only in certain, correct angles and specific intensities of light, betraying his otherwise youthful appearance. If Jessica had to guess, she would have put him somewhere just past thirty-five. Tom Lancaster was a living example of why age was so much fairer to men. The white hairs and the lines on his face only made him look better. They gave him that proverbially distinguished appearance.

"And I really appreciate everything you said about him before," Jessica said at length.

"When I started working for CVSU," Lancaster said with a warm, wistful smile, "your father had to serve as a sort of faculty mentor for me. They would match up a new professor with a senior faculty member from another department to sort of show him the ropes and create those connections across the various curricula. He was always such a warm and generous man. We've stayed friends all these years...." Lancaster paused and chuckled affably. "Even if we hardly understood anything about each other's work."

Jessica was moved by how much more natural charm and easy charisma Tom Lancaster had, how infinitely more appealing he was standing here talking about her dead father than all the scores of wannabe actors and future celebrities she always ran across in Southern California. The fact that he was above and beyond Dave Holloman in likeability just stunned Jessica. All the classes and acting coaches and technique couldn't give Dave and his ilk an ounce of what Tom Lancaster, a college professor in a sleepy Southern Illinois town, had in abundance by just being simply honest and decent.

"I would have liked to have been able to know more about this part of my father's life," Jessica said, sorry for all that had come between her and Brock Randall during the last several years.

"I know," Lancaster said evenly.

Jessica couldn't help but raise a quizzical eyebrow at that statement. There was something about its familiarity.

"Somehow, I just feel awkward saying this," Lancaster said, "but your father did tell me about you."

"Oh?" Jessica said simply. She felt surprised for a moment, but then realized it made sense. If this school, indeed, was the sort of close-knit family these people claimed, Randall was bound to have spoken to colleagues about his daughter.

"He had your pictures all over his office, you know," Lancaster said.

Jessica smiled lightly. Again, she was somewhere between feeling touched by this revelation and troubled by a stranger's familiarity with her history with Brock Randall.

"He told me about his divorce and how he rarely got a chance to see you growing up," Lancaster said. "That hurt him a lot. You know that, right?"

Jessica nodded but wondered how much Tom Lancaster knew about everything else, the problems that kept father and daughter apart after Jessica had grown up.

"Actually," Lancaster added, "talk of his office just reminded me of something else."

"What's that?"

"Well, I guess you can call it part of his verbal last will and testament."

"What do you mean?"

"Your father had been gathering together several collections of books and papers in his office. He told me that he wanted you to have them from a lot of old junk he was preparing to get rid of...." Lancaster paused awkwardly.

Yes, Jessica mused sadly, the ironic coincidences of life. Her father had been packing things up, and then he died.

"Let me give them to you, if that's all right," Lancaster said.

Jessica nodded. "Okay. Sure." She was taken, though, by a sort of abrupt end to Lancaster's statement. It sounded like there was more information he would have liked to have added, but something held him back.

"You will be staying at your father's house?" he asked at length.

"Yes, as a matter of fact, I am."

"It's on my way to work. Let me meet you tomorrow morning. I'll drive by the house, and you can follow me to campus. Is that all right?"

"Sure. That would be perfect."

A none too faint smile crept onto the right side of Lancaster's face. There was a warm yet somehow knowing look in his eyes for a moment. Jessica wondered if he was about to tell her whatever it was that he'd held back a minute ago. But they were interrupted when Tom's name was called from across the room. He sought out the source of the voice, regret obvious in his eyes.

And Jessica realized that she was glad to see that look. She was happy that he was reluctant to leave.

"Tomorrow morning, okay?" Tom asked.

"I'm looking forward to it," Jessica said.

"Let me just take care of this," Tom said, and started toward the part of the crowd that beckoned him.

But now she knew why she had originally felt a pang of discomfort when Tom Lancaster first came over to talk to her. It just wasn't right that she should feel a strong, stoking attraction toward this man as she stood here among all these strangers, stood here dressed in mournful black at her father's funeral.

But then Jessica's own name was called. It was called twice, once from seemingly right behind her, and then from further away.

"Miss Lafayette," the closer voice spoke again, quietly despite the noise. Almost...*furtively*, perhaps?

Jessica turned to see who it was and found herself next to another young-looking man in a grey, somewhat wrinkled sport coat. The dark green shirt, minus tie, underneath gave him a sort of thrown-together, lived-in look. Jessica got as far as noticing his longish, dirty-blond hair and lean face before her name was called again, louder this time, from further in the crowd. She caught a glimpse of a man waving at her from about forty feet away. She recognized him as one of the professors from her father's department. She couldn't recall his name.

"I'm sorry for your loss, Miss Lafayette," the stranger told Jessica, then grabbed and shook her hand.

His grip was much like Tom's, Jessica noted, quite different from all the other hands around here used to lifting nothing heavier than pens or chalk. The stranger's grip was strong and abrupt, though not as well-controlled, not as polite and subtle as Tom Lancaster's.

Jessica pulled away as the man relaxed his grip.

"That was a tragic accident that took your father," the man said in a voice that further disquieted Jessica. There was something conspiratorial, insinuating hiding among his words. "Did the police tell you it happened on a dangerous stretch of highway?"

"No," Jessica said, but before she could add anything more, the stranger spoke again.

"Very dangerous," he said. "Although there's never been anything like this head-on collision that claimed your father and Dr. Danziger, his companion in the car."

Jessica almost recoiled from these blunt words. How insensitive could this man be?

"You have to be very careful on those narrow country roads," he added.

"Jessica!" the professor with the forgotten name called again. Jessica saw that he was almost at her side.

Thank God! she almost said aloud. She felt extremely uncomfortable with the man in the shabby grey suit.

"My condolences again," the stranger said. "Your father was a good man."

But the moment Professor Whatshisname arrived, the stranger turned and slinked away into the crowd.

CHAPTER 5

Indeed, what a good man Brock Randall had been, the Predator mused, seeing how many people had come to his funeral. There were enough of them here, in fact, that no one noticed a stranger slip into the crowd.

He could sit and watch Jessica. He could observe her, study her from afar.

Actually, he could barely make it through the events. It had quickly become agony. He was barely capable of containing himself. To be so close to Jessica, to see her in the flesh…to see her…flesh….

The Predator had to leave the events at one point. He had to take a walk to calm down. He always knew how special Jessica was, felt her power over him when he could only see her through Brock Randall's thoughts. But the perfection, the beauty, the divinity he saw before him now was something he could never have been prepared for. His eyes had pored over her every line, her every detail. No matter how objectively he might have tried to assess her appearance, his only conclusion was that she was…*perfect*. Although she didn't look anything like a willowy, high-cheekboned model, her *realness* gave her a much stronger allure, a sort of raw sensuality. Her blonde, girl-next-door looks, an appearance that was closer to the prettiest girl in your high school homeroom class than some exotic runway model, made her all the more magnetic. Her soft, oval face and her somewhat sturdy, curvy body made voluptuous by those extra ten pounds or so women always wanted to be rid of made her seem so much more immediately, tangibly erotic.

But it would all be under control soon, the Predator knew. He had Jessica in his sights now.

CHAPTER 6

"Well, like any self-respecting academic's office," Tom Lancaster said after the communication department's secretary let them into Brock Randall's office and left them alone, "your father's workspace used to look like an over-exhaustive library given too little space for all of its books."

Indeed, Jessica realized, what remained of her late father's small office was a virtual maze of carton boxes stuffed by volumes of books and reams of paper sandwiched between flimsy file folders and into disintegrating interoffice manila envelopes.

"Did you pack all this up?" Jessica asked, her senses assaulted by the sheer bulk of all the books, boxes, and paperwork.

"Oh, no," Tom said, and chuckled. "These people would never let me in here that long."

"What?"

"Never mind," Tom said. "Private joke." After a pause, he added, "It's just a difference we have in perceptions of reality."

Yes, Jessica thought, Tom's comments certainly sounded like some esoteric academic joke, although the mildly condescending undertone was off-putting a bit. She, after all, did have a Master's Degree in Interpersonal Communication. Tom knew that. He should have trusted her to understand his sophisticated jesting.

"The hard science and…uh, *soft* science departments of this school can be funny," Tom said at length.

Jessica tested the weight of a box on top of the nearest pile.

"And those special books my father wanted me to have are somewhere among all this?" she asked as she found the box to be quite light. She could hear loose objects rattling around inside. Maybe things from her father's desk, she guessed. A pang of sadness coursed through her. She wondered if maybe one of those pictures Tom had mentioned was in there.

"Well, all of these things are yours now," Tom said gently. He must have caught a hint of her unease, Jessica guessed.

"Well, truth is, I'm not sure if I would really have use for a lot of this material. Even with my work." Then she thought of something. "Show me what my father wanted me to have, and maybe I'll just go through the other things later. Whatever books I can't use, I'm sure some of his colleagues or students here might be able to do something with," she said, then watched Tom test the weight of a large box. Almost immediately, the muscles across his wide, strong back strained and flexed from the bulk of the box. Wearing a casual, light blue short-sleeved knit shirt because of the relaxed dress codes for summer school, Tom Lancaster left enough of his impressive physique just slightly concealed.

"Sounds like a plan," Tom said, hoisting the box he was handling off a stack of similar containers.

Eventually, they had come to realize that Brock Randall's hand-picked items had been numerous enough to load both the back seat and trunk of Jessica's rental Nissan Maxima. However, the trips back and forth between her late father's office and the parking lot made Jessica think of the passage of time.

"Tom, you're teaching a class today, aren't you?" she asked as he squeezed in the last box that could fit into the back seat of the car.

Tom gently pressed the rear right side door of the Maxima closed. "Not until much later in the afternoon," he said.

"But, I'm probably keeping you from something important

in your office."

"Actually, not really," Tom said, and wiped some perspiration off his forehead. "I don't even have office hours today. I'm free until four this afternoon."

"So, I made you go out of your way so early in the day just to help me with this?"

Suddenly there was a sheepish look on Tom's face, and he let an embarrassed, endearingly boyish smile sneak onto the right corner of his mouth. "Well, I really didn't mind."

Tom paused, but Jessica could feel he wasn't through. There was something else, something more serious on its way.

"You know, this is quite awkward, but in a way, it's also part of what your dad had asked me to do."

"What's that?" Jessica asked when Tom paused again.

"When your father would have invited you down here, he would have tried to set us up for a date. I know, it feels just a bit strange in the middle of everything that's happening, but…I did want to do as he asked."

A surge of adrenaline stunned Jessica. Sure, she had sensed Tom's interest ever since they touched hands last night—she *wanted* his interest—but, nevertheless, his words of clear intent sent her heartbeats hammering.

Tom quickly broke eye contact. "If you call me an insensitive jerk, I'll understand completely, of course," he said. Then his eyes found Jessica's again, his glance eager, filled with anticipation.

"No, I don't think you're insensitive at all," Jessica replied at last. "And…." She paused, watching Tom hang on her words. She could see him, feel him wanting her. Her heartbeats raced out of control now. For a moment, she wondered if she would make a fool out of herself, stammering her next words, shaken by nerves, arousal, euphoria. "I know what my father wanted to do. He'd told me about it."

Tom chuckled at that.

"He didn't tell me who he wanted to set me up with, but...."

"Well, do you accept?" Tom cut in.

Maybe she was rambling after all, babbling foolishly, Jessica thought, but she welcomed Tom's words. "Yes," she said, grinning now. "Yes, of course, I accept."

CHAPTER 7

The Predator could barely split his concentration. In his hands he held the day's copy of the *Cedar Valley Journal*, news of his handiwork splashed across the front page. The *Journal*, just like the two big Chicago papers, had started calling him the "Inquisitor" now for his immolation killings. He burned his victims at the stake after vicious torture, just like they had during the Inquisition's reign of terror. The paper had meticulously detailed what he did to that girl in Carbondale, just like the way he killed the one in St. Louis and the two in Decatur and the one in Chicago. He would almost qualify as a particularly creative serial killer specializing in the Midwest, had he not done a few burnings in Idaho and Oregon as well. The Carbondale killing hadn't been planned as the others, though. He just couldn't resist this time. He had to do something before Jessica Lafayette arrived to be able to contain his excitement, his anticipation. But now here she was...*there* she was! The Predator watched her as she at across the street at the sidewalk café with the professor from Cedar Valley Sate.

The professor—whatever the hell his name was...Lancaster—was the only thing disturbing this perfect setting, the Predator seethed.

He leaned back on the bus stop bench, crossed his legs, and glanced down at the paper again. The bus wasn't due for another twenty minutes, so the Predator had a good vantage point for watching Jessica and her new friend across the street.

Friend, my ass, he almost muttered to himself. The two looked like they were practically lovers already. Lancaster couldn't get his mind off her crotch…and she didn't want him to.

The Predator looked at his newspaper again. He sulked and reread the best parts of the article. He was happy they got all the details correct. It reminded him how he imitated some of the ghastliest tortures of the Inquisition—and added a couple of original touches—once he took that girl to the decrepit warehouse so conveniently removed from the nearest sign of life on the farthest outskirts of Carbondale.

The Predator had started with the Old Standard of medieval torture—he imitated the effects of the rack. He'd often laughed to himself at the thought of having an actual rack and how comical it might be to imagine a serial killer trying to transport, maintain, and efficiently set up such an unwieldy device when he constantly needed to be on the move. Funny! The Predator, though, was creative enough to find a way to improvise the effects of the rack. He usually tied his victims onto a girder or beam of some sort by their arms, then steadily tied heavier and heavier objects to their feet. In Carbondale, he used large chunks of concrete—the abandoned storage area, after all, had been littered with them— slowly dislocating shoulders, elbows, knees, hips, and tearing muscles and tendons, created indescribable pain.

After stretching that little nightclub bimbo—the *Journal* said her name was Cecilia Monroe—until she nearly passed out, the Predator had removed the weights from her feet, but went about tearing up her skin. The coroner was commendable in deducing the exact order in which the tortures were applied, the Predator decided. In turn, the *Journal* didn't seem to flinch in reporting every little grotesque detail. They wrote how the girl was nearly skinned alive by the whipping the Predator administered to her naked back.

The paper, however, didn't explain how things had slowed down after the whipping. For a moment, the Predator had thought she was dead. Luckily, he was able to revive her after cutting her down from the overhead beams. The *Journal*, of course, couldn't have guessed that. In fact, he had revived her well enough to be able to administer even more arcane forms of torture afterwards.

First, he ran a red hot spike through her tongue. That really seemed to revive her. Her convulsive, hysterical shrieking resumed at that point.

Afterwards, letting no good hot iron go unused, he branded lines into both her cheeks. Much like the rack issue, the Predator reflected, something was just missing from that particular torture effort. He needed to be able to brand something more interesting onto his victims' bodies than straight lines. That would go on his to-do list: some type of a customized branding iron.

But the branding was followed by the grand finale, the *pièce de résistance*. Should those illiterate rubes in any of those hick towns where he was tasked with killing not be able to remember their history, he always finished the kill with a final move that quite obviously recalled the Inquisition. Or, perhaps, the Salem witch trials. It didn't matter, of course, as long as the killings looked like they were committed by a religious yahoo. Cecilia Monroe was finally dispatched by getting slow-roasted at the stake.

Before lighting the kindling, the Predator recalled with amusement, he made use of all that blood oozing from Cecilia's wounds to leave a message on a wall. Gauche, he personally thought, but the Handlers insisted on it. "If a man abide not in me," he wrote, quoting Scripture, "he is cast forth as a branch, and is withered; and men gather them, and cast them into the fire, and they are burned."

Then the Predator returned to Cecilia and used her blood

for his own purposes. He licked her wounds, sucked on her cuts and abrasions, and drank her delicious, hot blood. The blood tied him to the Handlers. The blood let him read others' thoughts. It fed the special powers that lay inside him, implanted by tiny droplets of the Handlers' own life force when they chose to share their gifts with him.

Afterward, he tied Cecilia's naked, scourged body to a stake and lit the fires around her. Just as witches or heretics had once been burned, so Cecilia was set to expire very slowly, the flames never big enough to consume her quickly and end her misery.

Holding the newspaper in his hands, the Predator almost forgot about Jessica. He was lost in his recollections, savoring the sounds of Cecilia's screaming as they started echoing through his mind. His nostrils seemed to fill once again with the tang of her burning flesh. He remembered how the blood flowing from her wounds started steaming and boiling. Her screams had been squelched when her perforated tongue had swollen so much it rolled out of her mouth. Her lips had burned off, her skin blackening, shrinking until they receded over her gums, revealing a ghastly, toothy rictus of death.

The paper mentioned something about the girl's parents being under sedation since the discovery of the body. Sure, the Predator mused, taking into consideration how all the ancillary devastation each killing created was satisfying in its own way, but he never did think about all that too much. He was usually focused on a singular event, a singular stimulus.

Although one thing the Predator was not happy with was the name, the papers had taken to attaching to his handiwork. "The Inquisitor." They had fallen for the religious façade, just like they were supposed to, just like the Handlers wanted. But it was all a lie. He wasn't motivated by any sort of religious mania, and none of that Biblical shit the Handlers told him to write in blood held any meaning for him. This posing had robbed him of some experience, the full satisfaction. The Handlers, though, had to be obeyed.

At least they let him have Jessica.

CHAPTER 8

Fitzpatrick's Refreshments was a peculiar but charming cross between a hip, modern café, and a quaint, old-world soda shop, Jessica thought. Maybe Fitzpatrick figured out that there was a market for both in Cedar Valley, but not enough investment capital, or imagination, in anyone else to specialize in just a trendy café or to compete with the *Happy Days*-style soda shop. Pictures on the walls inside revealed that the place had quite diligently maintained its "innocent middle America" image since its opening in 1954.

As they sat at one of the outdoor tables, Jessica mused at how much this place, this street, looked like she had just landed in the middle of Norman Rockwell heaven. The tree-shaded street, especially now with a backdrop of blue skies getting invaded by several blossoming anvil-headed cloud banks, appeared to be begging for someone to whip out a camera and take some pictures.

Jessica had opted for the café side of the menu, going for a cappuccino, while Tom ordered a tall chocolate milkshake.

He must have had the metabolism of a racehorse, Jessica guessed, watching Tom enjoy the insanely high-calorie, high-sugar refreshment. He drank that rich concoction with the guiltless gusto of a little kid, all the while looking so annoyingly fit and perfect. Jessica thought she would need an entire week of her kickboxing classes to even think about taking a sip of a shake like that.

"So tell me," Jessica asked, "how does a college professor like you fit in with a town like this?"

Tom cocked an eyebrow and smiled very coolly. "There are a lot of college professors here," he said, his smile growing wider.

Yeah, a lot of professors, Jessica thought to herself, *and they wear suits with sweater vests and tennis shoes.* "But you seem more cosmopolitan than most of them."

Tom laughed now, a hearty, full-throated, thoroughly masculine laugh. "Why, thank you, I guess. Our school is full of very hip faculty, though."

Jessica grinned and sipped her cappuccino. *So in that big, happy family,* she thought, *they were the only ones who didn't like my father and didn't show up for his funeral.*

"In your father's department, being cosmopolitan could be a strike against me, actually."

"How's that?"

"Long story," Tom said, and shrugged lightly. "They're just edgier than us science types."

Some more of that esoteric humor, Jessica thought. But somehow it didn't seem to bother her this time.

"But *you*," Tom said and poked a playful finger in her direction, "are trying to avoid my questions."

Sure, she was, Jessica had to admit, but she was so taken by the urbane Dr. Lancaster that she would just as soon avoid revisiting her problems with her father.

"I'm sorry if I'm being evasive," she said at length after another sip of her cappuccino. "But there's really not that much to tell."

"Or I guess I should be sorry if I'm prying into something that's none of my business."

"No, don't worry about it," Jessica said, hoping her easy tone would help dispel the issue altogether.

"It's just that Brock...that you seemed to be so much a part of his life."

Jessica thought about what he'd said about all the pictures and mementos of her in his office. And, indeed, they were all over his house, too.

"But not enough," Jessica elaborated at last.

Tom raised his eyebrows.

"You noticed how your jokes about the contentious relationship between your departments go over my head."

"They're dumb jokes, I know," Tom said with a dismissive wave of his hand.

"My father would have liked me to follow the same route into academia."

"Really?"

"I grew up away from him, as you know. We only really reconnected when I was going to college, and he got a kick out of the fact that I was interested in communication studies and human behavior and psychology, just like he was. Well, okay, almost like he was. But anyway, when I went for my master's, he was quite thrilled by it. He kept calling me the future Dr. Lafayette."

Tom smiled gently and nodded.

"Although he wasn't so thrilled when I decided against going for my Ph.D. and teaching."

"I'm sorry."

"So was he," Jessica said, and paused to finish the last swallow of her cappuccino. "I did an internship at a New York publishing company, and I was just completely hooked. Then, this editor I was working for thought my masters thesis had mainstream possibilities. She got me in touch with an agent, and the world of academia sort of disappeared in my rearview mirror after that.

And so did my father. Five months later, I had a book contract. My father probably thought I had sold out. Took the easy money and ran."

"Well, if he really wasn't a part of your life until that point, I don't believe he could seriously expect to have the right to dictate how you should live your life."

Jessica was relieved to hear this. Tom's perception and sensitivity just made her like him all the more.

"Now, I liked your father," Tom added. "Like I said, I think he was a good man, but he was just overstepping the boundaries of how much influence he had a right to exert on your life."

"Thanks," Jessica said and paused, hoping Tom would just get off this topic.

He, indeed, seemed to have no more desire to mine her past. He sipped some more of his chocolate shake instead.

Jessica was glad. But she was also intrigued by him. The attraction she felt for him was the best kind, she thought. She wanted to know more about him. She wanted to know who he was, what he was all about, what were the things he believed in, things that made him who he was.

Plus, she considered, turnabout was fair play. She wanted to mine some of *his* past.

"So what's life like in a town like this, anyway?" she asked.

"It's both peaceful and a bit boring at times," Tom said.

"Slow?"

"Sometimes. Chicago, of course, is an option now and again." Tom grinned and shook his head. "Well, okay, if you want to take a commuter flight up north."

"Peaceful's nice, though."

"Well, there are some good people around here, too," Tom said somewhat contemplatively. There was a glint in his eyes and a distant smile on his handsome mouth. "Except you have to be careful when they start talking to you about ghost lights and mystery beasts."

"How's that?" Jessica asked, thinking his last sentence was the most remarkable non sequitur, if there ever was one.

Tom let out a somewhat long, melodramatic sigh and took a healthy sip of his milkshake. "Well," he said at length, drawing the word out, making it long and belabored, sounding like he was about to expound on the nature of that proverbial cross he was condemned to carry. "Let's just say that Southern Illinois is very rich in folklore."

"How exciting," Jessica said, thinking that she always loved a good mystery story, a good enigma that seemed to exist somewhere outside the box of conventional thinking.

"If you remember that it's all folklore and myth," Tom said. Somewhat strongly, Jessica thought.

"What? People around here don't?"

Tom chuckled. "No, unfortunately, they don't. Or — let me be fair — a disturbingly large number of them don't. So just be careful if any wide-eyed locals come up to you and try to convince you that they can help you solve all the mysteries of the universe by channeling Gandhi's ghost through their crystal pyramids."

Jessica couldn't help but laugh. Tom's story sounded quite absurd, on the one hand — as hyperbolically absurd as he, no doubt, intended it. But, on the other hand, there was something of a frantic edge to his voice that made his recitation pricelessly funny.

"All right," Jessica said. "I'll be sure and watch out for those folklore zealots."

Tom sighed. "But no, these locals are not all superstitious kooks, no."

"Actually, if you want to know something my father said about you...," Jessica said, purposefully letting her voice trail off, teasing him.

"Absolutely!"

"Well," Jessica said slowly, "he said he needed to rescue you from them."

"I'm not sure how that sounds, actually," Tom said with a laugh and shook his head. But then he quickly added, "Although I'm really glad he chose you for the rescue operation."

"Thanks," Jessica said, was surprised to feel her cheeks blush.

"But it looks like your father had a mean, condescending streak, though. Well, truth be told, he did say to me at one point that a guy as young as I was when hired by CVSU shouldn't have moved here."

"What? Are the local girls not to your liking?"

Tom shrugged and smiled, but that smile was in no way condescending. "Maybe I wasn't to their liking. But yes," he laughed, amicably now. "I mean no, my relationships with the Cedar Valleyites just didn't seem to be working out. I don't think there's a whole lot we have in common." Tom paused and leaned forward, resting his elbows on the table.

Jessica sensed he was about to turn the conversation around to her again.

And Tom didn't disappoint. "What about you, though?" he asked. "Your father said those books you wrote were very successful, and you were doing guest spots on a TV show down in California."

Yes, the success of her books, Jessica reflected sourly. The books were the issue at the core of her father's constant criticism. Not only did he voice disapproval at Jessica's abandoning higher education, but she also became a convenient target for his academic inverse snobbery, intellectual snobbery. No book the great unsophisticated, unwashed masses embraced could be of any serious merit.

Or, Jessica *preferred* her father harboring that sort of animosity. She was fairly certain that academics hated all those books embraced by the great unwashed, not so much because of that work's dumbed-down inferiority, but because said academics would have liked to have collected those same over-inflated, vulgarly extravagant advances and royalties for their own work. But they, of course, couldn't. The green-eyed monster lived and breathed in the ivy-covered halls of higher education.

Jessica, nevertheless, would still have preferred the green-eyed monster to another possible root of their conflict. Did she just remind Brock too much of her mother? she wondered. Jessica had often mused over that possibility, too, chewed over it sadly. Her parents' marriage, Jessica found out eventually as she was growing up, had disintegrated for the basest reasons: money. Or, more precisely, because Brock Randall wasn't making enough of it for his wife's taste. Now Jessica would never know if that was at the core of their problems. Had she, in her father's eyes, abandoned his world, his ideals, to cash in on superficial, best-selling relationship advice, just like her mother had left him?

"It's radio, not TV," Jessica said.

"Fascinating," Tom said. He sounded quite impressed and genuinely interested.

"It is?" Jessica asked, just to make sure.

"Absolutely," Tom said eagerly. "How glamorous. Here I am on a date with a real radio star. This is exciting."

"Thanks," Jessica said, feeling a bit self-conscious now by Tom's attentions.

"And believe me, your father was very proud of what you did, too. I'm sure of it."

"In a way, I realize that. I just wish we could have had some more time to sort our problems out."

"Well," Tom said with a cheerful, goofy grin, "at least it pays better than academia, I'm sure."

Jessica forced herself not to react to the sting of that comment. Of course, Tom couldn't have imagined the complexity of all the difficult feelings between her and her father, but she still just wished they could steer clear of these topics.

"It makes me wonder why your father had to try and set you up on a date with someone."

"What do you mean?" Jessica had to ask, as much as she was hurting by now for the right word, the right phrase somewhere in this conversation for a segue onto another topic.

"Best-selling writer and radio personality? I would think those sophisticated California men are flocking after you."

"Thanks. But you'd actually be wrong."

"Oh, you're being modest," Tom gently teased, but leaned forward over the table still, attempting to get closer and closer to her.

Jessica was glad he did. "Well, let me tell you," she said. "The best-selling books and the radio show tend to drive a lot of men away."

"I have a hard time believing that."

"They think it's intimidating."

Tom raised his eyebrows. Jessica thought his stunned expression might have been done in jest, exaggerated, but she couldn't be sure. She didn't dwell on it, though, because of the jittery, wonderful fluttering sensation in her stomach.

"Even the successful ones, you know," she said. "Not just my ex-boyfriend, the struggling actor."

"Well, they're just not too smart in California," Tom said, and Jessica thought his beaming smile could just about melt her out of her seat.

"Thank you," she said, hoping Tom could hear the giddy happiness in her voice.

"I'd love to take a look at your books at some point. You know, the truth is that when your father told me what you do, a blind date with you was something I didn't need to be talked into. I'm not intimidated by you, Jessica."

"You don't know how much that means to me," Jessica said, unable to suppress a giggle that came with it.

Except something caught her eye then. Crossing the street. Very briefly, but unmistakably, he was looking their way. Looking *at* Jessica.

It was the strange man from the wake, Jessica realized. The one who shook her hand and commented on the way her father died in the car crash. He was crossing the street down by the end of the block. He was coming from the opposite side over to Jessica and Tom's side.

Despite the fact that yesterday he had stood only inches away from Jessica, only now could she take more accurate stock of his appearance. He, indeed, appeared to be somewhere close to Tom's age. Perhaps younger even. Dressed in a pair of jeans, sneakers, and what appeared to be a light cotton shirt, he had a solid-looking, but somehow rangy, build to his body. For some reason, he made Jessica think of a coiled snake, quiet, unassuming, but with an air of potentially explosive, potentially dangerous capabilities not too far below that still exterior. His unruly blond hair seemed to reinforce his youthful impression, and only now did Jessica consider that his face was not unappealing. She thought he reminded her of the seventies pop singer Andy Gibb, but with harder, more aggressive angles.

But he was keeping an eye on her, Jessica realized. She was shocked by the cold, inexplicable chill that thought gave her.

Will he come this way? she thought as the stranger hopped onto the edge of the sidewalk.

At once, Jessica wished she could move a few inches closer

to Tom, *and* she ran through her mental checklist of moves from her kickboxing class.

But then the guy turned abruptly and walked into the used bookstore in the middle of the block some eighty or so feet away.

It was a ruse, Jessica knew. He might have dodged into that store, but the guy had no interest in books, she was certain. Whoever he was, he had graduated from giving her the creeps up close in a crowded room to following her around.

"Well, you have to appreciate the fact that I'm asking this with an insanely elevated heartbeat," Tom's voice snapped Jessica out of her thoughts of dread and stalkers. "But," he said, "could we have a repeat of this day?"

His voice helped dispel the apprehension, Jessica realized. She smiled at him and said, "Yes, absolutely."

CHAPTER 9

The very woods, the bushes, everything around the Predator seemed to be alive and raging. He felt his face get lashed by a few droplets of rain, but mostly he was challenged to stand his ground against the gusts of howling wind that threatened to tear up everything around Brock Randall's house.

Five feet away, a gnarled branch, rendered from the tree above, crashed and splintered across the ground. But the Predator quested forward, approaching the Randall house. His adrenaline raced and prepped him for the kill. All of his natural senses were raised, honed in on the house, seeking out Jessica. With his ultra-human abilities, he tried to reach out, tried to enter Jessica's mind.

Can't do that yet, the realization pulsed through the Predator's mind. *Not strong enough for it yet. I don't have enough of the Handlers inside of me yet. I don't have enough blood in me yet. I don't have enough flesh in me yet.*

But this time, the Predator's limitations weren't frustrating him. He saw his condition as a challenge. It heightened the sport.

He quested forward, fighting the deafening, barreling assault of the winds as he tried to get through the thick foliage surrounding Brock Randall's house. He could see the lights from one of the windows already. Jessica was in there. She was almost moments away.

But this time, it would be different, the Predator promised himself. With Jessica, he didn't want to enact the Inquisition routine. He would rebel this time, he decided. He wanted to take Jessica on his own terms. He knew the Handlers didn't like it, but they owed him this much. He wanted to enjoy Jessica, wanted to savor her blood covering his body, its taste, its odor, the feel of her life force washing over him. He wanted to taste the sweet flavor of her flesh as he stripped it from her body, as he sliced it off her bones one delicious sliver after the next. But he would refuse to defile the act with tawdry, cheap theatrics. He refused to enact that ridiculous Inquisition make-believe with Jessica.

He could feel them in his head more clearly now as he skulked through the violently dancing, wind-ravaged underbrush. The Handlers were keeping an eye on him—or at least one of them was. The Predator felt a strong presence occasionally in his mind. Someone else's probing thoughts came and went, followed him as he forced his way closer and closer to the house.

Then, with one draining sheet, the rain exploded all over the Predator. The storm had arrived in full force now. More branches picked off the ground, torn off trees, or stripped from the bushes swirled around the Predator as he got soaked to the skin.

But none of that mattered because the Predator thought he saw movement inside. He caught a glimpse of Jessica. The rain, the winds, the branches, the blowing leaves, the phantom presence of a Handler inside the Predator's mind could all be blocked out. He was the true master of all the elements around him now. He stalked his prey, and he was unstoppable.

Incapacitating pain exploded through the Predator's head, and he was propelled to the ground. He could vaguely make out splinters of wood raining around him, spearing into the softening ground as he fell face down onto the forest floor.

CHAPTER 10

Jessica wondered if it was a hailstorm coming down outside. It sounded like solid objects were assaulting the window panes, peppering the roof overhead.

Bright flashes of lightning strobed through the night. Then, for a moment, there was nothing but silence and darkness beyond the living room windows. Jessica knew what was coming. A violent series of thunderclaps rattled the windows and clattered glass throughout the house.

The lights flickered on and off, and Jessica was apprehensive for a moment. If the storm knocked out the lights, how would she negotiate the house, especially the basement, until she found a flashlight? She barely knew this place and hadn't had the time to reconnoiter all of its rooms and storage spaces so far.

More blasts of thunder went off, but there were no more flickering lights.

"So how about you pass quickly?" Jessica whispered, abstractly speaking to the storm.

Breathing a sigh of relief that the lights seemed to be okay, she approached the mantelpiece below the living room's grand arched bay window. She placed her father's urn in its proper resting place while it still occupied this house. Until Jessica left, she would keep her father's ashes surrounded by the memories he had placed on the mantelpiece. They were a collection of pictures of himself and his late second wife, Carol, along with childhood, teenage, and recent pictures of Jessica. Brock's will had asked that after he was cremated, his ashes be scattered over the Pacific, off the coast of San Diego.

She wondered when Brock had made that addition to his will. Was it recent, or had he put that in a long time ago? Had he, in his own thoughtful, plodding way, been working on some private time table to try and get his daughter back into his life? So much didn't make sense, Jessica thought.

"Why did you wait so long?" Jessica whispered.

She wondered if that stab of a particularly unpleasant sensation spreading through her body was a wash of anger. She didn't want to be angry at her father. She so desperately wanted to gather and hold on to some remnants of who he was, and she didn't want them intermingled with bitterness, with anger.

Could he have felt such a grudge over her choice of careers? she wondered. It made no sense. It wasn't like she was a criminal or dancing topless somewhere. What kind of a stubborn allegiance did he have to this insular academic world of his?

Maybe Tom could help me figure that out? The thought automatically crossed her mind.

A bittersweet feeling followed. Her attraction to Tom Lancaster, she mused. The man she had fallen for when she came to collect her father's ashes.

We'll see what Tom will help me sort out, Jessica thought as she turned away from the mantelpiece.

Tom, of course, brought up another set of complications. Just what were her feelings for him? What could happen between them? What did they have time for during these few days she was in town? Did she really want time for anything else, or were her feelings for Tom all a result of her breakup with Dave?

Of course, that's part of it, Jessica almost said aloud as she ambled toward the coffee table and the *TV Guide* on top of it. She intended to watch a couple of hours of TV, dull her senses with a glass of wine, and get some sleep before wrestling with these issues some more tomorrow.

But Dave Holloman was still a ghost lingering over her fractured love life, Jessica thought. And of course, Tom looked all that much better because David had been such an insecure, neurotic jerk. Not only was Tom not intimidated by her stature and accomplishments, but he seemed honestly intrigued by them. In short, Tom Lancaster was all the good things David hadn't been.

A double crash tore through the living room, and Jessica nearly jumped into the glass-topped coffee table in thoroughly disorienting fright. Moments later, she realized the *TV Guide* was no longer in her hands. Apparently, her panic reaction had flung it away.

Gusts of wind tore through the living room, and Jessica could feel a light, yet stinging, spray of water lashing across her face. Looking toward the source of the chaos, Jessica realized what caused both crashing sounds that had nearly stopped her heart. The first sound came from the gnarled, creaking tree branch that had shattered the bay window and now insanely gesticulated back and forth like a giant, demonic hand. But the second crashing noise was caused by her father's urn. The tree branch and the inrushing wind had swept it, along with all the pictures, off the mantelpiece. It now lay on the floor, its lid open. Brock's ashes were intermingling with the torrents of incoming water on the Persian rug, the hardwood floor, and inside the confines of the jar.

CHAPTER 11

"The living room's a total mess, and God knows if I'm going to find water stains in the basement after this," Jessica explained to Tom over the phone. "I mean, there's hardwood flooring in here, and it's pretty old…."

"Oh, you're kidding," Tom replied. "It's cracked, you mean."

"Yeah. I've been mopping all this up since the rains stopped, and tried to throw every rag and piece of paper over it to soak everything up, but the water had to have seeped way down underneath." As a matter of fact, Jessica could still feel the stubborn, unrelenting moisture in the floorboards under her bare feet. "Just what I needed before I start talking to some real estate people."

"I think your main problem's that window, don't you?" Tom asked.

Jessica let out an exasperated chuckle. "Of course," she said, and looked out the empty hole where panes of glass used to stand a few hours ago. A brilliant sunny morning mocked her from beyond. "Have you heard if we're supposed to be getting any more rain today?"

"Actually, I'm not sure, but yeah, you're right. You need to get that covered up as quickly as possible."

"Which way to the local hardware store?"

"I think I've got some sheets of plywood in my garage at home."

Jessica felt a wash of warm euphoria spread through the center of her body. Tom Lancaster truly had her, she realized. In the middle of this calamity, the first thought of seeing him again made almost every frustration melt away.

Almost every frustration.

"Tom, listen." She had to shift the conversation to the other pressing issue that had just come up in the morning. "There's something else I wanted to tell you about."

"Yes?" he asked with that incredibly solid, reassuring, competent firmness in his voice she longed to hear.

"It's something real weird. Kind of troubling, actually."

"What is it?"

"Last night, when that branch got blown through the window, it swept everything off the mantelpiece. Including my dad's urn."

"Oh, no."

"Tom, the top of the urn came off, and some of the ashes spilled. And water got into the urn as well."

"Oh, *no!*" Tom reiterated.

"The thing is…," Jessica said and took a couple of steps toward the suspicious spot on the floor. She swept her toes back and forth over the spot, and it still felt different from the rest of the floorboards. She thought about the old towels she used to soak up the area on the floor where the ashes had spilled, and she thought about the spot on the wet Persian rug had where more ashes spilled. "They hardened."

"What?" Tom's voice turned incredulous.

"Tom, I don't know what's in that urn."

"You mean you don't think—"

"Almost all of it had completely hardened. In the urn, on the floorboards, on top of rags I used to soak up the mess, as well as on the rug. Kind of like…I don't know…cement or concrete or something like that."

Tom was silent for several seconds. Of course, Jessica realized that what she had said was not easy to respond to.

"Completely hardened," he said at length. "Well, let's take a look at this."

"Tom…," Jessica was about to begin but had to pause. What she was thinking was so strange had become hard to articulate. "I don't think I was given my father's ashes." She paused yet again, waiting for Tom's reaction, waiting for him to tell her she sounded completely insane. When he didn't reply, she said, "I don't know what they gave me at the funeral home, but I don't think these are my father's ashes."

CHAPTER 12

Jessica's world had taken a turn for the surreal and, she thought, with every passing moment, reality was slipping further away from her grasp. And now here she sat in front of another quaint Cedar Valley sidewalk café on Bridge Street with her father's funeral urn in a shopping bag next to her foot, a flier proclaiming the near-future construction of something called Heritage Gardens in one hand, and another flier asking her to help fight the pernicious threat of fundamentalist religious mind control in the other.

The anti-mind-control flier, handed out by a girl in a hippyish, flowing gypsy skirt and flower-embroidered shirt, seemed to have its specific ax to grind with Heritage Gardens, claiming it was going to be a "Concentration Camp for Fundamentalist Indoctrination."

Jessica crumbled both fliers into a tight ball, pitched them into a trash can a few feet away from her chair, and scanned the street all around. She searched for the silver Ford Fusion she was certain was following her.

"Dear God, I'm losing my mind," Jessica whispered to herself and looked around for the waitress she thought she saw a moment ago. She needed a cup of coffee fast if she was going to be able to figure all of this out soon.

She was certain a car had been following her. She thought she spotted the same silver Fusion at least three times in her rearview mirror on the way into town.

And what are the odds of that? she had to ask herself. Then she had to answer quite honestly and rationally by admitting, *The odds are quite good, actually. This is a tiny town. You're bound to run into the same people a lot.*

"It's not that tiny," she then muttered to herself, her overly-cautious side trying to assert itself. She preferred not to think of it as her paranoid side, only her *overly-cautious* side.

The fact was, caution suggested that although geographically the town was very small, it did have the Cedar Valley State University campus nearby. The small town, in turn, was usually overrun by the students. So, running into the same person three times, all over town, especially finding the same car in one's rearview mirror three times, was bound to be more than mere coincidence.

Or maybe not, she tried to retort. It was the summer and, even with the school, there were bound to be a lot fewer students around. Perhaps running into the same Fusion three times was within the realm of statistical probability.

Jessica was almost able to calm down until she glanced onto the street again. A cold, crawling wave of fear passed through her in a flash instant.

The silver Ford Fusion just cruised by. It seemed to move slowly, *too* slowly even for the speed limit. It looked deliberate, predatory. It looked like a menacing steel and glass hunter stalking her.

Then she wasn't sure if she saw what she did or if it was her imagination filling in the blanks with her now-deep-seated, dread fear. Although she couldn't make out the features of the driver, she thought he might have had an unruly head of shady blond hair.

CHAPTER 13

Almost the moment the Ford disappeared around a corner three blocks away, Jessica saw Tom Lancaster jogging across the street. It looked like he'd parked his Toyota Avalon at the only available parking meter on either side of Bridge street.

She couldn't help exhaling a breath of relief at the sight of him.

"Thank you for rescuing me," Tom said quickly as he rushed to Jessica's side.

"What's that?" she asked.

For a moment, they both seemed to be caught in an awkward position. How to greet physically, Jessica realized. They were too familiar for a handshake, but were they at the point of a kiss?

Tom took the initiative by giving her a light but decidedly possessive hug. Jessica leaned her right cheek toward him, and she felt his lips brush her.

"Thanks for getting me away from the office," Tom said as they sat down. "I let my students spend their day in the library working on a project, and I thought I could play some hooky. Then I get accosted by two colleagues wanting me to take sides in some equation they're arguing about."

"Actually, I was starting to feel bad for dragging you into this problem."

Tom smiled at Jessica with that slightly detached, placid smile he could ease into that seemed to suggest he was so far above life's mundane, petty concerns. Of course, what made this attractive to Jessica was that in no way did Tom appear to possess those obvious hints of barely-contained arrogance and condescension she remembered on too many academic gas bags from the days she was in grad school.

"Not at all," he said. "Your concern sounded very serious. I'd like to be able to help you out."

"Well...," Jessica said, and paused. She, in part, tried to make a mental list of all the serious concerns she had — and the ones she cared to share with Tom right now — and marveled at how much she just enjoyed hearing the sound of his voice. "First there was the concern of my missing window, and I'm liking more and more the idea that you have some plywood handy — "

Their conversation was interrupted by a waitress who took their orders for a couple of sandwiches and some coffee.

"So, where were we?" Jessica said after the girl departed.

But she was noticing Tom's gaze drifting toward the bag at her feet.

"That you think you have bigger problems than just your broken window," Tom said.

"Just take a look at it," Jessica said simply.

She handed him the shopping bag and the urn. He discreetly looked inside without removing the urn from the plastic. Jessica watched his face closely and saw it stiffening with discomfort, but only momentarily. Then he jostled the urn around, probably to see how much of the material inside had hardened.

In truth, the...whatever it was inside the urn, had not hardened into one large, blocky mass. Not enough water had gotten in for that to happen. The urn contained some light grey ash-like dust intermingled with several large, hardened chunks.

"Well, doesn't it look like...concrete?" Jessica asked before Tom appeared to be comfortably ready to offer a judgment.

"It's certainly unusual," he said at length and glanced up. His eyes were decidedly troubled, not merely curious after this weird mystery was handed to him.

"It doesn't look like ash, does it?" Jessica asked.

Tom seemed reluctant to answer outright. Jessica wondered why. There was no way anyone could look at what filled that urn, those rock-hard chunks, and conclude there was nothing out of the ordinary.

"Yes, it's strange," Tom spoke at last. He slowly shook his head. "As to what it is…."

Jessica couldn't help but drop her voice, even though no one sat nearby. "They're *not* my father's ashes," she said.

Tom just raised his eyebrows. *Why is he so reluctant?* Jessica wondered.

"Don't you think?" she pressed.

"Look, Jessica, that would be pretty serious…." Tom's voice trailed off.

Indeed, there he was right, Jessica knew. If one followed her suspicions to their logical conclusion, it raised a lot of very big, very bad implications.

"I know," she said. "What did they do at the funeral home?" Then she paused for a moment because the next part was difficult to articulate. "If those are not my father's ashes, then…what happened to his body?"

"Yes, that's the obvious question," Tom said, sounding a bit more resolute again all of a sudden. That calm, solid, self-control Jessica was looking for had resurfaced. "But, again, it's a pretty serious question, and it's loaded with a lot of implications and accusations."

"Of course. If those people at the funeral home didn't cremate my father, then what…what did they do with him?"

"Hard to imagine, right? With all due respect," Tom said,

sounding ever more grave and steadfast.

"Yes, exactly."

"And that's why, before we even try and go there, we have to be absolutely certain as to what it is that we have in our hands."

Somehow, Tom not only sounded determined but pedantic, actually.

"Sure, there seems to be something strange right here," he said, sounding like he was delivering a lecture in a classroom. He placed the urn in the shopping bag on top of the table, much like he would a piece of teaching aid. "But we need to understand exactly what this is. Could it be, in fact, an urn full of your father's ashes, but somehow altered by some sort of an uncanny chemical reaction?"

"Chemical reaction?" Jessica found herself blurting out. A moment later, she was glad she didn't blurt out something like "that sounds ridiculous."

Tom nodded slowly.

"But how? It was only rain water that got in the urn. After the window was broken and everything spilled over."

"Aha," Tom said and nodded. "The rain got onto the powder inside the urn. Or it *also* got onto the powder inside."

"What do you mean?"

"Well, it also got onto the urn itself. The walls on the inside of this jar."

"So?"

"So, could it be that what's causing the strange reaction, the rocklike hardening of the ash, is not the ash itself?"

"You mean the jar did this?" Jessica asked, *trying* to sound as incredulous as possible. She thought she knew where Tom was going with this, but it simply sounded too far-fetched.

"Why not?" Tom said with a raised eyebrow.

"That sounds like a stretch."

Tom smiled now, but he no longer seemed pedantic. It was a sweet, sympathetic smile, Jessica thought. "Could be. But I think it can logically be considered."

"How?"

"Shoddy craftsmanship. If this is a poorly made urn, if whatever glazes it's treated with are not applied properly, they could cause a reaction when touched by just the right amount of water for just the right amount of time, at just the right temperature. I think that if the proper conditions exist, you could have some really weird stuff going on."

Okay, so Tom's a what? Physicist? Jessica thought. *Which means...what? He should know about weird chemical reactions like this? Yeah, that's probably right.*

Perhaps, she considered at length. But *that* raised another obvious question.

"How can we be sure?" she asked.

"Good question," Tom said amiably. "We need to test this."

"Can you?"

"I think I can try."

"At your school, you mean?"

Tom nodded. "Yeah. There are some labs and a couple friends I can ask for a favor."

"And they can tell us for sure?"

"They can tell us what's going on with a very high probability. Then we can see where we go from there."

"A high degree of probability," Jessica mused, realizing that she might have sounded more incredulous than she intended.

Tom just smiled, though. "Yes," he said after a beat, "a high degree of probability. Actually, I would always advise anyone to be careful of people who give too many easy and absolute answers."

"I believe you," Jessica said, and smiled back at him.

"And, since questions raised about the funeral process can open a whole 'nother can of technical and legal worms, I say we try and first account for any other, more mundane explanations for what's going on here."

"Oh," Jessica said simply.

"Forgive me if I sound like I'm lecturing you," Tom said with a slightly embarrassed smile.

"It's okay," Jessica said lightly, making it sound playful. "It's your job, right?"

"Well, it's not very polite. It's just that...well, recently, after some of the things that have been going on around here, I just want to tell as many people as possible to always just try and keep their wits about themselves when met by any kind of a confusing or strange problem. There's a simple, elegant, and *logical* explanation to most mysteries."

Interesting speech, Jessica thought, but she realized there was also something else there between Tom's words. Something important to him.

"What's been going on here?" she asked.

Tom did a melodramatic roll of the eyes. "Oh my goodness, where do I begin?"

He brightened somewhat, though, upon seeing the arrival of the waitress and their lunches. A respite he welcomed from diving into a story he must have found very odious, Jessica speculated.

CHAPTER 14

"Don't worry, I'm not letting you off the hook, though," Jessica teased as Tom continued wolfing down his club sandwich in order to avoid getting into his story of the strange and frustrating things that had plagued Cedar Valley.

He gave her a lopsided smile that was actually more like a grimace.

"I'm getting more and more intrigued with every passing moment," Jessica said and nibbled on her own sandwich, then sipped some of her cup of strong, but very delicious, coffee.

"Nothing that intriguing, believe me," Tom said at last. "Just a lot of annoying, frustrating, and petty things people are all too capable of."

Jessica noted how strongly insistent his tone was. "Come on, what's happening?" she demanded.

"Well, you might have seen some ads and fliers around town about the future site of Heritage Gardens being close to our fair town, right?"

"Oh, yeah, as a matter of fact. But I've also seen some people not too happy with it, I think."

"Yes," Tom said, and smiled ruefully. "We, unfortunately, seem to be a magnet for too many people living in their own fantasy worlds. Heritage Gardens, you see, is the charitable project of the Reverend Jim Garnett. The recently image-revamped, ever-so-slightly-rationalized Jim Garnett and the Celebration of the Word

Ministries."

"Wait a minute," Jessica said. The name sounded familiar. "Didn't he try to run for the governor of this state some years back?"

"Yes," Tom said, very sourly. "When he wanted to use it as a testing of the waters for a possible presidential bid down the line." Tom paused and let a somewhat strained, awkward smile creep onto his face. "Now I know they say you should talk about religion and politics if you want to lose friends, but I just have to go to the mat with this one. I'm glad I never had to call him governor, let's just say. He's a nut job. The thing is that he's also a pretty intelligent nut-job, and that makes him dangerous. I think some of the most dangerous people in history've had that potent combination of qualities...but that's just me on my soapbox."

"No, I think you're pretty close to the mark."

"Thanks! Now I don't know if you know this, but the Reverend Garnett had first made his fortune, which he reinvested in his televangelical organization, as a writer of books on the coming Apocalypse."

Now things were getting colorful, Jessica realized. "No, I think I missed that."

"Yeah," Tom said, and shook his head in dismay. "Back in the seventies, Reverend Jim wrote this series of best-selling Antichrist books prophesizing the coming of Armageddon and the beginning on Satan's reign on Earth. Very scary stuff, except he called his books nonfiction."

Jessica couldn't help chuckling, although she was more amused by how near and dear this topic seemed to be for Tom. His sarcastic delivery belied a very deep-seated personal affront he seemed to be feeling from the writings and ideas—if not the very existence—of the Reverend Garnett. A very interesting glimpse into Dr. Lancaster's mind and personality.

"Well, Reverend Jim's books sold like hotcakes in the seventies. The age of *The Exorcist, The Omen,* and all that Satanic stuff in the pop culture. You can imagine how well the reprints sold in the years just before the millennium."

"Yeah, I can see that."

"Well, anyway, he made a lot of money over the years as a media-age fire and brimstone fundamentalist preacher warning of how the gates of Hell—opened up by sex, drugs, rock 'n' roll, legalized abortion, TV violence, and the commies—have let Satan's minions walk among us. Now the really twisted thing is that his followers are actually *looking forward* to the Antichrist and all these demons taking over the world because *that* will lead to the ultimate showdown between God and the devil.

"But anyway, once Reverend Jim developed political ambitions, he was smart enough to realize he had to distance himself from all the Antichrist and gates of Hell and demon rhetoric if he wanted to be taken seriously. Well, he became shrewd enough to also realize that his political platform had to go beyond the old standards like anti-abortion protests, school prayer, and teaching creationism in science classes. He's learned a lesson from his failed gubernatorial campaign, and he's now working on funding inner-city youth shelters and becoming a tireless crusader against racial bigotry and intolerance. It all seems to have reenergized his political prospects. It's broadened his base."

"Interesting," Jessica said.

"But, nevertheless," Tom continued quickly, "his Antichrist-hunting constituents from the old days are still following him around. A group of them have recently tried to start a grassroots campaign right here in Cedar Valley to abolish the UPC bar codes."

"Bar codes?"

"Yes, bar codes. They contain the mark of the beast. You know, six six six."

"I see," Jessica said with ample sarcasm of her own. She could see why a man of reason like Tom could be bothered by the anti-bar-code coalition forming right in his own back yard."

"Now this is pure speculation on my part, I'll grant you that much, but I would be willing to put some money down and wager that this murdering freak we've been hearing about—what did they call him, the Inquisitor—might one day possibly turn out to be a Reverend Jim fan."

Jessica was nauseated by the mention of the Inquisitor killings. She had heard about the torture and immolation killings going on over the past year.

"But of course," Tom said, "there's more! I don't much like the good Reverend Garnett myself, but we also have a group of his critics marshaling their forces in town. And they're just as off the wall."

Jessica laughed, recalling the fliers she'd thrown away. "And his critics accuse him of using the Heritage Gardens as a mind control concentration camp?"

Tom shook his head with pained, exaggerated disgust. "Ah, yes," he said wearily. "You've seen their handiwork. These people, you see, believe that the Celebration of the Word Ministry is the front organization for the New World Order and the fascist, corporatist power elite. Now they're trying to remind the world of all the mileage Reverend Jim used to get out of the Antichrist and the gates of hell and all that, to keep as many as possible thinking of Garnett as an unbalanced, fantasy-prone lunatic—which he might be, of course. But this group also has its own share of delusional conspiracy theories."

"So you have the fringe right-wing nuts going at it with the fringe left-wing nuts, correct?"

"Basically, yes," Tom said, but smiled affectionately at Jessica now. "We go from the Antichrist to the New World Order, corporate conspiracies that killed JFK, fluoridated water for mind control experiments, control of the weather by military satellites, and 9/11 orchestrated at the behest of the military-industrial complex."

"Okay," Jessica said with a chuckle after Tom's very funny litany. "So now I see why you don't like jumping to unsubstantiated conclusions."

"It shows, do you think?" Tom asked and grinned. "Along with my love for politics and demagoguery?"

Now there was an interesting turn of the phrase, Jessica considered for a moment. "Are they the same thing?"

"Today they seem to be," Tom said quickly. "To me, at least. But I've never been much of a political animal to begin with."

"Where is your sense of civics, Dr. Lancaster?" Jessica kidded.

"I *am* a civic-minded person," Tom said, "but I think politics just get in the way of that, really."

"Interesting...."

"I care about facts and data and the logical conclusions they lead to," Tom said, and Jessica noticed more of that fervent energy in his words. "Just like in a lab, the real world is full of problems that need to be analyzed logically, rationally. Problems have logical solutions. Any problem can only have one logical solution. Not a Republican solution or a Democrat solution."

"Again," Jessica said, impressed with the speech, "quite interesting."

"Just my two cents' worth," Tom said, and smiled now with a bashful shrug.

"Actually, I think it makes a lot of sense."

Tom glanced at the bag and the urn at the foot of the table. His face looked serious again. "Jessica, I really want to help you find out what's going on here."

"I know," Jessica said with a reassuring tone.

"And let's find the *truth*."

"All right. And you'll also help me fix that hole where a window used to be in my living room?"

Tom flashed a dazzling smile. "But of course."

CHAPTER 15

"Well, that's a start until the glass people show up and install the new panes," Tom said, and stepped back from the wall outside the living room. He had so expertly nailed the plywood sheet onto the window panes as to shatter all the stereotypes Jessica might have harbored about effete intellectuals once and for all.

She loved the way he put the accent on the finish of the job by cavalierly tossing and flipping the hammer in the air and catching it perfectly. She didn't know whether he did it ironically in mock imitation of the archetypal macho handyman, or if he just felt glad and giddy—perhaps a bit cocky too—to be done. Either way, he looked doubly attractive right now.

"My hero," Jessica teased. "How can I ever thank you?"

Tom grinned at her and wiped a sheen of perspiration from his brow,

It was getting humid, Jessica realized, although the temperature wasn't too hot. She was glad for it, too, because the humidity made Tom's thin shirt cling to his impressive upper body so perfectly. Of course, Jessica had also taken the time to fan herself at just the right moments when Tom was looking, by taking and fluttering the plunging neckline of her thin summer dress.

"Well, don't mind if I ask for some of that cold lemonade you promised before," Tom asked. While his words were innocent enough, *now* Jessica could detect traces of irony there, undercurrents of a suggestive tone.

Such a gentleman, Jessica thought. She appreciated it, though. However, she really didn't know how she would have reacted if he asked if they could share a shower right now.

"Anything you want," she found herself saying. She almost couldn't quite believe what had come out of her mouth.

"Thank you, ma'am," Tom drawled, playing the part now more obvious.

"Well, come on now," Jessica said and ran her fingers along his forearm, taking him by the wrist and leading him toward the front door.

But she led him only so far, quickly stepping in front of him and taking the lead up the porch steps. She wondered if she could actually feel his eyes checking out the swing of her hips as she took each step. Of course, she knew Tom would never believe one could literally feel another person's eyes on her. However, she would have gladly admitted to wishful thinking.

Despite the ever-thickening moisture in the air, Jessica and Tom did wind up sipping their lemonades on the front porch—on the wide porch swing, no less. Jessica still marveled at how her father's house so strictly adhered to the look and feel of a stereotypically small-town abode that it could have come out of made-for-TV-film on the Hallmark Channel. She wondered if the perfect quaintness was Brock's doing or maybe that of his late wife, Carol.

"I've told my friends back at school to hurry up with the examination of the urn," Tom said after taking a few very big gulps of the cold lemonade in his tall glass.

"Be careful drinking so fast," Jessica said with a hint of a tease in her voice. "You'll get a sore throat."

Tom grinned at her.

"But I appreciate it," Jessica added.

"Of course, you need to know this as quickly as possible, and I'm happy to try and help."

"Thanks."

"And do you also need to move on quickly after it's all cleared up?"

Jessica felt her heartbeats increasing at Tom's words. But she liked it. She smiled at him coyly. "Actually, probably not."

Tom stared straight into her eyes. "I'm glad, you know," he said strongly.

"Thank you, Tom."

"I know it's an odd type of a situation we find ourselves in — you coming in from the West Coast, living out there — but I'm really glad we met. And I want to keep seeing you."

"I'd like that, too."

"No matter the distance."

"There's no distance now."

Tom suddenly seemed to freeze, then glance at his watch. "I can't believe this," he muttered and hung his head. "Maybe a little distance for the rest of the afternoon," he added. "God, you can't imagine how much I'm regretting this right now."

"An appointment?"

"Retirement dinner at the school this evening. Incredibly boring."

"That's no problem," Jessica said, almost getting caught off guard by Tom leaning closer to her.

"Let me close the distance before I go," he said softly now, drifting closer to her.

Jessica could see his gaze drifting toward her lips. His eyes were filled with as much hunger as she felt.

She let her lips part and received Tom's mouth on top of hers. She could feel the passion, the excitement with which he tasted her, explored and savored her lips, her tongue, deep inside her mouth.

Finally, reluctantly, when he pulled away, she could feel how much he regretted having to leave her behind.

"I'll be crossing off the minutes in my mind until I can see you again."

"Me too," Jessica said.

CHAPTER 16

The only problem left by Jessica's last—and so blissful—meeting with Tom was the fact that she hadn't gotten around to bringing up her worries about the blond-haired guy from the wake and the street the other day.

And the silver Ford? a voice sounded off in Jessica's head. A nutcase stalker who's following you around? Minor little problem to forget, don't you think?

She had felt so good being with Tom yesterday, watching him hammer the plywood in place, kissing him on the porch, that she'd let all of her fears evaporate. There were no stalkers to obsess over when Tom was with her. There was nothing ugly, nothing sick or disturbing that could get to her when she was with him.

What if she was just misunderstanding a simple coincidence? she insisted on telling herself. Just like she reasoned yesterday, this was a small town. And what was it they said about towns like this? Everybody knew everybody else's name.

What was the guy doing at the wake?

Maybe the fact that he was at the wake proved her fears were unfounded. Who could he be if he was there? Maybe a grad student?

She had to ask Tom, Jessica decided. She had to go to the campus of Cedar Valley State, just as he had invited her, and come right out and tell him about this entire crazy business.

So Jessica glanced at her watch, saw it was a quarter to eleven, and decided she would head for CVSU right away. She would get her car from the lot behind The Organization packing store and drive straight to Tom's office.

It did make her feel better that as she approached the end of the block, she realized she had been feeling alone all day. There had been no silver-colored Ford Fusion anywhere. It wasn't in her rearview mirror, it wasn't rounding corners a block away or sneakily parked down the street.

And she hadn't seen any mysterious, off-putting blond men anywhere either.

The parking lot lay right behind The Organization's block and bordered an alley passing behind the store. As Jessica crossed the alley and headed for her car, though, she took notice of how quickly the traffic seemed to increase in such an unlikely spot.

She heard car engines behind her and directly off to her left as well. In an instant, though, the pitch of both vehicles' engines seemed to rise. There were two cars behind her, quickly accelerating.

Jessica walked further into the nearly empty parking lot while turning her head and trying to survey what was happening behind her. She was jolted with fright and adrenaline by what she saw.

Two vehicles were on a collision course at the intersection of the street and the alley. A mat-green, very-old-model van appeared to have been approaching the parking lot, having come from the same direction as Jessica. But as it passed the alley, what appeared to be a small Honda Accord sped right for it. The Honda appeared to be accelerating the closer it came to the van.

Jessica was surprised that she'd missed the Honda in the alley when she crossed it. But now the small sedan definitely made its presence felt as it hurtled down the alley, its engine screaming as the driver gunned it onto a collision course with the van.

The Honda clipped the rear of the van just as Jessica predicted it would. A blast of tearing, crunching metal echoed through the parking lot as the van was flung sideways across the alley and street intersection. The Honda skidded and swerved left and right as it moved further down the alley, eventually decelerating to a full stop.

More than the sight of the bizarre, suspiciously intentional collision, Jessica's own rush of adrenaline and her pounding heartbeats startled her, then inexplicably terrified her. For several moments she felt as is she had been possessed, her body invaded by some alien entity whose only agenda was to trigger every fear and panic reflex inside of her. She felt herself shaking, shivering in abject, inexplicable terror. Sure, some still-functioning, barely-in-control part of her rational mind told her, a car accident was a shocking thing, an unfortunate thing, but why was she so afraid of this one? Why this paralyzing panic attack?

But the paralysis soon passed. It was now countered by some subconscious need to flee. Almost as if her own life depended on it, Jessica instinctively knew she had to get out of there. Immediately, right that instant, more than anything in the world, she just had to escape that parking lot.

Isn't this illegal? that barely audible voice of reason in Jessica's mind spoke again, but by that time she was behind the wheel of her rental car.

Wasn't she obligated to stay and see if anyone was hurt? Leaving the scene of an accident…?

"Well, I didn't cause the accident," Jessica muttered as she started her car.

Besides, the Honda was moving again. Whoever was behind its wheel certainly seemed okay, and anxious to leave the scene of the accident *he'd* caused.

But what about the other guy? Didn't she have some ethical obligation to check his condition? Jessica asked herself as she put her Maxima in gear.

Except she was flooded by another startling, nearly incapacitating wave of panic. Something seemed to be telling her that the only possible way to retain her sanity was to get out of there right now.

Besides, doors had started opening on the buildings lining the alley. Other people had also heard the crash and were on their way to investigate.

CHAPTER 17

"But wasn't it, you know, illegal?" Jessica asked again, realizing with frustrated dismay that she still seemed to be babbling. "The way I left like that?"

Tom smiled at her and pulled his office chair closer to hers. Before saying anything, he pointed to Jessica's hands. She looked down and realized he was right. The can of diet cola was still trembling in her grip.

"Jessica," he said soothingly, "you need to calm down, okay?"

"Oh, God, I can't believe this," she said. "I'm a basket case, and I can't understand why. I've seen accidents before, you know. I mean, I've seen some real crazy stuff on the freeways in L.A."

"I realize that," Tom said calmly. As a matter of fact, his calm, logical, soothing "voice of reason" almost started sounding robotic now. "But you were startled. From what it sounds like, just moments earlier, you were walking in that same spot where these two cars hit each other. Right?"

Jessica nodded. Technically, he was right. She could imagine herself getting mowed down by one of those cars. Or getting pinned between them at the moment of impact.

"Yes, it's a terrifying idea," Tom said. "But I think you probably had some sort of a subconscious realization of what that crash would have been like with you getting caught in the middle. It's not easy to predict, or possibly even to understand, what can trigger panic attacks in people."

"You're probably right."

"Look, you said that one of the cars drove away, right?"

"Yeah."

"And the other one—a big van, right?—had its rear clipped. Well, I really don't think the van driver was hurt at all. And the other guy sure sounds like he was okay, correct?"

"I suppose."

"So there you go. Just remind yourself that this was such an inconsequential, stupid little intersection accident that no one even got hurt."

Jessica took a deep breath and nodded. She leaned back in Tom's surprisingly comfortable guest chair, then straightened out again. "Tom," she said at length, "you're absolutely right about the nature of the accident. Intellectually, I understand exactly what you're saying. But standing out there...I had something way beyond a panic attack. It felt like a nervous breakdown. Like something had crawled inside, wound itself around my brain, and flooded me with pure, near-paralyzing terror. There was only one thing I knew that moment, one thing I knew as certainly as what day it is, and that was that I *had* to get away from that place immediately."

Tom kept looking at her serenely throughout her speech, Jessica realized. He just looked in her eyes with those placid, light grey eyes of his and followed every word out of her mouth. He could have moonlighted as a psychiatrist, Jessica mused. He had a fantastic ability of putting her completely at ease. *And*, she honestly believed that it was more than the mere fact that she was a woman and attracted to him.

"Jessica," Tom said at last. "I realize I'm probably just taking wild shots in the dark here. I mean, human behavior and perception is more your field, right? But I think you need to very seriously consider a couple of things."

Jessica gave him a nod. Whether or not this was his field, his innate intelligence gave him a lot to offer.

"You've been under tremendous pressure lately, haven't you?" Tom asked. "You've been under pressure, and you've been holding up remarkably well. You just lost your father, you're trying to deal with it all alone out here, far from home, in a strange little town, and you're still trying to deal with the turmoil of your troubled relationship with him." Tom paused, seeming to study her reaction. "Does that about cover most of the issues you've been dealing with?"

Jessica nodded but gave him a smile as she did. He was actually quite good at a little impromptu bit of psychologizing. "That covers most of the big ones."

"Maybe these bottled-up pressures just somehow...I don't know, needed a release valve. Maybe a sudden panic attack was it." Then he grinned and shook his head. "I sound like I have no idea what I'm talking about, don't I?"

"No," Jessica said, but quickly added, "I mean yes! You do sound like you make a lot of sense."

Tom was laughing now. Jessica thought his self-deprecation was quite charming.

"See that?" she said. "I'm much better. You've been a great help. I just feel awful, though, that I keep running to you with one emergency after the next."

"Aw, shucks, little lady," Tom said, doing a remarkably corny cowboy imitation. "Always glad to be of service."

"Hammering plywood and psychologizing."

"I can be quite handy to have around."

"Yes, you are," Jessica said, feeling good enough now to start looking around Tom's small, windowless office and take note of its details for the first time. Although as well-stuffed with paperwork and books as most professors' enclaves, Jessica was impressed by how orderly and clean it was. "But, can you just tell me one thing?"

"Well, I'm certainly going to try."

"What's a naked ghost?"

Tom gave back a lopsided grin and threw a glance over his shoulder. "Oh, that little thing. A book I did a couple of years ago. Actually, it did quite well for something by an academic. Got me on a couple of radio and TV interviews, too, if I can brag just a little bit. Of course, it didn't give me my own radio show, but it did okay."

Jessica was looking at a framed cover of *The Naked Ghost: Modern Science and the Challenge of Superstition, Fear, and Unsubstantiated Claims*, by Thomas Lancaster.

"Quite impressive," she said. "And sounds intriguing."

At the same time, and for the first time, Jessica was taking note of the fact that Tom was actually a member of the Astronomy Program of the Department of Physics. Books dealing with things like astrophysics, stellar atmosphere, galactic structure, and astronomical data analysis were piled on his bookshelves. Posters about noteworthy astronomy conferences were on the walls, along with pictures of Stephen Hawking and Einstein, and autographed photos of *Star Trek* creator Gene Rodenberry and science fiction author Arthur C. Clarke.

"So, what *is* a naked ghost?" Jessica asked again.

Tom returned a bashful grin. "Well, it's actually about why certain ghosts *should* be naked," he said with an easy shrug.

It was nice to see an intellectual sounding so humble, Jessica thought. She had run across dozens of authors back at the KBLA studio in San Diego who talked about their books, full of mindless entertainment gossip as if they contained the secrets of the universe, the cures for cancer, AIDS, diabetes, Alzheimer's disease, and the key to ending war forever.

"Well, that sounds quite saucy," Jessica teased.

"It grew out of some articles I wrote in a journal criticizing the claims of some crazy medium who claimed to have found the most haunted house in America. It was supposed to be a house out in Tidewater, Oregon, by the way."

"And it was haunted by a naked ghost?"

Tom let out a rueful little laugh. "It sounds absurd saying it, doesn't it? But no, the house was supposedly haunted by three generations of a logging dynasty, a twelve year old girl who drowned in a creek nearby, and an Indian shaman."

"Crowded," Jessica couldn't help saying.

"You'd think, right? But the most active of these ghosts was said to have been dynasty patriarch Wendell Jefferson Carmichael. He was always seen wandering the halls of the old estate in his finest outfits, always cradling a top hat under one arm."

Tom paused, and Jessica felt his eyes on her. He made her feel a bit like he was expecting her to jump in and explain what was the biggest problem with the ghost scenario.

"Yeah, that sounds pretty wild," she said, feeling like it sounded more than a bit lame.

She thought she caught a glimpse of something in Tom's eye. A hint of disapproval, maybe?

"Ghosts, you understand," Tom said, "at least according to these mediums—or is the word actually media?—whatever. These people tell us that a ghost is actually an alternate-matter glimpse of the transformed energies of a living body. Or something like that. I have to double check my encyclopedia of pseudoscientific nonsense jargon. But anyway, I was arguing that if the ghost is created by this altered energy of a living body, then how come we're seeing Wendell Jefferson Carmichael in his Sunday best? Why are we seeing his stylish haberdashery? Do inanimate objects like cloth and leather have a ghost too? If we only see an altered version of a once-living being, shouldn't that ghost be naked?"

Jessica couldn't help but chuckle. Of course, Tom made sense. Although ghosts and the paranormal were not high on her agenda of issues to contemplate regularly, she would, most often, have admitted to being open minded to the notion. But of course, even in her own mind, a ghost was always a transparent apparition wandering around in period costumes. Tom just made her reexamine a set of her own taken-for-granted assumptions in a radical new way.

"Logic!" Tom said strongly. "That's what the book is really about. I'm saying that if you apply a little basic common sense, reason, and rationality to most claims of the supernatural, you would come to see how absurd it all is."

"Fascinating," Jessica said. "And quite impressive."

"Common sense and a little bit of level-headed thinking will give you the true answers to everything," Tom said, an affectionate tone to his voice now as he leaned closer toward Jessica. "Even mysterious panic attacks."

"Thanks to the brilliant Dr. Lancaster," she teased in return. "Although—"

"Although!" Tom cut in with a mock bombastic tone, stabbing upward with his right index finger. "I am able to commune with the mysterious powers from beyond and guess exactly what you are thinking."

"Well, let's see, what am I thinking?" Jessica played along, of course, knowing what Tom should have been bringing up.

"What's happening with the analysis of the urn," Tom said, leveling his tone now into something a bit more respectful.

"Hmm," Jessica said slowly, drawing out the exclamation. "Even clever and extremely rational scientists might have a hard time explaining that one."

"From what I was e-mailed this morning, we'll probably know for sure by tomorrow."

"Thank you again."

"It's important we know what's going on. We need to know the truth."

"I do have one more question, though."

"Yes?"

"Are you sure I'm not in trouble with the law for leaving so quickly?"

Tom chuckled lightly and winked at Jessica. "I'm pretty sure."

Before she could thank him, though, or compliment his skills as a counselor, the phone on his desk rang with a metallic chirp. Tom's exchange with someone named Bill on the other end was short, consisting of a couple of yes-es and uh-hums. He looked quite relieved when he put the phone down.

"That was a friend of mine from the solid state physics lab," he said with a smile. "We just got some good news about the ashes."

"What is it?"

"Those are ashes, Jessica. No doubt about it. The funeral home gave you your dad's ashes."

CHAPTER 18

Tom had recited some information and names of chemicals that sounded to Jessica like they might as well have been the names of intergalactic city-states in a science fiction novel. Quickly enough, the details of Tom's explanation became a blur. But the good part of all of this was the confirmation of the fact that the paints and the glaze on the urn had caused the solidification of the ash. To prove that case, Tom had gone into the chemistry lecture, detailing some stuff about chemical bonding and solidification, and some such jargon Jessica hadn't heard since the high school chemistry class she suffered through with a final grade of a C+.

"If you can meet me this evening here at say, about nine-fifteen," Tom said, gathering a pile of folders and binders he had to carry off to his afternoon class, "I can give you the urn back."

"Sure," Jessica said eagerly, marveling at the ever more precarious load of books and papers Tom was attempting to handle. "But can I help carry the teacher's books?" she teased.

"It wouldn't be gallant to make a lovely lady carry these heavy burdens," Tom said, attempting to balance the uneasy grasp he had on a lot of slippery binders while trying to pick his keys off his desk. "You could give me those keys, though."

"How about you keep the lovely lady from laughing at you when you drop all this stuff?" Jessica said, and took a pile of binders from him. "So come on, lead me to your class."

Tom did so, the two of them walking across the quiet, tree-shaded campus.

"Tom," Jessica said at last, incapable of putting the next question off much longer. Perhaps, she thought, what she might have been looking for was for Tom to put her at ease about it the same way he seemed to deflate and make vanish all of her other emergencies. "Do you know if there were a lot of graduate students attending my father's funeral services?"

Tom glanced at her with a raised eyebrow. "Why?" he asked after a beat. "I mean, I guess the Communication Department has a graduate program, but why do you ask?"

"Well, I think most of the students who were there looked like undergrads. Around twentyish or so," Jessica said, almost immediately realizing how strange and evasive it sounded.

"I suppose, yeah," Tom said. "But why do you ask?"

"Tom, would you...I mean during the whole thing—the funeral home, the reception—did you see anyone there you didn't recognize?"

"Didn't recognize?" Tom asked, an obvious edge in his voice now. He was catching on to the fact that Jessica was bringing up something sensitive.

"Well, you guys kept talking about the small CVSU community and family and everything." Jessica almost wanted to cringe at the realization of how ridiculously disjointed and rambling and evasive she sounded.

"Jessica," Tom said firmly. "What are you talking about?"

Jessica took a deep breath and decided to get to the point in one shot, no matter how paranoid and irrational it might sound. "I saw a guy at the reception. He came over, shook my hand, offered his condolences, and then vanished almost as suddenly."

"*Vanished?*"

"You know...disappeared in the crowd. But before you think I'm totally insane and having a panic attack again, the point I'm trying to get to is that I've seen that guy since. He keeps turning up in places I go to in town...." Jessica couldn't help but fade out in her explanation under Tom's piercing, skeptical, yet troubled, glare.

"Go on...please," he said as calmly as he had been speaking to her in his office.

"You can go ahead and tell me that I'm getting panicky again—and yes, I do realize how this is coming out, how this sounds—but there's just this feeling I was getting...that this guy was following me around. Like it wasn't a coincidence."

When Jessica paused, Tom asked, "How many times did you see him?"

"I think three, maybe four times?"

Tom slowed his stride and shifted his books in his hands. He looked genuinely concerned now, not so much rationally skeptical. "Four?"

"From my rearview mirror a couple of times."

"You think...."

"Yes!" Jessica said strongly, and nodded. "I thought he was *following* me."

"What do you think now?"

"I don't know. I mean, that's why I was asking you if you thought you saw anyone who looked out of place."

"Aha," Tom mumbled, obviously trying to search his memories of Brock Randall's funeral services. "Well, what did he look like?"

"About your age, I think," Jessica said, and tried to mentally sift through all the features she had been looking for in every crowd lately. "Maybe a couple of years younger."

"Early thirties?" Tom cut in. "Late twenties?"

"Early thirties. That's why I was wondering if he could have been a grad student. Kind of a sturdy build, you know...tough-looking."

"Big? Like a bodybuilder?"

"No, not really."

"Yeah," Tom said, and nodded vigorously. "Someone like that would have stuck out in a crowd."

"He just looked athletic. Like someone who could take care of himself. And he had this dark blond hair. Kind of long."

"Long?"

"Again, that's why I thought he might have been a grad student or something. Looked a bit unkempt. Wore a wrinkled suit."

"Are you sure he was the same man you saw...what? Three or four times?"

That, of course, was the rub, Jessica knew. She couldn't swear to it.

"I'm sure I saw him crossing the street when we sat at the outdoor.... God, what was that place, the café and soda shop?"

"Yeah, Fitzpatrick's."

"Yes! I saw him on the other end of the block then, and I swear he was watching us."

"You could swear to that?"

Jessica nodded. "I'm sure."

"You know—"

"I know! This is a small town, and chances are you run into the same people a lot. Everybody knows everybody and all that."

"Yeah," Tom said, but with less rational conviction this time. "And when you saw him from your car...."

"I don't know if I could swear to that. I thought he might have been following me. But in a real stealthy way."

"Stealthy?"

"Like he made all the right last moment turns and changed directions, so I wouldn't think he was following me."

"Did he look threatening?"

The sixty-four-thousand-dollar question, Jessica knew. And she wasn't sure what to say to that.

"Not overtly, no...I guess," she said.

"Except why the hell is he following you?" Tom was definitely agitated now. Or he showed something like immense self-control doing its best to contain tension, boiling anger just under the surface. "Look," he said at length. "I think the first thing we ought to do is check with the communication department and see if they know who this guy is."

"Sure. Let's make certain we're not jumping to paranoid conclusions."

Tom smiled at her. "Maybe he's one of them."

"And it's all a bunch of coincidences."

"That could be. I *hope* that's all it is."

He did it again, Jessica realized. He could put her at ease so well, so naturally.

"You're gonna hate me so much before long," she said with what felt like a crooked smile.

"Why?"

"I keep doing this to you."

"Come on—"

"It's true! I keep dragging you into all of my stupid problems and neuroses. Maybe I should just go and see a shrink."

Tom laughed. "Come on, Jessica, let's not go too far."

She couldn't help laughing too. "It's true."

"No, it's not. And, as a matter of fact, I was going to ask you if you would be interested in auditing my class. That way, you won't have to be alone until late at night."

Something warm and blissful washed through Jessica now. She was touched by his protectiveness, but she was also seared by a hot wave of anticipation...yearning. What were they embarking on now? Something inevitable? If he felt compelled to be with her, to protect her, even while he had to do his job, what would come later? What would the evening bring?

"That's very sweet...," she began.

"And I'm going to insist!"

"But I don't quite think I'm in mortal danger."

"Do we ever know when we're in serious danger? Do any of us ever choose to become victims of a crime?"

Good point, Jessica thought. And she thought his protectiveness was so sweet. But she couldn't let herself start feeling like a victim, someone who needed to be doted over.

"Come on, Tom," she said lightly. "I saw those books all over your office. Your lecture will start sounding like it's in Chinese in about ten seconds."

"So?"

"I'll fall asleep in your class. No offense!"

"I bet you're even more beautiful when you're asleep," Tom said without missing a beat, and Jessica could have sworn she saw that proverbial glint in his eye. The searing anticipation jolted her again. "Sleeping beauty in my own class," Tom added.

"I'll start snoring."

"I insist."

"Tom, I can't...I *don't* want to. I'm not going to start feeling like some fugitive. And besides, like you said, there's a clear, logical, rational explanation for everything."

"Oh, fighting dirty, are you?"

"Whatever do you mean, Dr. Lancaster?"

"Using my own logic against me. That's not fair, and you know it."

"Tom, really. Plus, I need to do more shopping in town. Have to pick up more packing stuff."

The concern, the deep-seated worry on Tom's face, was quite

touching.

"I'll be back here...when? At nine-fifteen did you say?"

"Be back here at eight. That's when the class lets out. I gotta go to a meeting after that, but I'll be out of there by nine-fifteen or so."

"All right, I give. That's a deal."

"Good."

"Now, get going to class, or your students'll walk out on you!"

CHAPTER 19

Small or not, Jessica realized as she searched for Mississippi Highway to take her to King's Bridge Mall, late afternoon tended to fill up the streets of any town. And rush hour, even in a place the size of Cedar Valley, presented a certain chance of traffic accidents. It almost happened to her when a Saturn cut her off on McCammon Street as it attempted to swerve around a slower car in the far-right lane of the four-lane street.

Idiots seemed to belong in a nationwide brotherhood, she thought as she stomped her brakes to avoid hitting the Saturn. No matter if they were in such thousand-mile-from-nowhere towns like Cedar Valley, or in San Diego, or L.A., the same kind of stupidity caused accidents everywhere. The guy in the Saturn made the risky move all for the chance to get to make the right turn at the upcoming intersection ten seconds earlier.

A split instant later, Jessica's heart was jolted by the sound of screeching tires from behind. Her sudden braking must have caught a driver on her tail off guard.

When her gaze darted into the rearview mirror, trying to see whether she was about to be rear-ended or not, her heart jolted in fear yet again. Her mouth went dry, adrenaline coursing through her body and a spectacularly unpleasant sensation, something akin to getting punched in the solar plexus by a skilled professional boxer, spread through her body.

It was the blond man!

There were no more questions, no more speculation in Jessica's mind. She was being followed! It was the same guy driving the same Ford Fusion, and he was stalking her, just like he had been since she got to town.

Something told Jessica that he knew she knew. Instinct, intuition, that inexplicable, unquantifiable something a hard rationalist like Tom wouldn't give much consideration to, whispered into her ears. The blond guy knew his cover was blown. He would make a move on Jessica very soon.

She had to make a move first.

She did so by hitting the accelerator. *Just get away from him as quickly as you can,* that same instinctive voice spoke to her again, *and think of something later.*

CHAPTER 20

The two right-side wheels of Jessica's car nearly lifted off the ground as she took the hard right onto the entrance ramp toward Mississippi Highway. But she couldn't believe this chase was still going on, she almost yelled out loud as she eased off the gas to avoid sliding out of control in the sharp turn. She had gunned her engine so hard she was sure she exceeded the speed limit on every road by at least twenty-five miles. She flew through two stop signs without so much as letting up on the accelerator. Where were the cops?

The joke about them never being around when you needed them the most was too cruelly ironic right now. She hoped her speeding would attract someone's attention. She hoped a squad car with its chaotically flashing lights would enter the fray, sirens wailing, and that slithering blond bastard's stalking and skulking would be brought to a stop at last.

No such luck on the side streets of Cedar Valley, though, Jessica regretted as she came upon the access to Mississippi Highway. Although she was leery of a chase on the open stretch of road, she had no choice. But maybe *there* a cop would turn up. Maybe if she barreled past a lurking speed trap, this insanity would be brought to a fitting end.

She glanced into the rearview mirror as she merged onto the highway. There was no sign of the Fusion. So *now* she let up on the gas. She looked at the speedometer and watched it report the car's loss of speed.

Then she looked in the mirror again. Where was he?

You son of a bitch!

Did he decide to give up for now? Had he figured out her game? Was he planning on disappearing again, only to strike at her from the shadows somewhere, ambush her on a street, break into her house in the middle of the night?

*God*damned *son of a bitch!*

Then, as perverse as it all felt, she was relieved to see the Ford emerge onto the highway. The chase was back on, and Jessica was glad for it. This would be their showdown, right here and now.

The Fusion seemed to accelerate back there, Jessica noticed. It was coming after her with full force again. Whatever lunacy was driving that stalker, Jessica figured—whatever demons, voices, alien programming, memories of his domineering mother, the girl who turned him down for a date in high school, the father who wasn't a strong enough role model—whatever motivated all these sick, sniveling freaks, it was too much for the guy right now. He must have been kicked into overdrive by his mania and couldn't give up on the chase now.

"Come on, let's get it on, you twisted piece of crap," Jessica found herself hissing through gritted teeth. "Come on, show me what a man you are."

And, indeed, the Fusion started closing the distance.

Jessica floored the accelerator. Her car's engine howled. It lurched forward under the power of its surprisingly well-tuned six-cylinder engine.

This was a chase to the finish, Jessica knew, except she hoped a cop would be on the end of that chase sometime soon. Speeding was the only way she could call attention to herself now. Her cell phone was in her purse, and that purse now rested on the floor under the dashboard. That was where it had flown when she first hit the brakes to avoid rear-ending the Saturn. Unfortunately, she had also forgotten to sync the phone's Bluetooth feature with the car after she had rented it.

CHAPTER 21

How much power and control she thinks she has...amazing!

The Predator watched Jessica make her moves, trying to escape. He felt some tiny measure of exhilaration at the thought of moving in for the kill, but actually a great deal more of dismay. It was a sad, regretful dismay.

Getting beautiful, flawless, exquisite Jessica wasn't supposed to have been about the thrill of the chase. He needed to take her quickly, smoothly, *quietly*, not pursue her all over the back roads of this miserable, godforsaken cowtown. The experience of Jessica was supposed to have been about elegance, precision.

Nevertheless, what had to be done, had to be done. He continued following her. With every passing mile, he was as surprised as she must have been that they hadn't yet caught the attention of a cop.

What an unbelievably bizarre turn of events.

"Events that are just about to come to an end," the Predator whispered to himself upon seeing the first sign advising those who aimed to get to King's Bridge Mall to stay in the right lane.

CHAPTER 22

Driving into the mall had been her first intuitive plan, Jessica admitted. Then she had second thoughts. Then she changed her mind yet again.

Going into the mall, she had reasoned, was the best way to snare her stalker. She was hoping to go speeding into the shopping complex's parking areas, barreling past some mall cops with any luck. Her pursuer, of course, would be hot on her tail. They would run into the chaos of the crowds, and everything would come to a head.

The further she drove, though, the more she hesitated. Barreling into the middle of a crowded afternoon parking lot with a homicidal, raving maniac on her tail started feeling foolhardy, irresponsible. Innocent bystanders could get caught in the middle.

Plus, Jessica wondered, what if he didn't follow her in there? What if the mall turned out to be too good of a place to lose a pursuer? Then she would be back at the same dilemma of not knowing when the twisted freak would be sneaking up on her again.

Keep driving? Keep speeding down the highway? she kept asking herself as the right lane was about to turn into the "exit only" lane to King's Bridge Mall.

The thinning highway traffic ahead, past the exit to the mall, started worrying her as well. Where would that road lead? Going straight must have led past the Cedar Valley town limits and out to the featureless, void-like flatlands beyond. How many cops were bound to be out there? She would be all alone with no one but a drooling sicko hot on her heels.

Jessica bore to the right at the exit.

CHAPTER 23

The Predator couldn't ignore the problem any longer. The fury was building within him, the closer he got to Jessica. Were the Handlers going to renege on their deal?

He watched her take the exit toward the mall, and he followed. She must have been thinking either that she could lose him in there, or a security guard would come and save her.

Of course, the Predator was ready for either of those complications. He, in fact, was ahead of both complications.

But the one problem that was harder to deal with was the presence of the Handlers. They were, for some reason, betraying him. They were going back on their word. After what happened outside Jessica's house the other night, during the storm, he could draw no other conclusions.

But why? he wanted to scream.

They had helped him, *requested* him to kill, torture, mutilate, burn enough women to put all the pieces of their plot into place. So why couldn't they let him have Jessica now?

It infuriated the Predator and made him glad that he had come prepared for more than just Jessica Lafayette. The fully-loaded .45 Smith & Wesson SW1911 pressed against his right side as it sat inside its holster. The Tigershark combat knife was tucked into one of the inside pockets of his jacket. In turn, his car's air-conditioner had to blast away on full power to keep him from getting too uncomfortable in his Kevlar bulletproof vest.

CHAPTER 24

Jessica had nearly sideswiped a car coming off the Mississippi Highway exit ramp, almost collided with a pickup truck as she ran a stop sign, and missed an island bedding of trees and shrubbery by inches as she careened into the nearest wing of the mall parking lot.

"Mr. Murphy's my copilot, and his laws are being enforced today," she whispered as she drove toward the mall's closest buildings.

She glanced into her rearview mirror, but couldn't yet see the Ford Fusion. Her heartbeats pounded, knowing some sort of a violent showdown with the stalker was only moments away.

But she had to *see* him at all times, she kept reminding herself. She had to keep the bastard in her sights to control the confrontation. She couldn't lose track of him, only to have him pounce at her without warning. Or she couldn't let him slip away, wise to her plan, only to have him come back another day.

Jessica pulled into an empty slot between an SUV and a tiny subcompact. She glanced into her mirrors, then turned and scanned every other spot—still no sign of the Fusion.

By now, it too would have left the highway, she knew. The stalker was somewhere down here. He was probably cruising the rows, ready to strike.

Jessica had to get inside the mall, but she also needed to do something just as important. It was time to take every possible precaution. She had to call for some kind of backup.

She lurched across the passenger seat and grabbed for her purse under the dash.

Tom! the thought rang through her mind as she rummaged through her purse for her cell phone. He was the first one she automatically thought of turning to. The realization of this was striking, of course.

Although he *was* indisposed at the moment, she realized as she grabbed her cell phone. He was right in the middle of class.

Her gaze darted toward the rearview mirror.

No Fusion.

Bastard!

Tom had told her that he would have his phone on its "vibrate" mode.

So Jessica tapped out a quick text message and transmitted it. If Tom noticed, he would read KING BRIDGE MALL. HELP!!!

The next step would be to call the police, but Jessica hesitated. How to do it so the psycho would be caught *today?* She didn't want him getting away.

No! Jessica thought. *Can't call yet.* Her heart pounded even more violently when she realized she had to make the decision. She couldn't call the cops just yet. If she did, chances were that they would place a call to the mall security. In turn, the mall cops would send several men right into the parking lot to pick her up and escort her to their offices. The stalker would see all of this and flee.

He had to be taken today, Jessica decided. It had to be here and now.

She put the cell phone into her slacks' right pocket and got out of the car.

CHAPTER 25

Jessica had to split her concentration as she hurried toward the nearest entrance into the mall. She had to split it three ways, actually. She had to try and look as natural and in control as she possibly could. She had to keep an eye on every part of her surroundings, lest her pursuer pounce and take her down from a blind spot, and she had to make sure that at least her hands didn't shake so visibly, so violently.

She had lived most of her life in big cities, the cruelly ironic realization needled her, and now, for the first time ever, she was afraid for her life and fleeing a psychopathic stalker in a sleepy rural town.

Just get out of this alive, and you can laugh at life's absurdities later, a voice went off in her head, warning her to pay attention to the problem at hand and stop analyzing the big picture.

She was just about to emerge from the rows of cars and approach the entrance to Target when she saw a group of people walking in the same direction. They looked like maybe three families that ran into each other, all going to the same place. There were several adults and a number of children. They looked like a tempting group, Jessica thought. She could pick up her pace and walk among them. She could use them as cover to enter the store. It was actually a good plan, she thought, and quickened her stride. She would throw the occasional glance over her shoulder as she used them as camouflage to try and spot her blond pursuer.

Except she saw him before reaching the group. It was the tall, tough-looking blond man, Jessica realized, the one from the street when she and Tom sat at the sidewalk table in front of Fitzpatrick's. Even though she was far enough away from him, she recognized him with one hundred percent certainty. The son of a bitch had had the same idea she did. He blended into the crowd and moved toward the Target entrance.

Jessica halted in her tracks, changing direction abruptly. She couldn't go for the same door now. It would be suicide. She was still planning on going into the mall, but she had to find another way in.

Off to her left, she thought she saw it. It was a cargo delivery entryway—it looked like a giant garage. Trucks could back in there and pull up to a loading platform.

Jessica's gaze darted toward the front door of Target. The stalker was about to enter with the group of strangers. He wasn't looking in her direction.

So Jessica bolted for the cargo area.

CHAPTER 26

Only one person took exception with Jessica using the cargo delivery entrance to the mall, but he had been left far behind. After she had vaulted onto the cargo platform, she thought she heard a gruff voice yell after her something about "authorized personnel only."

From there, she had run into a set of corridors, passed a few people who looked incapable of caring enough to give her the time of day or protest her presence in an off-limits zone and hoped to reach the mall proper within the next two or three minutes.

She soon found herself in a store selling high-end kitchenware. She quickly negotiated a maze of stylish bowls, cups, plates, and pots. But not too far ahead, she, at last, heard what she had been questing for. The noises of the mall were just beyond another few turns and dodges past display cases of cookbooks.

But did she now have an edge on the stalker? For a few moments, Jessica's heart blasted out its hyper-paced rhythm from excitement and relief rather than terror. She wondered if the stalker would be perched somewhere near the Target store's door to the parking lot. Was he assuming he'd gotten here first, and was he going to watch those doors, lying in wait for her?

One part of Jessica wanted to check. She wanted full control over the situation. But she knew it would be a foolhardy risk. Since the stalker was within the confines of the mall, she should be making the fastest possible move to take him out of commission.

She had to get to security and explain the situation. She knew they could then use the surveillance cameras all over the place to get a bead on him until guards could move in and take him down.

"So how do I get to the security offices?" Jessica mumbled as she neared the kitchenware store's access to the indoor promenade.

She slowed down at the door and looked onto the promenade. Off on the right was Target. The more she thought about it, going and looking for the blond pursuer before alerting security sounded more and more foolish. She would retreat back into the kitchen store and find someone who could tell her which way the security offices were.

She glanced over her shoulder, noting that store employees were a lot like cops. They were always there, asking if you needed help deciding whether or not to buy a thousand dollar coffee maker, when you didn't need them. She threw another glance out onto the promenade and toward Target....

And her breath caught in her throat.

The blond stalker was out on the promenade and looking in her direction.

This maniac was like some sort of a damned homing device, Jessica's mind screamed. He must not even have taken a moment to stay at the Target doors. It was like he knew it would be a waste of his time.

But now she couldn't go back into the kitchen store, Jessica realized. She would be trapped there. She had to get out onto the promenade and evade the sick bastard among the mall patrons. And luckily, there were quite a number of them around. So Jessica made her move, slipping out of the kitchen store, and headed left. As she did so, but just before walking away from the kitchen place, she threw one last glance toward the stalker. Of course, he, too, was moving. He was coming after her.

Damn him!

Jessica picked up her pace, weaving back and forth among the people. She tried glancing in display windows and opening and closing glass doors as often as she could, hoping to get a glimpse of her stalker's progress. And every time she saw him, he kept coming like a dog on a fresh scent—a true stalker.

Except for a moment when a large, rowdy group of teenagers came bounding out of a clothing store. Jessica saw it all from a reflection in a glass-covered display promising "50% off everything" in a shoe store. She and the blond pursuer had effectively been separated by the kids, a chaotic and volatile mixture of both guys and girls teasing and posturing and rough-housing with no regard for anyone else around.

So Jessica surged forward. She nearly ran, in fact. She headed straight for the nearest intersecting promenade and made a fast turn to the left.

She cast a glance over her shoulder, saw no one, and started running. She had to get to the nearest store, to its nearest employee, before the stalker made his way through the teenagers and came tearing after her.

And then her salvation appeared out of a furniture store some fifty feet or so away. A guy in a bright green jacket that made him look like a cross between a weatherman and a car salesman ambled out of the store, his eyes zeroing in and fixing on her immediately. Since Tom Lancaster, Jessica couldn't remember ever being so glad to feel a man checking her out. Sure, he must have known that the most he could hope for was a sale of a bedroom or dining room set, but he seemed to be glad for the eyeful that came along with a potential sale.

"Hurrying anywhere in particular, or can we take your time for a moment?" the furniture guy asked, taking steps toward her and lazily waving a flyer around.

Jessica thought the man could have made a wonderful spy as he approached. Aside from his quick, probing eyes that gave him the hopeful, desperate appearance of a hungry dog suddenly finding itself in the middle of a picnic with a lot of food, he really didn't have any other features that would stick out in someone's mind. Should someone see the salesman commit a crime, Jessica conjectured, the witness would have a hard time describing the perpetrator to the cops.

"Please, I need your help," Jessica said, hurrying toward the salesman, but tossing another look toward the intersection of corridors.

"Of course," the salesman said, already backing inside his store. "What can we help you?"

"Security!" Jessica said quickly. "You need to get security right *now!*"

"Is there a problem?" the salesman asked.

By now, they were inside the furniture store.

"I'm being followed," Jessica said as firmly as she could without sounding panicky and out of control. "I need you to get security here right now. There's a guy after me. He might have seen me come this way. He's a big guy. Real tough-looking, with blond hair and a denim jacket. You have to get security right now."

"Come on, this way," the salesman said, nodding toward the back of the store. Jessica saw one of the sales desks there with a computer and a phone.

As they hurried toward it, moving past some living room set pieces, Jessica couldn't help looking in their wake once more. It wouldn't take the stalker too long to figure out which way she had gone, even if he didn't see her take the left turn at the intersection.

Although she didn't see her pursuer, she missed an ottoman in her path. She just felt her left foot catching and losing balance. In an instant, it was too late to recover. She flailed at first in wild instinct as she went through the air, but then she was surprised by how quickly her self-defense training kicked in. She did a flat-palmed slap of the ground as she hit, performing the perfect fall maneuver, distributing as much of her weight as possible to avoid injuring any one spot.

Between the fall maneuver and the adrenaline already spilling through her system, she was springing back upright in a flash, even before the salesman had time to notice what had happened. He had actually gotten a couple of paces ahead of her, and now he was pausing, about to turn around and see what the problem was.

But Jessica was jolted by what she saw when she got a glimpse of his back. There was a cut in the middle of his jacket. It wasn't large, but it was noticeable. Along its edges and reaching down in an oblong shape was a dark, wet-looking stain.

Like a stab wound! Like a knife cut and a stab wound!

Jessica's mind screamed out these possibilities, yet, at the same time, she couldn't believe them. It seemed absurd, a fantastic, unrealistic....

But the salesman had turned around and had a look in his eyes that seemed to physically assault Jessica. It was knowing, somehow resigned and placid, all the while it looked utterly deadly, reptilian in its predatory intensity.

Then the salesman's left arm moved like a blur. It lashed out, his forearm smashing into Jessica's face.

CHAPTER 27

Splotches of white and yellow swam in front of Jessica's eyes. Before her vision cleared up, she was jolted again by the impact of concrete and the hard, slippery tiling under foot. Not only did the pain slash through her head now, but it raked her body as she took the hard spill to the floor.

And overhead, she saw when her vision cleared up, the furniture salesman — or whoever had stabbed the real furniture salesman in the back and taken his jacket — was lunging forward. He was moving with the desperate glare of an animal striking out of cornered rage.

What the hell is this? Jessica's mind shrieked while subconscious, thoughtless reflex moved to protect her. How could she be on the run from one demented stalker and meet up with a random killer who seemed to work by attacking and murdering people in a crowded mall?

She was certain those questions had complicated answers, and she could only have a chance of living long enough to figure them out if she fought like hell right now.

Jessica's right foot lashed out as the attacker pounced at her. That insanely angry look on his face, she thought, registered because he probably never intended to knock her to the ground. He probably only wanted to stun her with that punch. But whatever mania was driving him to do this must have gotten the best of him, and his strength surged out of conscious control.

But Jessica's kick caught him in the gut now, and it seemed to stun him. The madman staggered backward, his face contorting, reddening as he tried to endure the pain and desperately fill his lungs with air.

But contacting her foot with the attacker's midsection also shocked Jessica. Something just didn't feel right. It didn't feel like she was kicking someone's flesh. Her foot had made contact with something unnaturally hard under the guy's jacket. There were no abdominal muscles as hard as what she had kicked, and her assailant hardly looked like a gym-pumped hard body. Instead, this man had some sort of hard padding, some type of shield under his clothes—a bulletproof vest, perhaps.

But Jessica had to move *now*, she knew, and not sit on the ground conjecturing why her wild-eyed, hysterical attacker was wearing bulletproof padding. Moving immediately was her only shot. So she scrambled around onto her hands and knees and pushed off the floor. She had to move like a sprinter, she had to explode off the floor and run for the exit from the store like she had never run in her life. But before she could take more than three steps, a body crashed into her from behind, and she was back on the floor, pinned down.

Pain, combined with whatever malignant force it was that compelled psychopathic, murderous frenzy, had apparently let Jessica's attacker recover rapidly. She had barely gotten upright before the killer was lunging after her again, jumping on her and tackling her flat to the floor.

But this time, the maniac was intent on damaging Jessica enough to keep her from trying to flee again. He started by ramming a fist into the side of her face, snapping her head to the left, and driving it down into the floor again.

Jessica heard the crack of bone against the hard tiling echo through her skull before she even registered the pain. Her forehead hit the floor hard enough to bounce back.

And then her assailant struck again. A second blow landed on the back of her skull, smashing her head down into the floor for a second time.

The flashes of bright, disorienting color splashed in front of Jessica's eyes again, but this time they were blinding. All of the store, the mall, had disappeared from around her. Only the maddening pain remained. It engulfed her totally now and threatened to render her unconscious.

She only vaguely felt her body moving, but not of her own accord. As part of her vision faded back in, way too slowly, she saw disorienting glimpses of the store around her. It was all from a crazy angle, though. It wasn't from the floor.

Standing....

She was standing, Jessica realized, but she wasn't standing under her own power. She had been yanked upright by her attacker. He probably wanted to move her somewhere else, somewhere in the back of the store, into a storage area, no doubt. He must have been trying to move her someplace where he would have plenty of time to subject her to a full-on assault of all his sadistic fantasies brought to life.

What did the Inquisitor stories in the papers...?

Now Jessica felt herself choking, all the while getting dragged backward.

The killer must have an arm around her neck, over her throat, she realized. He was dragging her away by her neck. If the pressure kept up, she knew she would pass out.

Lashing out any way she could, in part guided by a recollection from her kickboxing class and in greater part sheer, mindless, reflexive panic, Jessica tried stomping on the killer's foot. If she caught him well enough on the arch of his foot, enough pain might stun him and cause him to loosen his grip.

Except she missed. There was nothing but the floor making contact with her heel. The maniac was still unscathed and dragging her backward with relentless fury.

Jessica tried kicking again, but this time from a different angle. She kicked backward, trying to swing her foot between her attacker's legs, hoping to connect with the bastard's groin.

And now she felt flesh! She had struck him. She could feel the man tensing, recoiling. She had hurt him! He paused in his backward movement, trying to steel himself against the blow, against what must have been stabbing bolts of pain shooting through his most sensitive pressure points.

Must have been...!

Disjointed thoughts of caution skittered through Jessica's mind. She was hardly free of the killer's grip, and she couldn't be sure how well she had kicked him. Did she really strike his genitals? Was he hopped up on enough adrenaline to make him impervious to the pain? She had to keep attacking. That's what they had taught in her self-defense class. She had to keep fighting, delivering blow after blow until her opponent was completely incapacitated.

So now she tried to stomp the arch of his foot again.

And it worked! She felt her heel connecting with the maniac's shoe, smashing down onto the bones inside his foot.

Now the madman screamed too. A wild, animal shriek of pain assaulted Jessica's ears.

And she struck again. She stomped his foot once more and felt the son of a bitch almost collapse to the floor. Only his grip on her body kept him upright. But even that hold had now been compromised. The chokehold he had over her had relaxed so much as to allow the killer to lose his advantage.

Jessica, of course, exploited her momentary victories by lashing out again. This time she did it with her teeth. Almost like the maniac, a feral, primal side had taken hold of her. Feeling the killer's loose grip, Jessica tried to get rid of it altogether by biting the man's wrist. She sank her teeth into his flesh and clamped her jaws as tightly as she could. She wouldn't let go, she decided, no matter what, until the attacker was in full retreat. Even if she had to bite chunks of flesh out of him, even if she had to sever skin, sinew, and arteries, she wouldn't stop fighting until the bastard was hurt and in retreat.

That did not take long. The attacker was screaming hysterically within seconds, insane from rage and pain. Not only did he let go of Jessica, but he shook her loose. He flung her away.

She stumbled away from the killer, almost spilling to the floor again. She was only stopped when she crashed into the table holding the inventory computer.

Getting her bearings, Jessica realized she had actually been thrown toward the back of the store, the maniac still blocking her path toward the main entrance into the mall promenade. But there was another way out, of course, she saw only a few feet away. There was still the way to the storage areas and, perhaps, those service corridors that led back to the mall's main cargo bays.

Without hesitation, Jessica took the alternative route and ran. She went out the back way, sprinting down a dimly lit corridor and into an even darker, shadowy storage area. Pounding heartbeats, searing adrenaline, and a suspiciously coppery taste in her mouth drove Jessica with such fury that she almost didn't need light to see where she was going.

Almost....

The faintest thoughts of revulsion at the idea that she might have been tasting her attacker's blood in her mouth, the blood she had drawn when biting through his wrist, whispered in Jessica's ear the moment she noticed something was amiss underfoot.

She had stepped into something that threw off her balance. In the murk of the storage area, she couldn't see that she had run into something slippery on the floor. The hard soles of her flats couldn't quite manage against whatever it was on the floor.

Fractions of a second later, her sprint was all over. Her right foot was flying out from under her. She was stumbling, falling out of control, unable to do anything but brace for the pain of the impact against the concrete.

But the agony of hitting the floor was the least of what followed. Realizing why she slipped and fell was worse. Seeing the lifeless gaze of a man some three feet away was much worse. Feeling the sticky, viscous pool of his blood under her, smearing onto her clothes, spreading all over her hands, was infinitely worse.

CHAPTER 28

Jessica recoiled at the sight of the dead man, at the feeling of blood all over her, the taste of it in her mouth. She kicked, she thrust, and she crawled backward, her awkward spasms all uncontrollable reflex reactions trying to distance her from the horror. She was staring at the murdered furniture salesman, she realized as she got to her feet. This was the man her attacker had killed and hidden in the shadows back here.

A moment later, she almost wretched, still tasting that maniac's blood in her mouth. Instead, she spat violently, trying to get rid of the salty taste.

But her rational mind was also working to reassert itself. She had to get out of there, its voice echoed in her head. As repulsive as all this was, she had to block it out. She had to suppress her rising gorge, a threatening onset of panic, and get moving again. She had to get moving as fast as she could because a killer was still back in the store. He might have been slowed down, he might have been hurt, but that also meant he was angrier now.

Jessica turned and ran further into the murky recesses of the storage area. She moved as fast as she could because her calculations quickly proved true.

The sound of running, trampling feet came from behind her — the killer had entered the storage zone. He was sprinting somewhere not too far behind Jessica, panting loudly when not letting out a grating, infuriated, unnatural noise. Jessica, for an instant, thought she would have said it sounded like an animal noise, but it wasn't quite that. The noise sounded more unearthly, like an alien distillation of pure, unalloyed evil, pure hate and rage turned into something that only registered on the auditory level.

Now it made Jessica run faster. Reflex, pain, and fear didn't spur her to run quite as fast as that demonic noise did.

And then she saw the target she had to aim for. It was a literal ray of light from a small window on a door in a far corner of the shadowy storage space. It was probably the exit to one of the service corridors. The one possible avenue to salvation, Jessica's mind screamed, and released a charge of adrenaline into her blood.

Maybe five seconds or so later, she slammed into the metal door, pain shooting through her right shoulder, but her left hand found the doorknob. She was twisting it immediately, fighting to push her way out of the storage zone. She, indeed, almost went through all alone, but she couldn't make it all the way before the killer was upon her.

Jessica finished the trip into a service corridor with the weight and force of her pursuer on top of her. He had caught up with her and lunged on top of her before she could make it all the way through the door. Now they were both flying forward, tangled up and stumbling across the hall and bouncing off its far wall.

When Jessica looked at what had come after her, she would have sworn to anyone, to Tom Lancaster and an entire army of smug, cynical skeptics and doubters and rationalists, that what had been chasing her was not human. Strangely enough, a part of her mind could still register irony in all this chaos, because Jessica could recall that barely a few minutes ago she thought this man looked dully nondescript. That impression couldn't have been any farther from reality now. His face contorted into a deeply creased landscape of rippling sneers. Every muscle in his face must have been stretching into unnatural places, displaying a barely-contained well of rage. His lips seemed to have disappeared, peeled away from teeth that were somehow animalistic. Glistening spider webs of spittle quivered and tangled from the madman's mouth as he let out a ragged, grating shriek. His nostrils flared, distorting into holes that seemed beyond the limits of a human face. But the most disturbing parts of this thing were its eyes. What should have been the whites of the rampaging killer's eyes were muddy, yellowish pools of corruption surrounding glistening black orbs. Jessica knew she would always swear to seeing glimpses of red flecks swimming within the killer's irises.

Jessica lunged upward and away from the lunatic what seemed like a microsecond before he tried to grab her. He missed her, but at the same time, Jessica realized he wasn't trying to catch a hold of her at all. He was trying to stab her or cut her with a large knife in his right fist.

The killer's knife hand lashed out in a left to right ark, barely failing to meet its target, but slamming into the wall. What Jessica caught a glimpse of in the moment of impact failed to make any more sense than the rest of this encounter. Unless the walls of the service corridor were made from criminally substandard building materials, the killer had tapped the sort of hidden well of superhuman strength one heard people possessing in moments of mortal danger, the strength that surfaced when burning cars had to be lifted off unconscious kids. The maniac somehow put a brick-and mortar-shattering crater in the wall, its noise sending an echoing shockwave down the length of the corridor.

Nevertheless, Jessica was on her feet, and the killer was still kneeling on the ground. So now she ran at an all out sprint again, putting what final reserves of strength, adrenaline, and white hot panic she still possessed into the effort. By now, she suspected she was about to die within the next few seconds, but she refused to lie down and let it happen without a final fight, no matter how futile it was. If that madman could summon enough strength to smash a hole like that in a wall, he would be coming after her like a hyper-charged juggernaut again. There was no escaping a creature like that.

Except Jessica was suddenly joined in the hallway by another door opening some fifteen feet in front of her. More accurately, the door slammed open violently, thrust, or kicked open with urgent force. A man lunged into her path a flash of a moment later, and things ceased to make any sort of logical sense.

"Get down!" the man yelled as Jessica stumbled, slid, and careened into the wall on her right. His right arm was snaking out from behind his back, yanking forward what looked like a large caliber, matte-black handgun from under his denim jacket. The man was flash aiming the handgun down the corridor, Jessica could see, but he was carefully aiming past her — taking a bead on the killer, she realized. He had come to rescue her from the assault.

Then the big gun went off, echoing three ear-drum-shattering blasts down the narrow corridor.

But it was neither the man's sudden appearance, nor the gunfire, nor her sudden salvation, that stunned Jessica the most. It was the realization that her rescuer was the blond man who had been following her. This was the guy she had thought was stalking her. This was the man from the Ford Fusion that had been following her around, the disquieting stranger from her father's funeral.

Jessica threw a glance behind her and saw her attacker on the floor, lying flat on his back. Except he wasn't lying still — he seemed to be stirring. Either unhurt by the gunfire, or....

"Come on!" the blond stranger yelled at her, snapping her attention away from the killer's form. "He's not dead yet. We have to get out of here."

Jessica stared at him in shock, not only unable to speak, but realizing she was barely able to formulate any coherent, logical thoughts, questions, or ideas at this point.

"Move!" the blond man yelled again, grabbing her arm and giving her a powerful, violent pull. "Move it!" he bellowed, trying to guide her down the corridor. "Move it now, or we're both dead!"

CHAPTER 29

They were leaving the mall by way of the same cargo platform Jessica had entered. The blond guy at her side kept urging her to move as quickly as possible, occasionally grabbing at her arm and giving her a violent yank that would nearly send her sprawling to the floor.

Certainly reflex and self-preservation were driving Jessica, too, but she couldn't help wanting to sort it all out, to try and ask questions. But too much thinking slowed her momentum now. It made her clumsy and uncoordinated, earning her an admonishing yell to move faster and one of the blond man's vicious yanks on the arm.

"He's gonna kill us both if you don't move," he spat over his shoulder. "So come on, damn it. Move faster!" As they neared the edge of the loading platform, the guy said something like, "I'm not gonna hurt you, goddamn it, but he will! So move!"

The rules of reality had departed long ago, Jessica decided, so she did as the man asked. At the edge of the platform, she did as he did, leaping into the air and plunging to the concrete some four feet below.

"My car," the stranger panted as they ran out into the parking lot. "Come on, or we're dead in the next five minutes!"

"All right!" Jessica snapped back this time. "I heard you."

After they had gotten into the silver Ford Fusion, the blond guy paused before starting the engine. He scanned the parking lot in their wake instead, trying to assess the situation back at the mall.

Jessica looked closely at his eyes as he did so. She thought she saw as much fear there as she felt. She didn't see aggression, she didn't see violent mania of the type she had witnessed in the eyes of her assailant.

"There are cameras here," the blond said as he started the engines. "Jesus Christ," he muttered, putting the car into gear. "They saw us. They saw you...." He paused at that moment and threw a frantic glance at Jessica. He didn't move the car yet. "But that might not matter if you get out of here quickly enough! Get out of town immediately."

"What are you talking about?" Jessica asked as the car took off, her chauffeur quickly gunning the engine and swinging the Fusion toward the exit leading to the Mississippi Highway on-ramp. "What's going on here? Who the hell was that?"

"A serial killer," the stranger said, not bothering to look at her this time. "He calls himself the Predator. In the papers, they call him the Inquisitor. You might have read about him."

A cold blade of revulsion pricked at Jessica's insides.

"He tortures and burns his victims alive. More complicated than it looks, though," the driver said as he took the ramp onto the highway.

Jessica noticed that he was heading back toward Cedar Valley. *Thank God!* "What do you mean?" she whispered.

"Not exactly sure. He was making his way here, to this town, for some reason. I don't think he's working alone. But listen to me!" Now the blond man threw a more jagged, more unstable look at Jessica than she had seen until now. "He's not going to stop. He'll keep coming after you. The best thing for you to do is get moving as quickly as you can. With that guy from the school if you can get him to believe you. What's his name? Lancaster, right?"

A nudging unease, a trace of fear surfaced inside Jessica's gut now. This man *was* stalking her. He had been following her around, keeping tabs on her, checking out her entire life, just as she'd thought.

"Who is he?" the blond asked. "Your boyfriend? I hope so, 'cause that way, he might actually listen to you."

"Stop!" Jessica said angrily now, although she realized she was unconsciously pressing her body harder and harder up against the door. "Just slow down if you don't mind, if you want me to listen to anything you have to say. Who the hell are you, who the hell was that maniac back in the mall, and just what in the *fuck* is going on here?"

The driver nodded quickly. "All right," he snapped. "Listen to me carefully! That man back there is a psycho, and he won't stop until he takes you down or he's killed. He's murdered a good handful of women all the way from the west coast to here. I've been following him, but I'm certain there are others he's working with."

"Are you a cop?" Jessica cut in. The information about her attacker was paramount, but the identity and motives of this man were just as important now.

"No. I'm a reporter, and I've been onto this for a while. But listen, I need to tell you the important details first."

"Just who the hell you are? And why you're involved in this is an important detail to *me*," Jessica said with what hopefully sounded like enough grit in her voice.

The guy threw a quick glance at her.

And there it was again, Jessica realized. It was the reason she was willing to sit here, inches away from him, and listen to his story instead of flinging the door open and lunging from the car. It was the look in his eyes. He appeared to be terrified of the story he was recounting. As driven and hyper as he might be, she decided, there was also a vulnerability there. He didn't feel dangerous. She had seen danger and madness and unfathomable evil in her attacker back at the mall. She sensed none of that in the man behind the wheel of the car.

"Fair enough," the blond driver said. "Like I said, I'm a reporter, okay? I've been following the story of these Inquisition killings all the way from the west coast."

"What's your name?" Jessica thought she needed to know right now.

"McPherson," the driver said. "You can also call me Buzz if you like. Most people do. My old man was a NASA and space nut, I'm told. Don't know for sure since he died when I was a kid. Is that good enough?"

"Buzz McPherson?" Jessica mouthed the name quietly.

"Yeah. Anyway, as I was saying, this nutcase is part of some, some...I don't know for sure—gang of killers of some type. But something big, something organized."

"What, like a cult?"

"Maybe," McPherson said, glancing into both inside and outside rearview mirrors, then taking down the car's speed. "Damn it," he seemed to be growling to himself, "if it's not that maniac, then the cops'll get us."

"So you don't think it's a cult?" Jessica tried to nudge him back on track. "And where are you taking me?"

McPherson threw a sideways glance at her. There was a sharp glare of irritation there. "I'm taking you back to that college and your professor friend, okay?" he snapped. Jessica could have sworn he sounded offended. "I'm *not* kidnapping you. That sick, sadistic bastard back at the mall, the one who apparently beat the crap out of you and was about two seconds away from cutting your heart out, is the one you have to worry about, not me. Do you understand?"

"Yes, all right," Jessica said, hoping she sounded placating enough. "I'm sorry," she added. "So you were saying?"

"Listen, the point is this: I'm pretty sure this maniac was coming to this town because he has friends, others he's working with here. I don't know if they're a cult. I haven't found out enough of the details about who they are and what they're doing besides the Inquisition killings, but there's something going on here."

"Okay, so there's some large, organized conspiracy here in Cedar Valley, though. This is their headquarters?"

"It might be, yeah," McPherson said and shot another quick, intense glance at Jessica. "And that's why it's not safe for you to be here. You have to get out of here, with or without Tom Lancaster. Or anyone else who might believe you. It's best if you don't even try and convince anyone else of what I told you. Just pack the hell up and go back to San Diego. Or better yet, go and take a very long, very far away trip."

Jessica was about to cut McPherson off when she felt the car lurching abruptly to the right. Then she felt the road dipping. She glanced out the windshield and saw they had taken an exit ramp back into Cedar Valley.

"All right," she said, at last, feeling a quick-rising well of anger now. McPherson's story had taken a very sudden turn into bad territory. "Just back up a second, pal, because you've got some explaining to do."

"We don't have time for —"

"Shut up," Jessica almost yelled. "Now what the hell do you know about me and Tom Lancaster, and how did you find out? You've obviously been following me around and checking me out. Why? If I'm in danger, why didn't you contact me? What the hell was that all about back at the funeral, watching me and Tom like some stalker, following my car? If any of what you're telling me is real, why didn't you come to us right away, and why didn't you go to the local cops?"

"All right," McPherson mumbled but didn't meet Jessica's eyes. He was taking furtive glances at the rearview mirrors again. By now, the late afternoon dusk had turned to almost complete darkness. "Here… The thing is…. Yes, I checked up on who you are once I found out that psycho was after you. It's not exactly hard to do, right? A quick Amazon.com search gives me all the titles of your books, and your web page and the KBLA web page are there for anyone to see, not just stalkers. The same's true for Tom Lancaster. I'd suggest you do a search of your own on his work and his extracurricular activities. Especially those articles he's been writing about rationality and logic. Has he given you any of his speeches yet about the logical approaches to strange phenomena?"

"What about it?" Jessica asked abruptly. She had just been talking about this with Tom earlier today, in the privacy of his office. McPherson's words were almost…*violating* her relationship with Tom.

"Well, I supposed he probably has," McPherson said with an offensive bitterness to his voice.

What right did he have to talk about Tom like this? Jessica wanted to yell at him. But at the same time, something instinctive urged her to hear McPherson out.

"What I've found out the hard way," he said, "is that people've had one hell of a time accepting some of the theories about this organized gang of killers. Someone who's as hardcore a skeptical zealot as Tom Lancaster would probably fight the idea tooth and nail." Now he paused and shot Jessica a cold, resentful glare. "If you don't believe me," he said, returning his eyes to the road, "go read an article about skepticism for the op-ed column of *Newsweek* two years ago. So, since I saw you two were close, I wasn't sure how open you would be to my suspicions. I decided to keep an eye on you, see how close the Predator was to catching up to you, try and make a move like this and take him when he showed up...."

McPherson paused for several moments abruptly. It sounded odd to Jessica, like he didn't know how to proceed with something extremely weighty, something particularly sensitive. "What is it?" she asked at length.

"But I made a mistake," McPherson said quietly. "I'm sorry about that."

"What are you talking about?"

"I should have come to you earlier."

Yeah, Jessica considered, it would have been the safe thing. If she let herself consider McPherson's implication in greater detail, it started sounding like he might have decided to use her as bait.

"I should have come after you this morning after you saw that accident downtown."

Jessica felt as if she had received a body blow. "You were...."

"I was there, yeah," McPherson said and glanced at her, gauging her reaction.

But Jessica was too stunned to be able to properly formulate words to reply.

"And so was the Predator. He was in the van. I was in the car that hit him. I had to stop him from going after you. But then I saw you taking off quickly enough, the place getting crowded, so I had to take off." McPherson looked at her again. "I'm sorry. I didn't know what would happen if all those other people got caught in the middle."

Jessica glanced out the window, trying to digest the ever more convoluted, surreal, nightmarish story McPherson was telling, and actually realized that the streets outside looked familiar. The

Cedar Valley State University campus, she realized. So at least he was keeping his word, bringing her back to Tom.

Then she wondered if Tom had seen her text message. Would the police already be here? How would they react to McPherson's paranoid story?

The car took an abrupt turn, swerving off the main drive and pulling into a dark, empty little parking lot. Jessica's attention snapped to McPherson. He brought the car to a stop in the middle of the lot, not bothering to park.

"What?" she asked simply.

"You know the way to Lancaster's class or office?"

"Yeah. What are you —?"

"I have to go. Just don't ask any other questions for now," McPherson said strongly. "If you trust Lancaster enough, if you think there's a chance he'll believe you, try and get him to take you away from here. But...." He paused now, apparently confused, wrestling between two impossible situations.

"This is insane," Jessica said, feeling that anger well up again. "After what you just told me, after what happened, we have to get the police involved. Hell, the police will *be* getting involved."

"Not yet," McPherson snapped. "It's...it's a long story, but there are other things I need to —"

"Listen, mister," Jessica cut him off. "Up to about a minute ago, I was with you. This story you told me made sense, and you didn't seem at all like a delusional head case. But right now —"

"Don't trust anyone, you understand me?" McPherson said, raising an index finger, waving it toward Jessica's face.

It was so dismaying, she realized because she *had* just told him the truth. She had been open to his story, she was willing to trust him. He had, after all, saved her life. But then, in a slip of a moment, he started unraveling in front of her, turning into a wild-eyed, gesticulating loon.

"You need to get out of this place as quickly as you can. This, this killer—the Predator, the people he's working with—there's something very wrong going on here. You can't trust anyone now. I don't know how much you trust Tom Lancaster...just be very careful."

Jessica pulled on the car door's release lever.

As the door swung open, McPherson leaned after her. "Only you know Lancaster, but if you have any doubts, ask him why we needed to know that she said 'no.' Ask him that."

Jessica didn't so much as step out of the car but recoiled from McPherson. Not only had he degenerated into a ranting madman, but his words no longer made sense.

"Ask him that if you have your doubts," he called after her. "Ask him why he had to tell the world that she said 'no.'"

Jessica's heartbeats kicked into overdrive when she saw McPherson's door swing open. What the hell was he about to do? Was he going to come after her?

He did get out of his seat, but instead of going after her, he just leaned over the top of his car. "And don't get anyone else involved with your father's ashes and your suspicions about the funeral home," he yelled after her.

But now Jessica's legs had virtually locked. She realized she was frozen in place by McPherson's words. Realizing that he had been following her, checking up on her and investigating Tom was creepy, unsettling enough, but this was too much. How could he have…?

"Whatever you do," McPherson said, "don't *ever* say another word about that to *anyone* around here. Anyone!"

He continued staring at her for a terrifying, protracted moment, but then he got back in the Fusion, put it in gear, and swung the car wildly around and out of the parking lot, disappearing into the night.

CHAPTER 30

The ache in Jessica's nose and forehead had been replaced by the cold bite of the icepack, but the throbbing, haunting pain in the rest of her head and neck refused to go. Maybe, she thought, her ongoing adrenaline surge and her pounding heart kept stoking the aches and pains.

"We're getting the descriptions of those cars out right now, and we'll see where they came from," Chief Simon Gainey told her and Tom. With the possibility that the Inquisition killer was in Cedar Valley, the chief of police had met Jessica and Tom at St. Anthony's Medical Center, along with the four patrolmen who responded to Tom's frantic call from the CVSU campus. Two of those patrol cops were now standing by outside the examination room while Gainey wrapped up the interview.

Despite the pains, Jessica wanted to get out of the hospital. The emergency room staff was able to give her a speedy once-over upon her arrival, but between the examinations and the cops, she thought she felt the walls closing in.

"Where they came from?" Tom asked abruptly. Just like the adrenaline surge spiking Jessica, Tom still sounded keyed-up.

"To check if they were stolen, sir," Chief Gainey said in cool, clipped, yet respectful tones. The well-contained politeness, Jessica thought, had actually started sounding mechanical by now. The "sirs" and "ma'ams" kept rolling off the chief's tongue with flawless frequency, as if coming straight out of the public relations manual. But then the chief's entire bearing had a starchy, military recruiting officer quality to Jessica. From the ramrod-straight, leathery stiffness of his posture to his pinched features and deadly-intense buzz-cut, Gainey looked like he might have switched careers from the service about two days ago. "Especially that van you saw this morning, ma'am," he said, his beady, bird-like little pinpoints of eyes snapping in Jessica's direction. "And you're absolutely sure you didn't see the van on your way to the mall?"

Absolutely, positively, one hundred percent certain beyond a shadow of a doubt, Jessica wanted to say this time. She had been asked that about five times already. "That's right," she said instead, lowering the ice pack from her nose. Sure, intellectually, she knew why they needed to ask the same things over and over again. People's recollections under intense stress, in moments of severe life and death trauma, could often be the least reliable. So Gainey had to force her to go over the events of the night again and again. But of course, it was still annoying as hell.

"Yeah, she only saw the mystery man who now claims to be her savior," Tom said acidly. He, apparently, was just incapable of seeing McPherson as anything other than an outright threat, someone almost as dangerous as the knife-wielding attacker.

"He *did* save me from—" Jessica began, not specifically aiming the words at Tom.

"Yes," Gainey cut in, "from whoever that guy was at the mall. And we *know* he was a killer."

Jessica's stomach still lurched when she heard those words. She was reminded of the blood smears on her clothes—the blood of the furniture salesman. The corpse tucked away in the shadows of the store's warehouse. "Dear God," she whispered.

"But there was something else I wanted to ask," Gainey said. "You're absolutely sure you didn't catch any part of the license plates of these cars?"

"Sorry, no."

"By the way, this man who drove you over to the campus, he didn't say anything about when he'll contact you again?"

"No, he didn't. You think he was lying about who he is and his name?"

"He had to have been," Tom said quickly. The bile was in his voice again.

Chief Gainey nodded calmly. "Most likely. But what bothers me the most is that it sounds like he's trying to insinuate his way into your life."

Perhaps, Jessica thought. On the one hand, McPherson — or whoever he really was — tried to urge her to get away from there as quickly as she could. But on the other, those bizarre questions, the secrecy, the cryptic comments about Tom's work, did sound like he wasn't planning on staying too far away from Jessica.

"Yeah!" Tom said. "And, as I was about to say —"

Nevertheless, Jessica was certain she would have been in the hospital's morgue right now was it not for McPherson, insinuating, bizarre questions, and all. So she cut Tom off. "But look! Like I said, there's no denying the fact he saved me."

"While he could have warned you ahead of time," Tom replied. "Instead, he comes skulking after you. Checking up on the both of us."

"Like your suspicions about the funeral home," Gainey's words struck like lightning.

Jessica couldn't do as McPherson had ordered. Once his speech began unraveling into an incoherent rant about not being able to trust anyone in town, she couldn't remain an ally in his strange, unbelievable agenda. It made no sense not to tell the police everything. She had told Gainey about her father's ashes, the storm, and her suspicions of some kind of a plot to mishandle bodies at the funeral home. She had told him about Tom's testing of the ashes.

But that part hadn't sat so well with the chief. He believed he should have been called first.

"Exactly," Tom snapped back at Gainey.

Jessica noted — with a raw consternation now — that a moment's silence followed between the two men, a moment of hard, unyielding stares going at each other. *Damn it!* she almost wanted to blurt out. *Are you two trying to out macho each other here?*

"And I can't even imagine," Tom said, "how the hell he could have managed to find something like that out. Was he bugging her phone?"

"Like I said, Dr. Lancaster, we share your concern, and my people are on this. It *is* damn strange how this man could know absolutely everything. But it's *our* job to do the investigating, not yours."

Tom gave a placating nod. "Of course."

"From now on, you inform us of absolutely *everything* that happens, correct?"

"I did the chemical analysis on the urn and the ashes hoping we wouldn't drag you into a wild goose chase."

Gainey, too, nodded, but said, "Understood. But from now on—"

"We call you about everything," Jessica took the words out of Tom's mouth. "But who do you think he is?"

"Believe me, ma'am, we'll know soon enough."

"You know," Jessica said, "I'm trying to figure out possible alternatives to what he told me, but I can't think of anything that fits."

"Anything other than he's a reporter following a story," the chief said. "But not turning to the local police for leads? With all due respect, that doesn't really make sense."

Of course, part of Jessica understood that too. Somehow, she still couldn't see McPherson as a real threat, a physical danger. Not the way Tom seemed to be so riled up about him. But then again, she had her reasons for not listening to McPherson, for not keeping his funeral home warning in confidence. Like Gainey said, McPherson's story just didn't add up.

"The chief's right," Tom said.

"A reporter needs any information he can get his hands on," Gainey said. "He should have been in my office the first day he set foot in town. Trying to get his hands on anything official, any leads if he thought the Inquisition killer's got some kind of a tie to Cedar Valley."

"Maybe someone knows him in the other places the Inquisitor's struck. Or the Predator, or whatever he calls himself," Jessica said.

"We're checking that out," Gainey said with a curt, efficient nod.

"Either way," Tom said, "this guy's bad news. Real bad news, bottom line."

"But for now, you won't have to worry about him. We might be a small town, but we know how to protect someone. As you know, Dr. Lancaster, there used to be a prison just eighty miles north of here some six years back. The place they're about to demolish. We know how to keep our eyes open for people who look like trouble."

Jessica felt Tom's hand on her back. "Yeah, I read the stories in the paper. But Jessica, the point is it was a *huge* prison just outside of town. Thousands of inmates. It's going to take them truckloads of TNT to bring the place down. They even had a couple of escapes over the years, but not *one* person in Cedar Valley's ever been hurt by them."

"That's right, ma'am," Gainey said. "Nothing for you to

worry about. And right now, we'll get a car to follow you home and keep an eye on you."

"Thank you, Chief," Jessica said.

CHAPTER 31

"Don't worry about anything, Dr. Lancaster," a young patrolman identified as Dunham by a uniform nametag said as he stood on Tom's porch, his hands on his hips. He then shifted his glance and gave Jessica an all-too-formal, regulation-efficient nod. "Ma'am," he added. "My partner and I will be in our car across the street. We've got other cars driving by as well. We'll make regular passes around the entire block. No one will get anywhere near this house."

"We appreciate that," Tom said, and backed across the threshold.

The patrol cop didn't move off the porch yet. He still stood with his arms akimbo, making Jessica think of Superman posed on a comic book cover. Then she noticed Dunham fix his stare precisely on her. "Chief Gainey will have a sketch artist available tomorrow. We'll get this guy's face all over town in no time."

"Thank you," Jessica told him. "I appreciate that."

With that, she took a tiny half step backward, hoping this was the end of the conversation with Dunham. She was troubled by her unease with the young cop. He was, after all, one of the good guys. He was one of her protection team.

Nonetheless, there was something off-putting about him. Maybe it was his stiff formality. Did the entire police department model its behavior on Gainey's anal, Marine Corps drill instructor bearing? Or perhaps it was something else, she told herself. She just didn't like the mindset that had taken over the entire police force. These people were approaching the night's events as if she was facing a mortal threat from not just one, but *two* assailants. Gainey and his entire force, she knew, had reached conclusions about this case they did not — would *never* — want to share with her. It was all about Buzz McPherson, she knew. Her insistence that this peculiar individual was no threat seemed to be falling on deaf ears.

Everyone's deaf ears, Jessica thought ruefully as she felt Tom's hand on her shoulder.

"Well, goodnight, Ms. Lafayette, Dr. Lancaster," Officer Dunham said, and turned to leave.

Tom closed the door.

"Just remember one thing," he said, and looked at Jessica, leveling his most placid gaze straight at her eyes. "What the chief said about being able to spot suspicious outsiders. They're really good at that."

"That's good to know," Jessica replied, and let Tom put an arm around her waist and lead her toward the living room.

At last, she allowed herself to relax enough to look around and actually take notice of Tom's exquisite home. *The Naked Ghost*, she surmised, must have been more successful than he so bashfully let on. Or maybe the astronomical sciences paid their professors fantastic salaries. Not only was Tom's house remarkably spacious, but it looked like it had been filled up by the most discerning New York decorator with a blank check to spend on high-end furniture and art. Tom did tell her, after all, that the school's science programs had for years been the recipients of enviably large government and industry grants to do research in partnership with the Argonne National Lab and the Fermilab particle accelerator in Batavia. The grants, apparently, attracted a lot of big names in the science fields who, in turn, could demand ever larger and larger salaries.

"Come on," Tom said as he led Jessica toward what appeared to be the kitchen in the darkness ahead. "I've got something to help you take the edge off."

When the lights came on, she found herself in a place that must have rivaled any celebrity chef's home kitchen. Not only was it gloriously spacious with yards of counter space, but it was fully loaded with every gadget and cooking apparatus a top-notch gourmand needed to do magic. This was the Super Bowl of stadium of kitchens.

"Now, *this* is a kitchen," Jessica said as she took in all the opulent details around her. "So, how is it you're not married yet?"

Tom chuckled lightly. "Come on, sit down," he said, and led her to a seat by the island table. "And just wait here a moment."

"A surprise? I'm excited," Jessica teased.

Tom disappeared through a doorway on the far side of the room. She could hear him descending into a basement. He returned a few short minutes later with a bottle of wine.

"Chateau Lancaster," he said, and swung the door behind him closed with one foot.

"Now *that's* exactly what the doctor ordered," Jessica said. She indeed hoped a glass or three of wine would help quell the adrenaline blast of the attack. In fact, she thought, at least three would be required to slow her heart rate back down to some kind of a normal level.

And then she nearly jumped off her seat when the metallic noise behind her slashed through the stillness of the night.

"Jessica!" Tom's voice called to her. "Easy! It's all over."

Her heartbeats hammering, Jessica turned to him with an embarrassed grin. She thought her face must have been giving off a brilliant red glow. The noise had only been the clatter of utensils in a drawer Tom opened to retrieve a bottle opener.

"Yeah, I'm a basket case," she said, and laughed at herself.

"I'm not surprised," Tom said, pouring the wine. "You've been through hell today. But you can relax now. There is absolutely no way on Earth anything else can happen to you." He handed Jessica an ample goblet of wine and stared deep into her eyes. "Do you believe me?"

"Yes," she said with a sigh, wanting so much to be put at ease by his calming, reassuring strength. But this time, it wasn't like the aftermath of the car crash. She had been through too much since then. "I believe you, Tom," she said, and forced a smile. She believed him, yet she could not feel it. Here she was, locked inside his massive, security-system-protected house, watched over by police guards on duty outside, yet so much was still so wrong. A rabid, maniacal killer was still out there. And Jessica was also certain that everyone investigating this case was heading down a very wrong path. *Buzz McPherson....*

"Here, drink," Tom said, and touched his wine glass to hers.

She did so, savoring a very sweet white wine.

"Good?" Tom asked.

"So sweet. Just the way I like my wine."

"Excellent," Tom said. "So, just drink up and forget about everything."

"God, I want to so much."

"Well," Tom said, sipping more of his drink, "just until tomorrow morning. Then you'll tell the chief's artist exactly what those two looked like. This will all be over before you know it."

Tom's words jolted Jessica out of the alcohol haze wanting to dull her senses.

"Look, Tom, I know this whole thing is so completely insane, but —"

"You're thinking about that guy who saved you," Tom

smoothly cut her off.

"Yes. The cops should *not* be looking for two criminals here."

"Jessica," Tom said, apparently trying to sound calming, reassuring, but unable to pull it off perfectly. There was something jagged, something severe shadowing his words. "That guy is not what he's claiming to be. I'm sure the police can check very quickly if someone with a name like Buzz McPherson is a reporter. And you know what?" Tom paused for effect.

Although his gaze was still so placid, the effect was anything but calming for Jessica. She was sensing something hard, something obsessively, zealously unyielding in him.

"They're going to come back here and tell us they can't find a Buzz McPherson reporting for any newspaper or TV station or radio or anything anywhere."

Well, let's see, Jessica wanted to say. She sipped her wine instead, wanting her senses dulled, her adrenaline neutralized.

It wasn't really working.

Tom seemed to sense that. "You have to get this whole horrendous evening out of your mind for just a little while longer. Just for tonight." He leaned closer and smiled at her. "Okay?"

"Tom, I really want to."

But soon enough, Jessica realized even the deliciously sweet wine couldn't go down past a second glass. She wasn't anywhere near to being drunk *or* sedated. Nevertheless, she should have been going to bed. Tom also realized this and showed her to one of the guest bedrooms upstairs.

When they stopped outside its door, Tom reached over and brushed a stray lock of hair away from Jessica's left eye. "Do you like this room?" he asked with a lopsided grin.

Maybe the wine had done something after all, Jessica realized because she didn't find the words to reply right away.

"I really don't want you to have it," Tom said ironically.

Jessica felt his fingers brush over hers. Their hands soon entwined. "I need it just tonight," she told him.

But she let Tom lean over to her. She *wanted* him to lean over. She wanted to kiss him, at least, to feel him. She let his mouth explore hers. She felt his hunger, and she felt her own.

But she knew she had to stop here for tonight.

When she lay in bed, she wondered why. After the horrors of this day, she wanted to feel the security of his body next to hers. Yet somehow that kiss was all she could take right now.

CHAPTER 32

The Predator had to keep it under control. This time, he had no choice. He had long known that he was a superior man, a superior being in control of an intellect that put him into a higher category than mere mortal human beings. Even before the Handlers had discovered him, before they had heard of his handiwork from all those bungling, clueless news stories of a seemingly perfect serial killer who might or might not have been a cannibal and a ritualistic blood-drinker, even before they endowed him with a fraction of their powers, the Predator had become fully cognizant of his exceptionality. But this time, he needed all of that self-control, that intellect, to quell his rage. He had to keep calm, he had to plot, he had to plan and strategize because the Handlers would only let him have one last shot at Jessica.

The Predator stood in the shades of the foliage and watched Tom Lancaster's house. The police protection around it was good, but not perfect. The trees and bushes between the properties on the block left an angle of approach that allowed an intruder to bypass the rowing police patrols.

Of course, the Predator couldn't make a move just now. He was too keyed up. He was too high on an adrenaline jag right now. Plus, he was fighting rage. He was struggling to stamp down the fury over his failure. He—the Handlers' instrument, their worldly emissary, the one superior being who was fit enough to help them achieve their ends—had been summarily threatened over Jessica. They had made the mistake of allowing him to indulge his fantasy of this woman, they told him, but they would not let him jeopardize the entire mission over his insignificant, useless sex fantasy.

And where would *they* be without him? The Predator wanted to rage back at the Handlers. How could they achieve their goals without his help? How dare they chastise him like this?

But the Predator knew the sort of weaknesses that bound the Handlers. Despite their powers, they were also alarmingly weak and limited. The short amount of time they could spend in this world was one such weakness. Plus, their reasoning capacity was severely limited. *That* was what frightened the Predator. There were times when the Handlers were no more than raving, savage animals.

The Predator had no choice but to do what he must. He had to take Jessica, and there could be no more failures. Therefore, he had to hold back tonight. He had to gather his wits and carefully plan his next move. That and....

The other one!

Jessica had protection now.

It was yet another obstacle thrown in the Predator's way, but it would be no match for his superiority.

CHAPTER 33

By the time Jessica had awoken, not only had Tom fixed a delectable salmon omelet breakfast, but he had returned from her father's house with her duffel bag and several sets of clean clothes. After a shower, she had changed into one of her flower-print sundresses.

The spectacular rays of the morning sunbathing everything in the kitchen with a golden, invigorating glow made Jessica feel like she had been transported into another world. This was a world of perfection and safety. The madness of the previous day had been washed away. She felt like she could safely let it fade from memory.

In fact, everything seemed so perfect that even the pains from her nose and forehead were gone. Where she thought she had a slight swelling on the bridge of her nose last night, everything had healed almost completely. It did feel slightly tender to the touch, but otherwise, she was almost as good as new.

Her sunny morning reverie with Tom, of course, did not remain perfect and uninterrupted. The cops were still outside, and Tom could not stay the entire day with her. But somehow it didn't seem to trouble her all that much here. She was in a place of sanctuary, even if the evil that tried to snatch her hours ago was still out there.

"We're taking this very seriously, ma'am, and that's why you'll be under constant, 'round-the-clock watch today," one of the Cedar Valley PD officers, a woman identified as Lieutenant Stansfield by her name tag, explained to Jessica before Tom was due to leave for school.

There was some state accreditation assessment meeting or something or other he could not get out of. Jessica had heard him arguing with the Dean of the School of Physics about it an hour ago. She appreciated his concern, of course, but ultimately, his absence didn't put her in any greater jeopardy. Twenty-four-hour armed protection just outside the house would do the job of shielding her from this Inquisition nutcase just fine.

Hopefully.

"We're sorry if it feels restrictive," Lieutenant Stansfield said with something of a perfunctory tone to her words, "but we don't want to take any chances until we catch this guy."

Jessica noticed how the woman rarely looked straight at her but rather scanned and evaluated the layout of the house. She was looking at all the points of egress, no doubt, mentally summing up how secure the place was.

"No, I understand," Jessica told her.

"Good," Stansfield said with a slight, professional smile. "And believe us, we *will* get him. Very soon. As a matter of fact, the sketch artist is being tracked down right now. We'll have him come by here within an hour." She paused for a moment. "We hope. He's actually an art instructor at Dr. Lancaster's school. We're trying to find him."

"Yeah, all those flaky academics," Tom kidded.

"You have nothing to worry about," Stansfield said before reassuring Jessica yet again that she would be just outside, sitting in her patrol car with her partner. Then, with a nod of reassurance, she left.

"She's right, you know," Tom concurred quickly. "This dirtbag is on the run now. And they'll have him behind bars in no time." Then, with a darker, somewhat frustrated shade in his eyes, he added, "And I'll be back before you know it."

"Oh, I know the danger's gone," Jessica said. "So don't worry about it, okay? Take care of what you have to."

Tom returned a lopsided grin. "You're a gem, you know. You're too understanding."

"I know," Jessica teased. "And I won't mind being held captive in here all day long."

Tom's look seemed to fade into something more serious, yet his tone remained light. "It's good to be cautious. Just for a little while."

Jessica nodded.

After Tom kissed her with a longing, regretful passion, he too left.

Jessica was unnerved by how quickly the entire house got to feel oppressively quiet. She understood the meaning of the cliché "deafening silence." Although she went on several walking tours of Tom's exquisite house, that feeling of disjointed vulnerable isolation only got worse.

It did so because her mind kept replaying the previous evening. She wasn't so much obsessing over the attack itself—oddly enough, she knew—but the implications of everything that came later. Her mind, her instincts kept screaming that Tom, the cops, everyone here was somehow dead set on being wrong about the attack. *About Buzz McPherson!* There was something much more complicated going on here that everyone was missing. They seemed to be almost willfully wrong-headed. They seemed to be insisting on charging down a completely wrong track because the alternatives did not mesh with their preconceived notions of what this investigation *should* have been all about.

But Jessica decided this train of thought needed to be brought to an end that instant. There was little she could do about anything at that moment, sitting in that large, silent house all alone. Futility was maddening, and she needed her wits about her until the entire insane mess—whatever it would all reveal itself to be—was sorted out and resolved.

She chose to do so by finding Tom's radio in the kitchen and tuning in to the local AM talk channel. In a half an hour, the highlights of Cassie Brynner's *Facts of Love* show from the previous evening would be replayed. The re-edited replay show was a rather absurd set-up, Jessica mused. The morning's encore presentation was a sanitized version of a show that could, on more than a few occasions, get unabashedly raunchy. Or "allegedly" raunchy, Jessica felt. Cassie ran a relationship and sex program, of course. But even the sex talk, in all its frankness, was non-exploitive and clearly health-and wellness-oriented. Naturally, in the twenty-first century, that still equaled "smut" to many "concerned media critics and family advocates." How a culture whose pop entertainment was so saturated with absurdly unrealistic images of sexuality could still be so squeamish about a level-headed, honest discussion of sexual health was beyond Jessica's comprehension. Maybe if she had listened to her father and gotten that Ph.D., she might have been able to figure that one out. Of course, the punchline to the whole "re-edition" of Cassie's show was that the *Facts of Love* was book-ended by a collection of ranting, fringe-extremist political talk shows. So unstable windbags who regularly called these shows with such well-formulated foreign policy proposals as "nuking the whole damned Middle East, taking their oil, and letting God sort them out" or "George Washington was a pedophile Illuminati Satanist" could be given free access to the airwaves with little concern about the pernicious effects on "children and the sanctity of America's families." Modern America had somehow gotten to the point where people who gave advice to men and women about loving each other were more frightening than those specializing in tearing people apart, starting fights, controversies, and fomenting fear and discord.

Go figure, Jessica whispered to herself as she turned the radio on, unconsciously bracing herself for what might come over the speakers.

Sure enough, once she found AM 1192, "the talk of the Midwest," the *Milton Lawrence Show* had, as usual, degenerated into a frenzied shouting match. The host and his guests were predicting the end of the republic if the other side's candidate won whichever election they were so fiercely debating.

"Let me tell you! Let me tell you, folks," the host was huffing and bellowing over the airwaves.

"You're wrong, Milt!" his guest was braying, trying to cut him off in mid-sentence. "You're dead wrong!"

"Let me tell you, folks, why my guest is *way* off base—"

"Dead wrong, Milt!"

"I gave you the chance to speak, so you be quiet, or you're off the air!"

"Whatever, Milt, except Hitler was saying the exact same things you are."

"Let me tell you what's wrong with this country, folks," Milton Lawrence pontificated. "Congress and the media! And who, besides this show, is keeping them accountable? I swear to you, folks, I swear to you right here and now—and may God, may our Good Lord strike me down where I sit if I'm lying to you—but I will buy a one-way, nonrefundable ticket out of this country if these idiots win reelection come November. This is my promise and my pledge to you. I will not live in their America. I refuse to be a citizen of the same country where liars and thieves and unprincipled cowards are running the show."

"How can one man be so wrong, Milt?" the guest retorted,

matching Lawrence's self-important diatribe with an equally-annoying, plaintive whine. "You just don't see what's in front of you and refuse to look at the evidence, so I hope that flight out of this great country will be very comfortable."

"Sorry," Lawrence shot back. "It's not going to happen because we're winning, folks. We're marshaling our forces all across the fruited plains, and we're taking back our country."

"The problem is, who's really in charge? You're refusing to see where the hegemony is consolidating its power. It's banking conspirators working hand-in-hand with a New World Order global power elite, working hand-in-hand with the global military power matrix that I'm talking about in my new book, and it's all run by—"

"Come on!" Milton Lawrence shouted. "Who can coordinate all this?"

"Who's already mastered the art of subliminal mind-control and behavior modification? It's a secret consortium of Las Vegas casino owners. They've been using nanotech to make you gamble away your entire life. People have been talking about this for years. It's all in my book, and now I have the documents from the Illuminati archives to prove—"

"Winslow, you've lost your mind!"

By now, Jessica was starting to feel that she was close to losing hers. She couldn't possibly listen to all this until Cassie's censored show came on.

"Vegas is the key to everything," Winslow protested. "If you look at the latitude and longitude coordinates of Vegas and understand anything about occult numerology, you'll see the significance of what I'm trying to say. But it goes much higher than that."

"How high, Winslow? Wait a minute! Don't tell me. We're talking about Vegas, so I suppose Area 51 is behind everything."

"Area 51 is a smokescreen, Milt! It's all in my book."

"Your self-published book, right?"

"Because the mainstream media won't touch my work! They're terrified of it."

"Sure, Winslow."

"I have the doctored photos. So yes, it has to go much higher than Area 51. I'm not convinced that Reagan died in 2004. The international banking conglomerates have too much invested in this scheme, and now their headquarters in Monte Carlo has been updated with third-generation high-frequency neural—"

Jessica turned down the volume at last. She would just need to remember to keep an eye on the clock until Cassie's show.

Maybe TV, she thought and padded over to Tom's living room.

Actually, she should try and give Cassie a call soon, she decided a moment later. It would be good to talk to her after all that had happened. Yet she also felt some trepidation about freaking out her friend with a story about being attacked by the Inquisition killer. And freaked out is exactly what Cassie would be. She had a way of letting her emotions run rampant, especially fear and panic. Well, Jessica considered, the last several years of Cassie's life had given her more than enough reasons to get panicky and emotional. The more Jessica thought about it now, the less comfortable she was with loading her burdens onto Cassie. Maybe if she could come up with just the right words to break the news to Cassie, she would call her.

So she continued into Tom's living room, hoping to find some way to break the unpleasant silence of the house without needing to turn to those lunatics on the radio.

The living room of the scholar, of course, Jessica thought with a smile, noting how the place looked much more like a library than a true living room. There were bookshelves along the two longest walls, with the shelves crowding either side of Tom's TV and electronic entertainment collection.

All the books gave Jessica an idea. She was going to take some of Buzz McPherson's advice, after all. She was curious to see just what kinds of things Tom wrote. Did any more books like *The Naked Ghost* help pay for his high-end lifestyle? she wondered.

Scanning the bookshelves on the right of the entertainment center, for a moment, she thought she was seeing the literary equivalent of the craziness on that radio talk show. *The Antichrist Conspiracy Hoax*, the spine of one book read. *The Media-fed Paranoia Industry*, read another. Neither of those books was by Tom, but she did find *The Naked Ghost* on a shelf above. Apparently, Tom kept a very strictly alphabetized collection—just like she did at home—the books coordinated by topics.

"Paranormal and unexplained," she mumbled under her breath. "Exactly what Mr. Call Me Buzz Because My Dad Liked Astronauts said."

She pulled a book by Tom, called *UFO's of the Mind*, off the shelf. On the front cover, she saw the subtitle, *Mass Hypnosis, Hysteria, and the Alien Contact Phenomenon*. It had a picture of a group of zoned-out people projecting images of flying saucers from their own eyes. So, apparently, Tom thought that all those alien spaceship witnesses were self-deluded and dreaming the whole thing. Since Jessica had never had a particular interest in the topic, she couldn't agree or disagree with Tom. She did, in fact, like reading "hard science fiction" and future-speculation novels—she had a collection of sci-fi novels and classic, pulp-era paperbacks at home—but she had never taken the time to read up on the whole alien contact and alien abduction controversy to form an opinion.

"*Cyber Age Mythology*," she read the title of another book by Tom as she put the UFO book back on the shelf. The table of contents promised a dissection and criticism of everything from retrieved flying saucers to New Age crystal powers, psychic phenomena, and angelic visitations.

Why We Want to Believe was a third book by Tom. Its cover design and script resembled the advertising artwork from the old *X-Files* TV show. Glancing inside the book's jacket, Jessica found that Tom was arguing that the belief in supernatural phenomena was all a result of a panic mechanism in people's minds against the horrifying implication that no higher power was in charge, and there was nothing beyond the here and now. Leafing through the book, she did find that Tom ended on an optimistic note. "The Beauty of the World Around Us," was the title of the last chapter. "We Can All Build a Better World for Ourselves and Others," went the subtitle.

"Hmm," Jessica mused quietly. "I thought human behavior was not your thing."

The next book Jessica looked at was called *Hogwash!* It was an edited collection compiled by Tom and someone called Earl Putney. Glancing through the table of contents — listing a long series of works criticizing various aspects of spirituality — she found Tom's own chapter, entitled "Near Death Fantasy Falls to Hard Science."

So he's a fanatical skeptic and debunker of the supernatural on his time off, Jessica realized.

Aside from the books, she found a collection of Tom's *Doubters* magazine, a publication devoted, apparently, to eradicating all beliefs in paranormal phenomena. Officially, the magazine claimed to "apply the scientific method to unsubstantiated claims of the unexplained for the advancement of a rational world." Among the issues on the shelf, she saw articles by Tom like "Exorcising the Peoria Prophet," claiming to expose a housewife believed to channel messages from a long-dead Tibetan holy man, and "The University of Seattle's Bigfoot Fetish: Why is a major university wasting its students' tuition dollars on a search for imaginary monsters in the forest?"

And then, something else caught Jessica's eye. It was another book by Tom, except it was smaller and thinner than the ones next to it. It was pushed farther towards the back of the shelf, going unnoticed upon her first perusal of the collection. Jessica pulled the slim volume out, and Buzz McPherson's rantings echoed through her mind.

It was a book called *She Said "No."*

"I don't believe it," Jessica whispered.

Now it all came back. It had caused a minor furor some years back. The book attempted to "set the record straight" about the deadly ending of a school bus hijacking. It was an all too familiar story. Some sniveling loser who had been shunned by his schoolmates for wearing nothing but black clothing to classes, and who had a nasty penchant for unloading "white power" rants on social media, snapped one day and took a school bus hostage. Armed with two shotguns, he had proceeded to execute ten of the kids on board before a SWAT team stormed the vehicle. One of the hostages, a fifteen-year-old girl named Jeanie Anderson, had been interrogated by the killer because he heard her say a prayer. Reportedly he asked her if she believed in God, even in the midst of this massacre. When the girl said "yes," the shooter murdered her on the spot.

The incident made a Christian martyr out of Jeanie Anderson, and she became the figurehead for a major wave of teenage religious revivals across the country. Her family, her church, and her admirers claimed it was proof of God's purpose in all things. Even tragedies and the horrors of the world had an ultimate, positive purpose, they declared. Jeanie might have died, but her martyrdom reignited the faith of thousands of young people across the country — across the world, according to some news sources. Hundreds of teenagers claimed to have found the power to kick drugs, throw away the bottle, get out of gangs, and one college coed claimed to have made the decision to stop stripping for tuition money all because of Jeanie's sacrifice and the power of Jesus Christ.

Except Jeanie Anderson did not say "yes." The panicking kid seemed to realize that her prayer enraged the psychopathic maniac and, hoping to save herself, she said "no" when asked if she still believed in God.

The ensuing firestorm of controversy accused the writer of the book — Tom apparently — of being part of nothing less than a Satanic plot to destroy faith and religion. His "outing" of Jeanie had, at one point, not only drawn the condemnation of Christians but several rabbis and Muslim clerics as well. Tom's book was quickly interpreted as a willful and malicious attack on the positive effects of faith and prayer, not just a specific targeting of Christians for criticism and embarrassment.

Jessica put the book back on the shelf with a sinking, unpleasant sensation somewhere deep in the pit of her stomach.

The truth of the matter was that she had never been overtly religious. While growing up, her church-going had consisted of a few rare instances on Christmas and Easter with her mother. Nonetheless, the *She Said "No"* controversy struck her as nothing but a mean-spirited, churlish attack on faith for no other purpose than to ridicule people the writer disagreed with. *Tom disagreed with!* What good reason could have been behind making this particular truth known? What greater good did the truth accomplish here? The family of that poor kid, the families of all those kids who had been killed, found some small positive ray of light to comfort them in what must have been the most devastating moment of their lives, and Tom had come along and stepped on it for...for what? To score some ideological point? Was he any different from all those fanatics on talk shows like *Milton Lawrence*, the people who would rather move to another country than see their political opponents win an election?

Jessica found herself backing away from the bookshelves as if they contained something horrendously gruesome, something that wounded her to the core. More than the content of the book, more than Tom's obviously zealous position on the age-old faith and reason issue, she was disturbed by the realization of the true nature of their relationship. She really knew next to nothing about Tom Lancaster. He was handsome and charming, sure, an accomplished academic and author, a man of eminence and respect. Yet aside from these surface details, she knew absolutely nothing about him. And here she was, virtually moving into his home, having fallen for him hard since the moment they met when he was really but a complete stranger to her. Had she not been attacked last night, what would they have done? Not for a single moment did she entertain real doubts. More than likely, she would have slept with him had he asked.

Jessica found herself aimlessly wandering around the house, heading back toward the kitchen. She was wrapped up in her thoughts, in her need to take an objective step back and try and find a way of slowing down her courtship with Tom until they could get a chance to know each other better.

And then she realized that amidst all this introspection, she had forgotten about Cassie's show. So she went into the kitchen, turned the radio on, and heard Cassie's familiar voice. Except it was somehow too familiar.

"Spring is almost here, girls," Cassie's voice came over the airwaves, "and guess what? As the weather's warming up, it's time to heat up your love life too. Well, we've got Dr. Amanda Cornwell, UC San Diego psychologist with us, and she'll tell us if the springtime really helps us relight those fires in the bedroom. And I'll give you some more info on the Wings of Angels Walk Across America for Breast Cancer project after your local news."

"It's a rerun," Jessica said to herself, actually feeling as if she had been abandoned by Cassie.

But why the rerun? she wondered. Cassie was supposed to have been doing live shows all month long. Last night they should have been live, and right now, Jessica should have been hearing Cassie's repeat.

Annoyed, Jessica switched off the radio.

What to do now? She needed something to occupy herself, something to get her mind off the fact that this house felt less and less like a warm, familiar sanctuary.

A sudden, unpleasant trickle of adrenaline buzzed her upon hearing two slight creaks of wood somewhere in the house.

Jessica stood stock still. She heard nothing but her own rapidly increasing heartbeats. *Two* creaks of wood, her mind screamed. As if someone was walking through the house and two of his steps disturbed the floorboards.

Somewhere close!

She stood rooted to the floor in the kitchen, trying to listen for every possible sound. The cops might have been close, yet she was completely cut off from them, the petrifying realization stunned her. Her heartbeats raced faster. Those cops might as well have been back at the police station if the Inquisition killer was in the next room.

Jessica continued concentrating on every sound around her.

Except there were none.

Deathly, empty silence.

Yet she stood still, letting time tick by, doing nothing at all but waiting.

And it was still silent. Not a creak, not a thump, not a single indication that she was not alone in the house.

Jessica's terror had passed, too. It passed, but only to be replaced by the warm, rising sensation of embarrassment. She had mistaken the creaking, shifting sounds of a large wooden house for the footsteps of a prowling psychopath.

Nonetheless, Jessica was glad she liked being barefoot most of the time, and she could move about soundlessly now as she was about to confirm how she let her paranoia get the best of her. She softly padded into the living room — the general direction of the creaking noises — and she nearly collapsed from shock as she found herself face to face with an intruder.

CHAPTER 34

"It's okay!" the intruder insisted, keeping his distance from Jessica. "It's *me*. I'm not going to hurt you."

She recoiled a tiny step, gradually overcoming the momentary shock-paralysis the appearance of this figure in front of her brought on—the appearance of....

"It's me!" he said. "It's okay."

McPherson! Jessica realized at last. Buzz McPherson. He seemed to be preferring a very casual, very dressed-down attire today. He wore jeans and a white T-shirt, indicating no place where he could have had any more large handguns hidden.

"You okay?" he asked, taking a cautious step toward Jessica.

"What the hell are you doing here?" she snapped. "How did you get in here? The cops—"

"Yeah, there's a nice blind spot among all the trees between this yard and the next. No matter where the cops are positioned, they can't see an intruder coming. Not good, you know."

"Okay, now you listen to me," Jessica said, feeling her strength, her composure returning. "I want some answers this time. I want some answers that make sense."

"All right, Jessica," McPherson said with a placating voice as his gaze darted toward the windows, obviously afraid of someone seeing him in there. "But *you* need to listen to me, too, because this is extremely urgent—"

"No!" Jessica cut him off. This time, she was determined to

do this on her own terms. "I said I want—"

"I will tell you everything," McPherson said, a beseeching tone in his voice. "But you're in great danger here. You must believe me. The attempts on your life are not over. You've seen too much. You can figure too much out."

"The police can help us here!"

"Can you and Tom get out of town? As soon as possible."

"Listen to me! I said the safest place for us is right here where the police can—"

"No, they can't."

"Listen!" Jessica almost yelled.

She was glad to see that got McPherson's attention at last. She was not going to let him go on with his incomprehensible rantings about deep mysteries in Cedar Valley.

"All right," he whispered, but his glance was snapping to the windows again. His body tensed like that of a wild, cornered, wounded animal.

"Now, I'm going to say this for the last time," Jessica warned him. "We do this *my* way. And I want some answers that make sense or I'm going to get those cops in here. You understand?"

McPherson nodded, but Jessica could see the muscles in his jaw knotting.

"I want the truth. Who are you and what is going on here? What you told me last night about the cops and the funeral home and you being a reporter does not make any sense. If you're a reporter on a story here, why didn't you go to the cops *immediately*? If you are here to investigate the Inquisitor, or the Predator, or whatever the hell he is, why didn't you turn to the cops right away?"

McPherson nodded deliberately. He even put his palms up, trying his best to calm Jessica. He shot a glance at the windows again. "Okay," he said. "I will tell you everything."

Jessica tried to give him her hardest, most challenging stare.

"I couldn't talk to the cops, I couldn't talk to Simon Gainey, because there is a major criminal conspiracy going on in this town. It's between the police and the funeral home." McPherson paused and fixed Jessica with his own hard stare. "You should *not* have told him that I talked to you about the funeral home!"

For a moment, that blindsided Jessica. How the hell could McPherson have known?

Almost as if reading her mind, he said, "I went out to the funeral home right after I left you. I thought every squad car in town was out there."

"And what does the killer, the Predator, have to do with this...this conspiracy?"

"I'm not sure."

"Yes, you are," Jessica shot at him. He was lying through his teeth.

"No, listen to me," McPherson pleaded again. "All I know is —"

"Bullshit! You're lying!"

McPherson seemed taken aback by her fierce accusation.

"I can tell, okay? That's what I'm trained in. I can tell when you're lying."

McPherson looked not just stunned now, but incredulous.

"I can read all the signs your body gives off when you're lying," Jessica exclaimed with as much force as possible. Actually, *she* was the one bluffing — *lying, for God's sake* — just then. Although she'd had training in and read a lot of the interpersonal deception research, it was doubtful that *anyone* could function as a perfect human lie-detector at the drop of a hat. Although there really *were* physiological changes betrayed when people attempted to deceive, there were also a lot of natural-born liars. Although she could tell that McPherson was not being honest with her, she couldn't pinpoint exactly where the truth ended, and the fabrications began. "I can see the things you can't control," she bluffed some more. "I know the direction your eyes will automatically move when you're telling the truth, and when you're lying. I can tell the difference in the rate your eyes blink, and how the depth and shallowness of your breathing changes."

"All right, I believe you," McPherson said quietly.

"Now, you told me that you've been following the trail of a serial killer. I could buy that. But after that, you've been telling me some completely insane things. A serial killer who's...what? *Protected* by the cops here and the funeral home? That makes no sense at all."

McPherson didn't reply immediately. Instead, he fixed her with a harder, somehow crafty stare. "Is that what Tom said?"

Jessica saw him glance at the bookshelf, and she was taken aback. It was almost—again—like he had been reading her mind—or more likely, peeking through one of those windows and watching her.

A stab of anger prodded her to yell at him, but her temper was kept in check by one fact: this man was responsible for her being alive right now.

"*No!*" she said more forcefully instead. "That's what any halfway rational person could tell you after listening to your completely absurd, illogical rantings."

"Listen to me, Jessica. The *truth* is that I *don't* have all the answers. I've been following this guy's trail from the West Coast as he made his way to Illinois. And yes, I've been talking to cops and getting their help. Except the Predator's always been one step ahead. Then, as I got to Cedar Valley, I thought I had him cornered. But then he disappeared. I was sure the people at the funeral home helped him."

"Why?" Jessica asked more calmly this time. McPherson

seemed to be opening up with some semi-plausible details, so she was willing to hold off on the antagonism.

"I don't know," McPherson said slowly, enunciating all his words. He wanted to add weight to them, to insist that Jessica just *had* to believe him. "It could be a lot of things, I suppose. Some sort of a body part, organ-selling ring maybe. That could explain a couple of things…couldn't it?"

Jessica didn't know how to reply. She supposed it could. And she appreciated the fact that his assertions sounded a bit more realistic now.

"There's a *lot* of money to be made in an organ black market," McPherson said. "Enough for a corrupt police force to get involved. Or maybe just a *few* members of the police force."

"The chief?" Jessica asked slowly. Indeed, a charge like this could be given some serious consideration. Of course, it left one more very important issue up in the air. "Do you have any evidence for this?"

McPherson nodded first. "Yes. I mean, I think I have a few leads. I've seen some things around the funeral home…you know, when I staked out the place." He stopped and slowly took a couple of steps toward Jessica.

Somehow, like last night, she could sense he wasn't a threat.

"Jessica," he said deliberately. "You know this puts you in a lot of danger now. You can't chance staying around here too long. It's extremely risky for you."

If there was any chance McPherson was right about any of this, she, indeed, would be in some real peril now. Jessica could understand this, yet, somehow, she wanted more. What evidence did he have? What proof could he offer that any of this was the truth?

"You have to leave town. Either with or without Tom Lancaster. You checked up on his work, didn't you?"

Jessica nodded.

"Good. So what do you think about him? Do you think he could be persuaded to believe you?"

"I hope so. Although I don't really see what his work, what his...*beliefs* have to do with him buying a story of a black market organ-harvesting ring." Sure, Jessica considered, Tom might have been given to extreme skepticism, but a crime was a crime. "I mean," she continued, "it's not like you want to convince him that the funeral home is being run by aliens and that the Predator is a werewolf or something."

"Well, he's quite a skeptic, isn't he?"

"Yeah, when it comes to the supernatural and —"

"Jessica," McPherson cut in. "I just wanted to see what you thought of that part of his life, and whether or not you could convince him to get out of here. And I mean now."

McPherson's eyes focused on something on her face. He frowned as he studied her.

"What is it?"

"You're bleeding," he said and reached toward her face.

Before she could pull her head back, he had swiped a finger under her nose. She saw blood on his index finger as he pulled his hand back

"Damn it," Jessica said, and wiped her nose, finding a thin film of blood on her hand as well. "That freak almost broke my nose last night."

"You better put something on that."

They went into the kitchen, where Jessica washed her face and her hand. She wadded up a piece of paper towel and pressed it against her left nostril.

"I didn't even feel the soreness this morning," she mumbled. After tearing off another piece of paper, she turned to McPherson. "Here, clean your hands."

He glanced at his index finger with an embarrassed grimace. She took note of his dusty, grubby-looking jeans. He must have crawled through a number of bushes in them, Jessica surmised. Now he must have wiped his fingers on them too.

But he took the paper towel and wiped his hand again. "Thanks," he said awkwardly. After throwing the paper in the garbage can, he turned back to Jessica with another determined glare. "You need to listen to me, all right? Either with or without Tom, you need to get out of town as quickly as you can." He threw a glance toward the window once again. "I need to get out of here. But you *have* to believe me!"

CHAPTER 35

Just as he had promised, Tom came home from school as quickly as he could, cutting his meetings with the dean and the state accreditation team short. In fact, he found Jessica in the middle of the session with the sketch artist.

Jessica, just like she thought the whole process would unfold, was asked to describe *both* the Inquisition killer and Buzz McPherson. Then, as she had predicted, Tom was adamant that she get McPherson's picture as accurate as that of her mall attacker.

Or more so? Jessica dared hazard a private, unspoken guess.

The growing gap she felt forming between herself and Tom after perusing his bookshelf threatened to expand more than a bit further now.

But what the hell's his problem? Jessica wondered, aching to know, but somehow she couldn't say the words. She was going to try and stay in touch with McPherson if he showed up again, and see how that played out before really confronting the issue with Tom.

And she concealed McPherson's true appearance in her instructions to the moonlighting art teacher/sketch technician from CVSU. Since she had given a broad description to Chief Gainey last night, she needed to stay fairly close to those parameters now. The youthful looks and overgrown blond hair had to stay. The facial features, which she still thought resembled a picture of the late pop singer Andy Gibb she had seen in an ad for an easy-listening station in Santa Barbara, mutated into something that might have been the result of a gene-splicing experiment between Matthew McConaughey and Brad Pitt.

"Good looking guy," Tom said somewhat dryly after seeing the picture. "We should talk to as many women around town as possible. I'm sure they'll remember him."

Now, in hindsight, Jessica realized what had troubled her the most about Tom's words. It wasn't the petulant jealously lurking behind his remark, but the word "we."

We should talk to as many women as possible? Since when had he become a member of the police force?

Soon after the sketch artist had finished, though, a message from Gainey had been relayed to them by Lieutenant Stansfield. The Honda Accord from the accident Jessica witnessed had been found in an empty lot behind an abandoned warehouse complex on the north side of town. It was the Accord McPherson had driven when he first tried to save her from the Inquisition killer, Jessica now mulled as she rode in Tom's car toward their rendezvous with Gainey. The police wanted her to positively identify the Honda.

"Are you okay?" Tom's voice interrupted her thoughts.

When she looked at him, she realized that although his voice was as warm as ever, there was a certain hawkish, probing directness in his eyes. Aside from being superbly intelligent, Jessica knew, he was also acutely perceptive of behavior and mood. She knew he could sense how troubled she was. She also wondered if Tom suspected she was not being honest with him.

Luckily, the radio was tuned to a news station, and she could try and use it as an excuse. The local broadcast, read by what sounded like a recent college graduate in his first on-air job in the sticks, was discussing her attack and the larger Inquisition case.

"I'm sorry," Jessica said, and tried to smile at Tom with something of an honest expression. "Just listening to this is so strange. I've heard myself on the radio, but not *about* myself as the subject of a sensational serial killer story."

Tom gave the radio somewhat of a rueful look. He was about to reach over and turn it off, but Jessica thought the story was about to take an unusual turn.

"Hold on," she said, and waved for him not to touch the dial.

"The King's Bridge Mall attack has not only put many locals on edge," the newscaster said stiffly, "but it seems to have ignited something of a political and spiritual controversy. The Reverend Jim Garnett of the Celebration of the Word Ministries has weighed in on the case in an interview with WSBC's Mindy Fletcher."

The next voice through the car's speakers came in the avuncular tones of a trained public speaker. There was a good-natured folksiness to the Midwestern inflection on the surface of the Reverend Garnett's words, but they belied something much harder, much steelier underneath. Upon first impression, he sounded like your favorite uncle who ran a country candy store, but he had an agenda-driven, combative grit not too far below that surface. It was the carefully-managed duplicity of a professional politician.

"These tragedies are obviously the work of a sick, *sick*, sad individual," Garnett said, putting special emphasis on the word "sick." "It's a reminder to us all that *evil* is a very real, very tangible force in the world. And yes, I pray that our superbly-trained, dedicated law enforcement professionals will be able to put this reign of *terror*, reign of *evil* to an end as soon as possible. And I pray to the Lord to give the families of the victims strength to make it through this difficult time."

Jessica noticed how the accent was also repeatedly placed on the words "terror" and "evil." A moment later, she thought she knew why.

Reporter Mindy Fletcher's voice segued over to another interview subject. "But it seems," Mindy said, "that some believe people like Garnett might be at the root of the Inquisition killer's reign of terror. Doctor Lyle Chambers, professor of political science at Cedar Valley State University, had this to say."

Dr. Chambers' comments were driven by as much force as the reverend's, but, unfortunately for the professor, his overall impression contained none of Garnett's polished, soothing charm. "Well, I'm not surprised that we have superstition, religious-fanaticism-driven maniacs running around in society obsessed with end-time prophecies and the Antichrist and the sort of exclusionary beliefs of extremists like Jim Garnett and his followers." Chambers' words seemed to rattle out of his mouth in an annoying, monotone grate. To Jessica, he seemed to be as much of a wound-up zealot as he accused Garnett of being. "I mean, look at what's going on here. This monster, this madman, seems to be killing people in some kind of a superstition-driven frenzy. Killing that girl from the nightclub? Is that a coincidence? I don't think so. He probably felt he was on a mission to eliminate sinners or punish the fornicators or some such nonsense. That's what people like Garnett have been preaching about for decades. That we're some sort of a decadent, wicked society, and everyone who does not believe the same things they do are evil and deserves to be punished. I'm sure they weren't listening to Christian rock in that nightclub. So she probably deserved to die, right? Or how about that woman at the mall? She writes about sex and relationships. To fringe extremists like Garnett and his flock, she's probably a smut-peddler. She deserved to die, right?"

Getting pulled into the middle of a surrealistic, outlandish debate like this caught Jessica like a punch in the gut.

In the meantime, the radio allowed Garnett a retort to Chambers' diatribe. "That's just outrageous," Garnett's voice came through the car's speakers, smooth, serious, and concerned. "Using tragedies like this to score some sort of a political point, some sort of an ideological jab, I just find absolutely disgusting. I've never in my life said that anybody deserves to die or that everyone who does not share my beliefs deserves to die. Now there *are* people whose lifestyles will put them in danger. There are people who choose to do reckless, irresponsible, or outright immoral things they can suffer from and eventually regret, but I never said anyone *deserves* to die."

This time, Tom did turn the radio off. He cast an inquisitive glance toward Jessica. "You don't mind, do you?"

In fact, she didn't mind, still too unnerved by the content of the exchange. She also wasn't sure how to position herself in the debate. Although sensing that someone like Lyle Chambers might have been given to grossly exaggerating and demonizing Garnett, her up-close experience of the "family values" crowd's attacks on, and subsequently forced censorship of, the rebroadcast of Cassie Brynner's shows made her think twice all of a sudden. The Inquisitor, after all, appeared to be killing in the delusional frenzy of some sort of religious fanaticism. He was leaving Biblical graffiti painted in blood, quoting the scriptures about the punishment of the wicked. Perhaps the fringe media-haters like Garnett and his ilk, harping on the pernicious effects of entertainment violence and sex, never considered the effects of their own sermonizing about the Apocalypse, damnation, and the tortures of Hell coming to all who were not of like minds. Once her own show debuted in San Diego, Jessica wondered if she would go onto all the moral watchdog groups' list of usual suspects responsible for corrupting Americans' values. Chambers, Jessica thought, was quite right in his assessment of how Garnett and his ultra-moralist followers would likely look at her own career. These considerations, of course, were dizzying and confusing all of a sudden. Just this morning, she had been outraged at Tom's senseless attacks on religious beliefs and spirituality. Now here she sat, listening to a baiter of religious fundamentalists, and realizing that Chambers would more likely be an ally to her than any of those people who had wanted to canonize Jeanie Anderson after they thought that she said "yes."

Fundamentalists. Extremists. That's the point, isn't it? Extremists, Jessica thought, dismayed. That was the state of the modern world, wasn't it? Chaos, hate, poison, paranoia, conspiracy theories. Where were the normal people today? Where were the true rationalists of the middle ground, the sensible center in a world ruled by fanatics praying for the Apocalypse?

Her eyes snapped toward Tom.

...Fanatics who used the deaths of teenagers to mock others' beliefs.

"No, I don't mind," she told him at length. "It's just scary how many crazy people are out there. And not only the serial killers."

She noticed a bitter little grin on Tom's face.

"Do you know this Chambers guy?" she asked.

"Actually, not too well, no."

"I thought your school was one big family."

Tom chuckled this time. The bitterness, the irony was still there. "Yeah, well, all families have their crazy black sheep. Although, I must say, Dr. Chambers did bring up some good points just now."

Of course, you would think so, Jessica almost said aloud. She was thinking of *She Said "No"* and Tom's own virulent attacks on spirituality. Where did he stand among the world's ever-growing population of zealots, demagogues, and uncompromising nutcases?

"Then again," Tom added, "even a broken clock is right twice a day."

"What's wrong with him?"

"You know those conspiracy fruitcakes I told you about before? The ones handing out the fliers all over town?"

"Yeah?"

"Lyle Chambers is their local patron saint. Since he's tenured, he can be. Somehow he even talked the political science department into letting him teach a class on it."

"He teaches a class on conspiracy theories?"

"Well, of course, he doesn't call it that. It's Critical Alternate Historical Paradigms, or some such pseudo intellectual collection of weasel words. Now, if he did it as an actual critical examination of all the 9/11 truther and crisis-actor Freemason conspiracy crap, that would be another story. But the good Doctor Chambers actually endorses those unhinged fantasies. Because they critique the so-called power structure."

"Well, I think you're right about staying logical," Jessica said as she noticed the glare of police lights in a parking lot not too far ahead. She, of course, didn't add that she thought what Tom *said* about staying logical sounded good. However, his own hints of being as much of an inflexible, agenda-driven extremist who could rival Chambers or Garnett or any conspiracy theorist he hated so much troubled her all the more with every passing moment.

"Thanks," Tom said as he made the turn toward the parking lot.

Jessica knew she was about to be given even more lectures about logic and rationality by Chief Gainey.

CHAPTER 36

The weed-infested parking lot where the police were waiting for Jessica and Tom belonged to an abandoned row of characterless, boxy office buildings and a complex of rusting warehouses. Even aside from the police cars, the place was far from empty. A collection of semi-truck-trailers and dump trucks—most of which were identified as the property of Axelman Demolitions—had been parked there beyond a cordon of quite new and well-kept fencing.

"It was stolen three days ago," Simon Gainey said, jerking his chin toward the car as Jessica and Tom joined him. "Belonged to a vacationing couple out of town until next week. Then he parked it here where the demolition crew members park their cars."

Jessica almost literally *felt* Gainey's eyes zeroing in on her.

"This is the car, correct?" the chief asked.

Indeed, it appeared to be, and Jessica told him so.

"Yeah," Gainey confirmed. "The damage on the front looks exactly like what you described."

Jessica felt Tom's hand on her shoulder. His touch somehow started as a caress, but slightly tightened into something possessive.

"Car theft doesn't sound much like standard operating procedure in investigative journalism, does it?" Tom asked.

Gainey returned a stiff, knowing smile, although Jessica

could hear Tom's comment was aimed at her.

"What about the van?" she asked the police chief. "Do you know anything about that?"

Jessica immediately noticed that the pointed tone of her voice had its intended effect. Gainey's eyes clouded over for a fleeting moment. His annoyance, of course, hardly bothered Jessica. She was plenty annoyed herself. The top cop in this town seemed smug and satisfied having found a car used by the man who saved her life, yet the serial killer who nearly murdered her was still at large.

"No, Ms. Lafayette," Gainey said, "not yet, unfortunately. But I can guarantee that will be the next thing you hear about."

"I know you're doing your jobs," Jessica said, somewhat placatingly, but only after a heavy beat. "I appreciate that."

"Absolutely," Tom said enthusiastically.

Gainey nodded and gave one of his crisp, recruiting poster smiles. "By the way," he said, "We also appreciate your help with the sketches. I've seen both pictures, and they're going out to all our patrol cars. As for that McPherson individual, we've been trying to locate any clue as to who he is or whatever organization he might be reporting for."

Gainey paused for a heavy, extended beat. Jessica could guess what was to follow.

"We've found nothing, ma'am," the cop said. "And you have to admit that sounds strange, doesn't it?"

"I'd say so," Tom replied.

But Jessica could concur on this one as well. Just like she could be traced through a simple Internet search because of her publications, a reporter should have left the same sort of cyber trail.

"Oh, and one other thing...." Jessica chose to touch on another issue instead. "Have you done any checking on the funeral home?"

There was a rueful look on Gainey's face. Jessica thought she might have heard Tom take an exasperated breath.

"Yes," Gainey said. "We checked on *everything* you told us. There is nothing suspicious or underhanded going on at that place. There *never* has been. We've never had a single complaint about that establishment. *Ever.* Even Dr. Lancaster told you your father had been cremated properly, did he not?"

Jessica knew she didn't need to look and confirm Tom's disapproving, pedantic stare right now, so she kept her eyes on Gainey.

"But it's something this McPherson person brought up," said the cop, "so we checked it out, believe me."

Jessica nodded.

"And please believe something else. This guy is seriously wrong. I realize you think he saved your life, but you don't want to deal with this man on your own."

CHAPTER 37

"I *think* he saved my life?" Jessica blurted out at last after walking through Tom's front door.

Sensing their post-Simon Gainey discussion was bound to get heated, she opted not to challenge the cop's statements while they were in a moving car.

"Look, Jessica, he probably could have done a better job of picking his words, sure," Tom replied, his tone so frustratingly patronizing. "I agree with you, but—"

"But *nothing*," Jessica shot back. "The next thing he's going to be telling me, and telling *you*, is that I imagined everything. That I'm insane or something."

"No, I'm sure he won't."

"I'm not sure about anything with this man. He said I *think* McPherson saved my life."

"Jessica, *please*," Tom pushed. "I think what Gainey meant, what someone with his experience of dealing with witnesses meant, was that the recollection of events after something sudden, traumatic, and stressful can be less than accurate."

"Oh, no you don't," Jessica said, feeling the heat rise to her face, raw anger taking hold of her. "You can't pull that debunker line on me. *Less than accurate?* I didn't see some flicker of light behind trees ten miles away and think it was a UFO from Mars. This guy was right up in my face, and he was trying to bury a knife in my throat."

"Jessica, the point I'm trying to make—"

"Is that you believe everything that cop is telling you because it's nice and convenient and safe. *I* was the one who got nearly choked to death, beaten up, and almost stabbed until McPherson showed up and tried to blow him away. Why is nobody hearing *my* facts? Why are you all trying to jump to your preconceived conclusions? Is what you're doing, Tom, more *empirical*, more *rationalist* than listening to me?"

Jessica saw the effects of her words. She could tell that suggesting Tom was betraying his own hyper-rationalist beliefs was starting to abrade him.

"Jessica, just please listen to me," Tom said with an exasperated, yet well-controlled little sigh. "Please? All I'm saying is that you need to stop obsessing over this guy. Isn't it just a little convenient—*too* convenient—the way he shows up to blow away your attacker? Don't you think there's something off here?"

"But, there's something off in treating him as if he were another serial killer."

"And the car theft? Avoiding the police? The fact that no one can find anything on him—?"

Jessica quickly cut in by saying, "He said there is some kind of a cover-up by the local police going on." But almost instantly, she realized what she had given Tom to jump on and object to. How vehemently he would do so, she could only guess.

"He did?" Tom fired back. His voice had the sort of edge Jessica expected. "And when did he say this? I might be off, but I don't recall that being part of your statement to the cops."

Jessica couldn't yet tell him that McPherson had talked to her today. Tom had to go on thinking that all of this information had come after the mall attack last night.

"Well, of course not," she said simply, yet resolutely.

"Of course not," Tom repeated. There was a condescending disappointment in his words. "You couldn't tip them off that you were onto the far-reaching conspiracy."

Jessica didn't reply. Tom was ready and eager, no doubt, to voice a line of retorts honed by years of work and experience as a professional skeptic. She hoped her set jaw and a strong glare might warn him, though, that she wouldn't let him psychobabble her into believing she did not see and feel and experience something she did.

"Jessica, Cedar Valley is not exactly Mayberry, but it's certainly no bustling metropolis either," Tom said in a surprisingly calm manner. "The police force is not run by a grand cabal of criminal masterminds." His voice seeming to plead, to beg for reasoned, logical reflection. "There are parking violations. There are speeders and drunken college kids. Some of us might do some pretty high tech research at the university, but we're not building space-based weapons systems for the military. There is nothing to hide in this place, nothing to cover up, no matter what a second-rate crank like Lyle Chambers might claim. These elaborate conspiracy theories you keep reading about are for simple minds and small people. Powerless people who can't accept the fact that the world is chaotic, messy, unpredictable, and just plain unfair. And, of course, conspiracy theories are also for a few undistinguished, invisible academics who are bitter over the fact that multimillion dollar book contracts are not coming their way, but given to semi-literate basketball players and teen idols...." Tom paused with a pained, ironic grin. "And relationship advice authors. And debunkers of UFOs and ghosts. *You're* a part of the conspiracy, don't you know? *I* am a part of it. Lyle Chambers might have all the revolutionary ideas to change the world, but a secret cabal is working against him, trying to keep him silenced.

"Jessica, don't fall for these over-complicated fantasies. The fact is that in reality, the most obvious solution to most problems is usually the correct one. If I see a man on the street screaming in pain, his leg bleeding, and a dog walking away, blood dripping off its teeth, what most likely happened was that the dog bit the man's leg. Period! I'm not going to look for another man hiding in the alley with fake blood he smeared all over the dog's snout, and yet another man who shot the pedestrian's leg with fang-shaped ice needles that leave perfect bite marks and create the illusion of a dog attack before melting and disappearing."

"Look, I understand what you're saying, Tom. And God knows, what you're saying is important, and the kind of skeptical thinking you're talking about is important."

"It's the truth," Tom said resolutely.

Like the truth about the fact that Jeanie Anderson actually said "No?" Jessica almost blurted out.

"That's what's wrong with people today," Tom said. "They just don't want to hear the truth. They'd rather run around trying to find confirmations of their preexisting biases than trying to uncover the truth."

"Tom," Jessica said emphatically, trying to match his plea for reason. "When someone has a knife in your face after he's chased you through an entire warehouse, you're not going to be less than correct about what he intends to do with that knife. That Inquisitor psycho tried to kill me, and McPherson shot him. I just don't think you and the police should insist on treating him like he is some criminal."

"You don't know what's going on with that guy. He could be some very dangerous part of this whole thing."

"Like what?" Jessica asked, trying to keep the empathy in her voice. She saw the perfect opportunity to turn Tom's own logic against him. She wanted to see how he would react. As she had mulled all morning, the problem with their relationship was the fact that they really didn't know each other all that well. She knew nothing about what hid within the depths of his character. A good way to try and determine that might have been to see how he handled it when he was challenged on one of his core beliefs. "I think what I told you is pretty simple. There's a psycho out there, and he tried to kill me. McPherson saved my life."

Jessica paused for a very tiny beat. She could see it dawn on Tom that he had been set on top of a logical trap door, and it had now been sprung. She could also see how mightily he fought to keep from betraying his anger.

"I mean, Tom, what else could there be? Do you or Gainey think McPherson's the one who's in league with the Inquisitor? That they're the ones orchestrating some diabolical conspiracy to—?"

"Jessica," Tom cut in, tense obviously, yet with his anger subdued until it had become invisible. "I *don't* know the full story, all right? But I don't believe in any diabolical cabals and master plans either. One thing I can see, however, one thing that I know, and what's obvious is what's happened to *us* since last night. And I don't like it."

Maybe what happened, Jessica wondered, was something that *needed* to happen. Maybe they needed to discover and confront parts of each other's personalities that had the potential to turn into the most painful obstacles between them.

"I think you said something really great," she replied. "We have to find the truth. We have to find out what's going on here. The whole truth, and not what we *want* it to be."

"Let's do that together," Tom said. "Let's try and sort this mess out and get beyond it. And also, let's promise each other that we'll do it safely, and we listen to what the police tell us."

Jessica nodded, but she was troubled by the fact that it was an insincere nod. She just didn't like the impressions she was getting from Simon Gainey. But then again, she was more than a little certain that Tom wasn't being entirely sincere either. She felt that he had already made up his mind about the truth, about Buzz McPherson and the connection to the Inquisitor. The arch skeptic, ironically enough, suspected some hidden, some nefarious connection between McPherson and the mall attacker. At the same time, Tom would be incapable of giving credence to anything Jessica would tell him about a criminal conspiracy between the town's top cops and the Benjamin-Mead Funeral Home.

So, where do we go from here? Jessica asked herself as she followed Tom into the kitchen upon the suggestion that they try to unwind and prepare something for dinner. *What comes next? We almost move around here like a married couple.*

But that train of thought was derailed when Tom's phone chimed through the kitchen. He took the call, and immediately his entire mood got a lot darker.

"God*damn* it!" he muttered and slammed the receiver into its wall-mounted cradle. "Sorry," he said a moment later, casting a glance at Jessica.

"What happened?" she asked.

"The school's just called the police. Someone broke into my office and trashed the place."

"What?" Jessica exclaimed. Somewhat inanely, she thought.

"I better get down there and see what they've got."

Jessica nodded.

"Gainey's officers are still outside, you know. You'll be safe here."

"Yeah," Jessica said simply, and quickly saw him out the door.

After she shut it behind him, she realized she was glad she'd gotten a reprieve from needing to figure out *what came next.*

But as she turned back toward the kitchen, she found herself face to face with Buzz McPherson again.

CHAPTER 38

"Do you always sneak up on people to talk to them?" Jessica gasped.

"I wish I didn't have to," McPherson replied, and waved for her to come closer. "Don't have much of a choice these days. Not around here." Again, he waved for her to come closer.

Instead, she paused.

"Come on," he said, "those cops out there can't see into the kitchen as well as they can into the living room."

When he backed into the kitchen, Jessica followed.

"Don't worry about his office," McPherson said. "It's just a distraction."

"You?"

"Yeah, I had to. To get him out of the way."

"Why? And how the hell did you get in here? There's an alarm system."

"That was turned off when you two came in. But the point is I had to do this because somehow I get the feeling that Tom would call the police chief if I just dropped in to say hello. Don't you think so? And that wouldn't turn out too well for me."

"I don't know about that, but they did ask some interesting questions about *you*. Actually, a couple of things I'd like to know the answers to."

McPherson frowned. "Like what?"

"The police tried to track you down, and they can't find

anything on you. They say Buzz McPherson doesn't exist."

"They're lying."

"And if I checked? Could I find anything on you?"

"Yeah. Of course. But listen, there's something much more important I need to tell you about."

Jessica didn't like the way he skimmed over the issue of finding data on him.

"You want to know why I came here?" McPherson asked.

"Why did you come here?"

"And thanks for not telling them that you saw me this morning," McPherson said with a wicked little grin.

"Why did you come here?"

"I think there might be a way to get a glimpse inside the funeral home. To try and see what they're really up to."

Jessica was stunned. "Tonight?"

"Yes, tonight. They had the cops all over that place last night. But the heat's off now. So do you want to come?"

CHAPTER 39

"Okay, we just stay under all these bushes, and no one will be able to see us," McPherson said. "Not the cops, and not the people in any of these houses."

As they crouched under the foliage at the rear edge of Tom's property line, Jessica could see a virtual crawl space among all the bushes, a hidden path that led straight to the eastern end of the block.

"Wait," she whispered. "What about when we get to the end?"

"Don't worry," McPherson said. "No cop cars parked there. Only in front of the house and an occasional second cruiser that takes a swing around the entire block. That one will be easy to spot and avoid. So come on."

"Okay...hold on." Jessica asked McPherson to pause one more time as she swept her hair back, flattening it against her skull as tightly as she could and tying it back in a ponytail. Trying to move through all the bushes in the dark would be rough enough without her hair getting snagged on something.

"Let's go," McPherson said when he saw she was done and grabbed for her left wrist. Jessica found herself automatically flinching and pulling free on his grip.

"Come on!" he said strongly, giving her a pointed, annoyed look.

Her reflex made little sense, Jessica knew. Here she was,

agreeing to crawl through bushes in the middle of the night with a perfect stranger — one who was more than a bit handy at killing — and she got antsy at being led by the hand.

"Just go!" she snapped. "I'm right behind you."

Slipping away from Tom's house and evading the police by following McPherson's lead did, indeed, go smoothly. They were soon another block away, running down an alley that was as spotlessly clean as the most upscale side of town could provide, and getting into a dark blue Toyota Camry with McPherson.

"Did you steal this too?" Jessica asked as McPherson started the engine.

He shot her a rankled, sideways glance.

"Well?" she decided to press.

"No," he said dryly. "I didn't."

"So, what was the deal with the Honda?"

"The one I used to keep the Inquisitor from killing you?"

Jessica thought the barbed sarcasm was just too obvious in McPherson's voice. "Yes," she said simply. "Where are you getting these cars from?"

"I bought this for cash from a used dealer in Marion. I didn't have time to buy a car when I had to stop that psycho from abducting you in that alley."

"What newspaper is paying all these expenses for you to carry on this investigation? Or is it a magazine? A TV station? And enough money to go around buying cars?"

McPherson didn't reply immediately. "It's complicated," he said after carefully weighing his words. "I need you to trust me on that a little longer. It could take a while to completely explain everything."

"I see. And *you* see why I had to think long and hard about how much of this I keep from Tom, right? Or why he wants to help the cops find you."

"All right, yes," McPherson said at length. Then he cast a quick, somewhat crafty glance at her. "But at least you're here with me now."

"Yes. I still trust you, I guess."

"Thanks. Just bear with me for now, all right? Hopefully, we'll unravel this whole mess very soon.... Shit!"

Jessica flinched at McPherson's sudden curse. She could see him looking in the rearview mirror frantically.

"What is it?" she asked.

"That intersection we passed...."

"Yeah?"

McPherson looked in their wake again. "There was a cop car at the stop sign."

Jessica slid down and peeked around the back of her seat. "Is he coming?"

And then she saw the police cruiser enter the intersection... but turn in the opposite direction.

"That was close," McPherson muttered.

"We've still got a while until the funeral home, don't we?" Jessica asked, and immediately saw McPherson's brows knitting together in tension.

"Just a bit," he said dryly.

"Well, the cop didn't recognize us. He probably wasn't looking for you in this car. Good thing for that generous expense account of yours."

"Nothing like humor to get us through this," McPherson said under his breath, his sarcasm weak and exhausted.

CHAPTER 40

"Just keep your eyes on the cops, and you'll be perfectly safe," the Predator mumbled as he rolled his car out of the small restaurant's parking lot. Since traffic was light, he could start following Jessica and McPherson's Toyota while using the occasional cars on the road to keep hidden.

"Just watch those cops, Buzz, because this whole town's after you," the Predator said as he nudged the accelerator. "This whole town is after you," he said through clenched teeth now. "And *I* am after you, and you'll *never* leave here."

The Predator accelerated yet again. The Toyota Camry had gotten too far ahead.

But, then again, he could use more than his eyes to follow Jessica.

CHAPTER 41

"Didn't you say we'd have to make that turn?" Jessica asked as McPherson drove past Fenton Lane. "Hey!" she insisted when he wouldn't reply.

"Sorry," he whispered under his breath. "No, I was wrong."

When Jessica looked at him, there was a distant, glassy stare in his eyes. He was staring off into some indistinct point in the darkness far ahead.

"Look," she said, "I think this road'll take us right out of town. I think we should have made that turn."

For a split second, McPherson gave her a start as he clamped his eyes shut and pinched the bridge of his nose.

"Are you okay?" Jessica gasped, startled by the prospect of him driving down this unlit, ever-more winding road with his eyes closed. "Hey, pull over if you're—"

"I'm okay." McPherson snapped back into what looked like a fully alert state now. "I'm sorry."

"There aren't even any street lights out here anymore. I think you got us lost."

"No," McPherson said simply.

Some three seconds later, he yanked the steering wheel to the right.

"What are you trying to...?" Jessica gasped as the car veered off the main road and plunged into the darkness of a narrow, unevenly paved lane snaking through a stretch of trees.

"Just trust me, okay?" McPherson said with an unnerving calmness in his voice.

"To take us where? This is an unpaved dirt road."

"No, it's not," McPherson retorted with a deadpan tone again. "Trust me."

Jessica didn't say anything, although the bouncing and the shaking of the car made it feel like they were on a bonafide country dirt road. She thought about telling McPherson to watch out for the Duke boys, who might come speeding past any second in the General Lee. A couple of times, McPherson's eyes darted into the rearview mirror.

"Is someone following us?" Jessica asked.

If there was someone on their tail, McPherson didn't seem concerned about it anymore. "No," he said coolly. "At least not yet."

"At least not yet? What's that supposed to mean?"

"Just bear with me a little longer."

"Are you sure you know where this road is going?"

As if trying to frustrate her even more, McPherson replied by switching off the car's headlights.

As far as Jessica could tell, they were hurtling headlong into a blind, inky black void. But of course, it was a void where the road snaked and curved all over the place, lined by rather thick, sturdy trees. They could be cut right in half by any of them if McPherson missed a swerve and went off the road.

"Okay," Jessica found herself stammering, her heartbeats exploding through her chest. "Are you trying to impress me or something, or have you totally lost your mind?"

"Just trust me," McPherson mumbled, seemingly unconcerned with whether or not she heard him. He seemed to be off in some private zone all his own.

But at least they were still alive and in one piece, Jessica wanted to thank all providence. McPherson had already flown through two sharp turns in the road with uncanny precision. He must have had the night vision of a cat.

"I probably should have asked you this," McPherson said all of a sudden, "but you're not still hurt too badly from last night, are you?"

"Why thank you for asking," Jessica gasped. "Chivalry isn't dead, I see."

"In case things get intense tonight."

"Intense? How intense? Just what exactly are you expecting to find?"

"Not sure yet."

"Listen to me," Jessica said. She wanted to scream it at McPherson, but she was afraid to do so. Startling him might make him lose control of the car, she feared, and they would both die instantly upon plowing into a tree. "You still know a lot more about all this than you're letting on, don't you? You're still lying to me about most of this Inquisitor business, and now you're dragging me into the middle of —"

"No, I'm not," McPherson replied in a flat, disinterested monotone.

Jessica hoped it was because he was concentrating on the road so completely.

"*What* could get intense?"

"Hold on," McPherson said calmly, then swerved hard to the right.

They went off the road, Jessica's mind screamed. For a moment, she knew exactly what they meant by the term "heart in your throat."

The Toyota jerked, shuddered, and bounced across the uneven, rutted landscape. But it was also slowing down. Thankfully, McPherson's wild ride was coming to a stop at last.

"Oh, thank Christ," Jessica breathed as the car stopped. A moment later, she turned to McPherson and said, "What is your problem?"

"Listen to me!" he shot back. "We're close to the funeral home. We can try and get in, but you need to listen to me and do exactly—"

"After all this, we *better* try and get in—"

"*Listen!*" McPherson yelled. "You have to do *exactly* as I say every step of the way from now on. *Exactly!* Do you understand?"

Jessica gritted her teeth and nodded.

"I think some of this mess could get cleared up right here," McPherson added, his voice calmer now, more reasonable. "But we have to watch our steps every second."

Except a lot of this mess is already clear enough for you, isn't it? Jessica thought. Then a much more unnerving realization dawned on her. About McPherson. About all this. He was bringing her here so she could see for herself, to find out exactly what he already knew. For some reason, whatever went on in the funeral home, whatever the truth behind the Inquisition killer was, it was so staggering McPherson could never truly convey it to her in words. Was that it? Did she just simply need to see this for herself to believe it?

McPherson reached under the left side of his denim jacket and brought out that large handgun he had used the night before. Without a word, he ejected the magazine from its grip. Jessica could see it was fully loaded. She wondered if he had an extra round in the chamber. He quickly set her straight when he pulled the weapon's slide back, exposing an empty breach. Then he jogged the slide back and forth a couple of times, testing its feel. He must have cleaned and oiled the weapon since last night.

After reinserting the clip of bullets into the piece, he reached across Jessica's lap, opened the glove box, and removed a second weapon. He glanced up, looking her square in the eye. "Do you know how to use one of these?"

"As a matter of fact, I do," she replied. Then, just to throw him off balance, she added, "That's a nine millimeter, isn't it? Smith and Wesson MP9. What...a seventeen round magazine?"

McPherson grinned. "Impressive."

"I dated an FBI agent a few years ago."

"Must have been serious."

"It's a long and complicated story."

In fact, it had been five years since she last shot a weapon at a gun club in San Diego. Given the adrenaline searing through her body, she didn't want to tell McPherson not to wager on how accurate she could be just now. "Do you have any spare rounds?" she asked calmly. She didn't add that if she had enough bullets to spray at a general area, they *might* stand a fair to middling chance of her actually hitting an intended target.

"That's the spirit," McPherson muttered and opened his door. "Come on."

They circled around to the back of the car, and McPherson opened the trunk. Jessica noticed several black nylon duffel bags inside.

"I don't believe this," she said quietly. "Are we going on some sort of an assault of that place?"

"I hope not," McPherson said. "But we want to be covered just in case."

"In case of what?"

McPherson opened one of the bags to reveal a cache of ammunition. "Just bear with me."

"Too complicated to explain, right?"

McPherson glanced at her.

"I just have to see for myself, correct?"

"You need to know what we're going up against."

Jessica could feel him studying her. "Well, I'm here, aren't I?"

He grabbed five clips from the bag and handed them to Jessica. "Actually," he said, "you don't have a place to put these, do you?"

"Didn't bring my purse," she said. The sundress she wore didn't have any pockets either. But it hadn't been designed for a major armed invasion. "Sorry."

"Don't worry," McPherson said, and reached for something in the back of the trunk. He lifted up some sort of a vest. "SWAT tactical vest," he said, and handed it to Jessica. "Put it on."

It looked like a black fishing vest, fitted with an array of pockets and loops and hooks. Jessica and McPherson filled the pockets with spare magazines for her handgun. Had McPherson been properly equipped, the vest could have held knives, grenades, and flashlights as well.

Wondering if they would be hiking to the funeral home, Jessica wished McPherson's Toyota assault vehicle was equipped with a full combat uniform. A sundress and thin-soled sandals were not made for the brushy, thorny wilderness all around.

After loading his own pockets with extra magazines, McPherson accessorized himself with a few more lethal pieces of equipment. One of them was a laser-targeting-device-mounted submachine gun. He slung it around his neck, letting it rest on his right hip.

"Woodward and Bernstein never packed heat like this, did they?" Jessica couldn't resist saying. The weirder and more frightening this entire night was getting, the more she needed to claim some grip on the situation with a bit of humor.

"What we're up against, they don't teach you about in journalism school," McPherson said stiffly, no humor coming back.

As he shut the trunk of the car, they were sideswiped by a

peculiarly sudden and warm gust of wind. Jessica noticed the odd way McPherson seemed to stiffen. He looked around carefully as if *feeling* his surroundings.

"Did you see lightning?" he asked.

"No. You think there's a storm coming?"

"Maybe."

More warm wind slashed past them, then died down yet again. Except this time, Jessica thought she smelled something peculiar. Something like ozone. Maybe a lightning storm was in the air after all.

When she looked in McPherson's direction, she caught another one of those pained, disoriented glances she had seen in the car.

"Are you okay?" she asked.

"Yeah," he said, snapping alert again. The transition was just as sudden and unnerving as before. "How about you?"

Jessica was taken by his bizarre question. "Yeah, I'm fine."

"Yesterday night…," McPherson said, then trailed off. "Your nose hasn't been bleeding anymore, has it?"

"No. I told you, I'm fine."

"How about the attacker? How badly did you hurt him?"

"What is this all about?" Jessica asked, feeling more frustrated than puzzled now. "Obviously, I didn't hurt him badly enough, right? Otherwise, you wouldn't have had to blast him full of so many bullets. Or his bulletproof vest, or whatever."

"Did you cut him? Scratch him? Bite him?"

Jessica stepped closer to McPherson. "What the hell is this all about? You think he's going to be *here*?"

"I don't know. Maybe," he said with more of that inscrutable weirdness all over his bearing, his words, the look in his eyes.

"I kicked him, I tried to punch him as many times as I could. I think I bit him when he tried to strangle me. Just so you know."

"Good," McPherson said simply.

"You're creeping me out, you know. And I don't like to be creeped out by someone with so many guns."

"Just trust me for now," McPherson said simply and nodded toward the area in front of the car. "We have to go that way."

"The funeral home's up there?"

"Yeah, but we're not going all the way up to the funeral home."

"Why?"

"We need to take a little detour."

CHAPTER 42

The Predator could feel Jessica, but he had to fight to see her exact location. She faded in and out.

"Damn you!" he screamed and pounded a fist into his steering wheel. He gunned the engine, hurtling the car down the murky, unlit, two-lane country road.

Jessica and McPherson had come this way, the Predator was sure of it. Except now, they were off the road. They had disappeared into one of the myriad little side roads, the dirt lanes or access roads that wound away to nowhere.

Of course, the Predator knew what they were up to. They were going to intrude upon the Handlers. While that in itself would solve one problem, it was something unacceptable, *intolerable* to the Predator. If Jessica and McPherson went stumbling into the ritual the Handlers were undertaking, the two of them would most likely get killed. But then the Predator would be denied Jessica. He couldn't let that happen. No matter what the cost, he could not let her be taken away from him. The Handlers had promised him Jessica, but they were angry at the way he'd let her slip away. They would not let her or McPherson or anyone jeopardize their secrets.

He would find her. The Predator swore that he would. All he had to do was reach out with his mind, find their link, and follow it to its source.

CHAPTER 43

"Did you see that?" McPherson asked as he dodged behind a tree.

As he did so, he grabbed Jessica's hand and nudged her to follow his lead.

Indeed she did see the flash of light. It looked like lightning, but at the same time, it didn't. It was off. Its location, the source of the flash, was somehow misplaced. It didn't look as if the light had flickered from the sky, but somewhere on the ground. Moreover, it appeared as if a single, very strong point of light had flown *across* the horizon somewhere ahead.

What are those weird electrical phenomena things called? Jessica wondered. *Ball lightning, or something like that?* "Yeah," she told McPherson quietly. "Except that's not lightning, is it?"

"No," McPherson murmured.

"And it's what we're looking for."

"In a way, yes," McPherson said, looking her in the eyes this time.

"What is it? What are they doing?" Jessica asked, although her frustration was resurfacing now. She knew McPherson would probably still not give her a straight answer.

"It's what they're doing to the bodies from the funeral home," he said, surprising her.

"They're bringing the bodies out here?"

"Yes. And we need to find the exact spot they're going to."

McPherson slid from behind the tree and skulked forward.

Jessica followed, her mind reeling at what part of the black market organ-harvesting scheme might be conducted in the middle of the night and in the middle of the forest surrounding the Benjamin-Mead funeral home. Except part of her suggested that she stop thinking about black market organ harvesting. That was a lie, wasn't it? It was a rational lie McPherson had told her. It was something plausible her mind could wrap itself around, something it could accept as a realistic explanation for what a funeral home could have been doing to stolen dead bodies.

After some fifty yards of scrambling through the brush, McPherson slowed down again and pointed to a clump of bushes on top of a slight elevation. "Over there," he said.

Jessica followed him, and they crouched behind the foliage.

"We're close," McPherson said a moment later. "Oh yes, we're close."

Jessica looked around, trying to take stock of their surroundings.

Then, a triple burst of lights flickered from some distance on their left. Jessica couldn't tell how far away the source was, except that it must have been pretty close. The bright strobes were more intense than ever before.

The lights, in fact, let her get a good look at their location. Beyond the bushes, she could see a small clearing in the woods. She also noticed how the weird, ozone-charged, humid atmospheric conditions seemed to shroud the clearing and its surroundings with thin patches of foggy haze.

"There's no one around," Jessica whispered to McPherson.

"Not yet," he said, "but they're coming."

"You sure?"

"Yeah, we're in the right place."

"How do you know?"

"Look," he said and reached off to his left.

He appeared to be picking something out from under one of the bushes, out from under the cover of broken twigs and fallen leaves. At first, it appeared to be a large rock. But then Jessica noticed it was too round….

"Oh my God!" She flinched, realizing what McPherson was holding.

It was a human skull, minus its jawbone.

"Oh my God," she could merely repeat, feeling as if she had been kicked in the solar plexus, all the air forced from her lungs.

"Sorry," McPherson whispered and lay the skull aside.

Whatever he was, Jessica seethed, regaining her bearings, at least McPherson was direct.

"They brought the bodies out here," she gasped, a sickening realization dawning on her.

"Yes," McPherson said quietly, leaning closer to her. "I'm really sorry."

For all she knew, Jessica shuddered—*literally* shuddered—that could have been part of her father's remains. They brought the bodies out here for disposal.

"Why?" she mumbled.

She could feel McPherson putting a hand on her shoulder. In his own strange way, he must have been trying to calm and comfort her, Jessica guessed. When it came to that skill, though, he was no Tom Lancaster.

"Why did they bring the bodies out here?" she whispered. Was it their disposal process after the organ theft? Was organ theft at the bottom of all this after all?

"We're about to find out," McPherson said.

Jessica could see him tense. His right hand moved toward the assault rifle at his side.

Jessica followed his gaze and saw a car approaching from

their right. As it rolled through the forest, she could appreciate the density of the foggy humidity enveloping them. The car's headlights became a pair of glowing, silvery rods spearing through the night.

As the car got nearer, Jessica saw that it was a large black SUV. It entered the clearing, turned off its lights, and shut off its engine.

"What now?" Jessica breathed.

"Look at that," she heard McPherson mumbling, shock obvious in his voice.

She looked at him and noticed his glance had shifted toward the left side of the clearing. When she found what he had been looking at, she couldn't believe her eyes.

CHAPTER 44

A man and a woman came sauntering into the clearing. Although they didn't hurry, they had a determined, purposeful energy behind their movements. From a distance of about forty-five feet, they looked to be in their mid to late thirties. They appeared to be relatively fit, of average builds. They could have been anyone you passed on the street. Except, just now, they were both completely naked.

"I don't believe this," Jessica muttered.

Sometime, a little while back, she and McPherson had crossed into *The Twilight Zone*, she guessed. Nothing here made any sense.

The nude couple approached the SUV. As they did so, Jessica thought she could pick up something in their glances, in their bearing. What was it? Anticipation? Need?

"What's going on here?" Jessica whispered and looked at McPherson.

He must have heard that her inquiry was more than a mere rhetorical question because he shook his head, but he did not reply.

Jessica looked at the SUV and saw its driver's and passenger doors swing open. A pair of men dressed in dark suits—funeral home staffers?—stepped out of the vehicle. There was no exchange between them and the naked couple, though. The men in suits quickly walked to the back of the SUV and opened its rear hatch.

Jessica thought the activity in the clearing had a sort of dull, perfunctory look to it. This must have been routine to everybody. The funeral home staff just came to make a delivery to a naked couple in the forest in the middle of the night.

From the rear of the SUV, the two men extracted a large cardboard box. A *very* large cardboard box, Jessica noted, her pulse quickening. Cardboard boxes, in fact, were used to move bodies into mortuaries from the coroner's office. Or to place a body into an incinerator for cremation.

After the box was placed in front of the naked couple, the men in suits retreated quickly. They both stood by their car but did not get ready to depart.

The unclothed man and woman quickly pounced on the box. They removed and tossed aside its lid and ripped its walls away.

Jessica felt her lips gaping open as a naked male cadaver was exposed in the tatters of the box. Her mouth and throat were dry. Her pulse pounded, roared in her ears. Terror and revulsion had her in their grip, raising gooseflesh all along her body.

A moment later, the already surrealistic scene transformed into a nightmare. Jessica could see the naked people baring their teeth like animals. They pounced upon the corpse, pawing at it, biting it.

The woman went for the dead body's left arm, seizing it in both hands and biting down on the bicep area. It looked as if she was trying to get as big a bite as she could from the meatiest portion of the arm.

Her companion likewise sought out as much meaty flesh as possible. He went for the corpse's right pectoral, tearing at the skin around the nipple area. As far as Jessica could tell, the dead man had been in fairly good shape, with a decent load of muscle on his frame.

And he must have died recently, too. As the cannibals tore at the flesh, blood flowed from the wounds.

Jessica felt her gorge rising. She would give herself and McPherson away any moment now, the mad, panicky realization jangled through her mind. She was going to start vomiting in another second, and they would be discovered.

Meanwhile, the man and the woman continued gnawing on the dead body, a frenzied, ravenous energy driving them. Although it was obvious that chewing through skin, muscle, and ligaments was much harder with human teeth than most zombie epics usually made it out to be. The cannibals, it appeared, could barely make a couple of modest gashes in the skin of their dead meal, occasionally clawing at the wounds with their fingers.

At one point, the woman working the bicep appeared to have gotten a good hold of some strands of muscle fiber and was determined to tear the flesh right out of the cadaver's arm. Like a dog, several times, she would shake her head left and right, jerk, and pull with blind, determined ferocity to bite away that choice piece of meat. But for the most part, the two had to make do with sucking and lapping as much blood out of the wounds as possible. Like rats, they gnawed and buried their faces in the wounds they created. Jessica's ears were assaulted by the gurgling, snorting sounds the two made as they attempted to drink as much blood as they could.

The man eating away on the corpse's chest appeared to have assaulted the nipple, bitten through most of the skin, then taken hold of that loose skin and yanked it further and further back, peeling it off the muscle below. Once enough raw muscle had been exposed, he buried his face in the fresh gore, licking and gnawing as much as he could get at.

"What is this?" Jessica heard her own whimpering voice. With her left hand, she clutched at McPherson's arm. She looked at him, trying to see if he had any clue as to the meaning of this monstrosity. "What are they?"

McPherson, too, appeared to be blanched, stress, revulsion, and terror racking his nerves. Yet there was something else there as well—a steeliness that Jessica could sense. What was it? Her mind raced to understand what she felt on some instinctive level. Familiarity? Had he seen this before? Could she have been right about McPherson bringing her here to show her something he knew all too well but could not put into words?

"Look," he said at length and jerked his head toward the bestial spectacle in the clearing.

Jessica was loath to do it, but she had to look. After coming this far, she had to understand everything.

When she looked back at the two human ghouls feeding, she saw the woman toss her head back and let out a guttural bellow. Somehow, it was a howl of pain and ecstasy all at once. It had an obscene, orgasmic quality to it. A spray of blood issued from her lips. But the most unbelievable thing Jessica noticed was the way the woman's throat and neck appeared to swell. Corded muscles laced by bulging veins and arteries pressed outward all over her neck.

Once her neck distorted like that, her face followed. Her mouth stretched open to its limits. Then her jaw seemed to snap, shudder to the left and right, and disconnect from the rest of her skull like that of a snake. Only skin and tendons held the jaw in place, the cavity of her mouth transforming into a blood-splattering maw. At the same time, her gums and teeth appeared to be undergoing a transformation as well. The gum line seemed to grow larger and larger, extending outward. Her teeth, in turn, seemed to grow, especially her upper and lower canines. Her entire dentition transformed into something like a shark's mouthful of chainsaw teeth.

"That's not possible," Jessica gasped. She felt her fingers digging into McPherson's arm. She glanced at him again, needing to see what all of this meant to him. He had that same uneasy look of disgust kept in check by resolve and monumental self-control.

"That's *not* possible," Jessica hissed through clenched teeth. "That's not *human*."

McPherson only nodded.

Jessica's right hand clenched harder than ever around the grip of the Smith and Wesson MP9 McPherson had given her to carry. She wanted to use it now more than anything. More than the urge to turn and flee, the urge to block all this out of her mind, she wanted to turn the weapon on those monsters only a few feet away.

Except she and McPherson were suddenly caught off guard by a raging shriek tearing through the night behind them.

CHAPTER 45

The dark form of a running man sprang from the shadows. He was holding an axe high overhead, propelling it forward and down as he threw himself at Jessica and McPherson. More precisely at McPherson, Jessica realized as she spun to her right, rolling away from the bushes to avoid the attacker.

In the middle of one of her turns, she saw that McPherson had only narrowly avoided the attacker's blade. The axe-head plowed into the soft soil under the bush a flash instant after McPherson lunged clear.

The axeman, Jessica also noticed, had made a costly error charging at them as vehemently as he did. The wild downward swing that buried the blade in the ground also threw him off balance, sending him headfirst into the bush.

But why this violent berserker attack? Jessica's mind tried to make sense of this as she raced to scramble upright. If this was the Inquisitor, she reasoned, and he was connected to that madness in the clearing, if the… *What? The cannibals? The creatures?* If those *things* were his compatriots, why not warn them of the intrusion more discreetly and have her and McPherson surrounded and taken out more efficiently?

The attacker's frenzied mistake was to her benefit, she decided as she kicked and scrambled to her feet, losing one of her sandals in the process. Now she and McPherson could just run for it and try to make it back to their car.

A shattering blast of machine gun fire erupted on her left, and flashes of bright light strobed through the darkness. McPherson had triggered his submachine gun, Jessica saw a second later. He had blasted a quick volley of rounds toward the bush as he, too, stumbled backward and away.

But almost immediately, more gunfire broke out in the woods. *Return fire!* Jessica realized, horrified. The people from the SUV also appeared to be armed—only with handguns, though—and they squeezed a searing fusillade of rounds in her and McPherson's direction.

"Move!" Jessica heard McPherson bellowing before he shot back.

She did so, but this time she was stunned by the whining slash of a pair of bullets whizzing past the left side of her face. The SUV's shooters' errant rounds! However, a warning seemed to rise from the back of her mind, trying to cut through the haze of panic, reflex, and the urge to flee. She had a gun!

She swung its barrel up, thumbed the Smith and Wesson's safety open, and squeezed off three quick rounds.

Indeed, she could feel it had been five years since the gun club. The weapon jerked, kicked, and vibrated in her hands. There was no turn of luck in this world, she guessed, that might have let a single one of her rounds strike anyone in the clearing.

But it would be useful enough, she realized, if her shots served as suppression rounds and kept the axeman, the SUV drivers, and whatever those two naked creatures were at bay. It would all be enough if she and McPherson could just get out there.

She blasted two more rounds into the clearing and turned to retreat. Before moving, though, she kicked off her other sandal to have the same feel of the ground under both her feet.

Apparently, McPherson was thinking about retreating as

well. A moment later, Jessica felt one of his hands on her left arm, pulling her to get moving.

A few paces ahead, McPherson ran while throwing an occasional glance over his shoulders. Twice he spun around and sprayed machine gun fire into their wake. Upon his third pause to shoot, Jessica, too, stopped, turned around, remembered the proper shooter's stance from years ago, and squeezed off three quick shots.

They managed to dodge and weave through the forest for another two hundred or so feet until McPherson yelled, "Take cover!" He shoved Jessica behind a large tree. He took position behind another one, then sprang forward again and blasted the last remaining rounds in his machine gun back the way they had come.

There was nothing but silence once the ringing echoes of the subgun faded away.

"Did we lose them?" Jessica asked. She was surprised to hear her voice stammering. Then she realized how she shook from the overdose of adrenaline coursing through her body.

"Don't know yet," McPherson said, and ejected a spent magazine from his subgun.

He reached inside his jeans' back pocket for a spare. He almost reloaded his weapon, too, except he was suddenly met by a dark form lunging out of the bushes. Like someone delivering a precision football tackle, the attacker slammed right into McPherson's midsection, knocking him back against the tree.

Jessica was stunned by the sickening crack of the bodies impacting the tree, followed by the sound of McPherson's gasp as the air was forced from his lungs. Within seconds, however, the hit was repeated as McPherson's assailant slammed his body against the tree yet again.

"Son of a bitch!" Jessica hissed through clenched teeth as she lifted her gun and realized how useless it was. She was aiming at two tangled bodies writhing, struggling in the darkness. She couldn't fire a shot. She couldn't risk hitting McPherson.

And then a blur of movement came her way, and pain shot up both her arms. Its epicenter was down in her wrists, her hands, her fingers. McPherson's attacker had lunged at her and knocked the gun out of her hands.

The hit was followed by a second incoming strike, a fist thrown at her head. This time, however, she was able to put up a minimal effort as resistance. Mostly on instinct, she raised both her arms toward her face. This lets her catch most of the blow on her forearms. The force of the hit was strong enough, however, to knock her off her feet.

As she went over, she did see something in perfect clarity. She, at least, caught sight of her attacker's face. It was the same man from the mall. That plain-faced psychopath, the so-called Inquisition killer, was back.

When Jessica hit the ground, she noticed — with as much relief as she was capable of registering amidst the pandemonium — that McPherson had not been completely immobilized. Just as the Inquisitor's weight shifted forward, no doubt getting ready to lunge at her, McPherson was on top of him. McPherson caught the Inquisitor in a bear hug, lifted him off his feet, and propelled him around.

It looked as if McPherson might have been trying to body slam the psychopath into the ground, but unfortunately, his gambit didn't work. Almost with the agility of a cat, the Inquisitor landed on his feet and remained upright the moment McPherson let go of him.

McPherson, though, did not let his momentary upper hand on the Inquisitor remain unexploited. He followed up by lunging forward and ramming a fist into the psycho's face. The Inquisitor stumbled back and collided with a tree. McPherson, in turn, moved in for yet another follow-up attack.

While the two men faced off, Jessica also tried to recover and scrambled to get off the ground. As she did so, she noticed the abrasive, flaky texture of a thick, dry branch under her right foot. Glancing down at it, she saw exactly what she had been hoping for. With her gun missing, she had found a new equalizer. A very brief moment later, she knew she needed it immediately.

As McPherson sprang forward to punish the Inquisitor yet again, the serial killer likewise advanced, lashing out with his right foot. The kick caught McPherson square in the gut. The blow doubled him over in what must have been excruciating pain. The psycho then struck again, propelling a wild backhanded punch at McPherson's face, driving him to the ground.

The murderer then set his deranged gaze upon Jessica. He sized her up in a split instant and lunged at her. His problem was that a split instant was too short a period of time to fully take stock of Jessica.

Jessica had been prepared for the Inquisitor with the massive branch from the ground. In some places, the branch was as much as five inches across. Now Jessica held it in both hands like a club. As the Inquisitor made his move, she swung her makeshift weapon with a precision honed by four years of college softball.

The branch connected with the madman's face, snapping his head and upper body backward, letting his legs fly out from under him. Once the Inquisitor was down, Jessica followed up by raising the thick stick high overheard, investing it with every ounce of strength and willpower she had, and driving it down toward the killer's head like a sledgehammer.

The downward swing was not quite as accurate as her homerun hit, but the Inquisitor did get a fracturing blow across his upper chest. He looked completely unconscious as a result.

Jessica could only hope he was dead.

Almost immediately, she saw movement behind the limp form of the serial killer. Buzz McPherson was rising to his feet, she saw. Although bloodied and bruised, he looked all right.

"Come on," he wheezed as he staggered toward Jessica. "Gotta get back to the car now." He spat a dark, gooey blood-thickened string of saliva. Blood flowed freely from his nose, and there was a nasty, glistening abrasion on his right eyebrow.

He did seem to regain his strength quickly enough, Jessica saw with relief. They had no problem making a quick dash for the Toyota.

CHAPTER 46

There was silence in the car until they could be certain that no one was following them. Neither the Inquisitor was on their tail nor the...the *others*.

"What the hell was that?" Jessica asked once she realized McPherson seemed unlikely to volunteer information without some prompting. As she spoke, she noticed how weak, how raspy her voice sounded. "What were those *things?*"

"They're connected to the Predator...or the Inquisitor... *definitely*," McPherson nearly whispered, throwing sudden, furtive glances into the rearview mirrors.

"But what *were* they?" Jessica almost yelled. "They...they *ate* that body. Is that what they do to the dead at the funeral home? Was my father eaten like that? By those creatures?"

McPherson looked at her this time. His expression had softened. It was pained even. "Yes. Most likely, yes."

For the first time in her life, Jessica knew what it felt like to have a knot in her stomach. The combination of adrenaline, terror, and maddening repulsion seemed to smash through her body like a devastating, icy fist.

But Buzz's words were but a confirmation. Jessica knew what those monsters' feeding had implied. The ashes that were probably concrete all made sense now. Too bad the chemical analysis equipment at Tom's school wasn't worth a damn.

"But why?" Jessica asked. "What are they? They're *not*

human. The way their faces changed...."

"No, they're not," McPherson said quietly.

Jessica had to address the other issue now. "And you know why they were out there?"

McPherson nodded first, then said, "I suspected."

"But what are they? I want to know the whole truth this time."

"All right, but first, we need to try and hide for a little while before he shows up again."

"What?"

"The Predator. He'll be coming after you again. He can track you wherever you go. Until we kill him."

"How?"

"I'll explain everything, but we need to try and hide."

CHAPTER 47

The Predator knew he had to flee and keep after Jessica and McPherson immediately. He had to leave the Handlers and pick up the trail of his prey if he wanted Jessica.

He wouldn't be allowed to keep stalking her, the realization tore through the Predator's mind as he ran through the forest. He was here to serve the Handlers, voices warned him, haunted him relentlessly. They had a job for him, and Jessica could not be allowed to interfere with that.

Surely Jessica would be killed, the Predator knew. They would never let her leave this town alive. She was not like so many of the others, the ones who could be counted on could be manipulated into protecting the secret for her own self-centered ends. But the Predator would not be allowed to kill her. The Handlers would take away his prize. They would take away his fantasy.

The Predator ran faster now. He rampaged through the forest, tearing toward his car to pick up the pursuit as quickly as he could.

CHAPTER 48

After checking the bathroom's tiny window, McPherson went over to their motel room's main window, gently eased the edge of the shade over with an index finger, and methodically surveyed the area outside. He had told Jessica that the seedy little Prairie Crossings Motel would serve their needs well enough with its hourly room rates. They should not be staying here any longer than that.

In a way, Jessica was glad for that. She knew it made no sense because their need to keep moving meant only that the Predator was still after them. Nonetheless, she was inexplicably put ill at ease by the unpleasant odors, the grimy whiff of corruption barely masked by a cheap, lingering hint of disinfectant in this room. The grubby little establishment hinted at a history of disparate economic times in Cedar Valley. From the defunct prison to the college town with its brand-new intellectual upper class of engineers and hard-science experts, this was a place that had its ups and downs. The downtimes left their lasting scars and left neighborhoods that were still the proverbial wrong side of the tracks.

Jessica quietly padded over to McPherson's side and looked over his shoulder. He couldn't possibly have spotted anything threatening out there, she wanted to believe. Then again, she also wanted to believe that she had killed the Predator, beaten him to death with that tree branch. But she just couldn't quite do so.

"How is this possible?" she found herself whispering. "How can he follow me everywhere?"

Buzz stepped away from the window, a tired, pained expression on his face. "God, it's so complicated."

She put a hand on his shoulder and pulled him closer. "I need to know everything."

"Yeah, you do," he said, and sat down on the bed.

Jessica took a seat on a worn-out armchair in front of him and pulled her legs under her. "What *are* they?" she asked. She knew the answer to that question would begin explaining everything that had happened to her since coming to this town.

Buzz rubbed his forehead. "Believe it or not," he said at length, "even after I've been trying to track them down for years, trying to track *him* down since these killings started on the West Coast, I can't answer that for sure."

So take a ballpark guess, Jessica almost said, but Buzz continued a moment later.

"I think the most accurate way you could describe them would be as something from another...another dimension, I guess—a parallel world or something. And the truth is I don't really know if that even gets close to what they really are."

"My God," Jessica whispered.

The shadow of a bitter little grin flittered across McPherson's face. "Or if you want a completely different world view—what's that high-flown word?—*paradigm* for it, you could say they're demons and devils. Then maybe they're from hell, from purgatory...I don't know."

"That's an impressive use of the word 'paradigm.'"

McPherson returned a thin, rueful little smile.

"Bad joke, I know."

"We might as well joke and hope to save our sanity."

Jessica didn't say anything more. With what Buzz had just

said, the only thing she could do was sit and give him time to explain everything. Or *try* and explain everything, from the sound of things. He seemed to be suggesting that he didn't know much more than what was the tip of a large, dark iceberg.

"They come in and out of our world," Buzz said. "Those lights we saw out there might have had something to do with it. But they seem to need to feed on the dead — the *newly* dead. Like that body in the forest. Did you see all that blood? He must have just died. But they need bodies like that and funeral homes like this sometime...they *somehow* get people to supply the bodies."

"Unbelievable," Jessica couldn't help whispering. All of reality seemed to be collapsing around her, and she just needed to verbalize the sort of disoriented, gut-twisting sense of vertigo she felt.

"Yeah, I know," Buzz said. Kind of strongly, Jessica thought. "Especially since these things are not always here. They...they go in and out of our world, so it's impossible to even prove they exist. To examine one of them. They're like ghosts. They're Bigfoot, UFO's, the Loch Ness Monster."

So, Jessica knew, you basically couldn't do to them what Tom would require to believe they were real.

"In a way," Buzz said, "our minds *can't* accept that they're real. Sure, maybe some people might, but most of us...no way." He paused, studying Jessica at length. "Do you think there might be a way of convincing Tom this is real? Do you think he would believe *you*?"

The million-dollar question, Jessica thought. "After what I've seen of his writings, I can't be sure."

"Yeah," McPherson said simply.

"But before we get to that, I need to understand this thoroughly. So these things, how often do they come over? Do they only eat humans? And why, for God's sake?"

"Not just how often, but where," Buzz said. "They try to stay hidden. They show up in places like this town. And they seem to prefer human bodies, it seems."

"I see," Jessica said slowly. But of course, there was another fundamental question that needed answering now. "But how do *you* know all this?"

Buzz nodded. There was a satisfied look on his face, Jessica noted. In the murk of the unlit room, she thought she saw something in his glance that reminded her of Tom in his pedantic moments.

"Because," he said, "I'm willing to believe what I see. What I *know* I see. Others have stumbled across these things before — for a long time, I think. I think these creatures might be at the root of a lot of legends — vampires, ghouls, shape-shifters, the undead, zombies. The old legends, folklore of blood-drinking, eating the body, possessing the body, I think it all comes from this. People have stumbled onto these things in the past, except their accounts are now legends and superstitions."

"How did *you* stumble onto them?"

Buzz didn't answer immediately. Jessica could hear him take a heavy breath. "I didn't," he said at length. "My wife did."

No end to Mr. McPherson's surprises, Jessica thought.

"She was a reporter," he said. "*She* was the one doing an investigative piece on what looked like a black-market organ harvesting ring tied to a prison in Wisconsin. Bodies removed from the prison for burial started disappearing. So she went after the story."

"Did you work on the story with her? You *are* a reporter, right?" Jessica had to ask. It was just unnerving how casually McPherson had been capable of fabricating one set of lies for her after another.

"Yes, I *am* a reporter," he said with something of a grudge to his tone. "But I understand what you mean, okay? I haven't been entirely straight with you about everything."

"All right," Jessica said quietly.

"I didn't work with her at first. You see, *she* was the star investigative reporter in the family. I was a couple of rungs lower on the career ladder at that point."

Something just occurred to Jessica. Why did he keep referring to his wife in the past tense?

"What happened?" she asked.

"Something kind of like this," McPherson said with a hard, distant sound to his voice. "She poked around the funeral home. Followed them around. Eventually followed them out to the woods, the way we just did."

McPherson paused, the silence hanging between them. Jessica didn't need to ask anything.

"And they caught her, and she was killed," McPherson said quietly, flatly.

Jessica could hear more than grief in his voice. In fact, he sounded as if he had dealt with the grief and come to terms with it a long time ago. Now, he had shifted into an entirely different mode. There was a cold, controlled, well-harnessed rage that had taken the place of grief. Buzz McPherson was out for revenge.

"But this Predator," Jessica spoke up suddenly, feeling as if something in Buzz's story didn't quite make sense. "He looked like he could be caught...or killed even. I mean, he was violent and strong—yeah, crazy as hell, but he seemed human."

"Yeah, he is."

"He's working with the creatures?"

"He's been...I don't know what you call it. *Infected...?*"

But McPherson paused all of a sudden and sprung from the bed. In a flash, he was over by the large window, peering past the edge of the curtain.

Jessica saw a beam of light from a car's headlights sweep past outside. "What?" she whispered, but hardly enough for Buzz to hear.

At length, he said, "Nothing. It's not him." Then he turned from the window and approached the bed and Jessica. "How can he track you so perfectly, you asked."

"Yes."

"It's part of what had been done to him. *And* to you."

"To me?" Jessica asked immediately. *Nothing* had been done to her. What was McPherson talking about?

"The Predator is a human who has some of the blood of these creatures in him. The creatures have some of his. That's how the process works. Plus, he drank human blood and ate human flesh. With a part of the creatures in him, it strengthens...." Buzz paused, appearing to be searching for the right phrases. "It gives him a degree of telepathic abilities. Especially if he comes into contact with someone. Physical contact. When he *touches* someone."

A cold stab of fear spread through Jessica's body. "Like me?"

She could see Buzz nodding in the dark. "Yes, that fight you had with him at the mall. For some people like him—humans that have been tainted by the creatures—there can be various degrees of psychic sensitivity. Some can just touch a person. Just make contact with a person, touch their skin, get in contact with skin oils or bodily fluids of any type, and the transformed, the tainted one, can have a long psychic link to their prey."

"This isn't happening." Jessica found herself gasping, sinking into her chair.

"Unfortunately, it is."

"And what can he do to me?"

"Other than track you, nothing. You don't have to worry about being controlled or harmed from a distance at all. And from what I've seen, even the tracking doesn't work well, or accurately, all the time."

"But right now, he's homing in on me," Jessica said, Buzz's skittishness, his surveillance of the windows making perfect sense to her.

"He's trying to."

"All because he touched me."

Buzz didn't reply immediately, and Jessica knew that was a bad sign.

"And because you bit him," he said at length.

"Oh my God." Jessica could barely get the words out.

"You might be tainted with him. With *them*."

Jessica was glad she was sitting down. She wasn't sure how long her legs would have supported her had she been standing.

"Look, Jessica," Buzz said, leaning over her chair. "This can be handled. This can be dealt with. Other than homing in on your location, there's nothing they can do to hurt you."

"But if I've been tainted, just like this Predator has been tainted," Jessica said, one petrifying realization building on another, "then that means I will be turning into one of them—"

"No!" Buzz cut her off strongly. "Doesn't work that easily."

"A killer," Jessica felt she couldn't keep the most horrifying conclusion of all bottled up inside her. "A murderer like—"

"No!" Buzz took her by the shoulders.

Jessica looked up at him. She needed to see his eyes. Was he being sincere? Was he telling her the truth about her condition?

"That man is a psychopath to begin with. He is twisted and evil, a monster by nature. That's why they're using him. Except these things just made him more powerful."

Buzz paused, apparently probing her reactions to his argument. As far as Jessica could tell, he appeared to be telling her the truth.

"You will *not* become one of them," Buzz repeated, "and you won't be a killer. For them to have a grip on you, you would need to drink a *lot* more of their blood. But then you would need to drink human blood too. You would have to eat human flesh. Do you understand, Jessica?"

"Are you sure?" Jessica asked, only having the strength for those three words right now.

"Yes. From what I've seen of them, changing who and what you are is a very long and difficult process, if it's really possible at all. Like I said, this Predator was a psychopathic killer to begin with."

Buzz's words were somewhat reassuring, yet Jessica's heartbeats continued hammering, shaking her entire body.

"Do you understand?" Buzz asked, and slowly let go of her. He sat back on the bed. "They *can't* hurt you."

"Yeah, unless that bastard's in my head. Unless he can see where I'm going and what I'm doing."

"But we're going to make sure we see him coming."

Immediately Jessica thought that Buzz had better have a lot more of those machine guns and pistols hidden away in those cars of his.

"Listen," she said a moment later, remembering another major problem they had on their hands. "You realize the cops in this town are gunning for you as eagerly as the Pre—" She froze, her mind jumping to that thought's logical implication. "The cops! The chief!" she almost yelled. "Are they...do they know about the creatures? Are they helping them get the bodies?"

"They could be," Buzz said gravely, although not resolutely. "From what you've told me about how gung ho the chief seems to be to get his hands on me, I think there's a good chance, yeah."

"What are we going to do? We have to get out of here as quickly as we can, but...." She paused. She tried to formulate some kind of a big picture, some kind of an idea of what she could do to get her life back.

"What comes next?" Buzz asked.

"Yes. What do we do about these things?"

"I've been trying to figure that one out for the past four years."

"We've seen them. They'll want to kill us."

Buzz didn't reply immediately. "That psycho, the Predator, definitely wants to kill you."

"But why? Why did he begin stalking me? It was by chance that I'm even here."

"Who knows. He's killed scores of women already."

"And I just happened onto his hit list."

"We have to kill him."

"And the others? The creatures that control him? If they want us dead, what do we do about a threat like that?"

"I don't know about that. To tell you the truth, whether or not they would...hurt you the way the Predator would is a fifty/ fifty chance. Although not one I'd gamble on."

"What?" This sounded a bit off to Jessica now.

"Others have seen them. Like I said, I think they've been around for a long time. Hell, maybe they've always been with us. Except...." Buzz's voice trailed off in a sort of contemplative momentary silence.

"Except what?"

"If you stand to be a serious threat to them. If you could make anyone believe...."

"Oh my God. You mean if I let it go...if I just walk out of here."

"Maybe," Buzz said quietly. "Then again, like I said. I wouldn't bank on it."

"Do *you* believe I can safely walk away from this?"

"After seeing what they're capable of? No, I don't. I'm sorry."

"I know."

"After all, *you're* a credible public figure. People listen to you. You have a following. They will see that as a threat."

Something dawned on Jessica. "If we want to take these bastards out, what if we got more credible people behind us? Like Tom. I know where he stands, but I *have* to convince him."

"That's what I was hoping for. But you need to understand something. It *could* put him in the same sort of danger."

"But this is too incredible — and too dangerous — to just keep hidden. These creatures are killing people. That's why you're after them. They killed your wife."

"Yeah," Buzz said quietly, but with an icy precision to his voice.

"She was close to proving they existed?"

"I think so. Although you need to know something else."

"What's that?"

"If you think Tom could be brought into this...."

"What is it?"

"You know that man who was killed with your father?"

The words about her father hit Jessica like a body blow. "What about him?"

"He was probably murdered by the Predator. He was a psychologist who believed that legends of demons and ghouls weren't all legends."

"He was one of the right people to try and convince the world."

"Yeah."

"So they killed him, and they killed my father."

"Your father was in the wrong place at the wrong time. Look, Jessica, it was only fair that you know that. But if you get Tom involved, or you seriously want to try and expose these things...."

"They'll keep coming after me, right? But they could keep

coming nevertheless."

Buzz nodded slowly.

"I could die in a freak accident myself. Just so they can be sure."

"We have to stop the Predator. He'll *never* stop coming after you. But afterward...."

"We can't just let this go on."

"All right," Buzz said, and got off the bed again. Once more, he checked the front window. "I think we've been in one place long enough."

CHAPTER 49

"I wonder if the cops are out looking for us," Jessica said, considering the fact that Tom might have returned home from his ransacked office by now.

"Good point, actually," Buzz said, keeping his eyes on the road and every side street, parking lot, or dark driveway they passed.

He had been driving as cautiously as he could since they left the Prairie Crossings Motel, obeying every speed limit sign exactly and coming to a full stop at every stop sign. The Predator was out there, Buzz had kept reminding her—he was closing in, but so were the cops.

"That's going to be tough, getting back in Tom's house to talk to him *and* to avoid the cops who must still be there," Jessica said.

"You're going to have to go ahead," Buzz said after thinking about it for a few seconds. "I'll drop you off a few blocks short of the place and try to get out of there as quickly as I can."

It was a good plan, of course, Jessica considered. Yet, at the same time, frustrating in what it made her recognize all too clearly. She had, in effect, become Tom Lancaster and the local police department's prisoner. They were expecting her to remain under 'round-the-clock police surveillance now. If she tried doing anything on her own—like simply taking off in Tom's absence— the entire police force would, no doubt, be mobilized to hunt her down. Buzz's supposition that the police chief was in league with the creatures started appearing to be more and more plausible.

"You know, if I can't convince him, things'll get a lot worse for you," she said and glanced at Buzz. She could see him doing his best to contain his frustration. Although he stayed stoic, Jessica could see the corded, hardened, veiny muscles in both his arms flexing as he gripped the steering wheel.

"Yeah, I know," he said at length, keeping his voice even, perhaps resigned. He was probably accepting the fact that Tom could not be won over, Jessica pondered, and that he just had to carry on the fight alone.

"But I *have* to convince him," Jessica said quickly. "This *has* to work."

Buzz tossed a quick glance her way. She saw a burdened little grin on his face.

"What?" she asked.

"You're optimistic."

"I think he knows me well enough by now that he will believe me."

"Well, excuse me if I'm being a bit forward, and it's not my place to say something like this, but have you two gotten...*close*?"

"Romantic?"

"Yeah, you know what I mean. Romantic. 'Cause it would really help things."

Buzz then looked at her probingly, obviously quite curious to know the answer.

"We're close, but not romantic," Jessica said, almost immediately shocking herself by what came out of her mouth. If she and Tom were not romantic, then what were those kisses last night and this morning and on the previous days all about?

Perhaps, she told herself, they were "not romantic," or she didn't want to consider the two of them romantic, because of the second thoughts she'd had about Tom. Maybe the realization she had that they really knew next to nothing about each other had been killing whatever romantic feeling she had been developing for him.

"Oh," said Buzz. "But you think you're close enough that he'll listen to you."

"Well, I hope we're close enough that he should realize by now that I'm not one of those UFO-spotting kooks he likes mocking so much in his books."

"Mocking, huh?" Buzz said and chuckled. "Yes, that indeed he does enjoy doing. But let me tell you something."

"What's that?"

"Since I got swept up in this whole world of craziness—the creatures, the Predator, alternate realities—I've gotten to do a little reading on things like UFOs and Bigfoot and unsolved mysteries and paranormal claims. Many of those people seeing UFOs are *not* kooks. Tom, of course, treats them as if they were."

Yes, he does, doesn't he? Jessica thought but didn't say aloud. She also didn't want to tell Buzz about how Tom had insinuated tonight that she couldn't accurately recall how the mall attack went down. If he was capable of doubting her like that, how would he really react to her claims that interdimensional ghouls were stealing corpses from the local funeral home?

Buzz grinned. "You really are an optimist."

Jessica chuckled now, liking how good it felt to release all the tension. "We have to try." But then something occurred to her that killed some of the optimism. "Buzz?"

"Yeah?"

"The legends, the monsters you talked about. The stories these things might have inspired. You said shapeshifters too."

Buzz just looked in her eyes for a protracted moment.

"What we saw them doing in the woods," Jessica said, remembering the way that female creature's face had distorted.

"It's much worse than that, isn't it? Much worse."

"Yeah," Buzz said without hesitation this time. "It is—"

He was cut off as the car was flooded with light from the left side. A tremendous impact followed.

CHAPTER 50

The oncoming car, flying out of the intersection, rammed the left rear end of the Toyota. McPherson's car spun around under the impact, skidding across the asphalt until its nose faced the direction they had come from.

As Jessica fought to regain her bearings, a loud groan of pain filled the car.

"Buzz," she gasped, and frantically tried to size up the extent of his injuries. Since the incoming car had come from their left and struck his side, he'd taken the brunt of the energy of the hit in his side. Luckily, Jessica saw, the side-impact airbag deployed next to his head, keeping it from smashing through the door's window.

"Where is he?" Buzz asked, his voice clearing, sounding like he was recovering from the trauma with no complications. "It's him. Can you see him?"

An added jolt of adrenaline seared through Jessica now. Buzz seemed to believe this was the work of the Predator. Could he track them down so quickly? As she glanced over the hood of the car, she saw that he could.

"Oh God!" she exclaimed in panic, seeing the Predator emerge out of a wrecked Ford Focus some forty feet away. He was gripping a large pistol in his right hand. "There he is!"

"We have to move," Buzz yelled and scrambled for a Beretta 92FS automatic in a holster under his left arm.

And then the Predator stopped dead in his tracks. He looked over his right shoulder, then quickly spun around. Jessica's stomach seemed to plummet upon the realization of what was happening.

"Oh no! No!" she stammered, watching the Predator.

The car wreck, she saw, had caught the attention of a man in one of the houses on the intersection. Wearing only a white tank top and shorts, he rushed out his front door. As he reached the middle of his lawn, the Predator calmly fired three rounds into the man's chest.

"Bastard!" Buzz hissed through clenched teeth, equally shocked by the casual murder. But by now, Buzz had palmed his own weapon and ripped his seatbelt free. "Can you move?" he asked Jessica.

"Yeah."

"I'm gonna try and take him out. But you have to run for it. Just get down the street as fast as you can. I've got you covered."

They saw the Predator turning around.

"Now! Move!" Buzz yelled and shouldered his door open.

Jessica did the same. As she slid out of her seat, she saw Buzz crouching beside his door, trying to use it as a shield. He had better be accurate with that gun, she thought because the door was not much of a hiding place. Weapons of the caliber they were using could slice through the skin of a car as easily as they could punch holes through paper.

A moment later, the thunderclap of gunfire drowned out all sounds on the streets. As Jessica lunged from the car, hoping to sprint away and toward the sidewalk, she *felt* the whizzing of errant rounds not too far behind her. The Predator's bullets added an extra burst of energy to her run, prompting her to put every ounce of willpower into pumping her legs and getting away from there.

When she reached the sidewalk and had the opportunity to dodge behind a tree for cover, she looked back toward the cars to size up the situation. By then, she saw Buzz at the rear of the Toyota. With one hand, he was tossing the trunk open. With the other, he aimed his Beretta over the top of the car and fired three wild shots at the Predator.

The Predator, it seemed, had also retreated to his own car for some added measure of cover.

From the trunk, Jessica saw Buzz retrieve a shotgun fitted with a combat-style pistol grip and its shoulder sling appearing to double as a bandolier holding extra shells. When the Predator shot back, Buzz ducked, racked the pump-action chambering grip, then blasted a searing volley of buckshot toward the psycho's car.

Jessica couldn't see what damage the shotgun blast had wrought, but she saw Buzz quickly backing away from the Toyota. As he did so, he moved at an angle that gave him a clear shot at the Predator. He pumped the weapon again, ejecting the smoking, spent shell casing, slamming a new twelve gauge round into the breach, then blasting away at the Predator's position once more.

After the second shot, Buzz turned and ran, casting a glance toward Jessica. "Move!" he yelled.

She did so immediately, sprinting down the street. Although the stretch of sidewalk felt poorly made, uneven and gravelly under Jessica's feet, she found running barefoot actually gave her movements, her ankles, her calves, her legs a more natural power, and her feet a more steady grip on the ground than any type of footwear could. Her usual warm-weather routine of long barefoot walks in the park had conditioned her to tolerate the run. Although her professional image was that of a glamorous sophisticate, Cassie Brynner had joked, she was really a hippie nature chick at heart.

But it didn't take the Predator long to send more shots after Jessica and Buzz. Four gun blasts went off behind them. Then, from somewhere not too far ahead, Jessica heard the sound of a metal projectile pinging off some other piece of metal, followed by the sound of breaking glass. The Predator's shots were impacting on people's cars and windows. Thank God, Jessica thought, she hadn't yet heard anyone in panic or pain.

Then she saw Buzz momentarily break his stride, spin around, and fire the shotgun.

"Keep moving," he screamed, obviously worried that she would slow down to survey his handiwork.

He needn't have worried, Jessica thought.

As they reached the end of the block, Buzz darted closer to Jessica and waved his arm to the left — he wanted her to take the turn down the intersecting street. She took a shortcut across someone's dry, scraggly lawn, running full-out into the new street. Buzz was, at first, fast on her heels, then catching up with his long-legged strides, running beside her. They seemed to make it halfway across the block in silence, their footfalls the only sounds in the stillness of the night.

"Is he coming?" Jessica panted, daring to hope.

Aside from the nature hikes in the park, she had been making the faithful daily pilgrimages to the gym for years now. The stair machines, the kickboxing, toning classes, and Pilates sessions, though, hadn't quite kept her in good enough shape for this kind of long-distance sprinting. Her college softball sprint-drills were too far in the past, and her current fitness routines were really along the lines of the average fad-follower.

"Yeah," Buzz said. "He'll never stop." His voice, Jessica thought, sounded reassuringly clear. He, obviously, was in as good a shape as he looked. His lung capacity must have been tremendous.

A half a minute later, the Predator reappeared with an equalizer.

A harsh white light bathed the sidewalk around Jessica and Buzz. The sound of an over-revved engine, protesting under the insistence of someone's heavy foot, joined by squealing, rubber-burning tires shrieked through the night. Three gunshots followed. Not too far ahead, Jessica heard the noise of more breaking glass.

Throwing a glance over her shoulder, she saw a car bearing down on them. Its headlights were on high beams, blinding with their glare. The psycho must have gotten back in his car, determined to run them down if he couldn't shoot them.

But almost immediately, Jessica's eardrums were traumatized by an explosion directly beside her. She saw a flash of sparks, and the night air blew the whiff of cordite into her nostrils.

Buzz must have still been on the very top of his game, she realized. That blast was his shotgun. Then she heard the metallic racket of a spent shell casing being ejected, a new round chambered, and a second blast following. Buzz then repeated the process once more, firing a third shot at the oncoming car.

While her ears rang painfully, Jessica looked behind her, hoping to see the Predator's progress coming to a halt. Instead, she was stunned to see his car swerving *toward* them.

Then she felt a shove on her right shoulder, Buzz pushing her hard and urging her off to the left, up onto the lawn of a small stucco house. He followed in her wake.

About two seconds or so later, Jessica heard the jarring racket of metal tearing metal right behind them. Out of the right periphery of her sight, she could see Buzz cut his pace and stumble to a halt. She gladly followed his example, her lungs searing in protest against this ultra high-intensity cardiovascular workout.

When she turned around, she saw that the Predator's car had swerved right into a massive-bodied Dodge Charger parked next to the curb. The two cars were a mangled heap of crushed, accordioned metal, shattered glass, and twisted plastic.

Buzz slammed a new round into the breach of his shotgun. "Son of a bastard," he growled. "You're not going anywhere, you piece of…."

It was probably a good idea, what he was thinking, Jessica considered coldly. She could not help it, and she didn't want to. The man in that car was a monster in every sense of the word. He had been an unfeeling mistake of genetics to begin with. Then monsters from whatever otherworldly beyond had made him into a living demon. He had killed countless numbers of innocent people. And he had murdered Jessica's father.

Except she now realized why the words froze in Buzz's mouth. More lights bathed the street. Except this time, they were colorful red and blue splashes.

"The cops," she muttered.

"Shit!" Buzz said in burning frustration.

"What are we going to do?"

"You stay here! I'll find you later."

"No…!"

"Listen!" Buzz said quickly, but with steely, forceful, uncompromising determination. "They'll just take you back to Tom. You'll be fine. But I can't trust them. You need to buy me time, okay?"

Jessica knew what he said made sense. She nodded quickly.

"I'll contact you. Just give me your cell number, quick!"

"Six one nine, five five three, nineteen twenty-seven. Can you remember that?"

"I hope so," he said and ran.

He dodged past the house on whose lawn they stood. A

moment after he was gone, Jessica saw a man and a woman cracking the front door open.

Chaos followed down the street. More people were emerging from houses, and the cops were closing in. Sirens echoed through the night.

Jessica started toward the street, steering clear of the wrecked cars and the sharp debris their collision had flung all over the place. As she walked away, she thought she could smell the piercing odor of gasoline.

Two police cruisers came to a skidding halt some thirty feet or so short of the wreckage. As Jessica walked toward them, she was surprised to see the cops were not getting out. In fact, both cars shifted into reverse and backed away about twenty feet. Then a cop from each car started waving frantically at her.

"Move!" one of them screamed at last. "Get out of there! It's on fire."

Jessica looked behind her and, indeed, saw that flames had engulfed the undersides of both cars.

"Oh, shit," she gasped, and started running toward the cops.

When the gas tanks blew, a searing hot shockwave knocked her to the ground.

CHAPTER 51

"And I promise you one thing, lady, the next time you withhold any information from me, I *will* charge you and book you for obstruction of justice," Simon Gainey railed at Jessica yet again.

They were joined in his office by Tom and one of the two cops who had driven Jessica to the station last night. The cop, identified as Jarvis on his nametag, was back because Gainey had ordered him to bring in a copy of the Cedar Valley Journal. Gainey wanted to drive the gravity of the situation home for her.

The local news media were surprisingly fast to print and distribute the latest breaking news. Although the shootings and the explosion of the Predator's car happened in the middle of the night, the Journal had a brief overview, with "developments to come as available" promised on the front page.

"Cedar Valley Streets a War Zone," Gainey read the headline and tossed the paper on the table in front of Jessica. The big block lettering of the headline landed perfectly under the morning's first bright golden rays of sunlight slanting through the blinds on Gainey's window. "That nutcase murdered two more people last night. Yeah, *two!*"

Jessica felt her pulse quickening.

"Not just the man he shot in the intersection at the crash. He shot a woman while making his escape."

Jessica had been stunned to hear that. After the collision,

the Predator apparently climbed out of his totaled car and ran far enough away to avoid the explosion. Jessica must have just missed seeing that as she tried to join the incoming cops. But the Predator had escaped, all right, Gainey informed her in a full-throated bellow once his men had brought her in. They checked the burned-out hulks of both those cars, and there were no signs of a body anywhere inside.

"He shot a woman a block away," Gainey seethed. "She was in his way as he tried to flee. He shot her in the stomach and in the chest. She died on her way to the hospital. You know, the second shot went through one of her lungs and severed her spinal cord on the way out. Had she lived, she would have been paralyzed from the neck down for the rest of her life."

A shudder coursed through Jessica's body now. Fear, revulsion, and *rage* all mixed inside of her.

"God*damn* it!" Gainey yelled.

"Chief," Jessica replied in measured tones. "I've told you everything I know. I *want* to help you."

"Where is he?" the police chief fired the question at her.

"I *don't* know," she repeated. In fact, Jessica had forgotten by now how many times she had told the cop that Buzz had just taken off without saying a word as to where he was going. Of course, Jessica wouldn't have told these people even if she did know. Once again, just like over the past twenty-four-hours, everyone around her acted as if the entire Inquisition killing case hinged on Buzz McPherson.

How many of them are in on it? a voice came from the back of her head. Was Buzz correct about that? Was it all a ruse? Was the chief in league with the funeral home and its scheme to supply bodies to the creatures?

"Did he tell you he would contact you?" Gainey beamed at her.

"No. Look, Chief, please…like I said, he saw the police lights, and he ran."

The cop glared at her for a protracted moment. He didn't believe her for a moment. It looked like he was hoping that she could read that off his demeanor loud and clear.

Then Jessica glanced at Tom. He sat next to her in one of the chief's uncomfortable office chairs. He still looked as inscrutable as he had since arriving at the station. More of that rage stoked in Jessica now. Did he look *embarrassed* to have to be here with this irrational, crazy woman?

"You know," Gainey said, dialing his outrage down several considerable notches. Yet a smugness remained in his voice. He sounded like he had a game-winning ace in his hand, and he was going to enjoy playing it. "We did get some stuff in about your friend. The one who calls you in the middle of the night asks you to go off and catch the serial killer without telling the police about it…." He paused, looking around with no small amount of melodrama. "Where is it?"

"Put it right there, Chief," said Jarvis, pointing at a folder on the left edge of Gainey's desk.

With the man's boyish, dimpled cheeks, slightly pointy chin, and wide, seemingly guileless eyes, Jessica thought he looked the least like a cop of all the men she had ever met. His features somehow reminded her of Alfalfa from the old *Our Gang* comedy shorts.

"Put everything together like you asked, Chief," he said, and nodded.

Apparently, Jessica realized, he was a natural yes-man for a martinet like Gainey.

"Found something interesting here," the chief said, and handed Jessica the folder. Its tab had "McPherson" handwritten on it with a black marker. "That's the closest thing we could get to a Buzz McPherson in journalism."

Jessica opened the file.

The first thing she saw was a clipping from a newspaper—she couldn't be sure which—about the quickly-building "Oscar Fever" some five years ago. Apparently, it was a regular column by an attractive, brightly-smiling woman named April McPherson. The name of her column was "The Daily Buzz from McPherson."

Sure, Jessica was shocked, but she knew there had to be an explanation for this. *There has to be?* her inner voice asked. *Are you sure?* Or had another one of "McPherson's" lies about his identity been just uncovered?

"That, by the way," said Gainey, "is from Miami. That woman was some local entertainment and gossip columnist. Seems our boy must have seen her column and thought Buzz McPherson sounded cool."

Jessica heard the cop who looked like Alfalfa snickering. She had the barely-controllable urge to punch him in the face.

"Yeah," Gainey said, drawing out the word, apparently enjoying this. "Maybe he had a thing for her. Maybe he's one of those stalkers or something." Then his eyes narrowed and zeroed in on Jessica. "Maybe he's doing the same thing with you. Saw one of your books...."

Jessica thought she was about to explode. "No!" she exclaimed, very nearly screaming at the cop. "He's not my stalker. That fucking maniac who shot two people last night is a stalker. You remember him?"

Gainey's expression darkened. "God*damn* it," he hissed. "You're the one who's getting in the middle of our investigation, and you have the decency to tell me—"

"What investigation?" Jessica snapped back.

As she did so, she felt Tom's hand on her arm and heard him call her name. She nearly shook his hand off.

"There's a serial killer out there, and you're more concerned with the man who saved my life!"

"Do you want to see the inside of a cell right now?"

Jessica wanted to launch into another attack, but she held back. She believed Gainey would do as he threatened. If she wound up behind bars, she would never get out. She was sure of it. If she pushed, she just might wind up a fresh meal for those things in the forest sooner rather than later.

"I suggest you think about every word out of your mouth right now," the chief warned.

"I'm sorry," Jessica whispered. But then she added, "He told me he had a wife."

Of course, what troubled Jessica was the fact that McPherson claimed his wife was a high-powered investigative reporter. This April McPherson looked like a low-level gossipmonger, someone who wrote fluff pieces and called herself an "entertainment and pop-culture journalist."

"Well, guess what?" Gainey dripped sarcasm. "Us hick cops've actually thought of that. You know, a connection between this woman and that guy who keeps following you around." He paused for a heavy, dramatic effect. "Guess what else? April McPherson ain't married. Or at least she wasn't. She died four years ago, by the way."

Jessica's heart raced a bit faster now. At least one part of "Buzz McPherson's" story checked out.

"We called that paper in Miami," said Gainey. "April McPherson died in a car accident."

"Buzz McPherson told me she died covering a story," Jessica said slowly, placatingly. She had to get out of the police station as quickly as she could, and the only way that was going to be possible was by mollifying Simon Gainey.

"Her paper said nothing about that," Gainey said briskly.

"He was probably lying," Tom said at last. He had opened his mouth for the first time in the last twenty minutes or so.

Jessica didn't reply.

"Chief," Tom said slowly. That embarrassed tone was clearly there in his voice. He sounded like a parent who had been called to see his miscreant kid's teacher. "This has been a big misunderstanding and a big mistake, sure, but can we just go on from here? We'll do anything we can to help you, and we'll contact you if we hear anything at all from this McPherson character...or whoever he is."

Jessica could feel Tom's eyes on her.

"Right, Jessica?" he asked with a patronizing tone.

She looked at him but didn't say a word. Instead, she turned to the chief. "Sure. I promise," she said curtly.

"Despite what impression you might be under," Gainey said, Jessica sensing that a good, deep, final dig at her was about to come, "we don't handle crimes out in the boondocks here with torches and a lynch mob. You *don't* take the law into your own hands, you understand? Unless you're really looking forward to some serious jail time."

"Yes, Chief. I'm sorry. I really do understand, and you have nothing to worry about."

Gainey nodded at last and glanced at the door. Apparently, Jessica realized, she and Tom were free to go.

CHAPTER 52

What an indignity it must have been for the good Dr. Lancaster to be seen like this, Jessica simmered as she and Tom walked out of the Cedar Valley Municipal Building. Not only was he seen at the seat of the town government with this bedraggled, filthy, barefoot woman, but a woman who had nearly been charged with a major crime. If indignity was indeed what Tom was feeling, Jessica wanted to revel in his discomfort, in his embarrassment. Not only had he basically sided with Gainey against her, but his patronizing behavior served to further humiliate her in front of the cops.

"Jessica, what in the hell are you—?"

"And what are *you* doing?" she snapped back at Tom. "You sided with them throughout this whole thing, and you treated me like some sort of an idiot child who made you look bad in front of everyone."

"What you did makes no sense at all."

"No, what the fearless police force in this town is doing makes no sense at all. God, Tom, doesn't it strike you in the least as abnormal that they're trying harder to find the man who saved me than the one who tried to kill me?"

"They're trying to find the one who's dragged you into a shootout in the middle of the night. Jessica, please! What the hell *was* that? Some midnight vigilante raid?"

Again, Tom's voice was no longer enraged or indignant, but

patronizing. It had a long-suffering parent whine to it. It had that "What am I going to do with you, young lady?" tone. Jessica even noticed his right hand reaching toward her shoulder like he wanted to take her firmly by the arm and give her a good shake and a lecture to impart some sense into her. Immediately, she stepped out of his reach.

But her next move had to be very carefully made, she knew. What she wanted to do, more than anything was to tell him to go to hell and walk away. But that was not an option. She and McPherson needed him. If he could be convinced — or better yet, shown the creatures — they stood a real chance of exposing what went on in this town.

"Tom, I know it was wrong," Jessica said, trying mightily to squelch her anger. "All right? I mean, those two people getting killed last night...I feel like it was our fault...*my* fault. Okay? Can you understand that?" This last part was not at all an act. To the contrary, if she ever made it through this, if she ever made it out of town alive, Jessica knew she would try and justify what happened for the rest of her life by telling herself that the deaths of those people were a result of her and Buzz trying to prevent more deaths. But that would never be a good enough excuse. It could never clear her conscience.

Tom nodded at last. He looked like his self-righteous outrage had deflated a bit.

"But Tom," Jessica said, much softer, more docilely this time. "I need to tell you some other things, okay?"

"What?"

"Some other things about last night. Things I saw."

She could see Tom's blood pressure surging yet again. "You mean things you didn't tell the police?"

"Yes, but listen to me."

"Oh, Jessica...."

CHAPTER 53

If the parking lot of the Traveler's Haven Inn hadn't been as full, the Predator would have marched into the lobby and blown away the people behind the counter. It wouldn't have mattered much. This morning's Cedar Valley Journal already carried a sketch of his likeness on the front page. The picture, in fact, looked pretty damned accurate. Those imbeciles working in the inn would recognize him the moment they picked up a paper, and they would call the cops. It was the reason he'd had to snatch all of his clothes from his room and take off through a side door this morning. His week, of course, had been paid for with cash, so chances were they might not even realize he was gone or who he was. But he could not take that chance. He could not take the chance on the cops. The Handlers had been vague about the local police force at first, then ordered him to make sure he did not come anywhere near anyone in uniform. The Predator, though, knew there had to be something going on between at least some of the cops and the Handlers. Someone of his intellect could not be kept under control by a few vague, simple orders. The extent of the connection, though, he couldn't guess, and the Handlers were not saying anything. For the time being, he had to remain a fugitive.

"If they even read the paper *about these here parts*," he mumbled to himself, adding a sort of generic, central casting hick accent to his last words.

BARNA WILLIAM DONOVAN

He sat behind the wheel of his stolen Nissan Sentra and kept staring across the parking lot at the motel's front office. One part of him burned, *ached* with the need to go inside and kill those two hayseed employees working the desk. He had been uprooted all of a sudden because these two witless bumpkins might remember him and decide to become heroes.

"If they can even read," he growled to himself. He knew he was wasting his time sitting here in the parking lot. "Huh? Do you *folks* read the papers down in this here down-home heartland town?" he drawled. "You shitkickers learn to read yet?"

The Predator almost went for it. He almost got out of the car, marched across the parking lot, and did it. Reason, though, got the best of him. The Traveler's Haven Inn lived up to its name today. The place was just off of I-24, on the southern outskirts of Cedar Valley, and it catered to cross-country drivers. Today, the motel was crawling with them. He had to control himself and not do anything stupid.

Or anything the Handlers considered stupid!

He started the engine and pulled out of the lot.

The Handlers considered shooting up the Traveler's Haven Inn stupid. Their reticence made no sense, of course. All he would have done afterward would have been to take some blood and write some random Biblical quotation on the wall. But the Inquisitor killer was not supposed to do rampage shootings in motel lobbies. It wasn't his proper M.O. He had to stick to the script. The Handlers would not allow him to deviate from the plan.

"Damn it!" the Predator shouted and punched his steering wheel. "Fucking damn it!" he screamed. "You want an Inquisition killing?"

The Handlers, of course, did.

So the Predator was going to give them one right now. He

was going to give them several.

CHAPTER 54

Despite the heat outside, Jessica had been wishing that Tom would turn down the air conditioning in the house. When she went to take a shower, she ran the water hot enough to prickle her skin. But she had been racked by shivers ever since she had gotten a sudden call from Cassie. On top of the madness, Jessica's life had been spiraling into, the emergency Cassie told her about had nearly pushed Jessica to the breaking point. Somehow, she reacted to it all through a spell of paralyzing cold shivers.

Cassie's breast cancer had come back. It was discovered during her checkup the day after Jessica left San Diego. This had been the cause of Cassie's absence from the radio.

The Wings of Angels project was something Cassie had organized and raised money for after her first diagnosis six years ago. At that point, the cancerous lump had been removed from her breast, and the doctors were optimistic that she was in the clear.

Jessica suddenly realized that she had lost track of how long she had been standing still under the cascading shower. It was as if she wanted to wash the entire world off her.

Something else that she almost forgot about was the sensation of stinging pain in the bottom of her right foot. She forgot about it because she could no longer feel it. During her long sprint away from the Predator last night, her adrenaline rush must have been so strong that she didn't even register having stepped on something sharp. By the time she was sitting in Gainey's office, though, she took a couple of quick glances down at the floor to see if she had left some smeared droplets of blood in her wake. She hadn't.

Nevertheless, she was sure that either a sliver of glass had lodged in her foot, or a sharp pebble or broken piece of sidewalk concrete cut the skin. Before stepping into the shower, she checked her foot but could neither see nor feel any damage. Of course, then her soles had been covered with a thick coat of black dust. Now, with her feet washed clean, she still could see nothing. There wasn't so much as an abrasion in the spot she had previously felt aching so severely. And the pain was all gone.

After she got out of the shower and dried off, Jessica put the lush, thick terrycloth robe on that Tom had given her. Its luxurious softness just swallowed her up. She wanted to collapse into bed, curl up in the comfort of her robe, and wish that somehow she could shut out the insanity, the chaos, the evil of the world all around her. We know that evil lurks just beyond the surface of so much of everyday life, she thought, but for her, this evil had to rise up through the veil of reality and threaten to overwhelm her right now.

She couldn't let it, she realized. She had to take control again, and it had to start right here in this house. She needed to make Tom an ally.

But she had to get dressed for that. She couldn't traipse around the house in this robe if she was going to talk to Tom about the unbelievable. It made her feel too exposed, both literally and figuratively. It made her feel vulnerable.

She returned to the guest bedroom, fished a pair of panties, a bra, a T-shirt, and a clean pair of jeans out of her travel bag, and got dressed.

By the time she padded down to the kitchen, Tom had

prepared a bagel, cream cheese, and lox breakfast for her, along with a halved grapefruit, French toast, and, best of all, fantastic-smelling coffee. She knew she would need the coffee the most.

For a few moments, they made small talk, but by the time she bit into the bagel, Tom asked, "So, you wanted to tell me something about what *really* went on last night."

CHAPTER 55

It would not have been accurate to say that the flawlessly postcard-perfect design, upkeep of, and scenery around the Valley View Bed and Breakfast soured the Predator's stomach. It would have been a cliché, really, he mused as he walked back toward his car with George O'Bannon. The cute little Currier and Ives look of the establishment actually excited the Predator. Like some supercomputer, his mind was reeling with ideas for destroying the place.

"Yeah, you can just pull your car around back, then come back in for those pancakes and coffee," George O'Bannon said and, for some reason, found it important to add an irritating little chortle on the end. "Believe me, more than one guest has said those pancakes made them consider packing up and moving down here."

"That's quite a pitch," the Predator said. He was proud of his performance. He thought he was doing an excellent job of approximating charm and friendly good cheer. He had, in truth, gotten sick a long time ago of O'Bannon's story of how he quit a job as a hedge fund manager in Chicago to move down here with his wife, daughter, and son to operate this B&B and the adjoining Comfy Nook Eatery. O'Bannon's endless insistence that his wife's homemade pancakes had inspired more than a few other relocations felt like a concert of dozens of nails on a chalkboard. "And right now, Mr. O'Bannon—"

"Name's George. Please!"

"George, I'm starving. Pancakes will hit the spot like nobody's business."

George let out a self-satisfied chuckle and even shook his head. "Well, let's get cracking. Just drive on back to the barn, and I'll let your car in." He pointed to a large, well-renovated, newly-painted red barn some two hundred feet to the rear of the main house."

"In the barn?"

"It's a garage, really," George said, and laughed again. "We're just trying to maintain the atmosphere," he said, a big folksy grin plastered all over his face.

"Nice," the Predator said simply, remembering to smile. "Well, come on, George, don't let me make you walk back there. Get in the car, and I'll pull right up."

"We're in business," the local said, laughing one more time.

The sound of that jackass bray, the Predator thought, was becoming unendurable. He was going to keep his mouth shut the entire five-second drive it was probably going to take to get from the front driveway to the barn, lest George be provoked into more conversation and more laughter. There was no cruelty even he could conceive of that could be worse than making someone endure this asshole punctuating each and every single sentence with a laugh.

"Now that's a smart idea," George said before opening the Sentra's front passenger-side door. He apparently noticed the pillow in the back seat. "Never could stand those hotel pillows myself."

"Yeah, they kill me." The Predator got behind the wheel and started the car.

"Won't have to worry here, though," George said and, of course, chuckled again. "I guarantee the most comfortable bed and pillows anywhere in the hospitality business in the whole

Midwest."

The Predator fantasized about lashing out and chopping the blade of his hand across George's throat. He wondered what it would be like to see him choking to death from a crushed windpipe.

The Predator wouldn't try that move, however. He had attempted it once on a truck driver years ago and had nearly gotten himself killed. The big dumb ape agreed to give him a ride after his rental car broke down at a TA rest area in Pennsylvania. The Predator wanted to try the hit to the man's throat after having rehearsed the move in his mind countless numbers of times. Plus, it just thrilled him to imagine what might go through the trucker's mind as he gasped and choked and died a very slow, fiendishly agonizing death.

The big witless buffoon had been a genuine Good Samaritan. His truck's cab was full of Jesus paraphernalia, crosses, the virgin on the dashboard, and a Christian suspense audiobook in the CD player about a doctor who counseled unwed pregnant mothers against abortion when not busting Satanic conspiracies by disproving evolution. What would a holy-roller like that think, the Predator had wondered, when his random act of kindness brought nothing but disaster? Thus, the Predator tried to smash the big shitkicker's windpipe…and missed. He caught the trucker on an alarmingly dense neck-muscle instead. The massive son of a bitch, at that point, reacted in a decidedly un-Christian manner. He had backhanded the Predator, nearly knocking him into a coma in that instant, pulled over to the side of the road, and proceeded to try and beat him to a bloody, quivering mass. Only the Predator's knife saved his life.

Although he didn't think George would be capable of beating him so badly, the Predator would take no chances this time.

Once he reached the barn, George got out and opened the

large wooden doors. He waved the Predator inside.

Indeed, he noted as he pulled the Sentra inside and shut off the engine, this was not a functional barn. There were some bales of hay in one corner and a couple of pitchforks hanging off a wall, but it was all for show. Here, George O'Bannon's roots in the world of Chicago hedge-fund-trading were evident. This barn looked like some big-city designer's conception of what a country barn would look like.

"Cute, though," the Predator murmured, and opened his door. "Looks right properly quaint."

After he got out, he was about to start toward George, but paused. "One second," he said, and opened the rear passenger door. He leaned inside for the pillow. "You know, George," he said as he removed the pillow with one hand and the Smith and Wesson SW1911 automatic with the other, "it might not look like anything special, but this is my late wife's pillow."

George raised his eyebrows quizzically. Whatever thoughts might have been going through his mind, the Predator made sure they were his last. He raised the pillow with his left hand and pressed the barrel of the handgun into it with his right. The pillow would act as an improvised silencer. The Predator had read about the trick. Although he couldn't remember for certain, he was sure he had seen the technique in a movie. But then he was reminded just how fake the movies could be.

The Predator couldn't aim accurately with the pillow in front of him, but that was only one of his problems. Another one was the fact that he was concerned with not shooting his own fingers off. Thus, his hold on the pillow was quite unstable.

The combination of the bad grip and the inaccurate aim served to deprive George O'Bannon of a swift death. He didn't get a bullet through his forehead, as the Predator had intended. The nine-millimeter Parabellum slug instead caught George in his right cheek. The round shattered his cheekbone and ripped nearly all of the skin off that side of his face. What remained was an enormous gaping hole. The Predator could perfectly see both George's upper and lower sets of teeth.

George O'Bannon stumbled backward several steps, then collapsed onto the dusty floor of the barn/garage.

Although George definitely looked like he was pretty much out of the game, the Predator knew it was smart to shoot him again, just to make sure all loose ends were tied up. Except the pillow was on fire! The muzzle flash of the gun had ignited the shredded pillow innards. The Predator was now out of a silencer.

He flung the burning rags onto the ground and stomped on them. He needed the fire extinguished for now. He couldn't afford to have the flames spreading accidentally before he was good and ready to do some burning. And oh yes, burning he would do. The O'Bannon estate would see its share of fire today. But everything had to be in order first.

By the time the flames had been stomped out, the Predator was reminded why he needed to deliver another killing blow to George. Despite his smashed face, George was still stirring.

"Bad move, my man," the Predator said, and took aim at O'Bannon. "You don't want to show me you're still alive."

But he couldn't pull the trigger. It would have been stupid to do so. O'Bannon had told the Predator that everyone was home. O'Bannon's wife, as well as seventeen-year-old Brenda and twenty-year-old Logan, were back in the house. He couldn't alert them to trouble before making it over there.

So the Predator improvised. He stuck the pistol in his belt and ran over to the wall. The pitchfork would have to do, he decided and hefted the tool off the wall. Although he didn't like killing with knives and edged instruments, the pitchfork couldn't possibly lead to trouble when applied to a semi-conscious gunshot victim.

Of course, it didn't. The fork's tines easily sank into George's soft midsection. He lurched under what must have been excruciating pain and let out a half-gurgling, half-squealing noise. Blood and spittle sprayed and gushed from his missing face.

After about two seconds, O'Bannon settled down.

But is he dead? the Predator wanted to scream.

This was the problem with stabbing people. It could take them too damn long to die. He had dealt with this before. The dilemma had come up with that hick truck driver. The Predator had managed to keep the big animal from beating him to death by getting to a hidden boot knife and sticking it in the trucker's groin. Although Trucker Clem was as stunned by that as anyone would properly expect him to be, it took the Predator three more stabs into the man before his life was completely snuffed out.

But the first time the Predator experienced this problem with knives was back home in Rochester, New York, during one of his first kills. That was the time when he was still Nick Gilroy, just before he came to accept himself fully as the Predator. He had wanted the kill to be not just exciting, but the extermination of something truly inferior. He had decided to kill his apartment building's black superintendent. He stabbed the knuckle-dragging gorilla twice in the back, yet some truly animalistic inner strength kept him going, kept him clawing and kicking at the ground, trying to escape. Eventually, the Predator had to kick him in the head three times, then straddle him and cut his throat from ear to ear. The Predator had damn near slashed his own wrist as he did so, but it had been an all-around bad experience, and no matter how many times he looked back on it, the frustration welled in him. He could recall the memorial vigils held outside the building for three days. At least four separate priests from two local parishes had given speeches right under the Predator's window about eradicating hate crimes forever, and remembering that Dr. King's dream was still not realized.

"Asshole!" the Predator hissed and stabbed George O'Bannon for a third time with the pitchfork.

O'Bannon didn't so much as twitch. He was a dead slab of meat.

But the Predator somehow liked the feel of the pitchfork in his hands. He liked the zigzagging pattern of blood its prongs painted on the ground next to George. So he decided to hold on to it a little while longer.

The Predator hurried toward the back entrance of the main house. He was going to rush inside and stab at least one more person with the pitchfork.

And then his second victim almost literally walked into him. A young man, someone who could only have been Logan O'Bannon, suddenly swung the door open in front of the Predator.

"Hey, man," the kid gasped. "What are you—?"

His words were cut off when the Predator plunged the pitchfork into his chest. The tines managed to neatly avoid any ribs *and* the sternum. They efficiently perforated both of young Logan's lungs, quickly filling them up with blood.

A thick crimson finger of blood gurgled out of his mouth, and the kid keeled over and hit the ground. The Predator delivered a vicious kick to the side of his head, snapping it off to the side at a grotesquely unnatural angle.

The Predator dropped the pitchfork next to Logan's corpse and rushed into the house. Some thirty seconds later, he ran into a girl—Brenda, it had to be—in a corridor leading to the kitchen. He smashed her across the bridge of the nose with the handgun and buried the weapon's barrel in her midsection. Essentially, he turned Brenda into a human silencer when he shot her three times.

In the kitchen, he found a startled Linda O'Bannon standing over a mixing bowl. She must have been whipping up some of those world-famous pancakes, the Predator thought as he rushed her and knocked her out with the butt of his gun. The woman hit the ground like a stout sack. She looked surprisingly chunky, the Predator thought. He would have expected a hedge fund hotshot like George O'Bannon to have snagged himself a cuter, slimmer woman back in Chicago. He had to have had enough money for it.

Go figure, the Predator mused as he took hold of Linda's thick ankles and started dragging her toward the living room.

"Fat bitch!" he yelled half a minute later when he felt a painful strain in his lower back as he had to maneuver the unconscious woman around a tight corner. He was going to set up the Inquisition scene in the middle of the house. That way, not only would Linda O'Bannon be put out of action, but the whole place would be burned to the ground.

He only had to get on George's computer and download an epic amount of pornography. The Inquisition killer was quite the moralist, of course. Or at least according to that ridiculous script the Handlers had written for him. In order for him to kill a nice wholesome family—exactly like the kind of people the O'Bannons turned out to be—he had to make it look as if they had some deep, dark, perverse secret in their lives. With the porn, the charade would be perfect. It would suggest that George might have been a sex freak who forced his wife to perform some of the more sick stuff from the magazines. Enter, stage right, a murdering religious fanatic like the Inquisitor and the Handlers' plot was perfectly pulled off; the "dark side" of heartland holy-rollers, like Reverend Jim Garnett's followers, was on display in living, revolting, sickening, bloody color for the whole world to see. The Inquisitor must have been causing the good reverend more sleepless nights—especially now since the killings had started in his own back yard—than all the evolution-espousing science books in all the schools across the country.

But once the Inquisitor claimed the O'Bannons, the Predator would go after Jessica again, no matter what the Handlers had to say about it.

CHAPTER 56

As Tom leaned against the edge of the kitchen's island table, he almost looked like a perfect picture of self-control. He almost looked like he was carrying on a reasonable conversation about an honest difference of opinion with the woman he cared about.

Almost, Jessica knew.

Only one part of his body betrayed the barely-contained well of anger inside him. While his right hand was wrapped around a tall glass of orange juice, his left index and middle fingers drummed incessantly on the tabletop. Upon second look, Jessica no longer thought his right hand looked normal either. He wasn't just holding that glass, she realized. He was *clutching* it.

"Jessica," Tom said with a deceptive, disturbing calmness in his voice. "Let me just start by reminding you that you have been through a series of incredibly stressful experiences, okay?"

But as angry as Tom might have gotten once she told him the entire story of the previous evening, Jessica was committed to standing her ground. "And that's why I'm insane, and I'm just imagining all this," she cut into his speech.

"No, that's not what I'm saying," Tom retorted with a sudden, spasmodic shake of his head.

"Yes, that's exactly what you're saying."

"Please—"

"No, you're just dressing it up nicely in your high-flown rhetoric," Jessica said quickly, feeling her own anger spiking ever higher and higher. "You're incapable of accepting the fact that I saw something that you cannot place into one of your neat boxes, something that doesn't stand up to the scrutiny of —"

"No, Jessica," Tom cut her off this time. "I'm saying that what you just told me is impossible. Okay? Do you want me to come out and say it? It is *not* possible. You could *not* have seen that. There is absolutely nothing in this world to indicate that the creatures you described have *ever* existed, or that they could exist today."

"Except that, I saw two of them," Jessica almost yelled.

"You think."

"Oh, you believe that I *thought* I saw two people barely forty feet away from me —"

"Change into monsters with mouths that —"

"And they started eating a dead body. I don't *believe* I saw it. I *did*. For me to have imagined anything like that, I would have to be completely, delusionally —"

Tom shook his head, violently again. "No, you wouldn't."

"Or I would need to have the IQ of a severely retarded baboon."

"No, that's not true. Remember your encounter with the Predator and McPherson's — or whatever the hell his name is — cars? Remember your panic attack?"

Tom's words hit her like a slap in the face. "You're going to use that against me?"

"I am not *using* anything *against* you. It's a fact — and you agreed before — that you've been under tremendous pressure and stress, and your perception of things —"

"Has driven me over the edge. And please stop denying that's what you're implying. I know semantics, I know word games, okay? That's my business. Communication, remember?"

"Okay, so you can go on and see and interpret anything you

want then. It still doesn't make it true. And it doesn't prove that shape-changing, corpse-eating monsters are running around in Cedar Valley."

"Tom," Jessica said, feeling the hard, metallic edge of her own anger rasping through her voice. Their verbal sparring had now escalated into full-out combat, she realized. Tom was making personal attacks now, and she was going to retaliate any way possible, no matter what it did to their "relationship." "I am *not* insane and not hallucinating shape-shifting monsters. I've *seen* them. And for someone to hallucinate creatures like this, she would have to be so far gone into paranoia, dementia, schizophrenia, that she would *always* see them. You don't hallucinate something like this once. You don't. Believe me. I have a little background in psychology, you know. Once I worked at a psych ward for three months while in grad school. I've met people who see things. I've met a woman who claimed to be getting stock tips from Richard Nixon. She was seeing him *every* day."

"Jessica, please, just listen to me," Tom said, his voice much softer now. He was taking on his "voice of reason and concern" again. This time it had an insufferable quality, Jessica thought. "I've seen some very intelligent, *brilliant* people make mistakes, misinterpret things right in front of them. It's not insanity. And this world is full of completely natural, mundane things that could be mistaken for something fantastic."

"Like a dead body being eaten in front of you?"

"And some not so mundane things can be seen by accident, seen under strange circumstances that make them look supernatural or unexplainable. There are demented, perverse sex cults out there."

"Look, Tom, I know the kind of debunking arguments you use. Do you think I saw a flock of wild geese illuminated by the moon through a cloud formation or something?"

A dark glance passed over Tom's face. "Let me ask you this. What if you would have seen mysterious balls of light flying over the woods? Flying and stopping in mid-air? Disappearing suddenly. Flying off at incredible speeds and taking ninety-degree turns. Making moves that no known aircraft could. What would you say? And I'll grant you that you saw it. You didn't hallucinate, and you didn't dream it, and you're not insane."

"What would it be?"

"Tectonic lights," Tom said with a shocking aggressiveness. He looked like he was trying to drive the sharpest, most lethal spear right into Jessica's heart. "Earth lights. Electric currents released in seismically active areas. It's a documented geological phenomenon. People have seen them around fault zones just before earthquakes. Which, by the way, you would have an excellent chance of seeing in this part of the country, since we're sitting just about on top of a major fault line. The New Madrid Fault. Remember when I told you about the rich folklore of Southern Illinois? Oh, yes, ghost lights are a part of it. Glowing apparitions, phantom lights, UFOs, the whole thing."

"And do these lights ever look like people?"

"No, but sometimes they look like the earth opening up and unleashing the fires and brimstone of hell. Oh yes! In nineteen eleven, massive earthquakes shook the southern Illinois and Missouri areas. I mean, holes opening in the ground, entire houses getting swallowed up. And what accompanied all this? Clouds of sulfur blasting out of the ground. Strange lights glowing in the night sky. Now, does that sound like hell itself opening up? And perfectly sane and normal people have said as much and come to believe that the end of the world and the Apocalypse and judgment day were here. They weren't, of course. Just a perfectly normal—albeit frightening and strange—geological phenomena that people have mistaken for something supernatural."

"Tom, you did not answer my question. Did *people* ever appear in these earth lights?"

Jessica could have sworn she saw Tom's appearance lightening again. However, it was not in a good way. He looked like a driven, frenzied competitor who felt that debating was verbal combat, a contest to the death, one where words were his weapons to mercilessly destroy his enemy. There was a look of levity on Tom's face because he was feeling like he was in the position to deliver the *coup de grace* to Jessica. "As a matter of fact, yes," he gloated. "Yes, they did! In nineteen sixty-five, a hunter said he saw balls of light fly through one of the forests nearby. And suddenly, the lights stopped, and two human figures materialized out of a bank of accompanying fog and flashes of light. The seismic meters at the University of Illinois indicated tremors along the fault lines at about the same time this guy — a church-going, God-fearing fellow, by the way — saw the mysterious phantoms appear. A creepy, cloudy night, some seismic activity, the appearance of earth lights, and just a dash of religious mania, and you've got yourself the recipe for a genuine, bona fide supernatural manifestation. Oh, and by the way, can I show you something you might find interesting?"

Without waiting for a reply, Tom marched into the living room. Less than a minute later, he was back, a triumphant spring in his steps and his iPad in his hand.

"Here," he said. "Website of the paper Gainey had in his office. Look at the bottom half, if you will."

Jessica did so and found a story about the seismic readings recorded at CVSU. There were some minor earth tremors in the area last night, the article's opening paragraph revealed. She did not bother to read the entire story.

"Everything's in place, Jessica," Tom said smugly and took a greedy swig of his orange juice.

"Not quite," Jessica retorted. "I'm not a religious fanatic. I haven't been to a church in three years, by the way. And I'm not a UFO-nut or a conspiracy theorist, and I don't spend my time looking at the dollar bill for hidden codes by the Masons."

Tom's face clouded over again. "You're just stressed out, and were dragged away in the middle of the night by a ranting madman who does believe in monsters and ghouls, and then you're attacked by a serial killer who's already tried to—"

"So I just imagine things that are not there. Thank you very much. We're back where we've started, aren't we?"

"We're back at one incontrovertible fact," Tom exclaimed with a petulant forcefulness. "That you're describing the impossible."

"Because no one's seen it before?"

"Yes!" Tom almost yelled. "Because no one's seen it before."

"Or because no one's bothered to try and look for it? No one's *tried* to find these things, no matter how many times people've experienced them. What is it you people say…?"

"*You* people?" Tom said suddenly with a plaintive, melodramatic, frustrated moan. "Oh, come on, Jessica."

"Extraordinary claims require extraordinary proof? Isn't that it? Well, you can't get extraordinary proof unless you conduct extraordinary investigations, can you? But your scientific method is unwilling to do that."

"It's not *my* scientific method," Tom snapped with genuine, undisguised anger. In fact, Jessica thought, he sounded as if she had just insulted his mother's honor. "It happens to be the truth."

"What are you so threatened by?" Jessica asked, looking Tom square in his eyes. She wanted to see his reactions to her question because she felt this question was at the bottom of his stubborn combativeness. "Is it your reputation? Is that it, Tom? Have you staked your name and written your books, and now the great Dr. Lancaster can't say he was wrong?"

Jessica was stunned at how the muscles in Tom's jaw were clenching, quivering. He looked like he was about to plunge into a fistfight or something. "Will you give me *one* scintilla of evidence that monsters, or aliens, or demons, or ghosts are real and —"

"And you will tell me they're earth lights. What are you threatened by? And why did we need to know that she said 'no'?"

Suddenly Jessica felt more stunned by what came out of her mouth than Tom appeared to be by the fact that she said it.

"Oh, come on, Jessica," he said with a weary, exasperated sigh and a roll of his eyes.

"Why, Tom?" she asked. The door had been opened, and she knew she couldn't close it. She didn't want to. She knew it could be the way to understanding why Tom's preference for a mindset ruled by admirable, logical scientific rationality had turned into fervent mania that could rival the obsessions of extremists who went around wiring bombs to themselves. "You see, over this past day, I've realized just how little we really know each other... no, that we basically don't know each other at all."

"Jessica," Tom said, softening his voice, but Jessica could see his tone wasn't genuine. He couldn't soften the burning anger, the uncompromising zeal flashing in his eyes. "I thought I knew everything I ever wanted to know about you —"

"Tom!" Jessica cut him off. She actually couldn't believe he was trying to romance her into seeing his point of view. "Please tell me. What were you trying to accomplish with that book? Why did we have to know that girl said 'no'?"

"Because it's the truth," Tom snapped. "That's the business *I'm* in. That's what I do."

"And what exactly did it accomplish in this case?"

"Why are you asking me this?"

"Because I need to know you. Was there any reason behind

that book other than cutting some ideological notch?"

"So you mean, why didn't I just let the truth be buried if the lie gave so many people hope?"

Jessica was caught off guard for a moment. Tom understood *exactly* what she found so objectionable about the debunking of the Jeanie Anderson tragedy. "Yes," she said, her tone losing its previous bite.

"Well, imagine yourself being asked for help by people very much like that girl's friends and family," Tom replied. He, too, sounded somewhat distant all of a sudden, his own combativeness dissipating. "Except this time it's someone's son who's getting sucked into a UFO cult. His new friends are waiting for the motherships from Zeta Reticuli to come and take all of their troubles away. So your *expert* opinion — as if you were a psychiatrist or something — is to start making one weak, qualified statement after the next about that kid's state of mind. Maybe if believing in these aliens brings him a peace of mind, a sense of purpose, then leave him and his friends alone with their delusions. Sure, intelligent life on other planets is theoretically possible. No, these idiotic conspiracy theories about men in black in Area 51 controlled by the Freemasons don't make any sense. But hey, if the young man finds meaning, structure, a moral code in his beliefs, then what's the harm? He and his pals have their First Amendment rights to believe in any invisible, magical alien visitors and conspiracies that control the world. Whatever makes them happy, they can believe it." As Tom paused, his eyes seemed to sear right into Jessica. "It's all good...until this Apocalyptic alien-worshipping cult commits suicide to be beamed up into the mothership and taken off to never-never land. So *that* is why I wrote the book."

"I'm sorry," was all Jessica could say somewhat flatly at that moment. "And I'm sorry to have brought Jeanie Anderson into this. This is not about her. But it *is* about me, and what I saw, and the fact that you can't even give me the benefit of the doubt."

"Jessica...," Tom said, and paused. She could see how uncomfortable he was. He was clearly trying to say something that went against everything be stood for and believed. "What if I came out to the woods with you, and we try to figure out — *together* — what it was that you *really* saw?"

Really saw? Jessica thought, her anger spiking again. What he meant was, "let's go out in the woods so I can get the chance to tell you that you saw swamp gas and earth gasses and star formations distorted by the moonlight. Just so I can live with my guilty conscience."

"Not now, okay?" she said quickly. "I can't right now. And I need to get out of here for a while. Look, I...I have to go find my father's lawyer and discuss his property issues."

Tom turned his back on her, retreating to the kitchen window with his orange juice. Jessica could see how stiff his entire bearing still looked. She thought she heard him mumble "Whatever" before he sipped some of his juice.

Whatever, she too thought. She actually almost said it out loud, but there was no reason to reignite the fight right now. She just had to get out of there.

But before she was able to do so, she saw something among a pile of fliers that must have come in among a batch of junk mail the previous day, and Tom had left it in one corner of the kitchen counter apparently reserved for junk mail and coupons. It was a light pink flier that made her freeze on the spot. The piece of paper was similar to all the special event and "used car sale" and "roommate wanted" fliers she had seen stapled and tacked all over the CVSU campus. It was similar to the anti-Jim Garnett flier she had been given by that girl a few days ago. Except this one was much, *much* different. It had a rather crude-looking hand-drawn picture on it that made Jessica feel as if the blood had drained from her face.

She quietly pulled the flier from the pile.

The hand-drawn picture was of a monstrosity. It showed a wild-eyed man with his mouth open inhumanly wide. His gums protruded forward, studded by massive, dripping shark fangs. As talentless as the drawing might have been, though, it was easy to see what it was trying to approximate. The similarity to the corpse-eating ghoul creatures she saw was unmistakable.

So someone else had seen them, Jessica thought, her mind racing to get a grip on all the implications. Others had seen the monsters and tried to spread the word, apparently, by sneaking these shabby fliers into the local papers.

But who? she wondered. *Those students protesting Reverend Jim's new park?*

Not quite, Jessica realized a moment later. The copy on the flier read, "Behold the Apocalypse! The minions of the Antichrist are already here."

CHAPTER 57

Jessica could have shown Tom the flier from some organization called The Celebration of Salvation Mission, but she didn't. She could have tried to explain the uncanny similarity between the drawing of the Antichrist and the two naked creatures she saw in the woods. But she knew it would have accomplished nothing. Tom could not entertain the notion of the creatures being real. He would, most likely, have talked his way around it, rationalized it by saying the drawing was a standard horror story caricature of a humanoid monster with big teeth, and Jessica's stressed-out subconscious saw last night's hallucinations reflected in that drawing.

Maybe if she and Buzz could capture one of those creatures, she had mused, but decided not to obsess any more about converting Tom. Sure, maybe if Tom actually saw one of the things himself, he could be swayed. Maybe then his sense of guilt could be assuaged. In fact, he could be the most powerful ally of all in trying to convince the world these things were real. If an arch skeptic like the eminent Dr. Tom Lancaster would vouch for their existence, it would stand to reason that there might be something to the claims of interdimensional monsters after all.

But following her argument with Tom, Jessica just didn't have the energy to go another round with him. She quietly pocketed the flier and declared that she would set out to the office of her father's lawyer.

At that point, the second major frustration of this entire Cedar Valley calamity set in. She really was like a prisoner here. If she wanted to leave Tom's house alone, the cops standing watch over the place were quickly at her side and objecting strenuously. She now sat behind the wheel of her rented Maxima, tossing occasional glances into the rearview mirrors and toward the CVPD cruiser "escorting" her toward the law offices of Plummer, Struan, and Boyd.

"Come on, Buzz, damn it," she whispered and glanced at her cell phone. "Where are you?"

She, indeed, had called Jonathon Plummer and made an appointment to meet and discuss her father's estate, but she wanted to give those cops the slip and meet up with Buzz instead.

At last, when her phone did ring, she almost missed it. The shrieking horn of a fire truck barreling down the street nearly drowned out the sound of the cell ring tone's jangling rendition of the *Rocky* theme.

"Yes?" she answered upon the third ring.

"Jessica? It's me." Buzz's voice came through the line.

Relief flooded through her. "Look," she said quickly. "I'm in my car, but I've got a problem. I'm being followed around by a police car —"

"Not for long, I think," Buzz cut in. Jessica could hear the frantic edge in his voice.

"Why? What's happening?"

"It might have been the Predator. He seems to have struck in a big way. Killed an entire family and set their house on fire."

"Oh, my God," Jessica blurted out, stunned. "That must explain the fire truck."

"All units are being called to the scene," Buzz said, "so maybe the ones on your tail will —"

Jessica saw the lights on top of the cruiser behind her turn on. "Hold on," she told Buzz. "I think something's happening. I'll call this number back."

As she shut the phone off, she noticed the cop car pull up alongside her. Glancing at the vehicle, she saw its driver gesturing for her to pull over.

She did so, and the cop ran over to tell her about a multiple murder and arson investigation, just like Buzz said he would. He wanted her to go on to the attorney's office immediately — or, better yet, back home to Tom's house — and call the police station the moment she got there.

"Yeah, right," she said quietly after the cop took off. Instead, she dialed Buzz's number.

"All right," he said after she filled him in on how the cop left her to her own devices. "It sounds like we're actually pretty close to each other. You need to go to a big, nearby parking lot next to a mechanic's place on the corner of Lathrop and Evergreen. The place is called Festinger's Garage. You can't miss it."

"Good. 'Cause I think I know what we have to do right away."

"What's that?"

"Go find someone. You can't believe the flier that's being stuck in the middle of this morning's paper."

CHAPTER 58

The Celebration of the Word Ministries was housed in a sprawling, Frank Lloyd Wright-style mansion of wide walls and sweeping horizontal planes imitating the spread of the Midwestern prairie. The compound, in turn, sat somewhere in the middle of an expansive stretch of property some ten miles northeast of Cedar Valley.

Jessica thought the place to be surprisingly approachable. With an organization as controversial as that of the Reverend Jim Garnett, she'd expected there to be more security. Or, Jessica wondered, had she merely been the victim of some unconscious prejudice? The fact was that Garnett's enterprise was "controversial" as far as fringe extremist college campus activists were concerned. Recently, Garnett had been befriended by everyone from the anti-media-sex-and-violence social conservatives to environmentalist liberals.

She glanced at Buzz after pulling into one of the parking slots close to the front entrance of the Celebration building, and asked, "By the way, what's your name?"

"Say what?" he asked.

Jessica couldn't help but note somewhat of a *sharp* edge to the look in his eyes. He did a fantastic job of hiding it, to be sure, but he definitely got a start from the question.

"I tried to keep your real face out of the paper," Jessica said, "but your name is in there. And the cops are quoted as saying that they need to find you urgently. You're a *person of interest* in the investigation."

Buzz gave her an easy smile. "Yeah, thanks, by the way."

"So, give me a name we should use in there."

"How about Owen?"

"Owen?" Jessica couldn't help asking, rather than taking the name at face value. It was an odd one to choose so suddenly and so randomly. Plus, she didn't think he looked like an Owen.

"My best friend from sixth grade all the way till senior year in high school."

"Owen, huh?"

"Owen West."

"Owen West," Jessica affirmed with a nod.

They walked through the building's main entrance, finding themselves in an atrium that was overpowering in its sheer size. The prairie design motif continued dominating, with the ceiling lying rather low in proportion to the length and width of the chamber.

"Where is everyone?" Buzz asked quietly, taking the words out of Jessica's mouth.

She, too, had taken note of the absence of people. "Don't know. It'll give us some time to look around."

The walls around the massive lobby were lined with display cases. Although she couldn't see everything behind all the glass quite perfectly, Jessica noticed that the room's perimeter appeared to be a testament to all the activities, causes, and values of the Garnett organization.

"Let's see," Buzz concurred.

They started toward the nearest display case on their left. Their shoes conspicuously squeaked atop the perfectly polished marble floor. Inside the case, Jessica saw a large photograph of a grandly smiling Jim Garnett surrounded by a group of equally ebullient men, women, and children—a lot of children, as a matter of fact. The group of people around Garnett, however, was properly multicultural. Several of the male and female pairings were African American, Latino, and Asian. A golden plaque under the photo read, "Saving our Families." Separate mini poster boards detailed the Celebration of the Word organization's "battle for" America's families. The enemies Garnett and his group apparently needed to battle, according to the display, were the "lascivious," "lewd," and "violent detritus" of popular culture and popular entertainment.

Not too far from the family display, however, stood another display made up of photographs depicting rolling acres of Midwestern prairie and wheat fields, mountains, whitewater rapids, and soaring eagles. "We're all stewards of God's land," a sign over the display proclaimed. The mini poster boards proclaimed the Garnett ministries' commitment to conservation and environmental protection.

"On second thought," Jessica heard Buzz saying quietly, "this could be tougher than I thought."

She turned to him and noticed he was still studying the family display. "How's that?"

"Your writing," he said, and glanced at her with a raised eyebrow. Then he smiled lightly. "You can get a bit saucy now and again. Which, by the way, I've been actually thinking about recently."

"Oh really," Jessica said, realizing that she said it with some considerable flirtatious heat.

"Yeah. Here I am on the lam with a leading authority on relationships. A very single one at that."

Now Jessica thought about how much more attractive Buzz was in this moment of levity. For the first time since they had been thrown together in this nightmare scenario, he was smiling in a way that wasn't motivated by a bitter sort of knowing irony. There was true joy in his glance, in his tone. There was joy in his eyes as he looked deeply into hers as he carefully studied her face, her features.

Then she felt her blood pressure surge. She felt waves of warm pleasure surging through her body. And it sure was a strange time and a strange place to feel these things, she mused, wanting to laugh out loud, wishing she could throw her arms around Buzz and they could laugh about this together.

"Let's just keep it under control," she said with as serious a tone as she could. But she couldn't keep a conspiratorial little smile from creasing the corners of her mouth. "We're not going to accomplish anything here if we're not wholesome."

But just as suddenly as they had been taken by this moment of pure levity, Jessica was startled by the staccato rapping of sharp, high heels echoing across the massive atrium. Both she and Buzz turned to see an attractive, slender young brunette woman in a conservatively gray—yet strikingly tight and form-fitting—business suit approaching them.

"May I help you?" the newcomer asked.

The closer the woman got, the more amazed Jessica was by how short her skirt was for someone working in a religious organization crusading to fight the "lewd" "detritus" of modern popular culture. A moment later, Jessica thought she saw a sparkle of recognition in her eyes.

"Hi, my name is Jessica Lafayette. This is Owen West. We need to be very direct with you. It's extremely urgent that we speak to Reverend Garnett."

"I'm sorry," the brunette said, "but the reverend is not in right now. How may we be of assistance to you? We definitely will try and help with whatever—"

"Look, I'm a writer and a radio talk show host—"

The young woman cut in. "*Jessica's Real Solutions for Real Relationships*? I thought I recognized you. I saw your book at the store the other day." The woman beamed a smile at Jessica. Somehow it was both pleasant yet off-puttingly distant.

"And the other day, I was nearly killed by the Inquisitor," Jessica said. "The Reverend Garnett said some very kind things about me during an interview, and I would like to have him involved in a special I'm planning on doing right here in Cedar Valley."

"I will make sure he gets your message. Do you have a card or some information where we can—?"

"And I would like the reverend to come on my show and help me discuss the nature of these killings," Jessica cut in this time. She realized that only very sharp, insistent directness and brutal frankness would cut through this woman's boilerplate stonewalling. "I believe the two of us—myself and Reverend Garnett—know what's really going on here. Actually, I'm so glad to finally find someone like Mr. Garnett who would be willing to even talk about the truth of the situation."

"I will definitely pass along—"

Jessica interrupted again. "Just like he very clearly implied in his statements during that interview with WSBC."

"I really don't know and can't comment on anything else. But if you can give me your card...."

"But you don't understand. We need to do our show in the *morning*. It's really extremely urgent that we talk to him right away."

Jessica could see the frustration in the brunette's composure. "Really," the woman said, the tension obvious in her voice as well. "The most I can tell you right now is—"

"Tomorrow I'd like to announce how both the reverend and I know what's *really* going on here, and what the serial killer, this man the whole world thinks is just an ordinary human, is really — "

"Look, Ms. Lafayette," the Celebration representative exclaimed. "I really can't — "

But all of a sudden, a new voice echoed across the atrium. "That's all right, Natalie," a solid yet calmly mellifluous male voice called. "Let me talk to Ms. Lafayette."

A man in his late thirties, tall, clean-cut, and dressed in a navy-blue suit, approached. He smiled just as pleasantly as Natalie had when she showed up. Yet, just like Natalie, he, too, had a bearing that was at once openly friendly *and* somehow guarded.

"Hi," Jessica said simply.

"My name's Scott Palmer," the newcomer announced and shook hands with both Jessica and Buzz. "And that's all right. If you can come with me, I think I can help you."

CHAPTER 59

Although Jim Garnett might have claimed to be a new-style fundamentalist minister in deeds and political and social agendas, his tastes in interior design and furnishing were strictly old school. Just like everything in the gargantuan Celebration of the Word headquarters, the reverend's office was oversized — moreover, stately dark oak, teak, and cherry wood and polished leather dominated. Leather-bound books filled bookcases like armies of sentinels, a leather-lined cigar box sat atop Garnett's desk, and swelling leather sofas and chairs filled the room. Dark wood-paneling covered all the walls, and the centerpiece of the room was an enormous obstacle of a work table.

Soon after stepping into the room, Jessica was struck by the fact that Jim Garnett not only sounded like your folksiest uncle on the radio, but he actually looked the part. The man was of average build with a slightly jowly, dimpled face and twinkling, quickly-probing, good-humored eyes.

After introductions by Scott Palmer, Garnett shook hands with both Jessica and Buzz. Jessica noted with some surprise that the priest's grip was impressively firm. Yet, again, just like he had when speaking to the radio interviewer, Garnett exuded a very distinct duality, she thought. Not too far beneath his country charm lay something tough and disciplined.

"Glad to meet the both of you," Garnett said after the handshakes. "And again, sorry about that misunderstanding of schedules in the lobby."

"Not at all," Jessica said lightly.

"So what can I do for you?" Garnett asked.

As cool and as serious as she was hoping to be, Jessica couldn't help taking a nervous gulp of air. "Well, I need to show you something, Reverend," she said, and pulled the flier with the Antichrist from her hip pocket.

"Very direct, Ms. Lafayette." Garnett smiled broadly and took the paper from her. "I appreciate that."

"Thank you," Jessica said as the priest studied the paper.

"And time is of the essence," Buzz said.

After poring over the paper for a prolonged moment, Garnett made eye contact with both Jessica and Buzz, then said, "Yes, indeed it is."

Jessica would have thought a line like that might calm her nerves. She had, after all, disciplined herself enough to walk into a very influential and public man's office and risk making a complete idiot of herself by declaring that she believed monsters were skulking around Cedar Valley. Yet Garnett's matter-of-fact reaction to the flier seemed to make her even more jittery. His words confirmed that the world Jessica lived in only a day ago had, indeed, disappeared. She was in completely uncharted territory now, a place much darker and threatening than she could ever have imagined existed.

"That thing is real, isn't it?" she said as evenly as she could.

She studied Garnett's face, his eyes. Although he said nothing, she was sure he gave a very slight, barely perceptible nod.

"What's your connection to the group that made the flier?" Buzz asked quietly. "And what do you know?"

Garnett gave them both a pained, dismayed little smile and handed the flier back to Jessica. "We live in a frightening time," he said cryptically.

"But the people who drew that—" Jessica began.

"The Antichrist?" Garnett asked with a rueful smile. It looked so odd, and his tone sounded so vague that Jessica somehow couldn't tell whether Garnett meant to mock the idea of the Antichrist with a sarcastic voice, or if he was confirming the identity of the creature in the drawing. "Well, I know quite well that evil is a very real thing in this world of ours."

"No," Jessica said with a strong shake of her head. "No, not a real *force* of evil. I'm talking about that *thing*. I don't know much about the Antichrist, but I do know that thing, that creature, is real."

"And so do you, don't you?" Buzz asked.

"Like I said—" Garnett began.

But Buzz cut him off. "Look, we know all about politics. We know you've distanced yourself from the Apocalypse stuff."

Garnett's eyebrows shot up. Jessica thought he might have taken Buzz's comment as a personal affront. "Mr. West," he said very strongly. "I take my beliefs very seriously. I always have, and I still do."

"Expect not everyone else might," Jessica said. "But this is real. We both know it, and I think that puts us on the same side. We've both seen these things. Haven't we? Somehow you've seen them too. These monsters exist. And now we need to warn people about them. I think between the two of us—you with your national visibility and platform, and me with my own books and radio show—we could convince the world that these things are real. That they're a threat, and they're killing people."

Garnett didn't reply immediately. In fact, Jessica could see his face looking more and more graven, more worried with every word out of her mouth.

"I think you're overly optimistic, Ms. Lafayette," he said at length. "In the world we live in, you're branded a crackpot, a zealot, if you start talking about the devil, about the Antichrist. Oh, yes, I know the devil is real. He's real all right, and he's right here, in Cedar Valley. That's why I set up our headquarters here." He swept his hand through the air. "In an out of the way place like this tiny town. This is where the enemy is. And his minions are real. Demented maniacs like this Inquisitor are really tools of the devil. Except I can't talk about the devil, Ms. Lafayette. I'd be accused of being the same sort of nut as the Inquisitor."

"Listen," Jessica replied, "You wouldn't be alone. I would also—"

"Ms. Lafayette," Garnett interjected glumly, shaking his head. "I've built myself a real platform now, a real national presence. I've put Celebration of the Word Ministries and its agendas on the verge of becoming a national political power. I can only work on putting our Lord back into the political system, to make faith a part of the legislative agenda, by being as grounded and rational as I can. *That's* the first step in combating the devil and the sort of insidious power he already has over this culture. My way, my rational, reasonable public approach, is the way to take this country back from the evil one. From the evil that already has a grip on so many Americans. To take it back from the pornographers, the atheist degenerates, drug addicts, and libertines.

"I hope *now* you know I'm right. *Now* you've seen the devil yourself, and you've seen his demons. Except, you see, we can't talk about them...just yet. That's what this—what do they call themselves in the Celebration of Salvation...*splinter group?*— can't understand. They keep following me around with their outlandish conspiracy theories and the UPC bar code and all that nonsense. They want me to speak out on their behalf, but they just can't understand that it's impossible. We would be laughed right out of any TV station, out of any talk show or—"

"Wait a minute!" Buzz cut him off. "Look, man! You don't have to talk about the devil then. These things aren't even the devil or demons or whatever. They're some interdimensional life forms."

"That's what those atheist rationalists would have you believe," Garnett snapped back. "Oh, yes! The Antichrist's tools aren't pitchforks, Mr. West. The tools are those gullible, hateful, spiteful people like Tom Lancaster and his kind. I take it you know about the Jeanie Anderson incident, don't you? Willfully trying to destroy people's faith in a time when…when *children* were murdered."

"But listen, Tom is not *that* powerful," Jessica said, realizing how much her voice sounded like a desperate plea. Like she was begging. Then again, she really was. There was a stunning, frightening, *depressing* realization dawning on her. "If you and I just speak out, if we tell the world that we're willing to put our reputations on the line, we can—"

"We will be laughed at and mocked," Garnett retorted. "Don't kid yourself. People who believe in demons and monsters are held up to ridicule, Ms. Lafayette. Your people have made sure of that."

"Excuse me? *My* people?"

Garnett coughed forth an exasperated little chuckle. "Oh, come on, don't be so outraged. You know exactly what I'm talking about. What the mainstream media have been doing all these years. Painted people of faith as a bunch of unstable, illiterate wackos. The devil himself can walk among us, and if you try to do something about it, *you're* the one who's crucified as a crackpot or a bigot."

"But this doesn't have to involve religion," Jessica answered. "We just need to stand up and tell the world that—"

"Life forms, Ms. Lafayette?" Garnett said, his voice edgy,

perturbed. His eyes honed in on Jessica, and all trace of their former good humor and folksy charm were gone. "These are *not* life forms. This is the final battle, make no mistake about it. These are the minions of the beast."

"I don't believe this!" Buzz exclaimed. He sounded as defeated as Jessica felt. He, too, had realized what was happening. Garnett knew exactly what was going on in this town, but he was refusing to try and do something about it because of his ironclad dogma, his prejudices and paranoia, and his belief in the media's anti-religious conspiracies.

Garnett looked at him with a bitter half-smile. "I know that full well, Mr. West. They've already been too successful in painting men and women of faith as lunatics and villains. I won't let them get away with it any longer. I can not jeopardize what we've been working for so hard."

"Jeopardize it, how?" Jessica asked, fighting to stay as calm as she could while she really wanted to scream in Garnett's face. "By trying to save some lives?"

"Talking about monsters is not going to save any lives. And let me ask you something else."

"What?" Buzz yelled instead.

At that, Palmer took a step toward them. Jessica noticed the man took a deep breath, doing his best to puff up his chest as well as he could, apparently trying to intimidate through size.

"Hey, Mister," Palmer said angrily. "That tone is out of line."

Buzz didn't even look at him.

"The Inquisition killer," Jessica told Garnett. "He's a part of this, isn't he?"

Garnett nodded simply. "Yes, that he is. He's a tool of the demons. He's a tool to discredit me. The demons are using him to bait me. That's what he's doing here. That's why he's killing the way he is. He's trying his best to look like some stereotypical religious fanatic. Some nonsense caricature out of some Christian-hating piece of garbage, second rate Hollywood slasher film. He's a tool, so a worthless little worm like Lyle Chambers can point to those crazy, intolerant Christians again. 'See what Jim Garnett's faith creates?' he says. 'See what religion creates?' Oh, no, Ms. Lafayette…no. I can't say a word about the creatures. I think in your heart of hearts, you understand me. The power of the devil is immense. And you know how they say that the greatest power of the devil is convincing the world he doesn't exist? Well, that's not all. An even greater power than that is to convince the world that anyone who *does* believe is a dangerous, delusional fanatic."

"So, you say the answer is to do *nothing*?" Jessica asked. "Is that better? Letting people get killed for the sake of your little political empire is somehow more righteous?"

"We must protect the power of the faith at all costs," Garnett said, indeed looking and sounding like all the unstable, wide-eyed fanatics he was so desperate to distance himself from. "We can't be discredited by—"

"So the Reverend Garnett *is* the faith?" Jessica asked. "Is that what you're saying? Without you, the faith is dead? And for that, people should die?"

"You just don't understand, do you? This is not a time of *death*."

Jessica felt a cold, sinking feeling of dread in her stomach. "Oh really?"

"The Lord won't let the Antichrist rule on Earth. Oh, no! The coming of the Antichrist is but a signal that our Savior is on His way back."

"So you're saying the Inquisition killer…these creatures—"

"Are doing a service for God. *That's* what he's saying," Buzz spoke up. There was both resignation and a barely-contained force of rage in his voice.

"Listen," Garnett said, "You need to understand—"

Jessica felt Buzz's hand on her arm, giving her a slight tug. "We need to understand that this guy is a certifiable lunatic," he said.

"Hey, pal," Garnett's man, Palmer, exclaimed. "That's enough out of you."

Buzz looked at Jessica. "Come on. These people are as bad as those things in the woods."

She knew he was right. There was nothing they could accomplish here.

"Please!" Garnett called as Jessica and Buzz turned to leave. "This is very complicated…. Look, you just have to leave this alone. You're in great danger, you know. They'll never let you leave this town alive."

Jessica paused now and looked back at the minister.

"You've pushed this too far," Garnett said. "They *will* kill you. If you…. I think—I *hope*—that if you stay, I can protect you. But you can never leave this town. They *will* hunt you down."

She turned to Buzz instead. "Come on."

CHAPTER 60

"So, are we feeling motivated just about now?" the Predator said to himself as he drummed his fingers along the steering wheel of his car.

Sitting here all alone, staring off toward the Celebration of the Word compound and talking to himself, someone would have pegged him as insane, he knew. So he laughed this time, enjoying his own biting sense of humor. But the point was he felt so good right now he couldn't keep it all inside. He wanted to gloat to someone about his victory. He wanted, more than anything, to be able to laugh at Jessica as he looked in her eyes, as he savored that distant, vacant look of hopelessness in those beautiful eyes.

"It's okay," he murmured to himself. "I can feel you. I can feel your fear."

He struggled to focus, to try and reach out to Jessica, to connect with her mind. He wanted to enter her mind until the chance to look her in the eyes came. He wanted to feel her despair.

And, indeed, he felt some of it. He couldn't quite maintain the mental connection for more than a few seconds at a time, but he could feel Jessica. He felt a cold, pulsing, overpowering tide of dread washing over her/himself.

"They're not gonna help you, Jesse," the Predator said, staring fixedly toward the Garnett compound. "You're on your own."

Jessica, the Predator could feel, was just realizing how truly alone she was in this town. Not only did Lancaster refuse to believe anything she said about the "monsters" in the woods, but now she was getting the true gut-kick of her whole terrible ordeal. Even Jim Garnett, who lived and breathed the spiritual world, an avowed fighter of the devil and the dark forces, had just turned his back on her.

"There is no way out of this, Jessica," the Predator said under his breath while concentrating on that connection with her. He struggled, he strained to will these thoughts into Jessica's mind. In case her panic, her pain, her despair were not complete, he wanted to flood her mind with complete psychic agony. "You're all alone here," he said, focusing all his concentration on a mental image of Jessica. "Nobody will listen to you, ever. And I'll always know where you are. I'll never stop coming for you, Jessica."

But the connection broke when the Predator thought of Buzz McPherson.

"Bastard!" the Predator growled. "Bastard asshole fuck!" he nearly screamed as his fingers tightened around the car's steering wheel. He could imagine his grip around McPherson's throat. He wanted to slice, to claw right into McPherson's throat, to slowly find his windpipe as his blood gushed and spattered, then crush it and rip it out of his neck. "You're a dead man!"

The Predator wanted to do it right in front of Jessica. *No!* he told himself resolutely. He *would* do it in front of Jessica. He would make her watch as McPherson, her last hope in this town—in the *world*—was slowly, viciously ripped apart. He wanted to bathe her in McPherson's blood.

Furthermore, the Predator swore, he would do this with or without the Handlers' blessing. He could still feel that they were angry with him. Despite what he had done at the O'Bannon house, they let him know he was still too close to being written off as a failure. Sure, Jessica's rebuff by Jim Garnett was a perfect example of how their plan, how *his* work had created the exact intended effect, but the Handlers still showed little more than cold, disapproving disdain for him.

"And I don't care," he breathed slowly. "Do you hear me? She's *mine*."

A sudden, belligerent tapping came from the window beside his head.

The Predator snapped out of his reverie. When he turned to look at the source of the sound, he found himself staring into the barrel of a very large caliber automatic handgun clutched in Police Chief Simon Gainey's fist.

"Open the door," Gainey said bluntly. "*Now!*"

On the right side of the car, the Predator just noticed, stood one of Gainey's cops. "Jarvis," his nametag read. He, too, had his service pistol drawn and trained on the Predator.

CHAPTER 61

Only after she pulled the Maxima's door shut and locked it, did Jessica reflect on the fact that neither she nor Buzz had said a word since they left Garnett's office. The shock of what went on there, of what the folksy preacher/politician had told them, left her drained.

"Four years, was it?" she asked at length.

"What?" Buzz asked.

Jessica looked at him slowly. He, too, looked drawn, but at the same time, he still seemed strong, ready, and committed. Jessica envied him. She was amazed by his ability to remain focused on this fight.

"You've been trying to...what? Expose these creatures? Trying to stop them for four years?"

"Yeah," Buzz said quietly. "And, you're right."

"What do you mean?"

"I know what you're thinking, and you're right."

Jessica didn't reply. She couldn't bear to say the words.

"I've been looking for them, trying to stop them, expose them, *kill* them, do whatever I could to fight what's happening, and I accomplished next to nothing."

Buzz just about hit her fears on the head, Jessica thought. This realization of their complete powerlessness was what had drained her, what made her feel so beaten down.

Then she felt as if rising and receding waves of panic tried to wash over her. It was much like what she'd felt two days ago, just before witnessing the vehicular confrontation between Buzz and the Predator. It felt like a nauseating, crippling sense of utter helplessness was attempting to invade her. The sensation, she was alarmed to realize, was almost alien. The fear did not seem to originate out of her own mind but appeared to be trying to... *possess* her.

Jessica took a deep breath, fighting to concentrate and *will* that incoming specter of panic away. She chose to concentrate on, *feel* the fire of determination burning inside of Buzz. He was not ready to give up this fight, she knew full well. She wondered where that will to keep battling came from. Was it his wife? Maybe he was telling the truth about that, after all. His wife's loss could have been at the core of Buzz's zeal. Revenge for a loved one could be a powerful motivator.

Just like the creatures had killed her father, Jessica mused. Aside from her stinging, frustrating despair ignited by Garnett's nearsighted madness, she was saddened yet again by how much she was reminded of her own superficial, nearly nonexistent relationship with her father. He was but an abstraction to her. His death was not fueling the sort of driven, focused rage inside of her that seemed to possess Buzz.

"He knows," Jessica said quietly, almost whispering. "He *knows*. Garnett knows what's happening here, and he's just going to sit by and do nothing. This is insane."

"Yeah," Buzz said simply.

"Because he's afraid of damaging his image."

"To live and die by P.R."

Jessica looked at Buzz. "And what were you hoping to do here? In Cedar Valley?"

"To catch him. The Predator. He's human, and he's a connection to the creatures. That's why I've been following him.

If I can get him, maybe—"

"The creatures will show?"

"Yeah. Or maybe he can lead me to wherever they cross over." Buzz shook his head in exasperation. "See what I mean about accomplishing nothing? I don't even fully understand where they come from."

"Well, wher*ever* they come from, you think there is one specific location? Someplace we can find and expose."

A low, quiet little laugh rolled out of Buzz's mouth. "Jessica, your guess is as good as mine."

"But we know for a fact that the Predator is here."

Buzz turned away from Jessica. Did he know what she was thinking again? Was he reluctant to talk about it? If he was, it was a sign, at least, that she could trust him a while longer.

"And he wants me," Jessica said, hoping that she could gain a better sense for this enigmatic man sitting beside her as she articulated the thought. He had continually lied to her—he was probably lying to some degree right now with that stuff about his murdered wife. Yet, at the same time, all her instincts told her that he could ultimately be trusted.

Buzz turned to her again but did not yet speak.

"He wants me," Jessica said. "Maybe we could use that to our advantage."

"Advantage, huh?" Buzz said quietly, reluctantly.

"I can be bait for him. Isn't that right?"

At length, Buzz said, "Yeah. But there's something else we can use as well. Something to our advantage."

"What?"

"Something that won't hang you out as bait."

"What's that?"

"Tom Lancaster. He could be our most powerful ally."

Jessica chuckled. She couldn't help it. "You think we can win him over to our side?"

"Maybe."

"Because I don't. Not anymore. I don't know, maybe I'm just too drained, but I don't think I could make it through another debate with him about scientific empirical proof."

"Maybe we could give it one more try."

"Maybe what Garnett said is true."

"Huh?"

"Maybe neither of us will have to *volunteer* to be bait because these *things* might hunt us down soon enough."

"Hell of a time for dark humor, huh?" Buzz asked ruefully.

"I just can't think of anything else right now."

"Don't you think Tom might start wondering where you are just about now?"

Jessica felt her cell phone in her pocket. "Well, he's not going out of his way to contact me. Anyway...."

"Anyway, what?"

"When you just looked in Garnett's eyes, you saw it, didn't you? The eyes of a zealot. An extremist."

"Yeah."

"I saw that this morning. When I was arguing with Tom. But, then again...."

"But what?"

Jessica could feel his eyes boring into her, studying her. "But I thought we were as close as a man and a woman could be without being...romantically involved."

"Unless he's the zealot you described."

"There's also something else," she said at length. "Not just zealotry. He's carrying some guilt around from a time when he wasn't skeptical enough. From a time when he *should* have been. But you said you'd still like to convince him to join us. Do *you* think that's possible?"

"What Tom Lancaster's always harping on is that no one ever gives proof. Or the right *kind* of proof, that is. Proof that he'll accept. Not the UFO witnesses, not the people who've seen Bigfoot."

"So what do you want to do? Take him out into the woods? To the funeral home? You think he'd go with you?"

"No, probably not."

"Yeah, probably not."

"But we *can* take him some evidence. *You* can give him some evidence."

"What…?" Jessica asked, realizing how quizzically her voice trailed off. Buzz seemed to be taking a sudden and very peculiar turn into left field.

"I'll take you home and show you."

"Home?"

"Well, I've had to stay somewhere since I came to this town. There's some stuff there I'd like to show you."

"What stuff?"

"I'll let it speak for itself. I'll tell you which way to go."

Buzz started sounding very weird again. Whenever that happened, Jessica had learned by now, things were bound to get very unpredictable…

…and deadly.

CHAPTER 62

The Predator sat in the back of Jarvis's squad car, astonished at how inept the cop had been when it came to frisking a suspect. Apparently, once Jarvis found a gun on his target, he immediately assumed his job was over. Perhaps in Cedar Valley, Southern Illinois, small-time hoods never carried more than one weapon at a time. So, as much as he disliked having to rely on one, the Predator could still use the Tigershark combat knife strapped onto his left forearm and concealed by his jacket. Not having been handcuffed also helped matters.

"I don't believe we're going toward the police station," the Predator spoke up at last.

Indeed, now he was sure their car was heading away from Cedar Valley.

Simon Gainey, sitting in the front passenger seat, turned to him. He had a look of disgusted, impatient condescension smeared on his face.

"*You*," the chief said, "are here to shut the fuck up and listen. You understand? You listen, you take mental notes, and do as you're told. If you've missed anything, you ask me to repeat it, 'cause you had better not get any of the instructions wrong. Now, did you understand everything I just told you?"

Of course, the Predator realized, *this all makes sense now*. He understood exactly what Gainey and his half-wit flunky were doing. The Predator was the one who should have been disgusted.

"Are these the new Miranda rights, Chief?" he asked. He was curious how Gainey would react.

The muscles in Gainey's jaw twitched. The Predator thought he would start snarling like a dog any moment now. Maybe foam at the mouth.

"Listen to me, you freak," Gainey said in slow, measured tones. "*You* are expendable. Do you understand? You are a tool. *You* were chosen for a job. But you can be replaced. Do you understand...you *freak*?"

The Predator could feel something hot flush through his face. This insect would have to die for what he just said. But the Predator couldn't allow this second-rate hillbilly crossing guard to get a reaction out of him.

"I did my job at the O'Bannon home," the Predator said calmly. "Did I not? Did I not set everything up as I was supposed to?"

"After you let *him*—and that woman—almost kill two of our Handlers," Gainey hissed.

The Predator wanted to spit in his face. This inferior, worthless maggot was not worthy of speaking their names. Neither Gainey nor Jarvis had even been blessed by any of the Handlers' essence. The Predator was sure of it. He could sense it. Neither of the cops had been given any of the Handlers' blood. If they had, it was so minuscule as to be insignificant. If they had gotten a taste of the Handlers, it was so small as to make them no better than the lowest street junkie who had been given a tiny hit of heroin. These imbeciles might have been granted a moment's exposure to the power, just enough to make them willing slaves. They were lower than the dog shit the Predator would scrape off the bottom of his shoe.

"*He* is not my responsibility," the Predator said, proud of his well-controlled tones, proud of his superiority. "*He* has been running around in your own back yard for days now, yet you don't even know what he looks like."

"What?" Gainey stumbled.

"The picture she gave you is not accurate. Looks nothing at all like him. She's been protecting him since the mall."

The police chief turned around to look out through the front windshield. After a moment's silence, he slammed a fist on top of the dashboard. "Bitch!" he roared. The cop's head snapped back toward the Predator. "Why was I not given more information?"

"I didn't even know who, besides the people at the funeral home, could be trusted. And until two days ago, no one sensed that he was here. He knows how to keep himself hidden."

"They didn't tell you about me and Jarvis? Or the other three?"

The cop left himself wide open for a nice little retaliation now, the Predator realized with great relish. So he coolly said, "I guess they didn't deem you important enough to mention."

"Ah, damn it," Jarvis spoke up at last.

The Predator decided not to even look at him.

"Because the Handlers probably thought you'd be competent enough to kill him on your own by now," Gainey said, glowering at the Predator, taunting him.

Of course, the Predator knew he was far too superior to rise to this peon's bait. He stared back at the cop with no show of emotion.

"You listen to me, you sick bastard," Gainey said. "I'm telling you for the last time — and this is coming from *them*. You understand? The Handlers themselves. You do your *job!* You do as you're told. And that means you better keep your pathetic hard-on under control. You know what that means? You carry out your assignments, and you leave the Lafayette woman alone. You had your chance, and you blew it. Now you stay away from her. The Handlers have their own plans for her."

The Predator remained impassive, but the blood pounded in his ears. He would *never* let Jessica go.

Then the car suddenly turned. They had departed the main highway along a stretch of wooded, overgrown wilderness, shuddering along a poorly-graveled access road of some kind. About a minute later, the police cruiser came to a stop. Jarvis was the one to get out of the car first. He circled around to the passenger side. There he opened the Predator's door and quickly reached inside.

The Predator saw Gainey opening his own door.

"Get the hell out," Jarvis said, and grabbed the Predator's right shoulder. The cop gave him a violent, jarring yank.

The Predator could see Jarvis's right hand balling into a hard fist as he pulled him out.

"And make sure you don't forget," Jarvis hissed while pulling his right elbow backward, cocking his arm to punch the Predator.

So the Predator struck first. He ripped the knife from his sleeve and thrust its blade into Jarvis while moving forward. To thoroughly incapacitate the cop upon first strike, the Predator did not merely stab forward, but upward. He slammed the knife's point under Jarvis's chin, stabbing through his mouth and impaling his entire head. Although short enough to disappear under a sleeve, the knife did have enough of a blade to skewer into Jarvis's brain once the Predator inserted it all the way until the hilt touched the bottom of the man's chin. Geysers of blood shot out of Jarvis's mouth, and nose as his eyes instantly turned glassy.

"Fuck!" Gainey screamed as Jarvis expired.

Out of the left periphery of his vision, the Predator could catch a glimpse of the chief going for his gun. That move, of course, was what the Predator expected and had been prepared for. So, before Jarvis hit the ground, he yanked the dead cop's service piece from its holster and turned it on Gainey, all the while thumbing its safety open.

Although the chief was quick on the draw, he wasn't quite quick enough. The Predator sent a nine-millimeter round into his stomach, doubling him over and letting him stumble back against the squad car. Gainey's weapon slipped from his fingers.

At that point, with Gainey still standing upright, the Predator pounced on him and jabbed Jarvis's gun straight at his mouth. Although it took some doing, the Predator was successful in what he had been aching to try for a long time. He thrust the pistol deep into Gainey's mouth, then pulled the trigger.

The blast removed the entire back of the chief's skull.

CHAPTER 63

Tom Lancaster did not believe that opposites attracted. The funny thing, Jessica thought, was that she and Tom were hardly such opposites. She was not a UFO cultist or a proselytizing religious fundamentalist, she didn't believe in astrology, and she had never consulted a psychic in her life. She even liked the idea of bringing the strictest, most rigorous rational scientific mindset to the exploration of uncanny, unexplainable phenomenon.

But unfortunately, she had also seen an interdimensional ghoul. She wouldn't have minded Tom questioning her about it in the most thorough, most rigorously scientific manner either. However, Tom's mind had already been made up. He just could not bring himself to keep an open mind, to give her the benefit of the doubt. That was the only way to explain his cold demeanor on the phone a half an hour ago.

He would be at school on a faculty function all afternoon, and all evening, he had curtly told her when she called. When she told him that she would be looking through financial papers at her father's house, that she was sure to be swamped with work, and she would much rather spend the night there, he hardly put up any objections. He appeared concerned that the police go out there and keep an eye on her, but even that suggestion had a dryly perfunctory sound.

Maybe, she reasoned, the "breakup" — if that was the proper word for it — could be compared to a man and a woman having radically different religious or political beliefs and being incapable of building a relationship around those beliefs.

"So, you still think we could talk him into taking our side?" Jessica asked as the silence in the Toyota seemed to stretch on and on. Aside from road instructions, Buzz had not said too much since they left the Celebration of the Word headquarters.

"We can try one last time," he replied.

Jessica glanced at him and wondered if he would mind all that much if they couldn't make an ally out of Tom. His flirtations back at the lobby of the Garnett base kept replaying in her mind. And she knew she did not mind Buzz's advances at all.

At the very least, she mused as she returned her gaze to the darkening road ahead—spared more and more by an ever-diminishing early evening sun—her stay in Cedar Valley was in no way boring.

CHAPTER 64

Buzz's "home" was a painfully old farmhouse that had been rented out on a monthly basis by the property's owner. The land it sat upon was on the market. If anyone bought it, chances were the house was going to be torn down and replaced by something much larger. Perhaps it would be an ultra-upscale, fully-loaded new estate house for some engineer or well-funded researcher doing high tech work at CVSU.

Aside from the kitchen and the bedroom, the house stood empty now.

"The bedroom, the kitchen, and the basement, actually," Buzz said after giving Jessica the less than grand tour upon arrival. "The things I have to show you are best kept away from prying eyes. Come on, this way."

After opening a padlock on the basement door, Buzz led her below on a disturbingly creaky stairway.

"You think this thing'll take both our weights?" Jessica asked as they descended into the basement.

"Don't worry," Buzz called over his shoulder. "The whole house is this loud, actually. But it's good for us."

"It is?"

"No one can sneak in without us noticing."

Once they reached the basement proper, Jessica noticed a setup that was, at once, both entirely functional and minimally accommodating. A small table in one corner of the room held a coffee-maker and a large supply of paper cups and filters, not to mention a very big canister of coffee. An unregenerate caffeine addict—Jessica liked the look of that. A small couch sat nearby. Underneath the coffee table lay a big red cooler. Coffee, food, and a resting place were all provided in case Buzz had to stay down here for long stretches at once.

But the rest of the basement appeared to be set up for the storing of information. There were cardboard boxes stacked in several locations. In the middle of the room, a large table held a thin laptop computer hooked up to a printer and a scanner. More file folders and newspapers sat atop the desk. Surrounding the desk were four large corkboards. Although she couldn't make out the exact details, Jessica saw that the boards were all covered by a mosaic of papers, note cards, photos, and newspaper and magazine clippings. Buzz McPherson had been quite busy down here.

"What have you been doing?" she asked as she tried to get a better look at the contents of the cork boards.

"Looking for traces," Buzz said vaguely and went to the nearest board. "Come on, take a look."

"Traces?" Jessica asked as she walked over.

"Yeah, traces of the Predator and the creatures pulling his strings."

A moment later, Jessica realized that the basement could just as well have been the editorial board of the most outrageous of supermarket tabloids. And not even a celebrity-gossip-style tabloid either. This was the realm of the wackiest of papers, the ones that fabricated stories of two-headed alien vampires and rock stars brainwashing their fans into Satanism at the behest of the Illuminati.

The first board was topped by a handwritten index card with the inscription "Wisconsin Werewolf" on its face. The rest of the space was taken up by articles clipped from newspapers, magazines, books, as well as pictures, both professionally painted and hand-drawn. Jessica was startled by whimsical renditions of hairy, glowering, fanged creatures that could have been displayed in a catalog of Halloween costumes. Upon closer look, she saw that Buzz had carefully underlined, highlighted, and annotated all the reams of printed materials on this "Wisconsin Werewolf." Sprinkled among all the clippings, she saw handwritten notes from notebooks tacked on the board as well. Had it not been for her experience in the woods on the outskirts of town, Jessica would have run for the door. She surely would have thought this collection of werewolf data was the work of a dangerously unstable mind.

"This looks like madness, but I know it's not," she found herself whispering.

"Unfortunately, it's not," Buzz replied quietly.

"So this werewolf business," she said as she tried to peruse the contents of the clippings. "This is really all about those things...the interdimensional creatures we saw?"

The newspaper stories, Jessica saw, were all written with the light, winking tone of fluff pieces local newspapers printed on a slow day when they had nothing to report from the local school board meeting or a parade sponsored by the Rotary Club.

"And that's exactly what they want," Jessica mumbled.

"What's that?" Buzz asked.

"The people in these stories. The ones who saw the werewolves; they all sound like babbling lunatics. I bet these creatures did their very best to be seen. They *wanted* people to think they're werewolves. I mean, what else have they imitated? Vampires? Aliens? The Frankenstein monster?"

"Check this out," Buzz said, and pointed to another board.

This one was dedicated to the West Virginia Mothman. The

one next to that was titled "Florida Skunk Ape." Jessica saw that it had a rather large subheading dealing with "Sasquatch/Bigfoot." The fourth board was a compilation of stories on "Cannibalism/ The Satanic Underground."

"Good God," Jessica gasped.

"Yes, these things do want to be seen," Buzz said. "In as many forms as possible. That way, none of them will be believed."

"Shapechangers," Jessica said as something occurred to her. "You said shapechangers last night, didn't you?"

She saw Buzz nodding grimly.

"That's why these things can appear as just about anything," Jessica said. "Isn't that right? They constantly alter their appearance."

"I think so, yeah. Something like that."

"You think so?" Jessica asked, realizing her voice might have been too snappish. But Buzz's constant equivocations were frustrating her.

"Look, I don't have some sort of a playbook, or an anatomy book on what those things are…how they function. I have some guesses, though."

"All right," Jessica said, hoping she didn't sound confrontational. "It's just that this setup…."

"Yeah. Makes me look like an expert? I wish."

"How do they change shapes?" Jessica asked, almost immediately thinking of the idea's truly horrifying implication. "And if they can, are they…?"

"Around us all the time? Walking next to you in the street?"

"Yeah."

"No. As far as I can tell, at least, no."

"But how do you know?"

"I think there's something—something in this world, in this atmosphere maybe…or maybe something's missing that they need to live—that prohibits them from just living around us all the time."

"Okay, go on," Jessica asked. "What else do you know about them?"

"Well, there's a guess I can make. And again, what we need is an expert, a doctor, a geneticist to comment on all this. But I think that might be the key to their flesh-eating—the blood-drinking. I think something's linked to human DNA. They can eat flesh, and they're able to instantly read...I don't know... replicate the DNA and become partially, temporarily human. Or they can look human for a very short time to actually move about in our world. And I would guess that if they exposed themselves to animal DNA—say wolves—then you have yourself—"

"The Wisconsin Werewolf," Jessica couldn't help blurting out.

"Exactly."

"Wait a minute," Jessica muttered, feeling like her mind was reeling, feeling almost literally thrust off balance by this information. "So if these things in the woods ate that dead man, they could assume his shape?"

"Yes," Buzz said quietly. "Of course, they looked human already when they started eating. But those...*shapes* they were in, they were merely the reproduction of others they had consumed."

"What do they look like in their true forms?"

"I'm not sure. I've only seen...partial transformations, I guess. Or maybe *deformations* would be the better word. Imagine the complete breakdown of the human body. Limbs, skin, skeleton, stretching, altering, reforming into something completely alien."

"I can't believe this," Jessica muttered almost involuntarily.

"I know," Buzz said. "It's unbelievable. And that's the problem."

"Dissonance," Jessica corrected.

"What's that?"

"The theory of cognitive dissonance."

"Oh?"

"Refusing to believe things that are provable through incontrovertible evidence because it makes you feel uncomfortable. Like people who believe that the earth is flat and it's impossible to change their minds."

"Dissonance theory, huh?" Buzz said with a cocked eyebrow.

"Yeah. Also known as having your head up your ass."

"It's a very good theory," Buzz said, and shook his head with a wry grin. "Come here," he added a moment later. "Let me show you something else."

He led Jessica to the cannibalism/Satanic cult board. Looking at some of the subheadings tacked on the board, Jessica thought Buzz might have been consulting with a team of unemployed horror movie writers. There were labels like "The World-Wide Satanic Underground," "Oscar Telecast is a Secret Satanic Ritual," "FEMA Concentration Camps for Human Harvesting," and "Blood-Drinking Cult Initiations."

"You can not be serious," Jessica gasped, looking at a lot of handwritten notes all over the board. "The Oscars?"

"I'm not," Buzz said. "Although I think I could sell some of this stuff to Hollywood for some really great movies."

"I was thinking the exact same thing."

"Documentation keeps cropping up to support this stuff. Mountains of allegations and true-life accounts all over the Internet. 'I survived Satan's death cult.' 'I was a bride for Lucifer.' 'I had sex with shape-changing she-demons that drank my blood.' 'Cannibal cults from hell.' That sort of thing. Again, if I were a movie producer, I could make a fortune off this stuff."

"So what is all this? The documentation, the allegations — all fake?"

"Yeah," Buzz said. Although his tone was light, Jessica could also sense that its levity was somehow forced. There was a frustration lurking underneath his words. "This stuff is so insane, so far over the top, that anyone who would even give it a moment's serious consideration would come across as an unstable fanatic."

"Like the Predator," Jessica whispered. "That's why he's doing what he's doing. And he's playing Garnett and that salvation splinter group like a Stradivarius. Make one of them look like crackpots and the other, the more powerful and respectable group, cover up for the creatures on purpose — "

"To avoid dissonance, right?" Buzz said with a bitter, ironic chuckle.

"How can we stand a chance against this?"

"Jessica," Buzz said, and got up from behind the computer. "These things are playing everyone. Driving us crazy with our own fears, private little hatreds, and paranoia. *Somehow* we should try and get Tom on our side, but do you think there's any chance of that at all? Any approach we can try and use?"

"I'm not sure. He's living with a lot of guilt over what happened in a UFO suicide-cult case years ago. But we're also up against killers. Killers who've murdered my father. Tom's *friend*."

Buzz nodded. "Hopefully, that's something we can use to get him on our side."

"But you have something else, too. You said that, didn't you? You can show Tom something that will help our case."

"Yeah," Buzz said at length. "There's something we can try."

CHAPTER 65

"Sure, I could have put this under some loose floorboards," Buzz said as he pulled the large, dark-blue duffel bag from a pile of similar bags in one corner. "There are loose boards all over the place."

"But you could hide it in plain sight," Jessica replied.

Buzz looked at her and winked. "Exactly."

"What is it? What's the key to winning Tom over to our side?"

"Come on," Buzz said, and carried the bag over to the table. He placed it on top and opened its zipper. "Right here. Hard, irrefutable empirical proof."

He reached inside the bag and removed what looked like a bundle of rags wrapped around something roughly the size of a handball.

"Hiding it in plain sight, all right," Jessica couldn't help saying.

"Yeah, looks like it could be my dirty laundry...but it's not!"

"So, what's inside?"

When Buzz removed the wrapping of old clothing, he was holding something jagged, misshapen, yet disturbingly organic. Upon closer look, Jessica thought....

"Oh, my God!" she gasped. "Is that?"

"Yes," Buzz said. "One of them." He met her gaze, looking deeply, grimly into her eyes. "It's the skull of one of the creatures."

"How did you...?" Jessica began, but couldn't finish the

sentence. Her attention was riveted to the monstrous, revolting, yet utterly fascinating object in Buzz's hands.

The skull looked something like a human skull — *roughly*, at least, Jessica reconsidered. Its size was somewhere in the same ballpark. However, it did have what looked like an abnormal bulge in its rear hemisphere. It appeared to be swept backward. It made her think of those ancient Aztec skulls, the remains of people whose heads were bound shortly after birth to flatten the foreheads. But, more than just deformed in its growth and development, the skull in Buzz's hands looked jagged, angular. There was an inherent *wrongness* about it. The words that came to the forefront of Jessica's mind were *alien* and *corrupted*. In fact, the closer she looked at the skull, the more and more disturbed she was by it. For one, she noticed that one of its eye sockets was larger than the other. That same socket was bordered on top by a protruding, simian brow ridge.

Moreover, the forehead and the top of the skull seemed to be spotted by tiny, jagged protrusions. The only way Jessica would have been able to describe them would have been as resembling horns. But their clustering around mid-forehead and reaching over the skull made them look vaguely saurian. They looked like the horned protrusions on the head of a crocodile or some such large lizard. Although the jawbone was missing, what remained of the creature's upper row of teeth offered no shortage of phantasmagorical spectacle. The gum line seemed to protrude forward. Much like the one oversized brow ridge, it looked perversely apelike, primeval. What was much worse, though, was the appearance of the creature's teeth. Much like the thing Jessica had seen transforming, mutating in the woods, the skull's teeth were pointed, elongated, and sharp. Although one of its canines was missing — broken, perhaps, in whatever calamity brought down the monster — its remaining counterpart

THE CEDAR VALLEY COVENANT

was impossibly long, wicked-looking, and sharp.

"This is incredible," Jessica whispered. "Absolutely incredible."

"Yeah," Buzz said, and placed the skull on the table. "But hopefully enough to get some sense into Tom."

"Where did you get this?" Jessica asked, still feeling beside herself with astonishment over Buzz's possession of the monstrosity.

He gave her an intense look before replying, "The good news is they're not indestructible."

"You killed it?"

"Yeah. They're very tough, but they can be killed. Actually, you can go as far as wounding them very badly. Making them unconscious. If they're stuck in this world long enough, they will die."

"And this one," Jessica said, nodding toward the thing on the table. "Did you kill it while it was in human form?"

"No," Buzz said with a frustrated wince in his eyes. "And there, you see, is the rub."

"I was afraid of that."

"Yeah, I guess you can see where this is going."

"If you suspect a person is...is one of them...."

"What are you going to do about it?"

"Oh, my God. Nobody would believe you. There *is* nothing you can do."

"Not if you don't want to be tried for murder."

"This is too much." Jessica couldn't help but mutter.

"Yeah, unfortunately, that's the case," Buzz said, and started wrapping the gruesome skull back in the collection of ratty old clothes.

Jessica drifted back toward the cork boards encircling the table. Looking at all the material tacked on each board, looking at all those clippings, claims, hypotheses, and outlandish speculations, Jessica realized that, indeed, the skull was the only hope they had. There was no other way any half-rational individual was likely to take them seriously. The creatures had done too good of a job of hiding in plain sight for that.

But staring at all the newspaper clippings reminded her of something else. She thought of a problem that had been nagging at her since the morning.

"Buzz," she said at length. "Can you tell me about your wife?"

He met her gaze but didn't reply immediately. She knew that he knew what she was thinking.

"How about I tell you everything over a cup of coffee?" he said eventually.

CHAPTER 66

Their heart-to-heart conversation was bound to go well, Jessica realized, upon tasting the coffee Buzz had brewed. He could make an incredible cup of java.

They had moved onto the porch and sat on its swinging bench, watching the pristine-clear western sky fade into an indigo darkness as the sun completely disappeared.

"April moved up from the police beat to covering celebrities on South Beach," Buzz continued his recollection of life with April McPherson in Miami. In fact, they hadn't been married at the time of her death, only engaged.

Just as last night, Jessica couldn't help but notice the even tones he spoke in. Again, she was taken by the fact that it was much more than the sound of a man who had learned to move on with his life and leave its greatest tragedy in the past. The loss of April was very much something that Buzz still lived with, still carried around, but it was manageable because of something else. He could move on — sort of — because of all the guns he had stockpiled in the basement. The computer, the databases, the newspaper clippings, the research, the mission of revenge, had given him something to replace the grief.

She gently brushed her forearm against his after lowering the coffee cup from her mouth. She wondered if something else could take the place of vengeance for Buzz to go on.

"She didn't care for it much, did she?" Jessica asked. "The

so-called entertainment journalism?"

Buzz smiled faintly. "Writing exposéss of who was seen eating lunch with who is not real journalism, she would say."

"She was a great reporter, wasn't she?"

"Yeah, she would have become one. This story about the cover-up in the disposal of the dead prisoners would have made her career. And I told her to go for it...." Buzz's voice faded out into a sort of edgy pause. "I'm not sure how to feel about it even after all these years."

"It sounds like she would have gone for it no matter what," Jessica said, and almost immediately noticed Buzz smiling.

"Yeah," he said quietly.

"And you loved her for that, didn't you?"

"Yeah. That...that drive, that fire, that's exactly why I loved her."

Jessica felt strange, conflicting emotions now. Her heart surged at what Buzz just said, but the feeling was haunted by guilt, too. She would have loved to have a man tell her that just once. Perhaps Buzz would do so soon. Was she being predatory longing for that, she wondered, sitting here knowing that the one woman Buzz did speak those words to would never be competition for her?

"She must have appreciated that," she said softly.

"I know...and for four years, I've been trying to survive without her."

"But at least for a little while, you two were perfect together."

Buzz didn't reply this time, and Jessica was glad for it. How was it possible to address anyone who'd been through Buzz's tribulations with trite platitudes you made up on the spot?

"You know," she said, deciding that perfect honesty was the only thing to speak right now. "I've never had a relationship like that. I envy you for what you had with April."

Buzz looked at her. The way he studied her eyes, her face, there was something still so inscrutable about him. "Oh really?" he said.

"I've been involved with very driven men who never put our relationship high on a list of priorities. Those were relationships that would usually end when I discovered their affairs—high-powered business types. World-beaters couldn't be tied down to one woman. And I'd always be dumb enough not to see the red flags when a guy told me on a first date that he loved to enjoy everything the world has to offer. My other relationships were the guys who were threatened by my accomplishments. It's not easy being a successful writer in a part of the country where one out of every three people is working on his big screenplay. And yes, I did become a successful writer giving others relationship advice. Makes you wonder, doesn't it?"

Buzz chuckled at that. Jessica loved hearing the easy, good humor in it. The man who stockpiled weapons in the basement didn't seem to be present right then.

"That's a statistical fact, you know," Jessica teased. "One out of every three people in Southern California is working on a screenplay. Most of the guys I meet are usually interested in getting to know my agent more than me."

"I'm sorry," Buzz said with another light laugh.

"Yeah, I know, poor little rich girl. Nobody loves her for who she really is. Not much sympathy for my problem, I know."

"No, there isn't," Buzz said with a quick, smooth deadpan.

Jessica couldn't—and didn't want to—hold back her own laughter. They needed to laugh at last. After all that had happened to them, what they needed to survive, perhaps as much as the guns and the battle plans, was the laughter now.

"So, you think your agent would be interested in a book based on our Cedar Valley adventures?" Buzz asked, and they continued cracking up.

After a few blissful moments of just looking into Buzz's eyes, Jessica said, "All of that sounds trivial now, doesn't it?"

"Relationships? Love? Not really."

After the jokes, Jessica was moved by the honest, weighty sincerity in Buzz's words. She felt her heart surging, as a matter of fact.

"I'm sorry," Buzz said. "I shouldn't have said that right now. With everything you're trying to deal with—"

"No!" Jessica cut him off. "I'd really like that too."

She could see what Buzz was about to do from the way his eyes studied hers, from the way he was probing her reactions, and she couldn't wait for him to do it.

Their lips met, and their mouths melted together. Buzz's kisses, his caresses, the longing in his eyes, in his touch, made it clear that the past was gone for both of them.

"And I was serious about that, you know." Buzz's whispered words brushed past Jessica's right ear.

"What?"

Buzz pulled away from her enough to look at her eyes. "Writing a book about this and getting your agent to sell it."

Jessica giggled back at him. "You're joking."

Buzz kissed her, then said, "No, I'm not. That could, quite possibly, be the only thing that might keep us alive."

"So let me ask you one thing," Jessica said, and returned Buzz's kiss.

"What's that?"

"What *is* your real name?"

"Well, Buzz *is* my nickname. That was the truth."

"Okay. And you are...?"

"Owen West."

The name from yesterday, Jessica realized. "That's *really*—"

Buzz leaned over and kissed the tip of Jessica's nose. "Yes, that's my real name. But I think Buzz would look better on the cover of our book."

"How about Buzz West?" Jessica asked, and kissed his lips, slowly thrusting her tongue into his mouth.

After enjoying her kiss for a very long, very arousing moment, Buzz winked at her and said, "Sounds like an insect infestation."

At first, Jessica needed to kiss him yet again, but then she whispered, "I don't think this swing is going to work."

"The bed upstairs will," Buzz replied quickly.

CHAPTER 67

The building the Predator took refuge in was not big, but it was big *enough*. In the midnight darkness, lying on an abandoned, weed-grown street in an area that had always been on the outskirts of Cedar Valley, what might once have been a store and an office facility was now a crumbling, decaying obstacle course no one in his right mind would have ventured into even in bright daylight.

Just as the Predator hoped, the car that came to meet him did not get too close to his hiding place. If the vehicle's occupant had designs on rushing him, coming into the dark hulk of the ancient building, a lot of blood was bound to be spilled. Sure, he knew the odds were against him in such a confrontation. The building was not that big. They could, soon enough, corner him and kill him, but not before he took several of his assailants with him.

Then the Predator concentrated, reaching out with his mind. He tried to *feel* for the people in the car. Who were they? *What* were they? Were they imbued with the Handlers' powers the same way he was? Simon Gainey had, after all, told him that there were at least three others on the police force who were in on the Handlers' secrets. If they had the Handlers' powers, the Predator realized, they might try and track him psychically. That was, of course, if he didn't notice them, and he couldn't block their mental probes.

But the Predator couldn't feel anything from the car. Perhaps the people inside were just like Gainey and Jarvis, the lowest of the low. They might have been helping the Handlers for a promise of one day being given incredible otherworldly powers. Straining his eyes against the darkness, the Predator recognized the shape of the car. He could see the outline of the lights on the roof. It was a police car, just like Gainey had suggested.

At last, the driver's door swung open. Only one person got out. Although the Predator could see the figure's hard, sturdy moves, he could also recognize a definitively feminine shape under the uniform. It must have been the woman cop on one of the "bodyguard" details posted at Tom Lancaster's house.

"That's far enough," the Predator called out once the cop was within twenty or so feet of the building. He instinctively tightened his grip on the pistol in his hand.

"Listen!" the woman cop called out. "We've obviously run into a problem here, but it can all be fixed. You understand?"

"By sending people to kill me?" the Predator replied.

"Gainey and Jarvis didn't want to kill you."

"Yeah, just rough me up, right? Teach me a lesson?"

"The Handlers are running this show, aren't they? They're the ones who give the orders."

The cop paused. She sounded like she expected the Predator to admit that he had come to see reason.

He wanted to do no such thing but knew that in a way, she was right. As powerful as he might have felt when on his own, the abilities granted by these otherworldly creatures were also their leash on him. They were, in every sense of the word, his handlers.

"But they don't want to kill you," the cop called out to him again. "They put an operation into place here that has to be pulled off according to their plans. The Handlers are calling the shots. We all know that. We have to listen to them, but they also need you. They need you to finish what you started." She paused once more.

"So we go on from here?" the Predator replied this time.

"Yes. There is one more thing you need to do here...and then you can have Jessica Lafayette."

The Predator's heart began to hammer. "No interference this time?"

"You do your job, and afterward, you get to do with her whatever you want."

The Predator tucked the handgun into the waistband of his pants and took a few steps forward. He could tell the cop saw him emerging from the murk within the building's wreckage.

"That's a good trade, isn't it?" the cop asked.

"Yes."

"All right," the cop said, and took a few steps toward the Predator. "Within twenty-four hours, she's all yours."

"And everything else is all set up?"

"You know the place. There will be a truck filled to capacity with TNT. All you have to do is walk in there and take it."

"The demolition company, right?"

"Yes. A truckload of this stuff will put a crater the size of Cedar Valley in the ground."

The Predator could feel sweat beading on his brows now. The ecstasy of contemplating such destruction literally put a sweet, sugary taste in his mouth.

"Well, more or less," the cop said, and chuckled. "We're going to want those forensics tech guys to find pieces of the rosary beads you'll leave in the truck's cab. We're going to find a crumpled flier from the Garnett ministries at the construction site. Crazy bunch of religious nuts finally go too far and cross the line into domestic terrorism. Has a nice sound, doesn't it? Blowing up nearly the entire Cedar Valley U campus when they want to kill a convention of those degenerate, Darwin-worshipping scientists.

Spectacular."

"Sure is," the Predator whispered.

He, in fact, was truly impressed. The plan was the Handlers at their best, playing all sides against the middle. After the P.R. blow this would deliver to all the holy-rollers across the country, the Handlers could emerge on their front lawns, take the shape of horned, pointy-tailed devils, and Jim Garnett and his ilk could still not utter a peep about demons and the Antichrist ever again.

CHAPTER 68

"I went to a hotel, actually," Jessica told Tom over the phone, her nerves tensing. She was getting worried about how much bluffing she could get away with. Was he going to ask which hotel? There weren't that many of them in Cedar Valley.

"You should have come back to my house," he said. There was still some of that reassuring warmth in his voice, Jessica thought, except now it sounded like he was *trying* to put it there.

"I was worried about the cops being occupied with everything that's been going on."

When Buzz had checked the web page of the Cedar Valley Journal this morning, they read about the full pandemonium that went on yesterday. First, an entire family got killed, then the police chief and one of his officers, Jarvis—the one Jessica thought looked like *Our Gang*'s Alfalfa—were ambushed and murdered.

"Look, Jessica, the cops would have protected you still. If this Inquisitor maniac is on a spree, they know you're a target—"

"Tom!" Jessica cut him off. "It's okay. I actually feel better this way. No one knows where I am, and I can stay on the move. I like it like this."

"It's not safe," Tom protested.

"It is for me."

"Jessica, the only way you can be safe is with the police looking after you."

"I bet they have their hands full with their own investigation."

"I just heard the state police, and the FBI will be sending people in here."

"Tom, you're at the school now, aren't you? Isn't that what you said? Until how long this afternoon?"

"To hell with that! It's some useless intercollegiate symposium."

"Whatever," Jessica said, unwilling to even try and decipher his academic, administrative jargon. When she glanced toward Buzz, he waved at her to hurry the conversation along. "Look, Tom, just stay there, and I will come to you later, I promise."

"When?" Tom demanded petulantly.

"Later, okay?" she insisted, making her voice sound strong and resolute, but hopefully not combative. "Listen, I have another problem I'm still dealing with, and I just need some space for this—"

"Have you been contacted by McPherson?" Tom asked suddenly. Actually, Jessica thought his tone had an angry, accusatory edge.

"No, I haven't," she fired back. This time, she made no effort to disguise her anger. "Tom, I said there's something I need to handle alone, okay? I'm in touch with Cassie, and it's very emotional...a very tough time for me right now, all right? Please try and respect that."

Actually, she felt her face burning all of a sudden. She wondered if she had flushed completely red. She felt angry, ashamed, almost, for turning to Cassie and using her as a part of a lie to keep Tom at a distance.

"All right, Jessica," Tom's voice softened. "I understand what you're going through—"

"Tom, please," she cut him off. "If you really understand, then please don't push me. I just need a little time to myself today. I'll come by your house...when? This afternoon?"

"All right," Tom said curtly.

"Around six o'clock or so, okay?" Jessica asked, and looked at Buzz.

He nodded vigorously.

They had decided the meeting should be as late as possible, preferably around the time the sun was close to going down. They didn't know how long it would take to try and persuade Tom, even with the show-and-tell they planned for Buzz's warped, monstrous skull artifact. In case Tom was not being swayed, in case the cops made a special guest appearance, Jessica and Buzz wanted the cover of darkness to help them make their escape.

"Sure, six o'clock is fine," Tom said.

"I'll see you then," Jessica said simply, and pressed END on her cell phone. "And let's hope we're not walking into a trap," she added and looked at Buzz.

He appeared to be stunningly calm as he let his gaze drift out the window and across the placid prairie landscape surrounding the house. Shirtless, barefoot, and with a head of tousled morning hair, wearing only his jeans, sipping a cup of coffee, he looked superhumanly—almost annoyingly—cool and collected, given the situation they were in. The fact that he looked fantastic should have lightened Jessica's mood. She would have wanted nothing more than to wrap her arms around him and coax him back into bed, had this been a normal day. But this was nothing even remotely close to a normal day. They were no longer living in a normal world.

Nonetheless, Jessica approached him and put an arm around his waist. She, too, was almost naked, except for one of Buzz's oversized T-shirts she had slipped on. It wasn't quite the time to entice him back into bed for a late morning retreat into love-making, but she did decide to make what she could of his ultra cool composure. She would try and use it for reassurance and inspiration.

Buzz looked at her and smiled lightly. "We can hope for the best," he said. His smile faded, but the look in his eyes was steely, utterly self-assured. "But we're already in a trap as long as we stay here. As long as we stay involved with these things."

"We have no choice. They'll never let us go. We both know that. And they've taken too much from both of us."

CHAPTER 69

The Predator found the lock on the trailer housing the explosives already broken open. He had no reason to look inside, but he could not help himself. He nudged the metal door open, urging its protest to issue from a pair of large metal hinges in bad need of some oil.

He glanced around for a moment, but he knew he was perfectly safe. It was the middle of the day, Saturday. The demolitions and construction crews were off work today. Only one guard had been left here to watch the explosives. He, of course, had been taken care of already. The Predator had killed him with the bolt cutter in his right hand. The dark, hilarious irony in that had been the fact that the guard was in on the plot, installed by Gainey's crew of collaborators. The guard had cut the lock off the trailer and stood by as the Predator cut the chains on the fence to this abandoned parking lot the construction crew had taken over. The broken lock and chains, the Predator had been told by Lieutenant Stansfield, the woman cop, last night, were required to make the charade look good. It had to look like the Predator cut the chains on the gate, snuck in at a time when the careless guard decamped to a local diner for some coffee and lunch, broke into the TNT container, and stole enough to blow up an entire building on the Cedar Valley State University Campus. The Predator, though, thought there should be a change in the script. He had freely improvised. He came before the guard's agreed-upon departure time and killed him.

But the Handlers' local minions had done their jobs, at least. The explosives that had to be placed in the box-truck had, indeed, been put in their place.

An equally large cache, though, remained in the trailer. The Predator dreamed of improvising further. He would love to have found a way to detonate the remaining explosives as well. The image of all the destruction the trailer's explosion would leave in its wake racked him with waves of ecstasy.

Instead, he took a deep breath and walked toward the box-truck he was supposed to drive out of here. There was nothing to be done now. He had to carry out his mission. He could improvise some more later. He could enjoy himself later…with Jessica.

CHAPTER 70

Jessica climbed the stairs to Tom's porch. The lights had already been turned on, despite the fact that the western horizon still had the peachy reddish glow of the last light of day.

Her heartbeats pounded in her chest as she reached the top. But it wasn't just fear she was feeling. There was sadness as well. The emotions battled inside her, tormented her the closer she got to the door. She recalled how good she had felt climbing these steps only a few days ago. She remembered how safe she had felt here with Tom. Despite his.... *Betrayal?* she asked herself. *Is that what it is? Or is that too strong of a word?*

Despite what happened to them, despite the feelings she now had for Buzz, she mourned the loss of the happiness she'd felt so briefly with Tom.

Then the door opened just before she could push the bell. Tom was waiting for her. She looked into his eyes immediately, curious about what she would find there. Did he, too, regret what they had lost?

She couldn't be sure when Tom returned her gaze. He looked tense, certainly, apprehensive. But she couldn't be sure of anything else.

"Jessica," he said quietly, and nodded.

As she stepped over the threshold, she couldn't help but throw a quick glance over her right shoulder. She did this as Tom turned to lead her inside. She hoped he wouldn't see, but....

"We're alone," he said, a clear edge to his voice. "I did as you asked."

Jessica didn't reply to this, quietly following him after she closed the door.

"So, are you going to leave now?" Tom asked abruptly a moment later. He turned around immediately and looked her square in the eyes.

Jessica didn't like the look of him this time. There was coiled, confrontational anger beaming off him.

"I have your duffel bag and your things upstairs," Tom said. "For what it's worth, I really am sorry things had to come to this."

"So am I, Tom…but listen…." She had to pause. That intense look in his eyes made it hard for her to start into what could quickly escalate into a fight.

"What is it, Jessica?" Tom asked. His words were quick, clipped, and impatient. "You see, I'm just sensing that you have a lot to tell me right now. Don't you?" He paused to study her.

There was a weird sort of glint in his eyes that somehow… *offended* Jessica. It was almost as if he was gloating. Did he hope to see how she would react once he demonstrated his superior abilities of perception?

"Did you see the monsters again?" Tom asked. His quick, sharp tone made his words sound like the verbal equivalent of a boxer's sudden, stinging jabs. "Did you come up with a way to prove their existence to the world? Or, wait a minute…." He paused again for a drawn out, melodramatic beat. "Does your friend, Buzz McPherson, have something to do with this? Did he materialize out of the shadows again and reveal more mysterious information?"

Jessica's heart was pounding again, but this time, not out of apprehension. It was time to knock some of that self-righteousness out of Dr. Lancaster.

"Yeah, Tom," she replied, meeting his gaze head on, hoping she was beaming an equal dose of attitude and defiance back at him. "That's right. Right to all of the above."

"What are you saying—? he began, but he was cut off by a banging noise outside. The noise was distant, but it was quite loud. It was unmistakably a small explosion.

"What was that?" Tom asked on reflex, his gaze skipping toward the windows.

Nice timing, Jessica thought.

Tom walked to the window facing the street in front of the house. "Sounded like it came from about a block away."

"Yeah," Jessica mumbled.

Tom suddenly turned to look at her. At first, he didn't say anything. He just stood there, studying her.

Jessica still hoped that Buzz's plan might work. Before the night was through, they needed to have a calm and reasonable discussion with Tom. Ever more, though, she wasn't sure how that would be accomplished.

"Jessica, what *was* that?"

"Look, Tom," she began, knowing she couldn't just keep standing there quietly like that. "I came here hoping we could talk...not fight."

Then she was interrupted by a popping sound from the kitchen.

Thank God! her mind raced.

It sounded like a metal bolt being forced open.

Tom's gaze darted toward the kitchen. "I don't believe this...," he began.

Jessica followed his glance and saw Buzz emerging from the kitchen.

CHAPTER 71

"All in one place, like a nest of roaches," the Predator mumbled to himself as he cruised along Flagstone street, the one street that bordered Cedar Valley State University for the longest stretch.

His problem right now was the fact that it was too early for the strike. Not all the principles were on campus yet. Luckily, it was almost completely dark. The campus, on a typical summer's weekend evening, was usually deserted. There were no classes and, save for a few special accommodations for a tiny handful of international students, the dormitories were almost completely empty. The Predator could try and drive onto the campus and pull into an out-of-the-way parking lot.

"Yeah," he mumbled to himself again. "Like a nest of bugs."

Or, he considered, *that* is exactly how a bunch of superstitious, inbred yahoos like the members of the Celebration of Salvation Mission would look at a gathering of Tom Lancaster and all his special friends. People like Lancaster were the spawn of Satan to the Salvation crowd. As a matter of fact, they were the spawn of Satan to Garnett's church as well. The faithful would need to strike like the lightning bolt of the Lord A'mighty Hisself and step on this little nest of devilish roaches and kill them with one fell swoop. Or, that was exactly what the world would be led to believe once the Predator got through with this place tonight.

He fingered the rosary beads on the seat beside him. He

hoped Stansfield was right, and the beads would survive the blast. After the FBI started sifting through the rubble, they would need to find these false clues and conclude that a demented group of religious nuts had blown the place sky high.

"Lancaster, you fuck! Where are you?" the Predator yelled suddenly as he made a turn onto one of the lanes traversing the campus.

He tried to reach out with his mind and remote-view all the people who were slated to attend Lancaster's little academic shindig tonight. The majority of the party was either in place or closing in on the campus.

"Jessica!" the Predator gasped.

He had a vision of her. When he tried to reach out to Lancaster, he saw her too. His heart pounded.

"Jessica!"

And then the vision collapsed.

The Predator fought to concentrate on Jessica. He put all his energy, all his will into seeing her. It didn't work! He could not get her.

Yet she was right next to Lancaster.

The Predator tore at the wheel of the truck and swerved into an empty parking lot. He had to stop the truck and only focus. He could not split his concentration right now.

And still, he could not get her. It was as if....

She's being blocked, the realization screamed in the Predator's mind.

Someone was willfully preventing him from seeing her. Someone was engaging him in deliberate psychic combat. They were blocking his scan of Jessica.

But why would they? The Predator couldn't understand. According to that dumb bitch, Stansfield, the Handlers had decided to let him have Jessica after all. So why did they...?

No! he realized. *It's not the Handlers blocking her out.*

CHAPTER 72

"Just a pipe bomb in a trash bin in the alley," Buzz said as he came forward.

Jessica glanced at the backpack in his hand. It would be up to the skull inside to defuse what was sure to turn into a nasty confrontation.

"If there *are* any cops outside, it would get their attention," Buzz added. "Get them out of the picture."

Instead of replying, Tom's gaze darted toward Jessica. There was anger in that look more than anything, Jessica thought, but also an undercurrent of hurt.

"No, there are no cops," Tom spoke directly to Jessica as if Buzz wasn't even in the room. "I *told* you it would only be us. I didn't set up a trap for you, if that's what you thought."

"Tom, I'm sorry," Jessica said as evenly, yet as emphatically, as she could. "But after our last couple of conversations, we just couldn't be sure. I mean, I know you were worried about the Inquisitor and everything—"

"Save it, okay?" Tom snapped. For the first time, he actually did take more than a cursory look at Buzz. The look in Tom's eyes, nevertheless, remained unsparingly hateful toward him. "What do you want?" he asked, but did so as he turned back toward Jessica. "What I don't understand is that if you think there are all these monsters running around in Cedar Valley, what are you still doing here? What do you want from me?"

"Tom, please," Jessica said. "This is a very dangerous situation. And we can't let this go on."

"What?" Tom snapped. "Are you saying you're here on some sort of a crusade? You're coming to me to help you save the world?"

"Tom, they're killing people. They killed my father. They killed Buzz's fiancée. They're stealing bodies from funeral homes. They're taking people's loved ones. Tom! They're *murdering* people."

Jessica had to pause, no matter how her blood pressure kept rising. She had to try and gauge Tom's reaction to anything she had told him. All she got back, though, was an unwavering, piercing, completely impenetrable stare.

"Tom, listen to me," she continued. "The worst of it is that there might be a lot of people out there helping them. Like this serial killer. The Inquisition killer. They — these...these *creatures* — they make promises of power, psychic powers and strength and immortality."

"Immortality?" Tom asked, condescending incredulity dripping off that word.

"I mean, they can't really make people immortal, but they make them promises. Tom, I need you to think about something very hard...please."

"What's that?"

"That person at your school...whoever it was that did the test for you on my father's ashes. He might have been one of them. He was lying to you."

A sort of sour, strained chuckle came from Tom. "Bill Clifton," he said quickly, almost as if talking to himself. "Bill in league with...what did you call them before? *Interdimensional monsters?*" Tom chuckled again and shook his head. "The heavens could part, and God himself could appear in front of

Bill, and do you know what Bill would probably do? He'd start debating why the existence of God is an irrational idea."

Buzz suddenly spoke up now and approached Tom. "Well, Bill might be a skeptic," he said, and Jessica noticed that his right hand was inside the backpack now. "But he's also a liar. What they gave Jessica was concrete powder." And now Buzz extracted the skull from the bag and shoved it at Tom. "And *this* isn't a figment of your imagination either."

Tom eventually took the skull in his hands, but he was silent throughout. The more he seemed to recognize, comprehend what it was that he was holding in his hands, the less likely he was, Jessica thought, of being able to speak. Although she had experienced the feeling not so long ago, knew what it felt like to see all of reality as she had come to understand it her entire life crumble and disintegrate around her, the experience must have been infinitely worse for Tom. She, after all, had never believed she knew all there was about life, the world, the universe, the way Tom had.

"So," Tom muttered at last.

Jessica thought a full five minutes had passed since he took the skull into his hands.

"So, what can I say to this now?" he mumbled again.

"Nothing," Jessica replied. "This is no longer about explanations and arguments and intellectual sparring matches. We just have to deal with this now. *This* is the truth." She pointed at the skull. "That thing in your hand is real. These creatures are real. And we have to tell people about them."

Tom looked at her, then shifted his gaze to Buzz. "Yeah," he said quietly. "The truth has to come out."

Buzz nodded. "Good. The truth."

"Tom, with your admission that these creatures exist, we'll have a real chance at being taken seriously," Jessica said.

Tom laughed with an inflection that sounded disturbingly unsteady. Jessica, though, couldn't fault him for it.

"From star skeptic to being the star of...." Tom looked back and forth between Jessica and Buzz again. "So, what are we going to call our little movement here? Contactees? Experiencers? Naw...that's for the UFO people. Already been used. Just what exactly are we? The ghoulbusters?"

Buzz laughed and shook his head. "Hell, I don't know. We'll think of something."

"Well," Tom said, "how about we drink to this? It's not every day that all of the rules of reality get rewritten, huh?" Then he paused and burst out laughing. "For me, at least. You guys must be used to this."

"No," Jessica replied. "I'm still not used to it, believe me."

"Although a drink does sound good," Buzz said.

They went into the kitchen, where Tom placed the skull atop the island counter. Afterward, he removed a bottle of wine from the refrigerator.

"I don't know why I'm feeling so...what? *Jazzed* over this," Tom said as he tried to rip the foil off the top of the bottle. "You guys are telling me that we're really in mortal danger."

"The more people we can convince," Buzz said, "the less danger we're in."

Tom thought about that, then nodded vigorously. "That makes some sense."

"We can only hope," Jessica said.

Tom looked down at the bottle in his hands with some frustration now. "Hold on a sec," he said. "Let me get a foil cutter so we can get around to a toast, huh?"

He began to turn, about to head for one of the counters along the wall, it seemed, but suddenly his move became strikingly fast. He was spinning around, Jessica realized. He was going into a full three-hundred-sixty-degree revolution and using his momentum to swing the bottle around. Before Jessica could utter a word, Tom used the wine bottle to club Buzz over the head.

Unlike in the movies, where full bottles of liquor could easily be smashed to pieces over people's heads in anarchic bar-room brawls, the wine bottle did not break over Buzz's head. It did, however, knock him down flat on his face. The sickening *thump* of the glass striking his skull almost seemed to echo across the kitchen.

"Tom!" Jessica gasped, feeling as if the mere sight of the assault on Buzz had given her the same type of physical blow.

Before she could react any further, Tom placed the bottle on the island, then lunged toward Buzz. He delivered a brutal, well-aimed kick into his midsection. Jessica found herself screaming as she watched Buzz's pain-racked body spin around and fall on his back.

"Stay back!" Tom yelled at her. Then he kicked Buzz again, sending a vicious blow to his ribs.

"Tom, no!" a scream erupted out of Jessica's throat. It was pure reflex, revulsion, terror, rage, manifesting in this explosion that tore out of her body.

Tom, though, was unfazed by her emotional outburst. He reclaimed the wine bottle and smashed it along the edge of the island counter. This time it shattered, spraying glass and wine all across the kitchen.

But Tom didn't stop there. Jessica was stunned to see him turning toward her. There was an animal, maniacal glare in his eyes. But what was worse was the remainder of the bottle in his right fist. Its jagged, rapier shards glistened dangerously. Then he lunged at her.

Jessica tried to react, to retreat, to recall a kickboxing counter-move, but her reflexive move was no match for Tom's deliberate attack. He was upon her in a flash. He lashed out with his left hand, reaching behind her head and seizing a palmful of her hair. The painful move arrested all her attempts at trying to move.

"You want to see monsters?" Tom shouted at her. "Then, take a look at him!"

Pain tore through Jessica's head, her scalp, her neck, her entire upper back as Tom spun her around by the hair.

"Look at him!" he screamed as he tried forcing Jessica's face in Buzz's direction.

Then Tom was pushing her downward. He was driving her down to the ground, onto her knees. Spectacular bolts of pain seared through Jessica's knees, her legs, as she was driven onto the floor. Luckily, she was able to brace herself with her two hands before Tom could press her flat against the tiles underfoot.

"Look!" Tom kept shouting for some insane reason. "Look at his face."

But Jessica saw that she wasn't the only one down on the floor next to Buzz's pain-racked, semi-conscious form. Tom was down on one knee, his opposite foot planted on Buzz's neck.

"Please," Jessica gasped. "Don't do this."

Then she saw the shards of the broken bottle hovering less than an inch from Buzz's eyes.

"Show her!" Tom seemed to be screaming at Buzz. "Open your eyes, damn you! Show her, you bastard!"

Buzz's eyelids fluttered. Jessica could see the very bloodshot whites of his eyes. In fact, his orbs seemed to be so badly bloodshot that "whites" were hardly visible at all.

"Open your eyes, you fuck," Tom continued with his insane raving.

Buzz's eyelids fluttered several times, and Jessica was horrified by what she saw. His eyes were getting redder and redder. That blow from the bottle must have done it, she realized.

Tom must have delivered some massive internal damage with that strike from the bottle. Buzz was dying before her very eyes.

"I said to open them, damn you, or I'm going to cut them out," Tom bellowed like a wild, deranged animal.

"Tom, no!" Jessica tried to plead with him, but her words only came out as racking sobs. "Please...Tom, please, no."

When Buzz opened his eyes, Jessica saw something that shocked her as much as the sight of the ghouls in the forest. All that seemed to lie under his eyelids were dark, angry crimson pools. His eyeballs were completely covered in blood.

"Oh, God, no," Jessica whispered.

But then Buzz's eyes changed again. His irises reappeared. They bloomed out of the middle of the redness at an incredible speed. Moreover, both reappeared at exactly the same moment. They didn't seem to be exactly circular anymore, though, and they weren't entirely black. They seemed to be flecked with a sort of gold patterning within oblong, jagged black fields.

And then Jessica felt Tom's hand letting go of her hair. Instead, he slapped onto her back and grasped her shirt. He gave her a violent, upward yank.

"Do you see what I wanted to protect you from?" he yelled at her.

Jessica looked at Buzz's wheezing, semiconscious form on the ground. She felt as if all the blood circulating through her body had turned to ice.

Then Tom spun her around and leaned into her face like a military drill instructor. "He's one of them!" he shouted at her. "Those monsters of yours? Look at him! He's one of them."

CHAPTER 73

"Goddamn you!" the Predator screamed and punched the truck's steering wheel.

His vision of Jessica was no longer blocked. He could see her, he could home in on her, but only because Lancaster had knocked McPherson unconscious. Lancaster had turned the tables on Jessica and McPherson, but now he was about to put her life in greater danger. He was going to bring her with him to the campus. That idiot was going to drag her into the path of a bomb that would put a crater the size of a football field in the middle of the Cedar Valley State U.

The Predator's eyes darted around in the darkness. He had to think of something. Jessica was *his*. The Handlers gave her to him, and he wasn't going to let that buffoon, Lancaster, deprive him of his prey.

CHAPTER 74

"So why don't you ask him the sixty-four-thousand-dollar question," Buzz wheezed, then spat a mouthful of blood on the kitchen floor. A grotesque mingling of saliva and blood drooled off his lower lip. He'd gotten the mouthful of blood after Tom punched him a minute ago. At that point, too, Buzz had tried to talk to Jessica. Nevertheless, Buzz persisted. "If he knows everything," he said, his voice defiant, "if he knows what...we are, why is he not doing anything about it? Why the skeptic routine?"

Tom didn't hit him this time but did throw an impatient look at Jessica. She thought the reason for his refrain from violence was the state of the kitchen towel wrapped around his right hand. Tom had been trying diligently to avoid touching Buzz. The towel acted as a makeshift glove. Although now it was starting to unravel from his fist and was well soaked with blood.

"Come on, open that thing," Tom commanded, nodding at the lock in Jessica's hands.

By now, Buzz was sitting on one of the kitchen chairs, wrapped up in a length of chains Tom had brought in from the garage. He had been able to do so because Jessica agreed to hold Buzz at gunpoint. She had been so shocked by the revelation of Buzz's inhuman nature that she barely heard his protestations of being in league with the ghouls in the forest. After Tom finished binding Buzz with the chain, he asked her to help finish restraining Buzz by securing the links with her own combination lock. The duffel bag she still had in Tom's house was actually her gym bag. It had only been at the San Diego airport, right as she tried to make her way through the metal detectors, that she realized she still had her gym lock attached to one of its handles.

She pulled the lock open and handed it to Tom.

Just as she heard it snap shut, she began to wonder why a single word Buzz had said sounded so odd to her now. "...if he knew what...we are," Buzz had just said. Yet he paused in a certain way before the word "we." There seemed to be such a sound of reluctance to that word. Or even more than reluctance; it was distaste, *revulsion*. He sounded like he was loath to associate himself with the creatures. But ultimately, what did that mean? Jessica needed to figure that out right now, but she didn't know how to try. Tom had already taken steps to eliminate Buzz.

"Tom," she said at last, "what's going on here?"

"Yeah, Tom," Buzz growled. "What do you know, and when did you know it?"

As angry as Buzz looked, Jessica was glad to see that at least his eyes looked human again.

"You shut the hell up," Tom told him in a menacing, volatile voice.

"Tom, please explain this!" Jessica replied, hoping her voice had enough command in it.

"This is too complicated to go over right now," Tom said quickly.

"Like hell it is," Buzz shot back, looking at Jessica. "It's quite simple."

"You can just lay here unconscious until they take you away," Tom threatened. Jessica saw his right hand clenching into a fist. "Choice is yours."

Nevertheless, Buzz persisted. "He's a coward," he hissed,

looking only at Jessica. "That's what this is all about."

"You asked for it, pal," Tom growled.

"No!" Jessica screamed. She needed answers right now, and she could no longer trust Tom. She had to prevent any more violence.

Tom flinched at the loudness of her voice. At least, Jessica was glad to see, he seemed dissuaded from hitting Buzz again.

"Jessica," Buzz called to her. "This is what they can do to you if they infect you enough. Remember, you asked me."

A cold shudder passed through Jessica now. Her bite of the Predator's arm flittered through her memory. But.... *It's more than that now,* she realized. It wasn't just the Predator inside her now. She'd had sex with Buzz....

"Oh, God," she whispered.

"But they can't control you!" Buzz said. "No one can. They can't change who you are. They did this to me after they killed April, but I'm not one of them. I swore I would destroy them all. Do you understand?"

"Shut up," Tom said suddenly.

"No one can control you!" Buzz insisted. "Not them. And not me!"

"Not you...," Jessica muttered.

And she saw Tom's gaze shifting onto her. There was a strange, somehow demented realization dawning on him. She saw...what? There was anger, *disgust* in that look.

"You and him," he said slowly. Then he nodded. "Well," he said at length. "I guess you'll find out how real they are."

"Jessica," Buzz's voice was rising. "Jessica, I did not hurt you. Do you understand?"

"He only wanted to turn you into one of those things that frightened you so badly out in the woods."

An involuntary shudder emanated from somewhere deep

inside her body.

"You damned liar!" Buzz bellowed. Now he tugged on his chains violently. He fought them like a rabid animal. "That's a lie, Jessica! Lancaster, you lying coward son of a bitch."

"They're connected in a telepathic web," Tom said, looking directly at Jessica, ignoring Buzz's tantrum. "You think it's not about control? That's what he wants."

"I'm gonna kill you!" Buzz shrieked, and futilely fought against his chains.

Jessica could feel those shudders increasing. She shifted her attention from Buzz to Tom, then back again, back and forth in an insane, frenzied succession.

"You lying sack of shit!" Buzz raged. "Jessica, I swear to God I did not hurt you. It's not about hurting you."

"No, he didn't hurt you enough," Tom came back. "Not yet. He hasn't infected you enough so they can control you."

"I'm *not* one of them," Buzz yelled. "Jessica, after everything we've been through, you can't believe that. I love you, Jessica. I would never hurt you."

"Then why didn't he tell you what he is?" Tom cut in, and, Jessica realized, he asked an excellent question. On top of all the other lies Buzz had told her, why this one? "Because," Tom said, "he's one of them. He wanted to infect you long enough until they all had you in their hive mind, in their telepathic web."

"That's bullshit!" Buzz thundered. "There's no hive mind. They can't control you. *I* can't control you. People like the Predator do what they do willingly. They can't take your free will from you. The Predator and all their allies do what they do for the power. For the abilities."

"And you believe him after all his other lies?" Tom asked.

"And what about *your* lies?" Buzz asked.

In fact, this time, Buzz's question was just as valid, Jessica realized as she fought with all her mind to resist the onset of panic.

"If he knew these things were in this town, then why his skeptical scientist act? Huh? Ask him that. Why did he fight you until the last moment?"

But the shouting came to a stop when the doorbell rang. Or rather, Buzz was about to shout something else until Tom lunged at him and cut him off with a brutal right hook to his face. Rivulets of Buzz's blood sprayed across the kitchen from his mouth and nose.

"No more words, Mr. McPherson, or whoever the hell you are," Tom said and started toward the door.

CHAPTER 75

The threats had shrieked through the Predator's head first. The onslaught of the Handlers' telepathic waves pummeled and buffeted him. At first, they merely ordered him to stay his ground to keep the truck parked in one place until Lancaster and Jessica showed up, and the final phase of this operation could go into effect. Then they tried to hurt him with maddening mental noise when he resisted. When that didn't work, they threatened. They promised to hunt him down and torture him for months in ways even he couldn't contemplate. Finally, they claimed his truck had a backup detonation switch built in. They could blow him up if he didn't do as he was told.

But finally, they relented and tried another tack. They promised him that Jessica could be spared from the blast. There was a way for him to still have her. If he only stayed his position and cooperated, he could still get what he wanted.

The Predator leaned back against his seat and quietly gloated over his victory.

CHAPTER 76

Jessica almost found herself lurching clear of Tom's attempt to put his hand on her shoulder. Instead, she pulled back, just an inch clear of his reach. She couldn't stand to be touched right now. She wouldn't let herself be controlled by him the way he had been controlling everything since Buzz's capture. Two men in a van had shown up from the funeral home and removed Buzz. Now, apparently, Tom intended to take her away himself, justifying everything through a hurried, rambling monologue about the dire threats and mortal dangers they all faced right now.

"Danger?" she asked as she took a step away from him. "What are you talking about? What danger?"

"Jessica, please," Tom said as he slowly stepped after her.

"No!" Jessica said, realizing that she was raising her hands in an awkward, self-defensive move. "Either you tell me right now, or I swear I'm not going anywhere with you."

"Jessica, for God's sake, please," Tom said in fake-calm, beseeching tone. Then he tried to reach for Jessica's arm again.

She recoiled. "No! I said either you talk to me right now, or I'm not going. You tell me the truth, or I swear to God I'm walking out of here and taking my chances with whatever's out there in this town."

She could see Tom's features hardening, frustration welling up in him. "Unless we leave right now and go to the school," he said in measured tones, "they—those things, those things like McPherson—are going to kill you. Do you understand me? They *will* come here, and they *will* kill you."

Aside from the anger on Tom's face, Jessica could see a strange measure of fear as well. It was the fear of a loss of power. It was the fear emanating from the fact that he knew there was something going on here that was much bigger, much more powerful than anything he ever hoped to contain. But she also took note of the fact that he did not say "kill *us*."

"Now," Tom said, his eyes begging this time, "will you please come with me? Please?"

"I want some answers," Jessica said as resolutely as she could. "I want to know—"

"Okay!" Tom said quickly. "All right. I'll tell you everything you want to know, but you have to come with me."

Jessica wanted nothing more right now than to run as far away from Tom Lancaster as she could, but rationality remained in control of her senses. She was in a trap right now, and she knew it. This town was somehow under the grip of those monsters, and they were intent on keeping her here. Under the cover of night, they had the best possible chance of doing so. On dark streets and dark roads, they had the perfect opportunity to ambush her. But somehow, Tom had some tiny—if ultimately illusory—degree of power as well. There was some sort of a truce between him and the creatures. Indeed, she realized, if she was with him for now, she could stay alive.

Although she still wouldn't let him touch her, Jessica followed Tom through the kitchen door and out to the driveway. They got into his Toyota Avalon, and he backed onto the street with the skidding, screeching urgency of a stunt driver hurtling his car through an obstacle course.

"So there are things you need to ask me," Tom said as they

sped away from the house.

What frustrated Jessica was a hint of anger, a hint of self-righteous indignation, that she could swear lurked under Tom's voice. He actually sounded like he was the one who was wronged by this entire affair. He was a liar and a fraud, he was in league with monstrosities that defied all sane imagination—he was, in effect, an accessory to countless murders—yet he was angry and indignant.

"Yeah," Jessica said, noticing how her voice almost came out like a hiss. "And I think you know what."

"Yeah," Tom said flatly. "Why we...*I'm* keeping their secret. Right?"

"Go on."

"I suppose other than the fact that he's one of them, McPherson told you about these creatures." Tom paused and cast a quick glance at Jessica. "More or less, right? He probably left out the part about their telepathic powers."

"Not entirely," Jessica said. She surprised herself by the sound of her own voice. It sounded defensive. More precisely, she sounded defensive of Buzz. As she thought of him, her emotions again clashed. She still fought to overcome the pain of his lies, the pain of betrayal that had cut through her, that felt like it tore through her flesh and scraped, shattered the bone underneath, yet there was something else that had come along with all his lies and manipulation. The bizarre, incomprehensible fact remained that he was also much more honest with her than anyone else in this town. He had told her much more about the creatures, about their nature and agendas, than Tom ever had.

"And he told you that they can assume all kinds of shapes?" Tom asked.

"Yes, he told me that," Jessica said, and watched for his reaction. She noticed a surprised arch of his right eyebrow. "They can change into things like werewolves and the…*whatever*… Mothman and Bigfoot. So people like you can dismiss everything about them. Call all the eyewitnesses crazy and delusional. So that you can be a great help to these things."

By the time the last words came out of Jessica, she realized how her tone had shaped them into daggers. She wanted to use them to cut into Tom, to hurt him. She realized quickly that she'd succeeded. He threw a quick glance her way, and she realized what the proverbial "dark look" really looked like. There was a narrowing of his eyes, a petulant stiffening of his lower lip, the self-pitying outrage of a man who knew he was *right*.

"Oh really," Tom shot back. "So how about this for shape-changing? What if one of these things shows up in your living room one night? A dark and stormy night. On Halloween night. Melodramatic as hell. Real theatrical. So damn theatrical, you have to laugh at it. I mean, Halloween? That's laying it on a bit thick, don't you think?"

"What happened?" Jessica asked simply, wanting to let Tom vent his spleen as quickly as he could.

"So one of these things shows up. Except now, it has two horns. It has a tail with a point on it. Reddish, scaly lizard skin. The whole works. Like every Sunday school description of the devil you ever heard. Like a second-rate Halloween costume. Then he recites some bullshit about astral signs adding up to six six six, that Lucifer has been given his chance to reign by our decadent world, that he thanks me for our world forsaking Jesus Christ, for corrupting our children with sex and violence on TV, music that—get this!—pleases the ears of Lord Satan, killing babies in thousands of abortions…I mean, this is every fundamentalist fruitcake's wet dream."

Suddenly Jessica realized what they meant when they said your "skin is crawling." A dreadful realization dawned on her.

"This is every demented Antichrist fantasy of Jim Garnett come to life," Tom continued. "I'm talking chapter and verse. I mean word for word. And do you know what happened then?"

Tom glanced at Jessica with a wild-eyed, outraged look.

"He...*it!*" he exclaimed. "That *thing* laughed at me. He *quoted* one of Garnett's books. You realize what it was all about, don't you? A put-on! Oh, but it was a good one. Because if those things are discovered, if the people who see them are taken seriously, we're going to be living in a Jim Garnett world. Believe me, Jessica, if anyone who's seen those creatures is believed, this world will be thrown back into some global-scale Puritan village."

Jessica's realization was proving true with every word out of Tom's mouth. "I don't believe this," she couldn't help but mumble.

"Oh, believe it, Jessica," Tom shot back.

"No.... *You*. I can't believe *you*. You are covering up their existence, you are helping to hide these *monsters* because you're afraid they will be interpreted as a religious revelation come true?"

"I am trying to protect reason and sanity in a world that is on the brink of falling into the Dark Ages. Jessica, just look around you. I mean, we put men on the moon, but we also have hundreds of fundamentalist zealots protesting museums because prehistoric life displays are not acknowledging the literal truth of the Bible. They believe in a massive Satanic conspiracy of scientists that's hiding evidence that the sun really revolves around the earth. And these aren't random trailer-park hillbillies. These are people who run school boards. These are people who ban textbooks that mention Darwin. These are people with political clout who make or break senators and congressmen...who can decide presidential elections. You want to know why so much of the world doesn't take this country seriously anymore? Maybe because we're on the verge of medievalism."

"But Tom, look at what you're allowing to happen!" Jessica couldn't help but counter his litany, all the while fairly certain her words could never have any sort of effect on him. "They're *killers*. They're killing people who don't look the other way like you. They killed my father. You know what they're going to do to me."

"No, Jessica," Tom replied, his words quick, brusque, dismissive. "You can be safe. If you listen to me."

"But that's not the *point!* I'm talking about people's lives. You're willing to let this...this evil go on because of your rationalist paranoia?"

"This is not rationalist paranoia," Tom snapped back.

"You know these killers are out there, but you're going to sit by and do nothing. Because a few creationist science books might wind up in a few schools? Because a few delusional halfwits blog about the earth being flat?"

"This is *much* bigger than that."

"It was all a lie," Jessica said, thinking of using one more tack to try and get through to Tom.

"What?"

"You lied to me. About my father's ashes, didn't you? You were the one who lied to me about that."

"I was trying to protect you," Tom said quickly. Jessica realized that her gambit had no chance of working. "I was trying to keep you away from this."

"Oh, dear God...you're just as bad as they are. All of you."

Tom glanced at Jessica again. His look was still angry, impatient, and condescending. "What are you talking about?"

She couldn't help but laugh bitterly now. "This would be hysterically funny if it wasn't such a nightmare."

"What?"

"You and Jim Garnett. You're exactly the same. You're no better than he is. You're no better than any fanatical, wild-eyed lunatic in this world. Like that...what's his name? That idiot conspiracy theorist professor in your own school." Now Jessica was just hoping to further anger and provoke Tom. It was useless, she knew, useless and immature. But she also knew these words were hurting him. And he deserved it.

"Jessica, you're not hearing a word I'm saying," he almost growled back at her. His words were acidic as well as hilariously pedantic. "It's the Jim Garnetts, the religious nuts with their visions and commandments from gods—and their bombs, if simple words of persuasion don't work—that I'm trying to save the world from."

"No, you don't detonate bombs. You just let people die. You just let them get murdered, and you look the other way. Because *you* know the truth. It's only your truth that can win, and to hell with anyone else."

"No!" Tom yelled. When his eyes flashed at her, Jessica could see unbridled rage in them. Apparently, she had just struck the core of all of his values, his beliefs. "It's not *my* truth. It is *the* truth. It's the truth because *I* can prove it. Everything I believe in, everyone else can observe. Everyone can look into my telescope and see the same thing I see. Everyone can do my equations and see the same things I see. I'm not more right or more special or more gifted or touched or blessed than anyone. I don't know what I know because I got special visions in a dream or because I hear voices no one else can hear."

What frustrated Jessica now was the fact that there were, indeed, truths in Tom's words. His worldview, his empiricism, was important—the world needed it. But what he couldn't realize was the way he was betraying those very things he believed in.

"But Tom," Jessica said, choosing to try and reason with him for the last time, trying to open his eyes instead of mocking and provoking him. "Why can't you fight these things? Why don't you try and convince the world that these are not demons and devils, but flesh and blood creatures?"

"Because we're living in a country where thousands of people believe that cavemen walked with dinosaurs," Tom raged in return.

"Then maybe try and understand why some people need something bigger than themselves to believe in."

Tom didn't reply this time, didn't even bother to look at Jessica, but shook his head.

Jessica wanted to tell him that the real horror of these monsters, the real tragedy, was taking place in this car. He was an intelligent man, someone who could say so many things that made logical, *moral* sense, yet someone who willingly aided evil now. He did so because evil, because covering up murders, had somehow become more acceptable than seeing his ideological enemies gain some ground. But telling him this, she knew full well, would do absolutely no good.

"Well," Jessica said instead, "like I said before, Tom. You *are* no different from Garnett. Do you know why? Because he knows the creatures are out there, too."

Tom gave her a quick glance, but this time it betrayed no emotions.

"It's true," she reiterated. "Buzz and I went to see him. Yesterday. We went to his compound for his help. You know what he told us? That he can't help us because it will let you win."

She paused to see how Tom would react, but he didn't.

"See what I mean?" Jessica continued. "This could all be one big hysterical joke if people weren't dying because of it. The Inquisition killer — the Predator, by the way…he seems to prefer the Predator — is being controlled by the creatures. He's doing the killings as an imitation of the Inquisition. So if Garnett speaks out about them, he loses credibility in the public eye. He comes off as an extremist nut. And *you* win. Do you see what I'm saying? Everyone's so obsessed with winning, with proving people they disagree with wrong, that it's killing us all. These creatures are taking advantage of it."

"I'm sorry, Jessica," he said at length. "But I can't risk Garnett winning. I just can't. It would destroy the world in ways you can't imagine. Please try to understand."

By now, Jessica couldn't imagine him saying anything else.

"So what happens now?" she asked after a heavy moment of silence hung between them.

"We're going to the CVSU campus. Because it's about to be blown up."

CHAPTER 77

Jessica felt like she was moving to take her position in front of a firing line, with Tom, the man who had professed his love to her only a few days ago, clutching her arm and yanking her to move along.

"Will you please make me feel at least a *little* less like I'm being kidnapped?" she said, and tried to pull her arm free as they walked down the corridor leading to the main conference hall of the Erskine F. Carlson Memorial Building.

"I'm not kidnapping you," Tom shot back and gave her an angry tug.

"And being held hostage," she said, finally twisting her arm free of his grip. "And get your hands off me, please. I came here of my own accord, didn't I?"

Tom glared at her. "You are free to go anytime you want. And then the Predator will go right after you."

Jessica felt a shudder pass through her at the thought of how much she had been drawn to this man in a time that seemed to have been decades ago. "Sure, Tom," she hissed back, "whatever you say. Let's just stay here and watch this school get blown up instead. So we can all live perfectly intelligent and rational lives, and all will be right with the world."

"You know, Jessica, I would love to hear you make jokes like this when you get sick, when you have to go to the hospital, but all you're allowed to have is a good prayer and trust in the lord's ever-loving, unknowable wisdom."

"Tom, let me ask you one question. When do *you* draw the line between following your convictions and becoming a reckless fanatic?"

He didn't reply. Instead, he marched with ever quicker steps toward the conference hall.

"Blowing up the school," Jessica pressed as she hurried after him. "For God's sake—"

"We're not blowing up the school," Tom called petulantly over his shoulder. "Only this building will get damaged, and—"

"And who else is out there? Wandering around the campus? Who could get hurt by a truck full of explosives going off?"

"You don't know what you're talking about," Tom said dryly.

"Well, excuse me," Jessica threw sarcasm back at him. "I'm just going on the information you gave me. What if one of your students happens by?"

"There are no classes tonight. It's the summer, and most of the campus is deserted."

"*Most* of the campus?"

Tom came to a sudden, abrupt stop now. He wheeled on Jessica and seized her by the arm again. "Do you want to leave?" He spat the words in her face. "I won't hold you back." Then, almost as if revolted, he shoved her arm away.

But the rub, of course, Jessica knew full well, was that she could no longer walk away. Once she came this far, once she let Tom drag her onto the grounds of the CVSU campus, she was stuck. She was in the full grip of a violent, murderous vortex, spinning faster and faster until she was irretrievably pulled under.

Her thoughts were suddenly interrupted by a voice from the entrance to the conference hall. "Cutting it a bit close, aren't we, Tom?" a man called out.

Standing under a banner with a mouthful of a title—the inscription reading "Intercollegiate Symposium on Humanities and Sciences: Mixing and Matching-Toward an Understanding of our Common Bonds"—stood a middle-aged man in a light grey summer suit. Upon a closer look, Jessica recognized him from her father's funeral—the chair of the Psychology Department. At the wake, he had given a speech about the common bond of tragedy between the psychology and communication departments, as they'd both lost people close to them. He wore a name tag on his jacket reading "Marshall Randolph."

"We got tied up," Tom said dryly as they met the anthropologist.

"Ms. Lafayette," Randolph said, and solemnly nodded at Jessica. "So you've come to see the light. Unpleasant business the truth can be. Unpleasant business. Well, in this case, it won't just set you free, but will keep you alive." He paused, shaking his head gravely before turning to Tom. As he did so, Jessica thought his face seemed to lighten up, take on some kind of a shade of joviality, in fact. "Tom, want to pick up your conference badge?" he asked. "Does make this whole thing look real."

"Let's just get this thing over with," Tom said in clipped, angry tones.

"Yes," Randolph replied, and nodded toward the interior of the conference room. "Let's go inside and wait until the proverbial curtains rise."

CHAPTER 78

Jessica noticed a small group of people milling around inside the Jules P. Mason, Esq. Commemorative Conference Hall.

"The truth will keep us alive, Dr. Randolph?" she asked suddenly. "Unlike Dr. Danziger, right?"

"What's that?" Randolph asked.

Jessica noticed the dark look, the scowling frustration on Tom deepening. "Dr. Danziger?" she asked Randolph and stared straight into his eyes. "The man who was killed with my father?"

"Oh," Randolph replied. Almost absently, Jessica thought. "Yes," he added quickly, "a tragedy I will have to live with for the rest of my life."

I bet you will, the thought slashed through Jessica's mind. "Who was about to be hired by your department, right?"

Randolph nodded solemnly. Jessica thought it was a shade theatrical, actually. It smacked of insincerity. "Unfortunately, yes," he said in grave, measured tones.

"Why did you make him that job offer if you knew the creatures would be threatened by him? He thought these things were real. So why do something that was tantamount to his execution?" As calm as she hoped to stay, Jessica realized her final words were getting more and more barbed, her voice outraged and confrontational.

"We didn't do anything of the sort," Randolph said, his face appearing to flush. "The man who was our department chair at the time did. He hadn't quite been...*enlightened* yet at that point."

"Oh, he wasn't in on it."

Tom nearly lunged between them. "Let's get inside, why don't we?"

"We never thought he'd actually, *seriously* consider hiring Danziger," Randolph said defensively. "That man belonged in the supermarket tabloids, not academia."

"Oh, you mean his books. Ones that people actually read," Jessica said. "How vulgar. My father said success like that could kill an intellectual's career."

"I'm sorry about your father," Randolph said, very stiffly, very uncomfortably. "I truly am."

In fact, a moment later, he looked glad that they had made it into the conference hall. Trying to read his fidgety body language, Jessica thought he was waiting for the right moment to slink away into the crowd.

Glancing around the room, Jessica was amazed at how real the whole setup actually looked. There were tables with finger-food trays and punch bowls set up. Most of the people — again, a lot of familiar faces from the funeral — actually did wear name tags. Given the fact that this was supposed to have been an "intercollegiate" symposium, it looked jarringly ridiculous. Furthermore, they actually had the gall to set up display easels with posters bearing charts, graphs, and various examples of their scholarly work.

"So this is all nothing but a great big sham," Jessica said, making no attempt to disguise her rising disgust at everything around her. "Congratulations. It looks real enough."

"Real enough to keep you alive," Tom grumbled.

"So now I'm part of the grand conspiracy," she said, giving him a challenging look, loading the word "conspiracy" with as much bile as she could muster.

"There are people from your father's department here, you know," Tom said coldly. "Maybe they could talk sense into you."

"Yeah, why don't I go and get acquainted with my new friends?" Jessica spat the words at Tom but took the opportunity to walk away from him as quickly as she could.

As she wandered among the men and women of the gathering, she was also taken by the fact that it was a relatively small group. She would have made a quick estimate of about thirty or forty people present in the room. Apparently, the ones tasked with keeping the creatures' secret were an elite few.

"Amusing what you said about the conspiracies, you know," a voice called out from behind Jessica.

In fact, she nearly jumped at the sound, it was so close. Whoever it was, he had virtually snuck up on her. It unnerved her. Plus, the somewhat oily tone of the voice—in a strange way both timid *and* arrogant—made her instantly recoil.

Spinning around, she was met by a tall, wiry man in a dark, wrinkled suit, nursing what might have been beer in a plastic cup. The look on his thin, angular face, the bearing of his entire body, communicated that same strange duality as his voice. He looked tense as he shifted about on his feet, giving the air of the pathological, socially inept nerd. But, just like the true nerd, there was a forcefully arrogant glint in his eyes. There was a ferrety, crafty slyness there, something indicating that he knew full well how much smarter he was than anyone else around. Furthermore, the glint suggested that this was the type of nerd who spent a great deal of time fantasizing and planning the sort of complex revenge schemes he would one day invest with all his intellect.

"The *conspiracy*," he said with a subtle, knowing nod. "Ironic, isn't it? Considering who you came here with."

"What are you talking about?" Jessica asked. Now she started to wonder if she might have heard this voice before.

"My name is Lyle Chambers," the man said. "I'm from the political science department. I was interviewed on the radio after the attack on you at the mall, and I argued that—"

Now it all came back. "Oh, yeah," Jessica said. "I heard that interview. You, uh, believe in conspiracies. That's what Tom said."

"Yes," Chambers replied with a humorless smirk. "Me and everyone else with half a brain. Lancaster probably told you we're a bunch of lunatics. *That* part wasn't a lie. I mean, Tom Lancaster really believes people like me are crazy. He thinks I'm an embarrassment to the school and a stain on the whole tenure system."

But what he just said, Jessica realized, seemed to make very little sense. "So why are you a part of this? Why not fight it?"

Chambers shook his head, his hands nervously fondling the cup in his hands. His movements were so spastic, both arms churning back and forth, that he reminded Jessica of a praying mantis. "Don't you think what I'm trying to do every day is hard enough?" he snapped. Jessica thought he was going to crush that cup in his hands. "Trying to convince the world we're all asleep and controlled by our corporate masters? This…this menace from beyond will be impossible to get anyone to believe. To believe and still take me seriously. This *must* be kept hidden. For now, we must not let anyone talk about it. Do you understand? We must keep this quiet."

Jessica's stomach turned. She might as well have been talking to Jim Garnett. Chambers was no different from the reverend. But then again, he was no different from Tom either. The whole damned lot of them, they were all exactly alike. They all needed to *win*.

"Keep quiet?" she muttered, amazed and repulsed by such destructive, willful stupidity trying to engulf her.

Chambers' crazy, vulture eyes glinted. "The true nature of these creatures can never be exposed. Or not in the foreseeable future, at least. They're too powerful. They're too advanced. They're too well plugged into all the corridors of power, all the organs of state and industry and the military all over the world."

"Corridors of power? You think—"

"They *are* the corridors of power," Chambers exclaimed. For a moment, Jessica thought he might throw his beer away, grab her by the shoulders, and scream his theories in her face. "They run *everything!*"

Jessica couldn't take this anymore. She had to cut him off. "No, they don't."

"Listen, lady," Chambers said, raw contempt blazing in his eyes. "You keep thinking that, and you'll be as brainwashed as all the idiots staring at their TV sets all over this country."

"These creatures are *not* that powerful," Jessica said, although she was no longer sure why she even bothered. Chambers, just like Tom, just like Garnett, just like everyone else milling about here, lived in his own world. They all had their agendas, they all had their private, well-nurtured rivalries and fears and hatreds, and there was no argument she could ever raise that could do any good. "Someone just needs to come forward and say—"

"Someone just needs to come forward and tear down all the institutions they have supplanted!" Chambers continued ranting. "The publishing houses that keep churning out all the mindless pabulum for a country full of morons. The TV networks, the radio stations, the movie studios. Wall Street, the bankers, the Pentagon, the White House, the CIA…these creatures are why we have wars. You're capable of realizing that, aren't you? They need wars to get their hands on dead bodies! That's why wars are started and perpetrated. To feed these creatures—"

Jessica cut him off, even as she knew her words would be

futile and carry absolutely no import for the conspiracy theorist. "But thousands — *millions!* — of people die every day anyway," she said, perhaps more to herself than Chambers. She needed to hear some semblance of normalcy — real, true rationality — to counter Chambers' delusions. "Nobody needs to start wars to get dead bodies. They just get them from funeral homes."

"You can see how impossible it is to believe, can't you?" Chambers fought back. "Even you are incapable of comprehending. That's why we need to overthrow the system first. To convince all those mass-media-fed degenerates in all their white picked fence-surrounded little two-car garage houses that they've been brainwashed and chained inside the hegemonic institutional matrix. Look, first things first. You're capable of understanding that much, aren't you? Most of your waking thoughts are hardly your own, I can understand that. We're all brainwashed."

"Except you," Jessica muttered, realizing her words hardly registered for Chambers. Of course, they wouldn't have registered even if she shouted them in his face. "You seem to be superior to everyone else, obviously," she completed the thought aloud. But, of course, Chambers could not be distracted with any counter arguments just now, she knew. He was in the middle of the best part of his dissertation. This was when he vented his rage at all the "morons," "idiots," and "degenerates" and their TV sets and radios. If you scratched the surface of any wild-eyed populist zealot, Jessica knew, every crusader who wanted to save the masses from themselves, every do-gooder who wanted to wake up the sleeping "sheep," you got to see pure, unbridled hatred. These crusaders, these self-appointed saviors of the weak and "brainwashed" — no matter where they were coming from, whatever end of the political spectrum — they were never really motivated by love for their fellow men and women. In fact, Jessica truly believed, they hated them. Those teeming masses, those hordes of the intellectually inferior, needed to be put under the control of the messianic, benevolent visionaries like Chambers. The true injustice of the world to Chambers was the fact that *he* wasn't the one in charge, the one running the world.

"So the battle can't be won if we come out and say that interdimensional monsters are controlling everything," the words kept tumbling out of Chambers. "People need to be awakened slowly. If you tell them about the creatures, they'll start thinking we're all completely insane and paranoid. That way, we'll never realize our agenda. The dream will never be achieved."

Jessica had to back away from him now. She knew that in another minute, she would either throw a shrieking, screaming fit or ram a knee into Chambers' groin. "I think I see now," she said quickly, and nodded enthusiastically. "We need to see the big picture like you do, right? But wait a minute!" She threw a haphazard glance over one shoulder. "I think I know that man… please, I'm sorry, I should talk to him right now."

With those words, she turned and bolted away from Chambers. She had to find a way to get lost in this small crowd, had to find a spot where Chambers couldn't come after her and couldn't talk to her anymore.

And then she almost collided with someone she really had met and talked to at her father's funeral. A balding fat man, nibbling on a crab cake in one hand, occasionally sipping from a flute of champagne in the other, just about missed stepping on her foot. Jessica remembered him explaining how he always asked Brock Randall to be the first one to give feedback and suggestions before sending an article off to a journal.

The corpulent professor's somewhat tired, hooded eyes seemed to light up in recognition for a brief instant. "Must be a tremendous shock for you. I can understand that," he said at length with a sort of sad, resigned tone before snatching the last bite of the crab cake off the toothpick.

There was something in his voice, though, that gave Jessica hope. The dejection, perhaps, she thought. She wanted to think that he might have had regrets over being a part of this obscene cover-up. Hopefully, he would soon prove to be less deranged than everyone else in the room.

"Don Renshaw, by the way," he said. "We talked at your father's funeral."

"Yes, I remember."

"The tragedy of this disgusting mess we're in," Renshaw continued with a weary, hangdog expression, but then his voice just faded out. He looked as if there might have been something else he had intended to say, but now it was just too much trouble to even try and remember.

The silence that hung between them was weird and awkward, Jessica thought, so she said, "At least someone's admitting it."

"Yes," Renshaw said with a tired nod. "That's where you're right, of course. This is all quite a pain."

But then he stopped again and just stared off into the distance.

After about six or seven agonizingly long seconds ticked off, Jessica realized that Renshaw did not appear to have anything left to say. Perhaps she had to reevaluate her first hopeful impression of the man after all.

"Although," the professor exclaimed suddenly, a sort of "here's my two cents, you can take it or leave it, I don't give a shit" tone gumming up his delivery. "Everyone seems to be missing the big picture here."

"What big picture?"

"Why we're so worked up over all this."

Jessica felt as if those words had slapped her in the face. Especially "worked up" stung the most with their casual insensitivity. "Come again?"

"With my heartfelt condolences for your father," Renshaw said calmly, almost indifferently.

"What are you talking about?"

There was a slack little smile on Renshaw's jowly face. "Makes me teary when I think Brock won't be jesting with me about how he'll find a way—come hell or high water, mind you—of getting his hands on my bigger office."

Jessica was about to grind her teeth in frustration. "Please explain what you mean by missing the *big picture,*" she demanded.

"Did your friend—Buzz—tell you what these beings are after?" Renshaw asked calmly.

"Actually, not in as much detail—"

"As you would have hoped, right?" Renshaw said, a bit more enthusiastically this time.

"What's going on here?" Jessica asked, realizing that the professor had some crucial information he might or might not have cared enough about to share.

"Our memories," Renshaw said, a sparkle of life in his watery eyes at last. "That's what they want."

"Memories?" Jessica exclaimed, feeling like she was about to get jerked around some more by someone who could turn out to be a chief contender for the title of the most deranged nut job of them all in this gathering.

"Are you familiar with the concept of racial memories? That the memories of an entire species can be locked in our genes?"

"Somewhat," Jessica said cautiously. She thought she remembered seeing a documentary discussing the theory on a cable science channel. Years ago, she read about the concept from a psychological approach; the Jungian collective unconscious, or a species' reservoir of experiences.

"Literal racial memories. An entire human species' memories," Renshaw said with a gaseous inflection of awe and wonder in his voice. "Well, really, the memories of all your progenitors. Imagine that. Not the metaphorical, collective myth pool of a culture or shared customs over centuries, but the real, literal memories of all your ancestors locked within your genetic code. Your mother's, your father's, grandfather's, grandmother's, and so on. Unlocked at will. Imagine remembering everything since the dawn of time on Earth."

Incredible, true, Jessica considered, but she wasn't sure where Renshaw was going with it. "And what has this — ?"

"Got to do with the creatures? Well, *that's* their ability. That's why they need our flesh, our blood. They get a charge out of absorbing our race's memories. It gives them a surge of power. Too bad they can't quite tolerate our world. But the more of us they absorb, the stronger they get, the longer they can stay here and live in our world. Don't even know if it's our air, our sunlight, or what it is they can't tolerate for prolonged periods of time. But they need *us* — our flesh. Aside from surviving, they can temporarily assume the shapes of the people whose DNA they take. Kind of like a group of chameleons. They will blend into their surroundings. And the most fascinating thing of all is that they seem to enjoy feeding on our experiences of conflict, discord, and fear the most."

"But they sound vulnerable. Too vulnerable."

Renshaw nodded with a thoughtful look before taking his time to respond. "That they are."

"Then, they could be *fought!*"

"Not *that* vulnerable."

"Come on!" Jessica blurted out. Renshaw's phlegmatic manner was infuriating. "Just think about it. They could be captured or incapacitated. Hell, killed even. Let our atmosphere, or whatever it is that kills them, do its thing."

"Incredibly complicated, isn't it, my dear lady?" Renshaw

mumbled slowly.

"No, it's *not!* We could try something, damn it, instead of all this dawdling."

"Dawdling?" Renshaw asked, his eyebrows knitting together. The look it created was at a strange midpoint between befuddled and irritated. "Oh, not quite. May seem like it, I know. But we are — or at least I am — doing something far more important."

"Like what? Hiding away in here? Letting their pawns, like that psycho, the Inquisition killer, run loose out there? Sitting by and letting innocent people get tortured to death so these things can cover their tracks?"

"Like what, you ask?" Renshaw replied, his eyes widening now, some true passion igniting in him. "Like thinking!" he added defiantly.

"What are you talking about?"

"Could it be that we're not seeing the bigger picture here, perhaps? Something much more complex than killers and victims? Sitting by versus charging into battle with guns blazing, all that sort of Hollywood stuff."

Jessica felt like the floor was dropping out from under her. She was in a true madhouse. She was surrounded exclusively by lunatics. "Oh, my God."

"Just think for a moment!" Renshaw said with a sharpness of voice Jessica thought he was incapable of. "Just think about what these...*beings* are capable of. Their wondrous nature."

"The nature that makes them kill people? Eat their bodies? Enjoy watching our hatred and fear of each other? You said so."

"Oh, please, Jessica — may I call you Jessica? — just think about their telepathic abilities. You know about that by now, don't you? Your duplicitous friend, McPherson, at least explained that much, didn't he? So just imagine their telepathy. If we could all communicate with each other through our minds. If we could all hear each other's thoughts. There would be no more secrets, no boundaries, no borders, no races, no genders...even the Internet would pale in comparison to this magical universal web."

"You think these things would ever share their abilities with you?"

"Oh, I'm fairly sure they shared them with the Inquisitor."

Jessica thought she was literally about to see red. Her blood pressure pounded in her ears. "The Inquisitor?" she almost yelled. "Who's a psychopathic killer? Are we talking about the same Inquisitor who murders innocent people? Who burns them alive at the stake?"

But Renshaw was unfazed. "Just *try* and see something more complex than that," he pleaded. "Of course, they need to procure...dare I say food? They need to stay alive somehow when they enter our world. So they've been relying on our dead. That would seem perfectly reasonable. The corpses from our funeral homes, hospitals. If you think about this rationally, does it really sound all that objectionable? People die every day. That sounds a lot more callous than I'd like it to be, but it's the simple truth. But do you think most people would ever accept a bargain like that with these beings? Can you imagine them coming out into the open and announcing they would gladly share with us so much of their wonderful abilities for only a slight payment? Only if we could just let them consume our dead? Can you imagine all those superstitious simpletons with their absurd religions reacting to that? Those creatures, by the way, are also quite unpleasant to our unaccustomed human eyes. Can you imagine the likes of Jim Garnett screaming 'demons' when he saw them? Quite honestly, I really can't see how else these beings could operate until the whole foolish, misguided lot of us on this planet can be reprogrammed. Please try to understand somehow that I genuinely wish these emissaries from beyond the best of luck in somehow overcoming so much of human stupidity, selfishness, superstition that's been conditioned into us over the millennia."

"Emissaries?" Jessica could barely get the word out. "Are you *completely* insane?"

Renshaw sighed and rolled his eyes with almost practiced melodrama. "Oh, please, just *try* and be reasonable. From what Brock told me about you — "

Jessica had to cut him off immediately. Just the thought that this lunatic even considered her capable of sympathizing with his sociopathic delusions made her feel unclean. "If what he told you makes you think I could ever accept this madness, I'm too happy to disappoint you. What makes you even *think* these monsters *want* to share anything with you? Their tool, for Christ's sake, is a serial killer! They're *murdering* — are you somehow capable in some part of your diseased mind of understanding what that means? — they are torturing to death, they are *killing* innocent people who were never given a choice to take part in this wonderful transformation of yours."

"Murdering? Killing?" Renshaw asked derisively. "So easily and so self-righteously we throw around those words. We will live in a world of no more killing, no more wars, no corruption, no injustice and exploitation if we can become one with these beings. You want to talk killings? How about all the killings in all the pointless wars our species ever waged? We just need to — "

"Yeah, make sacrifices, right? Break a few eggs to make omelets."

Renshaw shook his head and seemed to look past Jessica. He had the hopeless, exhausted look of someone who had tried his best to talk sense into a disruptive child, only to see the subject's sub-normal intelligence had him involved in a hopelessly futile exercise. "Well," he said wearily, "I can't think of any crisis in this world that can ever be solved by your simple-minded, black and white morality."

"But they can by just closing your eyes and marching off to be food for these ghouls," Jessica said, realizing that she was almost sputtering her words, barely able to string a coherent sentence together. "Have you all lost your minds?" she yelled, this time not just at Renshaw. In fact, she quickly backed away from him, noticing most eyes in the room, turning toward her. "Are you all completely insane?" she screamed at the top of her lungs, her voice echoing across the conference hall.

CHAPTER 79

Jessica had to flee the conference hall, even if it took kicking and punching her way past all of Tom's compatriots. The stares zeroing in on her, felt like those of wild animals. Insane, paranoid thoughts jumbled through her mind. She felt like she was the dead body she had seen devoured in the woods. No matter what awaited her outside, something like a susurrating voice echoed through her brain, she had to get away from the people in the conference room.

She spun around and bolted for the door. With a couple of voices chiming out behind her, calling her name, she ran for her life.

She sprinted along the hallway Tom had led her through, realizing that speed was her only option now. She had to get out of the building and move as fast as possible. It didn't matter which way she went, she just had to move.

The Predator! the thought flashed through her mind.

He was nearby. The threat he posed was almost palpable. She expected him to spring from the shadows any moment now.

But that was not the way he would come, she knew full well.

He's bringing the explosives, Jessica's mind reeled.

The Predator was going to drive a truckload of explosives into the building.

And he was on his way!

She had a vision of roiling clouds of fire, of debris, of total destruction in the building around her. Somehow she could see a nondescript white truck making its way through the campus, speeding up and rocketing toward a collision course with the Carlson building.

So Jessica pushed herself forward, ran faster still, and ran for the building's main entrance that was only some fifty feet in front of her.

"Jessica!" a shout echoed along the hallway, pursuing and catching up to her before she could reach the door. "Jessica, please!" the shout came again.

But she only came to a halt because she reached the plate glass doors. Her name was called for a third time, but she knew who it was that had been pursuing her.

"Jessica, don't do this!" Tom's voice came after her yet again.

She could hear his footfalls echoing down the corridor. As she pushed through the doors, she could hear that Tom was only a few feet away. But then he stopped. She could hear his exhausted breathing.

"Jessica," he said again as he fought to catch his breath.

Sensing the physical distance between them, Jessica turned around. She saw him panting, still struggling to breathe. And she was glad to see he had good sense enough not to try and come any closer.

"No, Tom," she said before he could say anything more. "I'm not staying here. This is wrong. What those people in there are doing is wrong."

"Look, Jessica," Tom said with a pained shake of his head. "This is too big to get out of now. If you walk away, you'll be a target for them. Come back inside, because we only have a few minutes left. There's a part of the basement that will survive the blast. We'll all be safe down there."

"Or we can run as fast as we can," Jessica said instead.

"No, you can't. They'll—"

"Find me? And what if I had help from someone who knows all about the nature of these creatures?" Jessica paused to study his reaction. "Someone who could keep them away by speaking out with me?"

Again, there was no reply from Tom.

"Or will that lead to a horrible new world you're committed to fighting?" Jessica asked.

And she knew there was no reason to stand there and waste time. There was only silence on Tom's part. She turned and walked down the short, three-flight staircase off the building's front entrance. As she was about to break into a full-out spring, she just had to take another look and see what Tom was capable of in a moment like this. She turned around and saw him disappearing into the shadowy interior of the building.

When Jessica turned to flee, she saw a pair of headlights spearing through the darkness, heading straight in her direction.

CHAPTER 80

Somehow, even more than the realization of the fact that a devastating explosion was only moments away, Jessica was stunned by the appearance of the incoming truck. It was a small white box-truck bearing down the wide footpath that led toward the Carlson building. When she pictured an explosive-laden truck making its suicidal run at the campus, it looked *exactly* like this. It was as if she was living out the realization of a perfect premonition.

Run! a voice echoed through her mind.

And, instead of breaking into a full sprint, she weakly, dazedly stumbled forward. She couldn't even focus on running for her life because a shocking realization threw her completely off balance.

Run, goddamn it! her mind screamed.

Except it wasn't her own mind. It wasn't her inner voice, her intuition, her instinct, or reflexes, or anything like that. It was a *voice* inside her mind. A psychic presence had entered her and was screaming at her to move or die.

Then the sound of a second car's engine roared out of the night from somewhere on Jessica's left. As she turned toward it, she was stunned by another pair of headlights. These, however, glared on blinding high beams. They also belonged to what sounded like a muscle car — might have been a Dodge Charger or a Mustang, Jessica guessed as the car got closer. The vehicle had been tearing up the lawn on a grassy stretch of the campus, its driver barreling off the paved driveways, over the grass, around trees, and finally swerving off to the left and onto the footpath. And it wound up on a collision course with the incoming truck.

"Oh, no," she gasped as she saw the two vehicles facing each other.

It looked as if the smaller car — indeed a Charger — was about to play chicken with the explosive-filled truck.

Jessica, in turn, bolted to her right, attempting to flee, yet her attention was riveted by the bizarre spectacle. Then, to add to the insanity, gunshots rang out of the Charger. But they did so a split instant before the vehicle skidded to a smoking, fishtailing halt. The driver, Jessica saw, was sticking a handgun out his window and pumping a quick volley of rounds at the truck.

The truck appeared to jink and swerve when shot at, but it remained on a more or less straight trajectory toward the Charger.

Then the Charger's driver-side door swung open. The man behind the wheel slid out, but took quick cover behind his open door. He was on one knee, Jessica could tell, and he blasted away at the truck with a large caliber automatic pistol.

Straight ahead, the windshield of the truck had been nearly obliterated. Plumes and flashes of sparks danced around the driver's cab. But, nonetheless, Jessica noticed in horror, the truck barely slowed.

Barely! her mind raced, realizing a moment later that the truck, indeed, was cutting its speed.

The shooter, in the meantime, having expanded his ammo, smoothly ejected a spent magazine and reinserted a new one with nearly eye-blurring speed.

"I don't believe it," Jessica realized she mouthed the word.

At first, she sensed it, as if by blind, thoughtless instinct, and then she actually caught a glimpse of the shooter's profile.

It was Buzz. Buzz…Owen…whoever the hell he really was, had escaped the funeral home men. Jessica's mind reeled at this turn of events. He had gotten loose and had come back here for this suicidal showdown with the Predator. Indeed, in the next couple of fleeting seconds, she saw him miss death by a hair's breadth.

After reloading, Buzz attempted to keep shooting, but it was too late. He recognized this because he only squeezed off two shots before lunging backward. He *had* to because the truck was still coming. The big vehicle had slowed considerably, but it was still moving. It kept rolling forward until it rammed the front end of the Charger. The strike was not spectacular, and certainly didn't seem to do much damage to the vehicle, but it did thrust it backward. In turn, its open driver's side door flew at Buzz.

He, it appeared, had realized that the impact was inevitable. He sprang back and away from the door. Although he missed the full force of the impact, he *was* struck. The door caught him across his right leg and hip and swept him to the ground.

Jessica gasped as Buzz was flung across the pavement. She could hear the clattering of his pistol as it escaped his grip. And then the driver's door of the truck's cab swung open.

"Oh, Jesus, no!" Jessica hissed. She was now rooted in one spot. One part of her logical mind screamed at her to flee, but the unreal spectacle of violence froze her in place.

The Predator leaped from the truck and palmed a handgun. He swung its barrel toward the Charger and lunged forward. His moves appeared to be a furious dance of barely-contained energy and semi-rational caution. He looked like he was aching to hurl himself right over Buzz's car and attack him, but he seemed wary of the fact that Buzz might still be armed and capable of fighting.

And the Predator's conservative attack plan was wise, Jessica could see when Buzz pulled out a second handgun. From a sitting position, he flash-aimed the weapon through the Charger's window and squeezed off two shots.

The psycho, in turn, recoiled from the assault but didn't retreat. He haphazardly aimed back and returned fire. His shots, just like Buzz's, were well off target.

A frenzied cycle of misfiring continued as Buzz, too, shot back. Once more, the Predator dodged his bullets on the opposite side of the car, then shot back at Buzz. Crazy flashes of sparks, chipped paint, shattered glass, and plastic zigzagged off the car as it was caught in the crossfire.

The shooting, though, could only go on for so long. At just about the same time, Buzz and the Predator were out of bullets.

Although she wouldn't have believed it was possible, Jessica's frenzied heartbeats surged once more. She was looking at the end game, and panicky comprehension dawned on her. Whoever reloaded first would live. In another two or three seconds, either Buzz or the Predator would survive.

And then Buzz made an unexpected move. He didn't reload but physically attacked the Predator. He sprang to his feet while his opponent fumbled a fresh cartridge of bullets from a pocket, jumped onto the hood of the Charger, and dived at the Predator. He tackled the serial killer—their collision flinging the madman's gun away—and they were quickly tied up in a brutal, violent tangle of flying, jabbing, pummeling, kicking fists and legs.

But how long will this delay the inevitable? Jessica's mind screamed. Someone was bound to die in the next couple of moments, and there was no way of telling who. Furthermore, while she had no reason to trust Buzz, the Predator's victory only meant her own immediate demise.

She should have run as fast as she could in the opposite direction, Jessica knew. That was the only option that made sense. But instead, she headed toward the showdown. As the fight got more and more frenzied, she rushed toward the Charger, slipped around its rear, and headed for the driver's side.

The gun! The gun! The gun! her mind raced. She had to find the weapon Buzz dropped after getting hit with the car door.

On the far side of the car, the Predator's otherworldly animal shriek tore through the night. The sound made Jessica feel as if icy blades had raked through her entire body.

And then she found the massive handgun. It was halfway in the grass on the edge of the footpath.

From the direction of the fight, she could hear the sickening sounds of punches and kicks pummeling flesh.

"Loaded...loaded and chambered," Jessica muttered to herself as she took the gun in both hands. She had seen Buzz squeeze off two rounds from the weapon before he went down. The gun should have been good to go. All she needed to do was point it and pull the trigger.

So she rose into a crouch and circled around the rear of the Charger once more. She had to sneak up on the fight and —

And what? a voice went off in her mind. *Which one will you hit as they're thrashing around?*

And as she made the turn to the combatants' side of the car, she found the two men standing upright, except Buzz seemed to be the one worse for the wear. Even though the Predator was physically smaller, he had Buzz by the throat with one hand and seemed to be squeezing with all his might.

Then the Predator thrust his hand upward and lifted Buzz off his feet.

"No!" Jessica screamed and jabbed the gun in the Predator's direction.

The Predator turned his head and glared at her as he propelled Buzz backward. Images from the mall flashed through Jessica's mind, except now the Predator looked even more otherworldly. A pulsing latticework of veins had risen all along his face and forehead. Both his eyes were glistening blood red.

The move of the Predator's arm slammed Buzz against the side of the car.

And Jessica squeezed the handgun's trigger.

Although not a perfect shot, the Beretta's nine-millimeter slug punched through the Predator's left shoulder and spun him around to face Jessica head on.

In turn, she fired again.

This time, a ragged, blood-splattering hole blossomed on the serial killer's chest. Apparently, Jessica realized, he wasn't wearing a bulletproof vest this time. She could see a geyser of blood spraying out his back.

So she kept firing. She squeezed the trigger over and over again, battering the maniac's upper body, reducing it to a raw, ragged hunk of bleeding flesh. One of the shots caught him in his left cheek, tearing away nearly half his face. Another round hit him in the forehead, drilling through his skull and blowing out the back of his head.

After the Beretta gave up its last shot, slide snapping back on an empty chamber, the Predator's lifeless form melted to the ground.

Jessica found herself frozen in one spot, enveloped in the reeking smells of death. The sharp tang of cordite rose from the gun in her hand. A puff of the night breezes threw the coppery stench of blood in her face.

Then she saw Buzz rising to his feet, still gasping for air, trying to recover from the Predator's chokehold.

When he approached her, Jessica couldn't help but keep the gun pointed forward. It was a useless, empty piece of metal, but she needed it to convey and message. She wanted it to look at least symbolically threatening. She wanted Buzz to know she wished she could be pointing a loaded gun at him. It was what he deserved for his betrayal.

He slowly approached and stood in front of Jessica. Then, without a word, he reached for her gun and slowly removed it from her slackening fingers. Then he took a full clip of bullets from his jeans' back pocket. He calmly inserted it into the Beretta's grip and snapped the slide forward. A new round was now in the chamber. Holding the weapon by the barrel, he lifted it toward Jessica. He took her right hand in his left and placed the gun back in her grip. He even guided her index finger onto the trigger. He only let go when she was aiming the weapon at his chest. He had put himself at her mercy.

"I'm not your enemy, Jessica," he whispered at length. "I swear on my life."

Jessica wanted to believe him, all the while she wanted to scream in his face and threaten to kill him. But all she could feel was a drained sensation of numbness. She lowered the gun.

"We have to get out of here and end this," Buzz said, his voice more pointed this time. "End what's going on in this town." He paused and gave her a challenging glare. "We can do it. Now I know how."

"How did you...?" Jessica summoned the strength to mutter.

"Tom shouldn't have secured me with your gym lock," Buzz said, and tapped an index finger against his forehead. "I could see the combination through your eyes."

Something frigid seemed to flood Jessica's body. What Buzz just said had implications she couldn't even try to fathom just now.

"And how do we end it?" she asked instead.

"We go back to the place they tried to take me. It's an abandoned house not far from the funeral home. But we have to take the truckload of explosives with us." Then he nodded toward the Charger. "I'll take the truck. Can you follow me in that thing?"

CHAPTER 81

Buzz pointed toward the treetops on the dark horizon. "See that?" he asked quietly. "Those flashes?"

Jessica had been straining her eyes to see something through the midnight blackness all around them. But then, just as Buzz suggested, flashes of light became visible. More than just flashes, in fact, but moving bolts of light appeared to be dancing across the sky. Within seconds of appearing, the lights would fade out. The phenomenon looked a lot like the lights they had seen the night when they spied the creatures feeding.

"Bolts of energy somehow…I don't know…escaping the point where they cross over," Buzz said.

"Cross over?" Jessica replied in a near whisper. She couldn't help but let her eyes wander as she did so. They stood alone at the edge of a gravelly access road winding into the heart of a peculiarly, eerily tangled, jagged stretch of forest. They must have been four or five miles east of the place they had last encountered the creatures and their flesh-eating. According to Buzz, this road led toward the area where they bridged the divide between this world and the alternate dimension they came from.

Aside from the fact that it was nearly pitch-black and they were intruding into the territory of an enemy mobilizing all its forces, all of its collaborators and acolytes, just the land itself seemed disturbingly otherworldly here. Jessica tried to tell herself—wanted to believe desperately—that it was only her nerves, only her fevered, terrified imagination that was projecting a haunted, alien-looking forest all around her. But this bit of self-discipline wasn't working. Straining her eyes against the darkness, she thought she saw trees that appeared preternaturally barren. Despite it being the middle of the summer, so many of the trees looked unusually defoliated. Underneath the trees—and all around Jessica and Buzz—wild, thick bushes sprouted everywhere. Almost all of them were barbed with wickedly sharp thorns. It was almost as if the land underfoot was corrupted, diseased.

"Are you sure about this crossing over?" Jessica asked. She knew her voice was thick with skepticism, but she didn't mind Buzz hearing it. On the one hand, she loathed standing out here in this lightless, forbidding landscape. More than anything, she wanted to turn around and flee. On the other hand, the story Buzz had told her about the reason he'd been taken out here was riddled with some formidable holes in logic. Moreover, she just could not bring herself to trust him.

"I saw it," he said quietly, and looked at her.

Jessica could sense that he was struggling mightily to keep his frustration under control. But he was also smart enough to know that he could not be any more imperious and insistent right now, right after his epic act of deception. He needed to stay as calm, as chastened and accommodating of all of her questions, demands, and insecurities as he could.

"This is where they tried to bring me," Buzz explained.

"To where they're crossing over?" Jessica quickly cut in.

"Yes."

"Why? Did they want to take you over?"

"I don't know," Buzz said, his frustration more evident now. "I assume so. This road leads to some crumbling old house. Pretty big one, as I could tell. Like some big old manor house.

And inside it—"

"Is the doorway?"

"Yes, something like that. That's where they came through. It's also conveniently close to the funeral home."

"And now you think that truckload of explosives will seal it?"

"I think it could," Buzz said with a strong, resolute nod.

"How? If this place is like a hole in…what? Reality? An opening in this dimension…." Jessica's voice trailed off. She hoped Buzz understood what she was trying to say. Despite everything, she just felt absurd, talking about holes in reality.

"No, it's not just a hole," Buzz replied. "They have a mechanism there."

"Mechanism? Like a device that opens the hole?"

"Yes. It's just inside the building. It's this silvery tower…if you want to know what it looks like. It's a machine of some sort they use to pass back and forth."

"And you think the explosion will destroy it?"

Buzz stared at Jessica for a protracted moment. "I have to try…there's no other choice."

If he was right about the interdimensional mechanism, Jessica considered, he was right about the attack as well. "But aren't they waiting for you?"

"No, I don't think so. They're back in town. Looking for us."

"But what about the psychic connection?" Jessica asked. This still remained the most confusing aspect of Buzz's story for her.

"I can block them…most of the time."

"Most of the time?"

"I can block them well enough. It's an ability I realized I had soon after they turned me into this. I can fight and block their mental probes. And I can fight their mental probes of others. Like you."

BARNA WILLIAM DONOVAN

"Are you sure they don't know we're here right now?"

"I can't be sure of anything. Not one hundred percent. But we *have* to do this. We have to do it now."

Jessica nodded. She knew he was right. "Okay."

"So get back into the Charger and get out of here," Buzz instructed as he started backing away toward the truck.

"And I'll wait for you at the spot you told me," Jessica said. They had agreed that she would wait for fifteen minutes at a campground off the main road nearby.

"Not if you know you have to flee! Do you understand?" Buzz asked strongly. "Do you understand?"

"Yes," Jessica said. If she suddenly had a powerful gut instinct, a panic reaction, if she *knew* she had to flee, they had discussed, it was really an instruction from Buzz. He could direct a mental panic alarm into her mind—just as he had done back in the middle of Tom's gathering, just as he had done days ago when the Predator came after her in his van—and she was to floor the Charger's gas pedal and speed out of town.

So she, too, started backing away toward the car.

"Jessica," Buzz said suddenly.

She didn't reply, sensing what he wanted to say.

"I'm sorry," Buzz told her. "I swear to you I never wanted to hurt you."

CHAPTER 82

The sound of the explosion reverberated through the night air. Its bass, demonic rumble carried all the way back to the Cedar Valley State University campus. Tom Lancaster watched the sky, wondering if he would see any faint traces of light from the detonation of all those explosives in the late Predator's truck. He couldn't.

The light pollution around the Erskine F. Carlson building might have had something to do with it, of course. Both local and state police cruisers crowded the area now, their red, yellow, and blue lights crazily bathing everything in color.

For a moment, Tom entertained an uncomfortable feeling. That explosion on the outskirts of town seemed somehow...*too* loud. Perhaps loud enough even to have been strong enough to bring the entire Carlson building down. Perhaps if the truck full of high explosives had gone off right here, all according to plan, he and his group might not have survived even the reinforced basement. Tom wanted to dismiss the thought, but it gnawed at him. He wanted to ignore it as unrealistic, as irrational paranoia. The creatures needed him. They *needed* all the people in this little arrangement. It made no sense that the creatures would want to betray them, double-cross them, and kill them for real.

Nevertheless....

"This belongs to you, I believe," Tom heard a voice next to him.

He nearly jumped from the sound, in fact. Whoever talked to him had snuck up in perfect silence.

It was the woman cop, Stansfield, Tom recognized. If he remembered correctly, her first name might have been Arlene. Arlene, or Amy, or something like that. He didn't particularly care. Although he also thought he heard it mentioned that she was slated to take over Gainey's position now.

"What's that?" Tom muttered.

"Here," Stansfield said and pitched over the small object she toyed with in her right hand.

It was Jessica's gym lock. Tom caught it in both hands.

"Nice going," Stansfield said.

"I was lucky she had the damned thing. Since she knew the combination, he was sure to retrieve it from her thoughts. So yeah, pretty lucky."

"Whatever," Stansfield said coolly. "All's well that ends perfectly according to plan. Well, more or less."

Tom took a close look at the woman cop.

She gave him a contrite look. "I mean, it would have been good if you could have convinced her to go along with the program."

"Yeah," Tom said simply. If only Jessica would have listened to reason, they wouldn't have to start dismantling her entire life and reputation the moment the first reporters showed up.

EPILOGUE - PART I

Jessica had been trying to make sense of what had happened between her and Buzz, what the experience had done to her, for weeks now. She was no closer to understanding or even deciding how she should feel about it, even now.

She could be sure of nothing, not even what she wanted to call him. For some reason, "Buzz" just didn't feel right. It was, though, possibly the only thing he had been honest about from the time they met. "Buzz" really was his nickname. Yet, in her mind, "Buzz" somehow just remained linked to his phony surname, "McPherson." That, of course, had been his fiancée's name. He had clung to that name because it was his only connection to her. He had loved her, and she had been taken from him. He had loved her so much that he gave up the life he had and devoted himself to pursuing her killers. He loved her so much that his mission of vengeance caused him to become tainted with an interdimensional infection. So, could she ever think of him by that name, McPherson, when it was but a ghost of his dead fiancée between them?

When Jessica tried sorting these things out, she came down to the beach and walked along the wet sand. It was only a block away from the house they rented under aliases.

She and Buzz/Owen — she wanted to start thinking of him as Owen, but she couldn't quite get used to the name change yet — had been sinking further and further into criminality. Their new home was but a symptom of it. They got the money they had been living off of for the past two weeks in Las Vegas and Reno. Buzz had made psychic connections with gamblers — men he had shaken hands with, whose loose hairs he could brush off a jacket sleeve, people he "accidentally" switched drinking glasses with at the tables — then cheated massive amounts of money out of them. He claimed he could just as easily get burglar-alarm codes, safe combinations, and bank account information out of people. He promised he wouldn't when he sensed Jessica's unease with the idea. Of course, he didn't say he hadn't made those forays into such pure, uncomplicated crimes in the past. Jessica, in turn, couldn't honestly know that such outright larceny would always offend her moral sensibilities. If it turned out they could never get their lives back, she just might let pure survival instincts take over sooner rather than later. Before they would get to that, Buzz said he would try his best to hunt down a premier hacker and learn how they could transfer all her money out of her bank accounts and into new off-shore accounts. But for now, crooked gambling let them live in a comfortable seaside cottage in the tiny Northern California town of Stewart's Point.

They, however, had no choice in the matter. The Cedar Valley authorities had gone out of their way to make both of them look like accomplices of the Inquisition killer. News stories shortly after the CVSU campus incident detailed how courageous police lieutenant — now chief of police — Arlene Stansfield had gunned down the rampaging serial murderer and religious fanatic.

But all these complications inexorably tied Jessica to Buzz/ Owen...her companion, her....

"Whatever the hell," she muttered to herself as she stopped, closed her eyes, and inhaled the ocean breeze. She hoped the sounds, the smells, the soothing beauty of the beach, and the water would help her sort through the twisted, unfathomable mess her life had turned into. It rarely did.

Just whatever the hell she and "Buzz" were had continued eluding her. She still grappled with the fact that she couldn't quite forgive him for sleeping with her without telling her what he was. His touch, his kisses, his body entering hers had drawn her further into his world, had passed his alien changes on to her.

Sure, he had rationalized it over and over. *She* had rationalized it to herself on good days. She had, after all, been tainted by the Predator. The sex they had could only have helped her break free of the psycho's connection to her. He even told her that when he wiped that drop of blood off her nose in Tom's kitchen, he had done it to gain his own connection and try and block the Predator's.

Except Buzz hadn't told her the whole truth *before* sleeping with her. How could he not have said anything about what he was? About how their love-making helped draw her deeper into the world of these monsters? It was the lie Jessica had an impossible time with.

You're looking at it like some sort of psychic STD, she had often told herself. And, in a way, that's exactly what it was.

Except, she wanted to believe Buzz as well. What went on between them would hardly harm her or turn her into one of those creatures.

Except he lied about it. Why couldn't he just tell me?

And, she often countered with herself, she probably would have slept with Buzz anyway.

But he lied.

She wanted to move on and forgive him. One part of her, at least, did.

Except she still hadn't slept with him since. But she wanted to…in a good moment.

And they had been feeling more and more like a married

couple with every passing day. She could guess his feelings, the things he was about to say next. She was able to finish his sentences.

It was all a part of the alien presence in her now. The sex, his body inside her, had done this. Created the ideal, literal psychic connection between two partners all people in love want to have for the rest of their lives? So what was so bad about it? she often asked herself.

The fact that he lied! He manipulated me. He forced this on me for "my own good." He took away my choice in the matter.

In other moments, Jessica's interpersonal relationship specialist self took over, and she thought these monsters might have had the ultimate answer to a long and happy relationship. Just a touch of the interdimensional infection and all the scores of romance-advice writers would be out of a job.

Then, when she found herself wandering down these logical byways, she would always eventually feel chills of apprehension passing through her. Was she actually starting to understand people like Don Renshaw and the rest of the utopian fanatics in Tom's little cabal? If the interdimensional virus made for a good relationship by bonding people together, could it not make for better citizenship? Could it not make people better friends? Better neighbors? Could it not make different nationalities, races, religions feel closer, less hostile, less likely to kill each other? Was Renshaw right? Did the creatures not deserve to completely infect our world?

But what of the people who did not want to be infected? Should it be forced onto them, whether they liked it or not? For their own good? For the greater good of humanity, peace, justice?

Jessica shook herself loose from these thoughts because they always led to dark, dangerous conclusions.

But then she often heard Cassie's words in her head. "Well,

another day has gone by, Jessica, and I still can't understand what you can't forgive."

And Cassie was "a whole 'nother story."

Jessica turned away from the ocean and started walking toward the edge of the beach and the sidewalk beyond.

Cassie had been giving her a virtually unchanging series of pep-talks about the "Buzz problem," as they called it. Cassie wanted her to put the lie behind her, accept the fact that she loved Buzz, and just move on. Life was too short, Cassie would invariably preach, to be stuck on past mistakes. She, of course, could speak from a unique perspective. Cassie had made a phenomenal recovery from her cancer. She was "one hundred percent" — she quoted her doctors — disease-free. "As if she had never been ill a day in her life," Dr. Lazarus Heinlein, Cassie's physician and miracle worker at the Renewed Life Oncological Institute in Los Angeles, had told her. Cassie usually spoke about Dr. Heinlein the way the newly converted spoke of their spiritual guides or gurus. In a way, of course, Heinlein had been exactly that.

Cassie was the only person from her old life Jessica still spoke to. Cassie knew the whole story about the Predator and the creatures in Cedar Valley. Although, most often, their clandestine communications made Jessica insane with paranoia. The FBI was bound to be keeping an eye on her old acquaintances. After the hell Cassie had been through with her cancer, the last thing Jessica wanted for her was to be arrested for aiding and abetting a pair of dangerous fugitives.

So now Jessica felt more like a knife was twisting inside of her, as she knew she had to confront Dr. Heinlein. Confront him and, most likely, kill him.

EPILOGUE - PART II

If you accept the fact that others could try and read your thoughts, enter your mind, Buzz had told Jessica, you could actually pick up their presence. You just had to believe it was true for it to *be* true. Belief opened a whole new world to your awareness, Buzz had instructed. Then, once you feel them, you can will them out of you. You can erect a mental firewall to keep them away.

It sounded almost like a religious sermon, Jessica had mused. If anyone would have overheard them talking like that, they would have been certain the FBI was right. They would have been instantly convinced that Jessica and Buzz were a pair of deranged, homicidal ding-dongs.

As Jessica stepped into the elevator to the fifth floor of the newly constructed Imperial Towers in Beverly Hills, she felt nothing at all. No mental probes, nothing trying to enter her mind. She couldn't be sure if she was just not aware, or if she was truly safe. Although Buzz, who was sneaking into the building at the same moment disguised as a delivery man, also felt nothing while they had reconnoitered the building.

Jessica was certain that presences *had* to be here, however. Very *bad* presences. As she would step off the elevator and onto one of the three floors belonging to the Renewed Life Institute, she would be stepping into the jaws of the beast. Or the *beasts*. The interdimensional ghoul beasts.

Dr. Lazarus Heinlein, my ass, Jessica had reacted almost immediately upon hearing about the "great man," "the genius," "the savior" from Cassie. The name was a joke to draw Jessica out. A fan of classic science fiction literature like her would catch the phony name. It was a combination of the names Lazarus Long, from the novel *Time Enough for Love,* and the work's author, Robert Heinlein. The book was about a character that lived a preternaturally long life.

One of the things the creatures can do for us, Jessica thought as she watched the number on the elevator wall change. *The supreme irony. They can strengthen our bodies, increase our longevity, while our world kills* them *if they stay here too long.*

She remembered how quickly the swelling from her punched nose had disappeared. And the cut on her foot.

Because of the Predator's blood.

But then Jessica thought of something that made her smile. She, at last, knew she had made the right decision. Before leaving Buzz behind outside, she had kissed him. She had whispered, "I love you" into his ear.

When the elevator doors slid open, the reception area of the Renewed Life Institute was not quite the way she hoped she would find it. Sure, the décor looked Beverly Hills through and through; ultra chic, ultra upscale, ultra expensive. Unfortunately, the place was also empty, except for a slim little receptionist giving Jessica a long, penetrating stare. The girl looked all of eighteen, and on her days off from the institute, she could just as well have been making some extra money as a model. Just like the décor and the furniture, she looked flawlessly perfect.

"Miss Gibson?" the receptionist asked with a spokesmodel's perky smile.

When the elevator doors slid shut behind her, Jessica couldn't help but think of the doors of a tomb sealing shut.

"Dr. Heinlein is waiting for you," the receptionist said smoothly, still smiling, and waved toward the entrance to a corridor on the far side of the room.

Jessica's heartbeats started hammering, her adrenaline surging. "Don't you need me to fill out some forms?" she asked.

"We can take care of that later," the receptionist said pleasantly.

Sure we can, Jessica thought. *If there is a later.*

As she walked forward, she concentrated on feeling the metallic impression of the Walther P99QA handgun tucked into the waist of her slacks by the small of her back. Her loose-fitting blouse concealed it. If anyone would have expected her to be carrying a weapon, they should have thought of her purse first.

Unless, of course, they know your thoughts.

But she couldn't feel any mental probes, Jessica reminded herself and recalled Buzz's words.

What if he's wrong? What if they're stronger than that? What if I'm not strong enough and can't sense them? What if…?

Jessica shook the thoughts from her mind as she entered the corridor.

What she wanted more than anything now was to feel Buzz's thoughts. She wanted to reach out to him. But, of course, she was afraid of that, too. She didn't want to give their plan away, didn't want to jeopardize his safety.

Jessica was startled by a metallic object getting jabbed into her back. Then a hand went straight for her pistol.

"Keep moving, and you'll live," a gravelly, emotionless voice droned into her ear.

Then the metal object at her back—no doubt a very large caliber firearm that could cut her in half—jabbed her forward.

"Not a word," her captor added a moment later. "Just keep walking."

At the end of the hallway, she was led through a darkly-tinted, pebbled glass doorway. On the other side, she found herself in a room so ultra-spare, so ultra-stylized it could have been designed by the interior decorator favored by most of James Bond's nemeses. The floor, the ceiling, the walls were all a very dark blue shade, and the illumination mostly came from bright pink lights behind large raised rectangular panels on the walls. There was an empty table and two chairs in the middle of the room, all a very bright cherry red. A banker's lamp atop the table gave off more light.

When the door on the left side of the room opened, Jessica saw something that made her feel as if she had been kicked in the stomach. She literally had to gasp for breath from the shock.

Tom Lancaster entered the room. Even stranger still, he was wearing a white lab coat.

"Hello, Jessica," he said calmly.

Jessica immediately noticed that something was off. His voice was not quite right. It was sort of close to what she remembered, but somehow different.

"Tom?" she whispered.

He smiled back at her in a way that was both soothingly placid *and* smarmy. "Sorry about the rough treatment," he said, "but we had to take your gun...for now." Then his gaze shifted to the man behind Jessica. "Apologize, why don't you?"

Jessica first heard metallic clicking and sliding noises behind her. Her captor must have removed the clip from her pistol. Then she heard the man's rough, thuggish voice. "Sorry," he said simply. Then, he added, "Here, take it."

When she turned around, she was jolted breathless once more. The man handing her the Walther was also Tom.

"How...?" she wheezed as she took the gun. Her hands shook now, she realized. For a moment, she thought she was going to drop the empty weapon.

"Yes, shocking, I know," the first Tom, the one in the lab coat, said. "Imagine if you told anyone," he added as he circled the desk and approached Jessica. "They'd say you were...."

"Insane," Jessica finished his statement. Not only had these creatures framed her as some kind of a would-be mass murderer, but if she ever left this place and told her story, she would appear to have completely broken from all reality. A Beverly Hills cancer treatment center run by clones of her former almost-boyfriend? Only in the fantasies of a psychotic.

He nodded at her with a cold, conspiratorial little grin.

He had gotten close enough for Jessica to see the name tag on his chest. "Dr. L. Heinlein," it read.

"Why don't you sit down," he said congenially. "You look like you need to." He pointed at the nearest red chair and put a hand on her shoulder. When she didn't comply, he slowly started squeezing. The pressure began to hurt a moment later. "Please?" he said.

So Jessica did as she was told.

"And I know what you're thinking," the Tom-like Dr. Heinlein said as he took the chair on the other side of the table. "Buzz is fine. We know he's in the building. We're just going to make sure he doesn't interfere with what we have to do right now. And no, we're not going to hurt him."

"'What we have to do'?" Jessica said, taken by the weakness in her voice.

The faux Tom smiled languidly. "Just talk. Discuss a few things."

"Aha," Jessica said at length.

"Discuss some of the options you have in front of you."

"Discuss options. And can our discussion include a few questions?"

The…*thing* in front of Jessica smiled again. This time it hardly made an effort to look friendly. It had a sort of generic, insincere celebrity grin. The key, Jessica thought, lay in its eyes. They were motionless, lifeless orbs.

"Questions," the Heinlein-thing said at length. "It depends."

Jessica took a deep breath. "I see. So why don't I just ask you a really basic one and see what happens? What the hell are you?"

"Several people have told you their ideas about that, haven't they?" Tom Lancaster's simulacrum asked with a quizzical raise of the eyebrows. There was even a slight, puzzled tilt of his head. "Really smart people, too. You would trust their conclusions, wouldn't you?"

He was mocking her, Jessica realized. She would have loved to have been able to lunge across the table and grasp his throat.

"Do you have reason to believe they're lying to you?" the creature asked. "Even Buzz? The man you love? Oh…you two *have* made up, I take it. Traveling around as you have."

"So, I *can* believe what I've been told?" Jessica asked, trying to keep her voice level and calm.

"You can believe whatever you want."

Bastard. "So, what do we need to talk about?" Jessica asked instead of cursing at him. She wasn't going to start playing word games with this thing. It was but another way for him to prove his dominance over her.

"Well," the creature began smoothly, "let me put it this way; some of us were impressed by what you accomplished back in Cedar Valley. Evading the Predator, fighting so doggedly to get to the bottom of the truth. Trying to convince…." The creature grinned as he waved at his face. "…*Tom Lancaster*…that there are interdimensional monsters running around out there. Bravo, Jessica. There's spirit in you we truly admire."

"Sure, you do."

"You sound so skeptical."

Jessica could feel rage flaring inside of her now. It felt hot and scalding. "All right, listen," she spat the words at the creature. "Just cut the crap, okay? You've got me. You have the upper hand. You have your partner back there with the gun, and I'm sure there are more of you all over this building. So how about you give it a rest and tell me what you want with me. Why am I still alive?"

"Because you fascinate us, Jessica," the creature said flatly. "I already told you that. And we want to know what you would do with this place if you could."

Jessica didn't want to tell him to cut the crap again, so she stayed silent, staring at him, waiting for him to make his full pitch.

"This place...that just saved your friend's life. We also saved a lot of other people's lives as well in our very short run here. And I think you know that happened, don't you?" The creature paused and studied Jessica for a few moments. "Of course, we're talking about very serious problems here. Not a couple of minor scrapes and bruises like you had. Killing cancer. Completely healing a person. You know what that takes?" The creature leaned forward and stared into Jessica's eyes. "*Blood*. Our blood. A *lot* of blood. Very special foods, too. A *lot* of it."

Buzz's words came back to Jessica now. Back in Cedar Valley, he had tried to convince her that the creatures couldn't control her. He told her that the Predator's blood she had tasted caused no more harm than a psychic link.

No more *harm? How screwed up does that sound?*

But Buzz had also said that complete control by the creatures would take a lot *more* blood. It would take the eating of flesh....

A very special diet?

So control was possible through copious amounts of the

creatures' blood, Jessica surmised. Perhaps it would take as much of the otherworldly blood as the body required to kill cancer.

Were the successfully cured patients of the Renewed Life Institute now in thrall to the creatures?

"But you can't argue with the results," the monster sitting in front of Jessica said. "*So* many lives saved. Like Cassie's. And so many *more* will be saved in the future. In fact, imagine the Renewed Life Institute becoming so successful that other branches open up. After all, it shouldn't be only the rich and famous of Beverly Hills who have access to this life-saving technology. Isn't that right?"

"Of course," Jessica said. "So many others deserve to be infected by your blood. To be controlled by you? That's what places like this will be used for. You will heal the sick…and make hundreds more flock to you. So you can keep feeding—"

The creature raised his eyebrows and affected a distant, contemplative gaze.

"You're already building more places like this," Jessica merely whispered.

The thing that looked like Tom even shook his head, as if unable to reach a decision in a dilemma that was complex beyond his capacities. "If you believe that," he eventually said, "you need to decide what you want to do about the unfortunate situation. You need to decide how much you can gamble. How much you can believe."

"But I don't have to decide," Jessica said. "Because I can't. Isn't that so? I'm your prisoner, and you're just jerking me around."

The creature across the table looked at her with another quizzical glance. In fact, he looked almost hurt by Jessica's assertion. "That's not true," he said. "In fact, my associate will leave the room right now. And the door he came through will be open for you. And then I will leave. Behind the door I will go through—on my way out of the institute—is a corridor to our labs. Our computers. Our medicines that help save so many lives...and do *other* things. So we will leave you right here, and you will decide what to do. You and Buzz that is. You'll find him down in the lobby, by the way. He got the same pitch you just got. He also listened very patiently, because we promised him we wouldn't harm you."

The creature looked at his "associate" and waved him over. "Tom, please give back what belongs to Jessica."

The other Tom-like creature came over and placed the clip to her Walther P99QA in the middle of the table. Afterward, he turned and quickly left the room.

"Oh, and here's one more thing," the Heinlein-creature said and reached into the right pocket of his lab coat. He brought forth a hand grenade and placed it next to the magazine of bullets. "It's real and live, I can assure you. I'm sure you know how to use it. Buzz has a few of these, I suppose. Or you've probably seen enough movies to know what to do with it. If not, just pull that pin there, release the lever, then...run quickly, I suggest, because you'll have about five seconds until it blows. It could be quite helpful, I think...depending on what you're going to decide on."

The creature then got up and, just as he'd promised, left the room.

EPILOGUE - PART III

Oct. 23, 9:42 EDT
FORMER RELATIONSHIP AUTHOR BEHIND BEVERLY HILLS
BOMBING, FBI SAYS

By John Hargrove
Associated Press Writer

The bombing of the Renewed Life Oncological Institute in Beverly Hills, California, was the work of fugitive religious extremists Jessica Lafayette and Owen "Buzz" West, according to the FBI.

"Surveillance cameras have captured the duo entering and exiting the building," Special Agent Charles Foxworth of the FBI's Los Angeles office said in a press conference. "West was seen entering the building through a cargo exit, disguised as a delivery man. The video shows him clearly trying to evade detection. One of the cameras also shows Jessica Lafayette throwing a grenade into a laboratory."

Jessica Lafayette and Owen West are believed to have met in Cedar Valley, Illinois, where they became romantically involved. According to the Cedar Valley police and Lafayette's acquaintances, it was there that the two committed themselves to religious extremism and violence.

Their reasons for allegedly attacking the cancer treatment

center are not yet known.

Dr. Thomas Lancaster, an acquaintance of Lafayette's late father, Brock Randall, said that Lafayette was "obsessed" with apocalyptic religious theories. She was especially drawn, according to Lancaster, to the ideas of the Celebration of the Word Ministries and its controversial splinter group, the Celebration of Salvation Mission.

"Jessica was fixated on prophecies of the coming of the end of the world," Lancaster said. "She was always reading some book or other, some pamphlet or reams of papers printed off the Internet about the Antichrist, Judgment Day, and demonic possessions. She read all the old Antichrist books by the Reverend Garnett, and she was convinced that demons were taking over the world."

How the successful author of a series of relationship-advice books could take a turn into religious extremism and domestic terrorism is baffling to many of her friends and former colleagues.

"What I want to know is what role this Owen West person plays in all this," said Helen O'Brien, a producer at KBLA radio in San Diego. Lafayette was slated to start hosting a relationship-oriented talk show at the station this fall. "The media keeps putting the focus on Jessica through all this," O'Brien said. "And the Jessica Lafayette I knew could never hurt a living soul. I do believe she was forced into this by whoever that man, West, is, and that Inquisition killer."

According to Thomas Lancaster, however, Lafayette had a particularly strong fascination with anything otherworldly, even before coming to Cedar Valley for her father's funeral. "At one time, I joked with her that she should start living in the twenty-first century because it's a pretty nice place here. By her own admission, she was a science fiction fanatic. UFOs, ghosts, Bigfoot, she was a junkie of all the paranormal stuff."

When the FBI searched Lafayette's home in San Diego, they found a very large collection of science fiction novels on her bookshelves. They did not, however, find any paranormal literature.

Lafayette is the author of six books on relationships. Three of them, including her latest work, *Jessica's More Real Advice for Real Relationships*, have been Los Angeles Times and Amazon. com best sellers.

No one was injured in the bombing.

# # #

HIGHLIGHTS OF REVEREND JIM GARNETT INTERVIEW – WGN TV, CHICAGO
Oct. 23

BEGIN TRANSCRIPT

KEVIN RICHMOND: A number of people who have known the fugitive Jessica Lafayette said that she had a connection to your church and was motivated by your books. Do you think this is true, and have you ever met her?

JIM GARNETT: First of all, the connection is completely false. It's all fake news.

KR: But you did meet her.

JG: Yes, I did meet her, but again, she was never a member of my church, and I am certain that she in no way believed anything I wrote or ever spoke about.

KR: How can you be sure?

JG: Well, let me explain. She and her male companion, this Owen West, came to the Celebration of the Word headquarters over the summer to convince me that monsters from another dimension were taking over the world. It immediately struck me that both of them were occult, New Age extremists. Absolutely not one word out of their mouths sounded like scripture. Now, let me say that I am not trying to cast any aspersions on New Age beliefs, unlike some evangelicals have in the past. I don't believe that they are evil people—New Age followers, that is—or that they're Satanic or anything like that. But this Lafayette woman was completely taken with ideas like channeling and aliens and alternate dimensions. Her beliefs were certainly not Christian, is my point. Definitely occultist, but not Christian. As a matter of fact, I asked her and her friend to sit in on one of our services, but she became very hostile at that point.

KR: She refused?

JG: Oh, to put it mildly. Her friend, Owen West, became abusive. He shouted profanities right in my office. He called us a cult. We had to get security to escort both of them out.

KR: Did you get a sense that the Inquisition Killer might have been connected to them?

JG: As a matter of fact, I'm glad you brought up the Inquisition Killer because a connection between them and Jessica Lafayette and Owen West makes perfect sense to me. I believe the Inquisition Killer was doing what he did to damage religion, to make all of us look like fanatical, murderous crazies. There is an agenda behind the way he planned and executed his crimes. So a connection between him and Jessica Lafayette makes perfect sense.

KR: But she did not mention him?

JG: No, she didn't. But that's my guess. There was probably a connection.

KR: Well, thank you, Rev. Garnett, for speaking to us.

JG: Thank you, Kevin.

# # #

JESSICA LAFAYETTE ACCUSED OF MASTERMINDING CVSU BOMB PLOT

By Robert Masters
Cedar Valley Journal

In light of the Renewed Life cancer center's bombing, FBI officials have been looking into the attempted attack on Cedar Valley State University this summer, and the role fugitive Jessica Lafayette might have played in it.

Nick Gilroy, identified as the "Inquisition Killer," was shot to death this summer by Cedar Valley police while trying to crash a truck loaded with explosives into the CVSU campus. Jessica Lafayette, a best-selling author, and Owen West, a former Miami reporter, believed to have been accomplices of Gilroy, tried to steal the truck after the foiled bombing attempt.

Cedar Valley police and agents from the FBI are now seriously considering that Lafayette had masterminded the bombing, as well as the Inquisition Killer's reign of terror, from the beginning. Several of her Cedar Valley State University acquaintances paint a disturbing picture of the woman who was once a star author.

"She definitely struck me as being extremely unstable," Dr. Thomas Lancaster, a professor of astronomy, said. "I don't know what might have been going on in her life, but she appeared to be unraveling very fast. From what I've read about how her California friends are supporting her, it just amazes me how well people can conceal their mental illnesses from those closest to them."

Dr. Lyle Chambers, professor of political science, also believes he might know a reason for Lafayette wanting to blow up the school. "I find it amazing that religious extremists like Jim Garnett are saying she is some occultist, fringe liberal wanting to hurt religion. Although I only met the woman twice, it was impossible to talk to her about anything other than the Antichrist and Biblical end-time prophecies."

Chambers also believes Lafayette was a political zealot. "Well, you know she was estranged from her father because she couldn't stand academics. She believed that college campuses were some sort of a hotbed of communist subversion. She sounded like some kind of a McCarthyite out of the nineteen fifties. Once I brought up the issue of the JFK assassination in a conversation, and she just about screamed at me. Told me all those crazy conspiracy theorists are a bunch of un-American communist sympathizers who can't get a job in the real world, so they want to destroy the minds of young people."

On the issue of Lafayette's beliefs in demons trying to take over the world, Chambers adds, "She definitely believed that they were fallen angels from the Bible. She talked about demons that were all a part of one great connected overmind. It is just like communism, she kept saying. That's why she seemed to think that academics were in league with the demons, to bring about world communism through this supernatural mind meld."

# # #

www.latimes.com/
11:51 AM PDT, Thursday, October 24
CANCER CENTERS PUT ON ALERT AFTER BEVERLY HILLS BOMBING

By Bruce Nash | 7:35 a.m.

Following the attack on the Renewed Life Oncological Institute in Beverly Hills, FBI officials have put all cancer research facilities on alert.

"Cancer centers have not traditionally been targets for domestic terrorism," said Phillip Talbot, spokesman for the Bureau's Los Angeles office, "but protocols law enforcement has in place for dealing with threats to abortion clinics will be called on to deal with this problem."

Although he would not comment on any specific threats the FBI is focusing on, he did say that the Beverly Hills attack and the fugitives Jessica Lafayette and Owen "Buzz" West are a top priority.

The FBI is offering rewards of $50,000 apiece for Lafayette and West. If anyone has information that could lead to their arrest, they are urged to call their local FBI office. Lafayette and West should both be considered armed and extremely dangerous.

THE END

About the Author

Barna William Donovan, a professor of communication and media studies, is a graduate of the film school of the University of Miami, and he earned his Ph.D. from Rutgers University. His books on film and fandom include "The Asian Influence on Hollywood Action Films," "Blood, Guns and Testosterone: Action Films, Audiences, and a Thirst for Violence," and "Conspiracy Films: A Tour of Dark Places in the American Conscious." His commentaries on film, television, and popular culture have been quoted in media like the BBC, Variety, LiveScience, Forbes, Yahoo News, HLNTV, and various publications from Europe to Latin America.

Made in the USA
Middletown, DE
29 September 2020